Tor books by Melissa Scott

Burning Bright
Dreamships
Shadow Man
Trouble and Her Friends

MELISSA SCOTT

TOR®

A TOM DOHERTY ASSOCIATES BOOK / NEW YORK

Copyright © 1995 by Melissa Scott

A Tor Book
Published by Tom Doherty Associates, Inc.
175 Fifth Avenue
New York, NY 10010

Tor® is a registered trademark of Tom Doherty Associates, Inc.

Design by Lynn Newmark

ISBN 0-312-85800-0

Printed in the United States of America

1

mesnie, mesnies:
> (Hara) basic unit of (traditional) Haran society, a group of households (i.e., a man, a woman, and their children) living together in a single compound and usually working together at a profession or industry; all the households in a *mesnie* are related, and marriage within the *mesnie* is considered incest and forbidden.

clan:
> (Hara) one of the fourteen political, social, and familial groupings that form the basis of Haran society; although the people who formed the first clans were not actually related, but rather chose to affiliate themselves with one of the original fourteen founders, at this point the clans are interrelated in complex and often confusing fashion. Each clan controls a particular territory, which varies in the quality and abundance of its resources; the Stane clan has parlayed their original good luck into economic and political dominance of the planet.

Watch:
> (Hara) largest division of Haran society, based on the original divisions of the ship that brought the first colonists to Hara. There are five Watches: White (command), Blue (medical/scientific), Black (engineering), Green (land-trained colonists), and Red (ocean-trained colonists). Watches retain certain administrative duties, and are also used to determine marriageability; the larger clans are split between Watches to help keep the genetic mix stable.

WARREVEN

The White Watch House was built like any other *mesnie* hall, but on a much grander scale. Warreven leaned on the railing of the gallery that ran around three walls, looking out over the crowd below. They still filled the open area at the center of the hall, though the crowd around Aldess Donavie had thinned out a little. She looked grateful, if anything, though it was hard to tell beneath the drape of the white-and-silver *shaal* that covered her dark hair. Still, she was doubly alien here, a Stane only by marriage, Red

Watch rather than White; it couldn't be easy to perform the rituals of mourning and absolution without the comfort of her own clan's ancestor tablets, her own kin to offer advice.

And that, Warreven thought, was just the sort of sentiment Aldess herself would never tolerate. She had gone into her marriage clear-eyed—eager, even—for the power of being married to the son of the Most Important Man, and if she regretted this miscarriage, it was largely because it put off the day that she confirmed her status by becoming the mother of his child. If she had looked worn-out when he had paid his formal regrets, the lines on her face suddenly stark, it was only the physical stress. This was her fourth miscarriage in nearly eighteen bioyears of marriage; she would have to be worrying about her ability to carry any child to term, wondering whether to seek off-world help. They had been at school together, years ago, and he remembered her ambitions: if she had to go off-world to find a way to consolidate her position, her rank within the most important of the Stane *mesnies*, she would do it without hesitation. At least Stane was rich enough to afford that intervention.

Warreven heard laughter from the north end of the hall, a familiar, rich sound intended to carry, and leaned forward a little against the railing. Temelathe Stane, Speaker for the Watch Council, and the Most Important Man on Hara in fact as well as in sour jokes, stood on the low dais, head thrown back, still laughing at something the man at his side had said. As Warreven watched, Temelathe clapped the stranger on the shoulder, said something, still grinning. The stranger smiled back—an offworlder, almost certainly a representative of one of the outsystem pharmaceutical companies that dominated Hara's economy—and stepped away. Temelathe stood alone for an instant, hands on hips, legs spread wide, surveying the hall. Consciously or not, his pose echoed the Captain carved on the wall above him, and Warreven allowed himself a rather bitter smile. The massive carving—it was a famous work of art, commissioned a hundred years ago by Stane from his own Stiller clan, showing all seven of the spirits who mediated between God and man—had recently been repainted. The colors glowed in the sunlight that streamed in through the gallery windows and the wide-open doors, and there was no mistaking the resemblance between the Captain's face and Temelathe's broad bones. He had even pulled his gray hair into an old-fashioned knot at the nape of his neck, imitating the carving. Duredent Stiller, who had carved the piece, would be turning over in his grave if he could see it, Warreven thought. The rivalry between Stane and Stiller was old and deep, dating from before the first days of settlement, from the colony ship itself and the legendary animosity between Captain Stane and Chief Stiller; the fact that Stane had in effect won that ancient battle only made the situation worse. In the carving, the Heartbreaker turned her face away, smiling at Caritan crouching at her skirts, and Cousin-Jack, the spirit of the land, shaded his eyes to look into an invisible distance, but even Duredent had been unable to blunt the Captain's authority. The rest of the spirits— Genevoe the Trickster, stolid Madansa of the Markets, even Agede, the keeper of the door between life and death—stood shoulder to shoulder with the Captain, their domains meaningless without the Captain's strength to support them.

There was a movement in the crowd then, and a young man in the traditional tunic-and-trousers suit forced his way to the dais, said something quietly to Temelathe. The Most Important Man nodded, and then clapped his hands loudly. Heads turned all across the hall, conversation stopping instantly as people realized who was summoning their attention.

"Miri, mirrimi," Temelathe called. "And our distinguished off-world visitors. If you haven't yet paid your respects to my daughter-in-law, this is your last chance to do it." He paused then, but no one moved. From his place in the balcony, Warreven saw Aldess lean sideways, murmuring something to another woman he didn't recognize. Tendlathe, Temelathe's only son and her husband, was nowhere in sight.

"The wheel has turned," Temelathe went on, "and the doors have opened. We welcome the spirits who carry us as we carry them in our hearts." He nodded to the young man beside him, who lifted a bell in a carved and painted frame. It was metal, forged from the salvage of the ship that had brought their ancestors to Hara, and its odd, resonant note carried weirdly in the stillness. It was answered by the shrilling of a whistle, and then the beat of drums. The people by the entrance gave way, clearing a path, and familiar figures danced in—two *vieuvants*, the old souls who served God and the spirits, moving as though carried on the heady rhythm. The first *vieuvant* was dressed as Agede, all in black, one eye blinded by a dark patch, the second as the Heartbreaker, her cheek scored with the three parallel lines that marked that spirit. She carried a new *shaal*, brilliant saffron silk embroidered with glittering glass beads and shells and even a scattering of metal, and spun it into the air as she twirled through her dance. All around the hall, people began clapping, picking up the rhythm of the drums.

Agede led her up the hall, three drummers following them, and then back down again, stopped at last in front of Aldess. She touched her lips in dutiful acknowledgment, lowering her *shaal* to her shoulder, and the *vieuvant* produced a bottle of sweetrum from under his tunic. He lifted it in salute, drank, then sprayed a second mouthful of the liquid over Aldess's face and hair. She accepted the blessing without flinching and there were cheers and scattered, off-beat clapping from the onlookers. The second *vieuvant* spun forward then, skirts belling as she turned, dipped, and extended the length of saffron silk. Aldess touched her lips again, and took it, wrapped it in place of the other, over her head and shoulders. There were more cheers, and the *vieuvants* turned away, dancing back toward the doors, the drummers following at a respectful pace.

"What—exactly—was that all about?" a woman's voice said quietly at his elbow. She had spoken *franca*, but the liquid offworld vowels were unmistakable, and Warreven was not surprised to see a woman in the drab coat of a pharmaceutical leaning on the rail beside him. He knew her slightly: Sera Ax Cyma, her name was; she was new to the planet, and they had had dealings in the traditional court where he was an advocate in a matter of trade. Those dealings had been settled with satisfaction for both sides, and he answered willingly enough.

"It's the end of Aldess's mourning. Agede—the Doorkeeper,

he holds the doors of life and death—has released her, and the Heart-breaker is reblessing her marriage."

"I guessed some of that," Cyma said, and sounded faintly pleased with herself. "But why'd he spit the rum on her?"

"It's a blessing," Warreven said. "Traditional." In the hall below, he could see Aldess discreetly wiping her face with one corner of her new *shaal*.

"I see. And the dancers—*vieuvants*—" She corrected herself hastily, and Warreven nodded. "They're representing the spirits?"

"More or less," Warreven began—he never quite knew how to explain the spirits to off-worlders—and felt a hand on his shoulder.

"Raven."

There weren't many people here, in the White Watch House, who would call him by his childhood nickname. He turned, already smiling, to see Tendlathe Stane beside him. "Ten. It's good to see you. I'm sorry for your loss."

"Thanks." Tendlathe looked at him, refusing to match the smile. "Father wants to talk to you."

"Why?" Even as the word slipped out, Warreven regretted it, but knew better than to apologize.

Tendlathe shrugged. "I wouldn't know," he said, and tilted his head toward the off-worlder in unspoken warning.

Warreven sighed. Everyone knew that Tendlathe opposed the pharmaceuticals' influence, but there was no point in being actively rude. He nodded to the woman. "If you'll excuse me, mirrim?"

"Of course," Cyma said, backing away, and sounded relieved to be clear of their conversation.

"So what does he want?" Warreven asked, and followed Tendlathe along the length of the gallery toward the stairs.

"I don't really know," Tendlathe answered. "He just said he wanted to be sure to talk to you before you left."

Warreven made a sour face. A summons like that from the Most Important Man could mean almost anything, from a trade case—and the advocacy group was handling half a dozen right now, in both the off-world and the traditional courts—to some business between Stane and Stiller. He had acted as a go-between for Temelathe before. . . . He shook the thought away. There was no point in speculating; Temelathe would tell him soon enough.

Now that the main part of the ceremony was over, *faitous* had appeared in the main hall, carrying trays of food and braided feel-good and jugs of sweetrum. Warreven stopped to snag a cup of sweetrum from a passing woman, and Tendlathe looked over his shoulder, showing teeth in a not entirely friendly smile.

"Think you'll need that?"

"You tell me," Warreven answered, and this time Tendlathe did laugh.

"I told you, I don't know what he wants. But—" He stopped abruptly, tried again. "Look, Raven, I haven't seen you in ages. Can we get together after this? We can talk properly then, not like here."

Warreven hesitated. There were a lot of reasons he hadn't seen much of Tendlathe over the past eight or nine years. They had been at the Concord-sponsored boarding school in Riversedge together, and they had spent holidays together at Temelathe's *mesnie* outside Gedesrede, along with half a dozen other children of Important Men and Women. They had come of different clans and Watches—collected, Warreven had realized very early, to improve Temelathe's position as Speaker of the Watch Council—but for some reason Temelathe had taken a liking to him. When he had turned eighteen—human years, bioyears, not the longer calendar years—Temelathe had proposed a marriage between him and Tendlathe. It had been contingent on a change of Warreven's legal gender, of course: a great honor, but an even greater sacrifice, given the patrilineal structure of both his own and Temelathe's *mesnies*. Luckily, Tendlathe had been equally unenthusiastic about the proposal, and it had been relatively easy to decline. Though if he had not been the one to become the wife, Warreven admitted, it would have been a tempting offer. But now there was too much between them, not just politics, but the marriage that hadn't happened as well as the one that had to make it simple to retrieve the old ease. He had waited too long, and Tendlathe looked away.

"It's not that important."

"What do you want, Ten?"

Tendlathe looked back at him. They were much of a size, both thin and slight, so similar in looks and coloring that when they were children strangers had usually assumed they were siblings, to their mutual disdain. Tendlathe had grown his beard as soon as he was able, but the narrow dark line, coupled with the long hair pulled back into a severe braid only seemed to emphasize the matching length of chin. "It's Aldess," he said at last. "I want to talk to someone who deals with the off-worlders regularly."

So Aldess was thinking of going off-world for help with her next pregnancy, Warreven thought. It made sense: the Concord Worlds had better technology anyway, and they were used to dealing with these complications. He said, "All right, but I don't know what I can tell you. When?"

"After this is over," Tendlathe said. "Come by the house— our house, not here—I'll give you dinner, if you'd like."

"You don't have to feed me," Warreven said. "Besides, I have plans." Something flickered in Tendlathe's eyes, disappointment, maybe, or annoyance, and Warreven couldn't quite repress a sense of satisfaction. And that, he knew, was ridiculous: he and Tendlathe had defined their relationship years before, and they had both ruled out anything more than friendship. He grinned, at himself this time, and said, "I'll come by at the twentieth hour?"

Tendlathe nodded. They had reached the dais then, and he stopped a calculated distance from the Most Important Man. Before he could say anything, however, Temelathe turned to face them, waved one big hand in welcome.

"Raven! Come up here." He turned to the man at his side, an off-worlder in the severely cut uniform of one of the Big Six. "This is Warreven . . . Stiller, the one I told you about. The one who might have been my daughter-in-law."

Out of the corner of his eye, Warreven saw Tendlathe freeze for a fraction of a second, his handsome, bony face going absolutely still, and then he turned on his heel and stalked back through the crowd, heading toward the table where Aldess was holding court. Warreven allowed himself a sour smile and stepped up onto the dais. "That was a long time ago, my father. I decided against it, and so did Tendlathe. I remain a man, thank you." He saw the off-worlder looking at him, saw the familiar movement of his eyes checking the shape of hips and shoulders and chest, looking for the indicators of true gender. "Legally, at any rate, which is what matters."

The off-worlder's eyes snapped away, fixing on something in the distance, over Temelathe's shoulder, and Warreven was pleased to see a faint color rising under the man's fair skin. If he'd been on Hara long enough to be doing business with the Most Important Man, he'd been there long enough to know better than to be so obvious about it. Harans might actually have the same five sexes as any other human beings, but law and custom admitted only two.

"And in the process," Temelathe said, "you missed a chance to serve your clan and Watch. But, no matter." He gestured again, drawing Warreven closer. "I want to introduce you to Ser Wile Kolbjorn, of Kerendach. The two of you may be doing business together."

Kolbjorn held out his hand, the off-world greeting, and Warreven took it warily. He knew Kerendach, of course, any Stiller did: Kerendach was the largest of the Big Six, held most of Stiller's harvest contracts. They paid the clan in metal and in concord dollars for the various products it gathered from land and sea; if anyone thought Kerendach could pay more, they were careful not to say it. Kerendach had Temelathe's backing, and that meant there was no point in negotiating. Though why Temelathe thinks I'll be doing business with them, Warreven thought, I don't know. Unless they've been dabbling in trade. That was more than likely—the Big Six didn't need the extra income, or the hassles with their own agencies, IDCA, the Interstellar Disease Control Agency, chief among them, that trade inevitably caused, but it was equally inevitable that low-paid clerks and shipping techs would take their chances at that game. "Mir Kolbjorn," he said, and braced himself for whatever the approach would be.

To his surprise, however, Kolbjorn merely nodded, releasing his hand, and looked from him to Temelathe. "A pleasure meeting you, Mir Warreven. I'll look forward to further acquaintance. Mir Temelathe, thank you. Please give my best wishes to your daughter-in-law." His eyes flickered a little at that, darting toward Warreven, but he controlled himself instantly and turned away.

Warreven watched him go, tilted his head to one side. "And what was that all about, my father?"

Temelathe laughed, and flung a heavy arm across the other's shoulders. "Insurance, my son, for both of you. Trade's a nasty business, you should have more strings to your bow."

"If you say so," Warreven murmured, not bothering to hide his skepticism. Temelathe laughed again, and drew him down from the dais with him.

---

fem:
(Concord) human being possessing testes, XY chromosomes, some aspects of female genitalia but not possessing ovaries; ðe, ðer, ðer, ðerself.

MHYRE TATIAN

The room was artifically lit, and dim, the curtains and sunscreens drawn tight against the day's fading light. The environmental system rumbled in the next room, churning cooled air into the three rooms of the apartment, and the apartment's current owner listened with half an ear, judging the output. Nothing on Hara was ever quite cool enough—he had been born on one cold planet, had spent his childhood and adolescence on another—and he had reconfigured the room plan so that he slept next to the main cooling vent. It was noisy, but it meant that he could sleep— and it also meant that the current main room, which had been intended as the bedroom, was warmer than he liked. He looked around the table, wondering if he could afford to turn the system down another notch. His employer, New Antioch Pharmaceutical Design, was reasonably generous with its housing allowance, but cooling costs were always astronomical this time of year. Arsidy Shraga sat opposite him, frowning over his set-up pad, lights flickering under his fingers as he tried out three different configurations in quick succession. He looked hot and bothered, but then, he was losing this game, and losing badly. Eshe Isabon, on the other hand, was looking cooler than ever, smiling faintly as ðe studied the board. ðe met his gaze, and ðer smile widened for an instant, before ðe shifted the next block of pieces into position. Shraga threw up his hands at that and blanked his pad.

"Shit, that finishes me. I'm out."

"Tatian?" Isabon looked at him, eyebrows lifting.

Mhyre Tatian reached for the dice arrayed on the tabletop in front of him, palmed them without taking his eyes from the pattern of pieces, and selected two of the ten-sided dice. "I'll go again. Once."

Isabon smiled more openly. Shraga said, "Remember, the red one's the tens."

Tatian acknowledged that with a grin—among friends, it was almost acceptable to cheat a little at queens-road—and rolled the dice. The first, the brown, the single digits, bounced off Shraga's random-number box and came up five. The red rolled farther, came to a stop above the cluster of blue lights that marked his own home camp, and showed a two.

"Oh, bad luck," Isabon said, without sympathy.

Tatian made a show of studying the board, but he had needed at least forty to stay in the game. "I'm out."

Isabon looking sideways, fingers busy on ðer wrist pad as ðe called up the bets and side bets. "You owe me ten-point-two cd, Tatya. Shraga, you owe me nineteen-nine, and you might as well make it twenty."

"Like hell," Shraga answered, his fingers busy on his own pad. "Nineteen-nine is right—or I'll make it fifteen in metal."

Tatian gave a rather sour laugh at that—he spent too much of his time making and assessing similar offers; Hara's indigenes were desperate for metal—and Isabon shook ðer head slowly. "No, nineteen-nine—and in dollars, thank you."

"Never play queens-road with a fem," Shraga said, with mock bitterness, and reached into his pocket for his card.

"Never gamble with a fem," Isabon corrected amiably, and mated his card to ðer own. Lights flashed as the transfer went through, and Isabon freed the cards, offering Shraga's to him with a flourish. "Thank you, ser. And yours, Tatya?"

"Ten-two, you said." Tatian reached for his own card, pressed his thumb against the veri-lock, and quickly entered the transaction. Isabon took it and returned it a moment later with the green light flashing: transfer complete. Tatian switched it off and stuck it back into his pocket. "Anyone want anything else to drink?"

"I'll take another beer," Shraga said promptly, and Tatian suppressed a sigh. Beer—real beer, not the narcotic-spiked, fermented grain drink the indigenes called beer—was imported from off-world and correspondingly expensive. Still, there was no going back on the offer, and he went on into the apartment's narrow kitchen.

"Isa?"

"Whatever I had before."

"All right." Tatian rummaged in the coldbox, brought out three frosted bottles, Shraga's beer and a bottle apiece of *quatra* for him and Isabon. *Quatra* was a local drink, one part sweetrum to three parts ruby melon juice; like all the local liquors, sweetrum was strong and rough, and not very consistent, but the sweet melon juice cut the worst of the flavor. After a moment's searching, he found a tray and filled a shallow bowl with the sour-sweet mixed-fruit relish. He added his last package of flatbread and carried the precariously balanced cargo out into the other room, setting it on the table beside the playing board.

"Did you hear the news? Aldess Donavie had another miscarriage. Today's the whatever-they-call-it, the ceremony."

Shraga winced visibly, and Tatian remembered too late that the other man had a partner and child at home on Cassandra. The same mutation that had produced the five sexes had increased the incidence of miscarriage; almost anyone who had successfully had a child would have lost another early in pregnancy.

"Tendlathe's partner," Isabon said, and grimaced. "Sorry, wife."

Tatian nodded.

"I wonder what Temelathe is making of all that," ðe went on. "I mean, if the dynasty's going to continue, he's going to need a grandchild."

"A grandson," Tatian said. He still wasn't completely used to the system, found himself insisting on the gendered words as if that would help him understand.

"Whatever." Isabon reached for ðer *quarta* and took a long swallow.

"It's not really a dynasty," Shraga said. "There must be somebody else in the clan who could take over, if Tendlathe and Aldess don't have kids."

"I can't see Temelathe letting the position go to anyone outside the direct line," Isabon said. "In fact, I wonder if the indigenes would accept someone who wasn't a direct descendant."

"Do you mean of Temelathe, or of that Captain of theirs?" Tatian asked.

"Is there any difference?" Isabon grinned, and Tatian nodded.

"True enough. Still, I'm surprised they haven't had kids by now."

ðe shrugged. "For my money, he looks like a herm—Tendlathe, I mean. Which would explain a lot."

It was a common and constant rumor, circulating through the Nest and the off-world community on the average of once every four-and-a-half kilohours. "It doesn't really matter," Tatian said, and bit back the rest of the sentence. *It doesn't really matter what he is, as long as the indigenes say he's male:* that was stating the obvious, and in any case he was tired of dealing with the oddities of the Haran system. Let the Harans deal with it, he thought—no, let Temelathe deal with it. It's his son and his dynasty: his problem, not ours.

"Another game?" Shraga asked, and reached for his beer. "Isa owed me a chance for revenge."

"Sorry." Isabon shook ðer head, glancing sideways as ðe triggered ðer implants, calling up some display visible only to ðerself. "I have to work tomorrow."

"I thought you had tomorrow off," Tatian said.

"I did," Isabon answered. "But then I heard there's a textile fair in the Ferryhead market. I'm curious to see what's on offer."

Tatian nodded, accepting the excuse, and switched off the queens-road board. The fields that shaped it and formed the playing pieces collapsed, and he began to roll the now-limp board into a tidy cylinder.

"How can you make money exporting that stuff?" Shraga asked, and reached for a wedge of flatbread. He broke off a manageable piece and dug it into the relish, then said indistinctly, "I mean, doesn't mass alone eat up half your profits?"

Isabon gave another of ðer austere smiles. ðer company was small, but growing; in five years, Tatian thought, ðe would probably pass NAPD on the gross-profit list. He was just glad ðe didn't run a rival pharmaceutical company.

"It would—it does, on the biggest pieces, the premade things, quilts, bodices, other clothing, and we don't buy much of that. We only take the best for the art market. But the silk isn't that massy, and it sells very well. The same goes for flaxen."

"But—"

Isabon shook her head. "Sorry. Anything more is trade secrets."

Shraga lifted his hands in instant apology, and Tatian slipped the dice and the random-box back into their cases. "Are you doing anything tomorrow, Shraga?" he asked, and the other man shrugged.

"I took the day, too. I'm going to sleep late, eat real food, play a few games of basieball, and then I'm going to watch a vidik on the big screen downstairs."

"Want to hit the Glassmarket before the vidi-show starts?" Tatian asked. "There's going to be drumming and a dance."

"I don't plan to leave the Nest tomorrow," Shraga said. "That's *my* idea of a holiday." He set his beer aside—empty already, Tatian saw—and stood, stretching. "And, since I have such strenuous plans, I think I'd better get my beauty sleep. It was a good game, people."

"See you next week?" Isabon asked, and Shraga shook his head.

"I'm off to the Estcote—three days in Estaern, and then four on the road, bouncing around the Delacoste *mesnies*. I'm free the week after, though."

"That's good for me," Isabon said, and looked at Tatian.

He touched the input pad between the bones of his right wrist and flinched as a wave of static rose from the failing connection. Static danced in front of his eyes, but resolved itself almost instantly to the familiar scheduling grid. "I'm free then, too. It's your turn to host, Shraga."

"It would be," the other man said, but grinned. "I'll have a four-pack just for you, Tatya."

Tatian laughed, acknowledging the offer, and touched the sequences that unlocked the main door. Shraga let himself out, waving, and Tatian closed down his implanted system, feeling another wave of cold static rise to break over his shoulder.

"You should get that seen to," Isabon said.

"I will." He didn't add—he didn't need to add—that it was hard to find technicians on Hara who were both competent and affordable. And the system was his own; NAPD would pay for the surgery, but not for replacement parts.

Isabon gave a knowing smile, and took another sip of ð er *quarta*. "So, you're spending an evening at the Glassmarket. Going with Prane Am?"

"We're not seeing each other at the moment," Tatian answered. And maybe not ever again, but that really wasn't Isabon's business.

"I'm sorry," ðe said. "I hadn't heard."

Tatian couldn't help raising his eyebrows at that. Hara's off-world community was small and intimately connected, practically incestuous.

Isabon shrugged. "People don't gossip to me, Tatya. Nobody told me."

ðe left a silence more compelling than a question, and Tatian found himself filling it after all. "It was the usual thing. She thought I was going native, playing trade on her. And then I heard from Kaialis that she's seeing some mem up at the port."

"I thought she was man-straight," Isabon said, startled.

"She was when we were dating."

"I'm sorry." There was another little silence, and then Isabon sighed and put aside ðer empty bottle. "Kaialis isn't the most reliable person around anyway. It may not be true."

"I know." Tatian managed a smile that was almost real. "I just don't need my life to be this complicated right now."

"Ah, the joys of the Midsummer contract," Isabon said. "I don't envy you druggists."

"And I don't envy you at the Quarter-days," Tatian answered. He worked the door controls for ðer—using the wall box, this time—and ðe pressed the latch.

"See you in two weeks," ðe said, and the door slid shut again behind ðer.

Left to himself, Tatian slid the rolled-up board and the boxes of dice and number generators into their place in the storage cells that filled the inner wall, and then gathered the empty bottles and fed them one by one to the apartment's recycling system. He rewrapped the flatbread, poured the relish back into its jar, and tucked them both away in the narrow cabinets. Then he went back out into the main room, and crossed to the single large window, dragging Isabon's chair back into its proper place as he went. He unlatched the curtains and drew them back, so that only the sun-screen remained between him and the glass. He could feel the day's heat radiating inward and released the screen as well. It slid up into its housing, and he had to look away for a moment before his eyes adjusted to the brilliance. His apartment faced east, overlooking the city of Bonemarche—his choice; the other option had been to face the starport, and he had known he would be homesick if he could see the shuttles leaving. He looked out between the two towers that made up the Nest, the Expatriate Housing Blocks One, Two, and Three, across the maze of low buildings to the Harbor proper. The sky was white with haze, the red spire of the lighthouse at Blind Point all but lost in the milky radiance.

He had not particularly wanted to think about Prane Am, or Jon's Kaialis's gossip: it was bad enough to be falsely accused, but worse to think that Am might really be doing what she had charged him with. He slapped the window controls, lowering the sun-screen again, and turned to the media console as the fierce sunlight dimmed. Rather than risk the implant, he pulled out the little keypad, paged through the menus of his personal datastore until he found the file he wanted. He flicked the shadowscreen to retrieve it and reached for his bottle of *quarta*, settling himself on the couch opposite the display screen. Codes flickered, mere sparks of light, and then the main screen windowed. Lolya Masani, the Old Dame who had built NAPD, looked out at him, ðer dark face drawn into a frown. Of course, it was rare to see Masani smile: he thought he had seen it twice, once when ðe hired him, and the second time when he had brought in the Uldamiani job against all odds.

"Welcome to Hara," ðe began, and Tatian braved the failing implant to speed-search the file. A progress bar appeared, going from green to red, and the face in the screen writhed soundlessly until he'd found the section he wanted.

"—two things that fuck up people on Hara," Masani said, "and those are sex and drugs. Drugs—you know my policy. You play in the illegal marts, you're out. I can't afford what a run-in with Customs, or ColCom, or the IDCA would eventually cost me, and don't kid yourself that you'd make enough to cover the fines. You want to fish in that pool, you do it outside of my company. That's my final word on the matter." ðe drew breath then, and the fierce stare eased a little. "The only gray area I'm prepared to see is where new drugs are concerned. You find something interesting, you bring it in, develop a product, and I'll back you to the hilt—as long as you file the proper papers, and keep me informed. I'm not averse to recreationals as long as I have lead time to get Legal to clear it. But make sure you keep me informed."

There was more, but Tatian touched the implanted pad again, dragging the file forward a little farther.

"—sex," Masani said, "and sex is likely to be the biggest prob-

lem. Now, everybody knows the facts about Hara. They were settled late, right at the end of the First Wave, and then when the
First Wave collapsed, they were one of the colonies that got lost
in the chaos. So by the time we reestablished contact, we'd pretty
much resolved all the issues around hyperlumin-A, and they'd
never even heard of the problem. Which means that, while they
look normal enough, they only admit to two sexes. And that's
where the problem comes in. The indigenes don't understand our
expectations, and we don't understand theirs. You can meet a perfectly normal-looking person of your personal preference—because, remember, they actually *have* five sexes, they are normal
human beings that way—but if that person's an indigene, they
won't know how to respond. And neither will you."

Tatian lifted his bottle in silent toast. It had taken him most of
the first year to learn to look not at bodies when he met an indigene but at the clothing that signified "real" gender.

"Now, if that were the only thing, I wouldn't bother doing
more than mentioning it," Masani went on. "You're all grown-
ups now, and if you want to fuck things up for yourself, that's your
business. But I will not have my company involved in trade. Hara
attracts a lot of players from the Concord Worlds. They've found
a whole planet just as abnormal as they are, and they're willing to
pay for sex. They'll pay the indigenes in metal, and anyone with a
backcountry exploration permit for the use of it. This is illegal,
and the IDCA runs patrols and spot checks and does everything it
can to stop it, so you will get offers. People will try to buy your
landing permits, your exploration permits, your housing vouch-
ers, anything that will give them an excuse to go into the city. And
I won't have it. Anyone caught playing trade will be fired. No appeal. Do trade, and you're out."

ðer face softened again. "This is not to say that I care what you
do yourselves. As long as you're not selling NAPD's rights, you
can screw what you like and in whatever combinations. One thing
Hara has going for it is no native HIVs. I know you're going to
meet indigenes who are attractive and intelligent, and I know
some of you are going to fall in love, and that's fine. But I want
you to remember a couple of things before you let yourself take

this too seriously. Hara's a funny world, with funny morals; you may find yourself doing things here that you'd never think of doing on any of the Concord Worlds. And the people are even stranger. So my advice to you is, whatever you do on Hara, don't take it off-world with you."

There was more but Tatian flicked the screen off again. Masani had been one of the people who had built NAPD's Haran business in the first place, and ðe clearly knew and loved the planet. And ðe had been right about one thing: people felt free to do things on Hara that they would never dream of doing at home. Trade existed everywhere in the Concord Worlds, of course; in the Concord, it was more a matter of how much space each world allowed it, and how much the players were looked down on, how much they had to hide their tastes. The Concord was relatively rigid in its roles, its acceptable sexualities—it had to be, with the dozens of HIVs that circulated among the planets despite the IDCA's best efforts at control. . . . But there were always people who didn't fit in, always some desires that weren't fulfilled. The biggest group were the ones who couldn't quite accept the new roles that came with the five sexes, the ones who looked back to the good old days when there were only two genders, two roles, two complementary parts to play. Even if those days had never truly existed, it was still a compelling image to a certain minority, and in Hara, those people had found their sexual paradise. On Hara, players could always find someone of the sex they desired who was willing to play boy to their girl or girl to their boy, regardless of actual sex and without the complications of Concord society. In effect, Hara was a whole world that practiced boy/girl trade, and it was no wonder that even the most secure and normal people found themselves occasionally doing something outside their norms.

Like Prane Am, who had called herself man-straight, a woman who liked men, but was now seeing, maybe even sleeping with, a mem—if, of course, Jons Kaialis had the story right. Tatian stared back out the window, at the cityscape only partly obscured by the sun-screen, suddenly, violently disgusted with it and himself and everything around him. There was only one cure for that, as he knew perfectly well. He reached for the keypad again, tied a secondary screen into the Nest's housekeeping systems, and called up the schedules for the racquet courts. At least two people at his rating were currently seeking partners, and he hastily put his name into the system. A moment later, the screen beeped, and offered him the chance to play Lefsin Morley if he could get to the EHB Two courts in ten minutes. He pressed the accept button, and headed for the door. The confirmation chimed as the door closed behind him, and he grinned, anticipating losing his bad temper in a simple, physical, game.

---

man:
> (Concord) human being possessing testes, XY chromosomes, some aspects of male genitalia; he, his, him, himself.

WARREVEN

The library was cool, the night breeze blowing in through the open windows. Warreven could smell the ocean, the pungent smell of Ferryhead at low tide, could smell, too, feelgood drifting in from the braziers in the compound itself. The *faitous* and other workers at Stane house were celebrating Aldess's return to normal life. He stretched his legs, feet digging into the thick carpet. It was imported from off-world at God and the spirits alone knew what expense—carpeting wasn't common on Hara, especially not along the coast, where mildew was a constant problem—and the deep wine-red color matched the strips of silk between and above the tall bookcases. Tendlathe saw him looking, and grinned, reading the thought.

"Yes, it cost a small fortune. Father's idea." He gestured to the jug of wine that sat next to a platter of fruit on one of the low tables. "Help yourself, I remember you could always eat sweets."

Warreven smiled back, acknowledging his weakness, and took one of the chunks of sourcane. He turned it so that the fibers ran perpendicular to his fingers, and bit carefully into the sour-sweet flesh. It had been soaked in sweetrum, but the natural flavor was still there. The juice sweet was as the sweetrum, the plant itself sour, with a bitter-sharp aftertaste that clung to the tongue. Tendlathe lifted the jug in silent query, and Warreven nodded, waited while the other filled a pair of tall glasses. He recognized the work—out of the Stiller glassworks, sand from their miles of beachfront tinted with sea salts and blowers' clays and the powders ground from half a dozen plants—and wondered if Tendlathe was making a deliberate point, or just using the best he had.

He hadn't seen Tendlathe in a while, not up close, and took the chance to look carefully again. They still looked much alike, though Warreven had broadened through the hips and chest at puberty, while Tendlathe had stayed slim as a reed; their skins were the still same shade of golden brown, unmarked by the fierce sun. Tendlathe was still dressing as traditionally as ever, in the shirt-vest-and-loose-trousers suit that was popular in the Stanelands, but the material was better than before, showing off-world colors and an off-world eye for cut and form. Only the jewelry remained the same, the wide etched-steel bracelets, cut from the interior hull of the Captain's cabin before the hulk that had been the colony ship broke up and fell flaming into Hara's seas, and the matched steel hoops, each with a pendant square, faded blue etched with lines of gold, which might have been part of the ship's computer. Warreven touched his own bracelets—smaller, darker, carved from the outer hull but still part of the ship—for reassurance and thought again that Tendlathe was an extremely handsome man. Not that there was anything between them beyond that admiration: anything more had been put firmly out of bounds the day he himself had refused to change legal gender. He accepted the glass that Tendlathe held out to him and sipped the wine, nodding his appreciation.

"This is nice."

"It's Delacoste, they've planted a vineyard outside Estaern, with off-world rootstock," Tendlathe answered. "They paid a near fortune for it, mind you, and it has to be tended daily, but the result seems to be worth it." He paused, looked away again, concentrating on setting the jug of wine back in its place. "I'm sorry about Father, by the way."

Warreven nodded. The marriage was a sore point between them; he hadn't expected even this oblique reference. "What's he up to, anyway, bringing all that up again?"

"I wouldn't know." Tendlathe's voice was cold, and Warreven sighed, accepting the rebuff.

"So what did you want, Ten?" he said, after a moment.

Tendlathe grinned, exactly the expression, amused and slightly abashed, that he'd always had when they'd both known he was speaking out of turn. "Like I said, it's Aldess. She wants to go to an off-world doctor, maybe even go off-world, see if they can help her carry to term."

"It's not a bad idea," Warreven said. "They probably can."

"I don't think she should." Tendlathe took a deep breath. "I think it's dangerous, and I want you to help me talk her out of it."

Warreven blinked. "Ten, Aldess is never going to listen to me—she doesn't like me, she's never liked me, and she doesn't listen to anybody once she's made up her mind to something. Besides, I think it's probably a good idea."

"It's dangerous," Tendlathe said again. "We're not really like them."

"The off-worlders have been dealing with the problem for centuries," Warreven said. "It's the same mutation that made the odd-bodied. Hyperlumin causes miscarriages and intersexual births, everybody knows that. And if anybody knows how to get around it, the off-worlders do—they're still taking the stuff, you can't go FTL without it."

"I don't want her going to them," Tendlathe said.

"God and the spirits," Warreven began, and Tendlathe went on as though he hadn't spoken.

"The off-worlders—hyperlumin's their excuse, it justifies what they are. But we're not like them. We're not the same."

"We're not that different, either," Warreven answered. "You talk like they're aliens or something."

"Well, they are," Tendlathe said. "In every way that really

matters, they're aliens. That's what Aldess and I have been arguing about, Raven, that's why I want your help. We aren't like them, and we can't afford to become like them. We're all that's left of what people, human beings, are supposed to be, and if we change, that's lost forever."

"Ten—" Warreven broke off, shaking his head. "I agree with Aldess on this one. If she wants to talk to the off-worlders, I think she should—if she wants to go off-world, I think she should. It's stupid not to take advantage of their skills."

Tendlathe sighed, shook his head. He lifted the wine jug again, and Warreven held out his glass automatically. "When we were back in school," Tendlathe began, "remember the *vieuvant*'s daughter, Coldecine—they were Black Stanes from way up north in the Stanelands, remember?"

Warreven nodded. He remembered the girl, all right, a year younger than either of them, but clever, so that she had been in most of their classes. She had been striking at fifteen, long-necked, skin like polished wood, her face already losing the roundness of childhood, fining down into the serene planes of a statue. He hadn't thought of her in years, wondered vaguely if she had retained that beauty.

"Remember when we were studying the end of the First Wave?" Tendlathe went on, and Warreven nodded again. "The off-worlder they hired in to teach us—what was his name?"

"Sten something," Warreven said, wondering where this was leading. "Or something Sten." The Donavies, Aldess their leader, had joked that he was a *blake sten*, punning on the name and his nearly black skin: a stupid thing to remember, after all these years.

"Colde's father wouldn't let her come to those classes," Tendlathe said. "Said they might tell facts, but they weren't true, and he didn't want his daughter having to say they were."

Warreven felt a chill run down his spine, told himself it was only the night breeze on his skin. The First Wave of Emigration had ended in 207, when people had finally made the connection between hyperlumin—hyperlumin-A, he corrected himself, remembering the classroom, the smell of *shaefler* outside the window and Sten-something's dry, accented voice—and the increased rate of miscarriages and intersexual births. FTL travel had ended almost overnight—no one had wanted to risk the mutation, but it was impossible to travel through the jump points without taking hyperlumin to suppress the FTL shock—and hundreds of colonies had been virtually abandoned. Hara had been one of those, a minor place, settled late, at the end of a particularly unpleasant and ill-charted jump point. It had taken nearly four hundred years for the Concord Worlds to find Hara again: too many records had been lost as the old Federation split apart, each colony slowly losing touch with its neighbors. Planets are big: most colonies were well planned, well settled, and they survived; even Hara, as mineral-poor as it was, had thrived. What was the loss of technology, compared to the riches of the seas and jungles? But over that time, the rate of intersexual births and of miscarriages had remained just the same, something that could be ignored only as long as Hara was out of touch with the rest of human-settled space. He said, "It is true, Ten, and you know it. We're human, they're human, we all come from the same stock, we've all been exposed to hyperlumin. They just know how to handle it better."

"They've let it take over," Tendlathe said. "And that's why we—why Hara can't sign the Concord." He took a deep breath. "The point I was making is, I think Colde's father was right. Kids shouldn't be taught this, not the way we were—I think that's what ruined Haliday, Raven, and it'll ruin you, too, if you're not careful. We need to be very careful that we understand the difference between fact and truth, and I'm not having a child of mine exposed to that."

Warreven stared at him for a moment. They'd had this argument before, in one form or another—it defined the basic difference between Traditionalists and Modernists, and Warreven had been a Modernist from the day he'd walked out on Temelathe's offer—but this was the most extreme version he'd heard Tendlathe espouse. "Well, if you don't go to the off-worlders, I doubt you'll have that problem."

"What do you mean?" Tendlathe's face was tight and set behind the narrow beard.

Warreven sighed, already regretting the words. "Just what I said. Aldess has had four miscarriages already, not a live birth yet in, what, eighteen bioyears? She's not stupid, she's never been stupid about this sort of thing, and if she says she needs help from the off-worlders, then I'd trust her."

"Then you won't help me."

"I won't try to talk her out of it," Warreven said.

"You never liked her," Tendlathe said.

"No, I don't," Warreven answered, "but I think she's right."

"I might've known you'd be jealous," Tendlathe said. He sounded remote, almost thoughtful—*you would have said calm*, Warreven thought, *except for the grip of his hand on the arm of his chair that made his knuckles stand out white against the gold of his skin*.

"I'm not jealous—"

"It was you who turned me down."

Warreven took a deep breath, no longer bothering to keep control of his temper. "I said I wouldn't marry you, and I wouldn't change my sex. That's my right, under law and custom, to say what I am, and I made my choice to be a man. And I would still have slept with you. Then."

Something ugly writhed across Tendlathe's face, and for an instant Warreven thought he'd gone too far. He let his hand slide down the stem of the wineglass, ready to smash it into an improvised dagger. It was a trick he'd learned in the *wrangwys* bars and dance houses, never expected to use in Temelathe's house— Then Tendlathe slammed his hand against the arm of his chair, the sound very loud in the quiet space, and Warreven let himself relax.

"I'm not wry-abed," Tendlathe said, through clenched teeth.

"Fine," Warreven answered. *But I am.* He let those words hang, unspoken, not needing to be spoken, set the undamaged glass carefully on the table beside the half-full jug, and pushed himself to his feet. "We both made choices, Ten. Live with it."

Tendlathe looked away, tight-lipped, said nothing. Warreven hesitated for a moment, wishing there were something he could

say that would bring back the old days, said at last, "Good night."
Tendlathe muttered something in return. Warreven sighed,
and turned away, letting himself out into the cool dark of the garden.

player:
> (Hara) an off-worlder who is involved in trade, or who is willing to pay for sexual favors; not a common term outside of Bonemarche and assimilated areas.

trade:
> (Hara) specifically, the semi-organized business of sex (paid for in money or favors) between off-worlders and indigenes of either legal gender; because these transactions take place outside the normal social systems, and involve unusually large sums of money and/or metal as inducement, an indigene in trade, whether a man or a woman, is not necessarily considered to be a prostitute. By extension, the term also covers indigenes and off-worlders who facilitate the buying and selling of sexual favors, and the various permits that allow off-worlders to stay on Hara.

WARREVEN

Lightning flickered beyond the windows, too far away as yet to hear the thunder. Warreven counted the seconds anyway, to fifteen, and then to twenty—more than eight kilometers away, too far to worry about—then dragged his attention back to the courtroom. No one had noticed the lapse: the judges—one from each of the clans involved in the case and a man from the White Watch to arbitrate—were still murmuring over their noteboards, heads close together, bodies inclined toward the center. Behind them, the notice board displayed the particulars of the case in letters and a machine-read strip for the off-worlders that flashed brighter than the lightning. Warreven wasn't wired; he looked instead toward the table where the brokers were waiting. Beyond them, he could see the IDCA agents and their advocate, Dinan Taskary, punctiliously respectful in his formal suit; they were technically the greater danger to his client, but he was more concerned with the brokers. All three of them—all men, or maybe the third, the slight one who wore no jewelry, was only passing—were sweating, and that was a good sign. They were all indigenes, Green Watch men, two Maychilders and an Aldman; if they were sweating, it was not from the heat, but from worry.

Thunder grumbled, and Warreven glanced again toward the window. The storm was getting closer, a darker band of cloud shouldering up beneath the gray outriders, blue-black against the orange tiles of the roofs of Ferryhead on the far side of the harbor. As he watched, lightning flashed again, a jagged, multiforked bolt from cloud to ground. He counted again and reached fifteen before he heard the thunder.

One of the judges looked up at the sound, an older woman, dressed in an off-world shirt and narrow trousers, but with strands of shell and glass beads woven into her graying hair. She beckoned to the nearest clerk, and said, "Lights, please."

The young man nodded and crossed to the central podium, where he fiddled with the room controls. The lights came up strongly, blazing to life in the inverted bowls of the hanging lamps, and threw a distorted reflection of the courtroom across the lower half of the window. The clouds still visible in the upper half looked even darker by contrast.

Warreven stared at the reflection, picking out his own image—common enough, distinguishable only by position and by the loose mane of hair—from among the line of lawyers and advocates and the brokers and *seraalistes* that filled the spectators' seats at the back of the room. In the imperfect mirror, the groups of people waiting for their cases to come up looked like shapes in a kaleidoscope, the bright colors of the indigenes' traditional clothes vivid against the duller off-world palette. By contrast, the three judges behind their tall bench looked like a painting formally composed, the triangle of bodies leaning together over the one man's noteboard, blending, through the brown arms outstretched to balance the women on the ends, with the polished wood below.

"Æ, Raven."

The voice was barely a murmur, but Warreven winced and turned his eyes back to the courtroom.

"Are you all right?"

Warreven nodded, knowing perfectly well why the question had been asked, and made a show of recalling something on his noteboard. The Stane judge, who as the White Watch spokesman had ultimate authority over the court, was a stickler for the proprieties and would be looking for an excuse to throw the case to IDCA. Under the cover of the gesture and the flickering text, he answered, "Sorry."

Malemayn—they were both Stillers, and closer kin than clansmen, had been born in the same *mesnie*—nodded, and touched the noteboard's screen, highlighting a meaningless bit of text. Warreven pretended to study it, and brought himself back to the matter at hand. So far, they had succeeded in keeping the case out of IDCA's hands—the Interstellar Disease Control Agency had a deep and bitter interest in matters of trade—but they still had not convinced the judges that their client, a Trencevent from the Equatoriale, had been duped by the brokers and deserved his passage home. He could still see Chattan, a thin, wiry herm who looked almost convincingly male, sitting in their office, seascarred face composed, only his knotted hands betraying his embarrassment as he tried to explain his problem. The brokers had promised him a sea-factory job, he said, but had told him it wouldn't start for another week; in the meantime, they suggested, he could make quite a bit more money playing trade for the offworlders. Chattan had agreed—though he was *not*, he had said, lifting both hands for emphasis, *wry-abed*, had only gone with people who called themselves women—but when the week was up, there had been no factory job waiting. The brokers had shrugged off his complaint: they had found him a job, after all; they would neither return his fees nor find him something else.

Of its type, it was an unusually easy case, Warreven acknowledged—trade wasn't a real job by anyone's definition—but he couldn't afford to let his attention wander, especially after his run-in with Tendlathe three days before. Temelathe was vigorous, but he wasn't getting any younger; it was important to get precedents established now, while the Most Important Man could still be relied on to accept them as part of customary law. Still, it was hard to concentrate in the warmth of the courtroom, with the edge of thunder, the faint sharp smell of the coming rain that seeped into the building through the ventilators. He had always liked thunderstorms, had been born in one, or so his aunts said, and even at his age the promise of a storm was like a drug.

The judges settled back into their places, and Warreven fixed his eyes on the bench. Malemayn—he was the speaker for this particular case, as the most traditionally acceptable of the three partners—rose to his feet at the Stane judge's gesture. The brokers' advocate stood too, expressionless, showing no sign of the defeat he had to expect, and Taskary copied him at the IDCA table. Warreven touched the edge of the noteboard, closing files, and then folded his hands over the screen. The gray-haired judge—she was the Maychilder judge, closest kin to the brokers—was watching him, and Warreven met her stare without regret or anger. The brokers had a job to do, and a difficult one; people lied to them, would say anything to get out of the Equatoriale, if they were at the bottom of their *mesnie*, or their kinship, or just hated knowing that in Bonemarche, not quite two thousand kilometers from the jungle tracts, anyone could have all the technology, all the luxuries, just for ready money. And people lied to their advocates, too: he and Malemayn had learned early to verify the stories of anyone who claimed they had been lured into trade unwillingly. But this time, it was the brokers who had lied, and Chattan deserved some recompense.

The Stane judge nodded to the nearest clerk, who reached across to sound the court's bell. It was metal, like the bells at the White Watch House, and its note silenced the murmured conversations in the back of the room. Even Warreven, who had heard it and other metal bells many times before, shivered at the sound. In the sudden quiet, thunder rumbled.

"The court speaks," the clerk said. "Archer Stane speaks for the court."

"The court decides," Archer said, "that the Carrier Labor Brokerage, represented by Langman and Richom Maychilder and Bellem Aldman, are required to repay the fees paid to them by Chattan Trencevent. The question of fares back to his *mesnie* is continued until after the Midsummer holiday."

"Mir Archer," Malemayn said, "Chattan is living in the Red Watch's holdfast here in the city, he has no means—"

Archer shook his head. "The case is continued," he said, and gestured to the clerk. "Ten-minute break, Aldane."

The clerk repeated the words, touching the metal bell again, and there was a rustle as the people in the back of the room began to move, some turning back to conversations, others moving forward as their cases were called. Overhead the display board changed, announcing the next case. Warreven looked instead at the brokers' advocate, who met his stare with a bland smile.

"How much do you suppose he . . . contributed?" Malemayn said, bending over the table to collect his noteboard.

"More than we did," Warreven answered. Malemayn managed a sour smile at that, and behind him, Warreven could see Taskary shaking his head as he joined the other IDCA representatives. "The Stane *baanket* should be lavish this year."

"It had better be," Malemayn muttered, and turned away. They all knew how the case would end now. The brokerage would return the original fee, and Chattan would vanish, ready to pay his own money to be back in his own *mesnie* for the approaching Midsummer holiday. The brokerage would demand at the continuation that Chattan appear, and—since it was unlikely he'd return—the case would be dismissed for lack of a plaintiff. Chattan Trencevent would get his money back, which was most of what he wanted, and the brokers who provided the off-worlders with a lucrative service weren't unduly embarrassed. It was, Warreven thought, an elegant, if not an ethical, solution.

"We'll send the voucher as soon as it's processed," the brokers' advocate said. "Will tomorrow morning be convenient?"

Malemayn nodded. "Fine."

"I have every confidence in you," Warreven said, and meant it. The sooner the fee was returned, the sooner Chattan would head for the Equatoriale, no matter what any of them said to him about court dates.

The other advocate nodded in ambiguous acknowledgment, the hint of a smile just touching his thin mouth, and turned away.

Malemayn sighed. When he was sure the brokers and their party were out of earshot, he said, "Well, so much for this one."

"We got the fee back," Warreven said.

"True." Malemayn glanced at the window and the massing clouds. "You want to catch lunch in the district? I doubt we can get back to Blind Point before that breaks."

Warreven nodded, and they threaded their way through the crowd to the door. Outside, in the wide hall, it was suddenly dark. Warreven blinked twice, and nearly walked into a woman in full traditional dress. The hem of her weighted skirt, heavy with shells and glass, slapped his shins, but she was hurrying and did not look back. He made a face, and a tallish person—male by dress, but as ambiguous as Warreven himself in face and body—gave a sympathetic smile. Warreven smiled back, glad as always of the odd-bodied's unpredictable kinship, and started down the stairs to the central lobby.

The air smelled abruptly of rain, the thread of breeze from the main doors suddenly cool and cleansed. Malemayn muttered something under his breath, but Warreven threw back his head, enjoying the change. The noon rains would bring no more than temporary relief from the day's heat, but even that was worth savoring, with Midsummer so near. Thunder rumbled outside, a long, sharp roll like the sound of a *tonnere* drum, and Malemayn said, "So much for getting in before the rain."

Warreven shrugged, and pushed through the doors onto the narrow portico. It was raining, all right, the big soft drops that preceded the main storm, and the clouds were almost blue in the eerie dark. A breath of wind wound around the columns that held up the roof, tasting of sea and storm, licking at his skin like electricity. He suppressed the desire to run out into it, down the five stairs that led up to the courthouse and out into the open space of the plaza, and turned his face to the clouds. A drop of rain struck his cheek, carried by the fickle wind; he blinked, and lightning split the clouds overhead, a great streak of light followed half a heartbeat later by the crack of thunder. He stood dazzled, and someone ran up the steps into the shelter of the porch, colliding with him at the top.

"Sorry—"

They had caught at each other instinctively to keep from falling, and Warreven found himself looking up into a handsome, bearded face. He smiled, and the stranger smiled back and released him.

"That was close."

The voice was off-world, as were the fair skin and hair. Warreven let go with some reluctance, and answered in the off-world creole, "But off the ground, anyway."

The off-worlder nodded, and looked back over his shoulder at the clouds. He was breathing hard from his dash across the plaza, and his shirt was splotched with damp patches the size of a child's hand. A few drops of water clung to his neat beard, and some of his golden-red curls were flattened against his skull. He was, Warreven realized, extremely handsome.

"Still too close for me," the stranger said, with another smile that showed white and even teeth—off-world teeth, Warreven thought, automatically. The stranger nodded, still casually polite, and walked past him into the building.

Warreven watched him go, and Malemayn said, from the doorway, "Do you know him?"

Warreven shook his head. "I wish I did."

"God and the spirits." Malemayn looked quickly over his shoulder. "Do you mind, Raven?"

"Anyone would think you were wry-abed, not me," Warreven said. "There's no one here, Mal. Relax."

"You should still be more careful," Malemayn said. "What if one of the judges heard?"

"If they haven't take my license yet," Warreven began, and Malemayn shook his head.

"They haven't taken your license yet because Temelathe likes you. Don't push it—"

The rain came down in earnest then, drowning his words in the rush of water. Warreven looked out across the plaza suddenly obscured, as though by fog; overhead, the clouds were already lighter. He raised his voice to carry over the downpour. "Do you know him?"

"Æ?"

"Him. The guy who ran into me."

Malemayn gave him a look, exasperation and affection compounded. "You don't give up, do you?"

"No." Warreven looked up at the sky, gauging the storm's progress. Lightning flared again, and Malemayn's curse was covered by the thunder. "Do you?"

"Yeah, sort of," Malemayn said. "He's a pharmaceutical— NAPD."

"I don't know them."

"No reason you should, they're not that big—one of the Fifty, I think. This one, he runs their local office."

"Do you know his name?"

"Raven—" Malemayn stopped, shook his head. "Titan, Tatian, Tatya, something like that. I think his family is Mhyre. Can we go now?"

"I thought you didn't want to get wet," Warreven said, and heard Malemayn swear again.

---

player:
    (Concord) one who participates in trade; a person who does not conform to any of the culturally recognized patterns of sexuality or who wishes to indulge in sexual behaviors and roles not acknowledged by Concord culture, and who is willing to pay professional or semi-professional prostitutes to take on the reciprocal role(s).

trade:
    (Concord) commercial or "specialty market" sexuality; on Hara, specifically the practice of paying indigenes of any gender for sexual favors and to assume sexual roles not usually taken by persons of that particular gender. Commercial sex is normally regulated by the IDCA, which provides medical and legal recourse for all parties, but Haran trade remains outside Concord law. In conversational usage, "trade" can also refer to the various quasi-legal markets for residence papers, travel permits, etc. that make it possible for Concord citizens to remain on Hara.

Tatian shook himself as he passed into the dimly lit main hall. His shirt still clung to his back, and he shrugged his shoulders until he'd freed the damp cloth. Then he glanced sideways, waking his system and bringing up the sleeping file. The time and place of the meeting blazed against the shadows, and he blinked them away, the room confirmed. At least he had gotten to the courthouse before the worst of the storm had hit. He could hear it now, a steady roar against the roof, filling the near-empty hall with the sound, and he wondered if the person he'd run into at the top of the steps had far to go. Whoever—she? it had been a long time since Tatian had seen an indigene who did not dress to demonstrate legal gender, but he had distinctly felt breasts beneath the thin silk of her tunic, in the moment they'd collided. Still, whoever she was, she was rather nice looking. It was just a pity she—or 3e? 3e could be a herm, which would be too bad—was an indigene. Of course, working in the courts, she might be assimilated— He broke that train of thought sternly. She might also be a herm, which would mean he himself wouldn't be interested. And, anyway, Masani was right: even the most assimilated indigenes were very different from off-worlders. Besides, he had work to do.

He reached for the control pad buried between the bones of his right wrist and fingered it, summoning a second display. A summary of the last two years' licensing agreements, with the legal and extralegal payments that had accompanied them, flashed into the corner of his vision. The display was accompanied by the tingle deep in his nerves that meant that the failing connection was getting worse. He shook his hand tentatively—it had helped before—and felt another jab of static. Isabon was right, he was going to have to get it repaired soon, but where on Hara was he going to find techs who could do that kind of microsurgery? There were techs in Startown, sure, but too many of them stayed on Hara only because they weren't good enough to get hired offworld. The technicians in the port itself were good, but they were hardly surgeons, and they charged what their monopoly would bear. NAPD would pay for the surgery, but he himself would have to buy the parts, with no guarantee that the Old Dame would reimburse him for anything. And on top of that, going to the port would mean seeing, and probably dealing with, Prane Am. It was an old problem, new indecision. He put it aside again and passed through a green-painted door into the maze of inner corridors.

These halls were brightly lit and narrow, and the sound of the rain was abruptly distant, as though someone had thrown a switch. He blinked in the sudden light, then found his bearings and turned down the first of the corridors that would eventually lead him to the Licensing Bureau. It was always tricky dealing with Wiidfare, and NAPD's general export permit was up for renewal in another year; it was going to be awkward to turn down the extra personnel permits without jeopardizing next year's negotiations, or this year's harvest permits. All in all, he thought, it promises to be an interesting meeting.

The door of the Licensing Bureau was half open, as always, and the waiting room was crowded. Half a dozen indigenes were sitting in the lesser chairs toward the left side of the open space, and Tillis Carlon was already waiting in the place of honor beside the empty secretary's desk. Tatian lifted an eyebrow at that—Carlon was chief-ops for Norssco, NAPD's closest current rival—but schooled himself to present an indifferent front. Carlon nodded a greeting, but said nothing. Tatian matched the gesture and looked through the glazed greenglass wall behind the desk into the clerks' room. It was as cluttered as ever, crowded with indigenes and old-fashioned datadisks the size of a man's palm and binders and folders crammed with realprint. The computers were plainly visible, boxy monsters dominated by their display screens and touch- and keypads, and half the secretaries wore dark viewlenses that made them look blind. That was the best there was, on Hara, and Tatian wondered again where he would find someone to repair his implants.

Wiidfare's receptionist was nowhere in sight, but before Tatian could ask, the door to the inner room opened, and the young mem appeared, tucking þis datalenses into þis pocket. *His* pocket, Tatian amended silently, and *his* lenses. Beivin Stane was clearly a mem—þis real gender was obvious in þis beardless face, þis slight, almost boyish build, even in þis temperament, the stolid precision with which þe managed Wiidfare's business—but on Hara, þe was legally and culturally a man.

"I'm sorry to keep you waiting, Mir Tatian—Ser Mhyre, that is," Beivin said, þis light voice completely without expression. "Ser Tillis, I'm afraid the appointment is filled after all. If you come with me, Ser Mhyre?"

þe held open the inner door, but Tatian looked at the other off-worlder. "Poaching?"

Carlon shook his head. "Call me."

"I will," Tatian answered, and followed Beivin into the inner rooms.

Wiidfare rose from behind his massive desk as the door opened and gestured expansively toward the visitor's chair. "Mir Tatian, how good to see you. I trust everything was in order, that the package met your expectations?"

Tatian seated himself, leaning back with a comfort he didn't entirely feel. "The permits came through fine, thanks, Mir Wiidfare, but the numbers seem to have gotten garbled in the transmission. I have two more exploration tags than I need, and an extra residency permit for Bonemarche. I need to clear this up before I can authorize the release of payment."

Wiidfare made a production of consulting his desk. It was a recent model, Tatian realized, had been standard in the Concord Worlds as recently as five years ago: one more reminder of Wiidfare's status. Wiidfare was Temelathe Stane's nephew, and Temelathe was the unofficial master of Hara's indigenous government—the Most Important Man, the indigenes called him, with bleak humor—but then, Temelathe had a dozen nephews. Not all of them were as close to Tendlathe as Wiidfare was, either, Tatian thought. I'd give a great deal to know how many of them have desks like this one.

"My records show that you requested five exploration tags," Wiidfare said, "and four residency permits. One for you and for each of your employees. I'm rather surprised you're able to manage with so few people."

"We hire locals where we can," Tatian said. "Company policy. Which is why Stane Derry—Derebought Stane—doesn't need a permit. It's an easy mistake to make, but I do need to clear it up. And we only want three tags."

"There must have been a transmission error." Wiidfare looked at his desk again, one hand moving gently over the shadowscreen embedded in its polished surface. "I can withdraw the tags without a problem, but rescinding a residency permit is always difficult—almost as hard as issuing one. The Colonial Committee, IDCA, they make it very tough to grant them on the spur of the moment. I should warn you that if you find you need a permit on short notice, I can't guarantee that you'll be able to get one. I would suggest that you keep it—you never know when you'll have visiting staff, technical advisers, coming in."

So that was what this was all about, Tatian thought. Wiidfare was playing trade—not for the first time, either—and playing the game rather crudely. Tendlathe's people didn't usually participate, but then, Wiidfare was in a position to make serious money, metal money, out of it. He said, "I understand. The permits are expensive, though, and we're not projecting bringing in anymore staff for at least a couple of years. Under the circumstances, I'll have to pass."

"It wouldn't be that hard to find someone to split the costs," Wiidfare said. "I know, oh, at least a dozen people who have been trying to get permits for years."

And all of them are players, Tatian thought. And probably high-paying players, too. He hesitated for a moment, considering his options, and then smiled widely. "Mir Wiidfare, let me be blunt. We've had a good relationship in the four years I've been on Hara, and I don't want to do anything to jeopardize it. But you know my boss's position on trade. I appreciate the opportunity, but I have to refuse."

"There are other companies," Wiidfare said.

"I know," Tatian said. "But thank you for thinking of me."

There was a silence, and for a moment Tatian wasn't sure if he'd gone too far. Then Wiidfare leaned back in his chair and laughed, and the off-worlder released a breath he hadn't known he'd been holding.

"All right, suit yourself," Wiidfare said. "Three exploration tags and three residency permits, one a semi-permanent for Shan Reiss, who was born in Irenfot of off-world parents." His hands were busy on the desktop as he spoke; an instant later, a diskwriter whined to life on the far wall. "Though if your boss so disapproves of trade, I'm surprised Mir Reiss has lasted this long."

"Really?" Tatian said, and made his voice as bored as possible. Reiss was hardly a player, except by the Haran definition; he was omni, but that was all—and he'd been raised as a Haran and, could be excused a little confusion. More to the point, he didn't profit from his games.

Wiidfare snorted, and pointed to the diskwriter. "The forms are there, if you'll sign them."

Tatian collected the disk and, at Wiidfare's impatient gesture, spun a secondary reader to face him on the desktop. He fed the disk into it and paged quickly through the files, making sure all the codes were correct. "Thank you, Mir Wiidfare, this looks perfect." He touched the locking sequence as he spoke, fixing the text and signing his name and various identification numbers at the same moment.

Wiidfare nodded, his expression sour, and accepted the disk. "I'll need payment within twenty-four hours."

"I'll transfer the—processing fees—this afternoon," Tatian answered. He did not need to add that they would include a sizable payment for Wiidfare himself.

"Excellent," Wiidfare said. "Then, if you'll excuse me?"

"Of course."

Tillis Carlon was no longer in the outer office, and Beivin was cloistered behind þis viewlenses, fingers busy on an analog pad. For a moment, Tatian was tempted to interrupt him, to demand to know where Carlon had gone, but controlled his anger. Haran corruption was like nothing else in human space; one paid what one had to and put up with the side games. But he would call Carlon and find out what he had been doing here.

The rain was still loud in the main hall, and Tatian was not surprised, as he pushed his way through the doors onto the narrow porch, to find the two indigenes still waiting, both looking out into the rain. One was definitely male, legally and in reality, a tall man, light-skinned for a Haran, with close-cut black hair and a beak of a nose that dominated his profile. The other, the one he'd run into on the stairs, was shorter and darker, and the loose silk shirt and vest and soft trousers effectively hid the relative sizes of hip and breast and shoulder. Deliberately hid? Tatian thought, and wondered again about a Haran who would conceal legal gender. Haran law and custom demanded that everyone belong to one of the two acknowledged sexes; society enforced that artificial distinction rigorously. It was even rumored that there were still *mesnies*, along the southern coast toward Fariston and in Pensemare on the Southland, where children born mem, fem, or herm were surgically altered to conform to the parents' wishes. That seemed unlikely—even on Hara, the child's health was usually considered paramount—but the thought was discomfiting. It was almost as odd to imagine a Haran embracing ambiguity of body.

The stranger saw him looking then and smiled. Tatian smiled back, but the expression was cut off by a sudden static pain in his wrist. It ran quickly up the molecular wires and reached his elbow, spreading a tingling numbness before he could grab the control pad and shut the system down completely. The stranger had been watching, curious as a cat, and Tatian felt himself flushing. To his surprise, however, it was the other indigene who spoke first.

"Are you all right?" His voice, cultured and almost accentless even in creole, held nothing but a mild concern, but Tatian felt the color deepen in his face.

"Fine, thanks." That was patently a lie, and he added reluctantly, "I've got a loose connection in my implants, that's all. It stings a little sometimes."

"I would imagine." That was the first stranger, the ambiguous one. The voice was as indeterminate as the body and clothes, in the midrange that could mean almost any gender. He could just see the swell of breasts beneath the silk, not quite concealed by the drape of the vest, but the stranger was too wide through the shoulders, too narrow-hipped, to be a woman. Probably a herm, then, Tatian thought, with regret: 3e wasn't busty enough, or long legged enough, to be a fem. 3e probably passed for male, though—most herms did—but it was still hard to be sure from 3er clothes. It was too bad; 3e would have been a striking woman.

"Do you think the rain bothers it?" 3e went on, and Tatian shook his head.

"I doubt it. Though anything's possible."

"There's a woman over in Startown," 3e said, slowly, and tilted 3er head to one side. In that position, 3e looked more than ever like a cat, pointed face and wide-set eyes framed by a mane of coarse black hair. "She does some work on implants."

"Oh?" Tatian said, without much hope, and the indigene nodded.

"Starli—Starli Massingberd, her name is, she's no kin of mine. But she works the *kittereen*, the jet-car circuit, cars and racers. You might talk to her."

That sounded promising, after all, and Tatian nodded. "Starli Massingberd—in Startown?"

"She has a shop there. She'll be on the rolls."

"I'll look for her," Tatian said. *And I'll also check her out with Reiss.* Shan Reiss raced *kittereens*, when he wasn't driving for NAPD. "Thanks."

The indigene smiled again. "I'm Warreven." 3e nodded to the other indigene. "And Malemayn. We're both Stillers."

"Ser Mhyre Tatian." Tatian held out his hand in automatic reflex, lulled by the creole, and Warreven took it gingerly. Assimilated 3e might be, but the handshake was still unfamiliar.

"We were heading out for lunch," Warreven went on, releasing the other's hand. "Care to join us?"

Behind him, the other indigene—Malemayn—made a soft noise that might have been laughter or disapproval, or both. Tatian considered for an instant. It wasn't a proposition, exactly, more of a first move, but the hints of interest, of trade, were unmistakable. "Thanks," he said, "but I've got to get back to the office."

"Maybe some other time," Warreven said, and Tatian nodded. The rain had almost stopped, and watery sunlight was beginning to show through the clouds. Curls of steam rose from the puddles in the plaza, and the air smelled suddenly, violently, of seaweed.

It wasn't a long walk from the courthouse to the Estrange where NAPD had its offices, but the sun was fully out by the time Tatian reached the arcade that led to Drapdevel Court. All but the largest puddles had evaporated, leaving wet shadows that shrank as he watched, and his shirt clung damply to his body in the revived heat. The old woman who owned the rights to the vendor's pitch at the mouth of the arcade nodded to him, but didn't stop rearranging her stock, disordered when she'd covered it against the rain. Tatian knew better, after four years on Hara, to hope for much that he could comfortably eat or drink, but he scanned the trays anyway. She had dozens of braids of feelgood, some in sheaths, the rest coiled for the smoking pot, and sticks of sourcane soaking in *liquertie*, a pottery jug heating over a candle flame, and, at the base of the cheap clown-glass statue of Madansa, the spirit who controlled the markets, a plug of odd fibrous stuff he didn't recognize. That was worth investigating—he could name four proprietary drugs that had been discovered as an unknown plant in a marketwoman's tray—and he paused to examine it. Up close, it seemed to be a web of close-growing, hairy cords wound over an inner object the size of a child's fist. He picked it up curiously, turned it over in his hand. The cords were leathery to the touch, the hairs prickly in his palm; the dark brown skin seemed almost warm to the touch. He sniffed it warily, and grimaced at the familiar musty odor. Hungry-jack, he thought, and in the same instant found the cross-shaped mark at the tip of the ovoid where the pod's pseudomouth had been. He pried back one lip, using the corner of a fingernail, and found the scarlet flesh of the inner pod. The old woman was watching him narrowly, and he handed it to her, saying, "Hungry-jack, grandmother?"

She nodded, weighing the pod in her hand. "They clean the pods when they take them in the *seraals*. This is the whole thing, dried in the sun on a sandbed."

"Is there a difference?"

The woman shrugged. "It's different—milder, but you'll still fly, my son."

There was no point, Tatian thought, trying to explain off-world physiology to the indigenes. Harans used the full pharmacopeia almost from the cradle; they grew up chewing poppinberry for a stimulant and drinking nightwake and sweetrum to relax, and a ten-year-old was as likely as an adult to throw a braid of feelgood on the kitchen fire after a hard day's work. An offworlder couldn't hope to match that inbred tolerance. "I'll take it."

The old woman looked him over. "Three megs a decigram. Or all of it for fifty grams of metal."

Hara was metal-poor, and the little that lay close to the surface tended to be tied up in the ironwood trees that grew along the slopes of the central mountains. It was hard, sometimes, for Tatian to imagine the relative worth of the off-world coins in his pockets. And Warreven, he thought suddenly, had been wearing metal bracelets—not glass or carved and painted ironwood, but bright, silver-colored metal. And so had Malemayn: they were Important Men, then, in the Stiller clan. He reached into his pocket and produced a handful of coins. The old woman set up her scale—placing it politely in front of the statue of Madansa, though, equally politely, she made only a perfunctory invocation—and set a fifty gram weight in the seller's pan. Tatian counted out coins, six quarter-dollars from Joshua, and then five copper hundredths stamped with the Ansonia Corporation's monoglyph to bring the scales into balance. The woman eyed the scales and took her weight away.

"Enjoy the hungry-jack, my son."

"Thank you, grandmother," Tatian answered, and tucked the pod into his trousers pocket with the remainder of his coins. He hadn't saved much, given the exchange rate, by paying in metal, but then he could afford it.

He went on into the arcade, grateful for the fugitive cool of its shadow, and came out into the sudden brilliance of the court. The bricks that paved the central space were still a centimeter deep in water, and the sunlight glanced from its surface as if from a mirror. The walls of the surrounding buildings were patched and flecked with the reflected light. Tatian sighed, anticipating a flooded cellar, and waded through the blood-warm water, scattering the sky's bright image and making the shards of light dance across the red brick walls. He fetched up gratefully on the low doorstep of NAPD's office and stooped to free himself from his wet shoes, peering in through the open door. Stane Derry—Derebought Stane, the office's only full-time botanist, looked back at him from the door of her own office, her broad face eloquent in its lack of expression.

"How's the cellar?" Tatian asked, and stepped barefoot into the building, leaving his shoes to dry on the stone sill.

"Don't ask," Derebought answered, and then relented. "The pump's screwed up again. Reiss is down there now, trying to get it going. We've got a couple of centimeters of water wall to wall."

Tatian nodded, already relieved of the worst of his worries. The backups and other records were stored in watertight cases that stood a quarter of a meter off the stone floor: there would be no real damage from this flooding. "I thought Reiss was in Irenfot for the races."

"He was," Derebought said, and shrugged. "But I guess they got a bad storm, and it washed out the track. So when he showed up here, I figured I'd put him to work." She looked down at her desktop. "Did you get the permits straightened out?"

"I think so." He reached for the secretary cube that stood inside the doorway and ran his hand over the input strip to trigger the output nodes. Images blossomed in the air before his eyes, mixed icons and text, nothing of immediate importance, and the failing connection surged again, sending a wave of cold down his arm. "Have you heard anything about Norssco moving into any of our areas?"

Derebought shook her head. "Not a thing. Why?"

"Tillis Carlon was in Wiidfare's office when I got there. I thought maybe someone was sending a message."

"I wouldn't have thought so," Derebought said, and shrugged. "Then again, maybe Wiidfare's dabbling in trade again."

"Oh, he's doing that." Tatian reached for the keypad, used it to move to the next screen of messages, not wanting to risk his implanted control pad. "Reiss is downstairs?"

"Yes. Are you all right?"

Tatian lifted his sore arm. "The damn connection's getting worse. I'm going to have to get it looked at."

Derebought nodded. "Good luck finding someone."

"Yeah. Ask Reiss to stick his head in my office when he gets through in the cellar, would you?"

"Sure."

"And I bought this on the way in," Tatian said, and pulled out the uncleaned pod. "It's hungry-jack, dried whole. Have you ever heard of preparing it that way?"

Derebought frowned. "I don't think I've ever seen it dried like that. I've seen it whole when it was fresh, but I always thought you had to clean it before you could use it. We always did in my *mesnie*, anyway." She held up her cupped hands. Tatian tossed it across to her, and she turned back into her office. Tatian followed, leaned against the door frame. Derebought set the hairy pod on her desk, pulling her mag-lamp down over it, and peered down through the lens. "Interesting, though."

"Run a full analysis on it, covering and all," Tatian said. "See if anything turns up."

Derebought mumbled agreement, already probing the web of cords with a blunt glass rod, and Tatian sighed, recognizing her absorption. He flicked a toggle on the secretary, setting the system to forward calls to his desk. "I'll be in my office," he said, and pushed open the door.

The desk woke at his approach, sensing his presence, and Tatian flinched as the recognition pulse tingled through his skin. The desktop lit, producing half a dozen working screens scattered through the clear surface, and Tatian scanned them as he sat down. Most were old business, and none was urgent; he reached for the shadowscreen, splaying his hand across its virtual surface to fit his fingers to the current control configuration. He flicked a "button"—a literal hot spot, a bump of warmth under his finger—and a new screen appeared, offering access to Bonemarche's

communications system. It was primitive by comparison to the
systems current on most of the Concord Worlds—even now, a
hundred years after contact had been reestablished with the rest
of human-settled space, most indigenes who lived outside the
urban areas didn't have access to the planetary net; it had only
been last year that all the *mesnies* had gotten a terminal—but it was
at least adequate for communications within Bonemarche itself.
He ran his fingers over the shadowscreen's shifting spaces, summoning contact codes for Norssco and then for Tillis Carlon.
That matter needed to be settled now: Carlon needed to be dis-
abused of the notion that he could poach on NAPD's territories.

A panel slid aside on the wall, revealing a meter-and-a-half-
square flat screen. A red dot appeared, indicating the camera position; Tatian slid his finger down another control, fading it to
near-invisibility, then flicked the control away. Glyphs swam
across the base of the screen, and then a face appeared, a stocky,
dark-skinned woman with a Norssco badge at her collar, the camera dot centered like a misplaced caste mark between her eyes.

"Can I help you, ser?"

"Ser Mhyre Tatian, for Tillis Carlon."

"Ah." The woman's eyes flickered as she consulted some internal display. "I'll patch you straight through, ser."

That was a good sign. Tatian waited while the screen went
blank and then reformed to reveal Carlon sitting at a desk that
very nearly matched his own. A line of icons flickered in the upper
left corner of the screen—security programs currently running,
save-file protocols in effect, nothing out of the ordinary—and Tatian noted them with one corner of his mind, intent on the image
in front of him.

"Tatian." Carlon sounded distinctly relieved.

"You said I should call."

"Yes. I thought I owed you an explanation."

Tatian nodded once, and Carlon gave a smile that was almost
a grimace. "Wiidfare asked me to come in then, said he'd had
someone cancel an appointment. We—I've been having a little
difficulty with our residency permits lately."

From Wiidfare, or from ColCom and the IDCA? Tatian wondered. Norssco had always had a reputation for doing trade in a big way. Not that people of Carlon's rank were involved—at least, not that much—but Norssco employed a good seventy-five or eighty junior staff, secretaries, technicians, backcountry brokers, most of whom supplemented an inadequate income by selling permits to players. But that was none of his business, as long as Carlon wasn't interfering with NAPD. "So have we," he said, voice neutral, and Carlon's smile widened briefly.

"Sorry to hear it."

"Wiidfare offered me an extra permit, with the usual string attached," Tatian said. "I hope he didn't get any ideas about that from you."

Carlon shook his head. "If there are any extra permits, Tatian, I want them for me."

"One other thing," Tatian said. "I will take it very badly if Norssco reps show up in the peninsular *mesnies*. Clear?"

"I—" Carlon stopped, closing his lips tight over whatever else he would have said. "Clear enough. I don't appreciate threats, Tatian."

"It's not a threat," Tatian said, and smiled. "It's a promise."

"Clear," Carlon said, face grim, and Tatian broke the connection. He leaned back in his chair, watching the panel slide closed again over the flat screen. Norssco would bear watching now, at least until after the harvests that were due at Midsummer had all been delivered, but it had been important to state NAPD's position as explicitly as possible.

He reached for the shadowscreen again, trailed his fingers through the varying sensations, cold and hot, rough and smooth, adjusting the desktop to a more comfortable working configuration. Lanhoss Mats, the shipping wrangler, as well as Dere-bought's partner, had left a long, thickly annotated file updating his projections for the weeks following the harvest—storage space available, accessible, and already rented, and the ships scheduled to land and the backup craft available. Tatian sighed, looking at it, but dragged it to the top of the file. The sooner he looked through it, the sooner he could turn it back over to Mats, and he tapped the icon to open it.

The soft sound was echoed, more loudly, from the doorway, and a familiar voice said, "Derry said you wanted to see me?"

Tatian pushed the file away with some relief. "Yeah. Come on in."

Shan Reiss seated himself warily in the visitor's chair. He was young to be NAPD's chief driver, and looked younger, so that Tatian frequently had to remind himself that Reiss had been born on Hara, and knew the backcountry as well as any indigene. He was a thin, tall man, all whipcord muscle, brown skin burned darker by the planet's fierce sun— Could have passed for an indigene, Tatian thought, not for the first time, if it weren't for the vivid blue eyes. At the moment, those eyes were very worried, and Tatian wondered just what he'd been up to. As Wiidfare had implied, Reiss hung out in the trade bars and dance houses; if he was in trouble, it would involve sex. But if he wasn't selling permits, it was no one's business but his own.

"Do you know anything about a tech named Starli?" he asked, and saw Reiss's shoulders slump fractionally. "She's a Massingberd, I'm told."

"Yeah, I know her." In spite of himself, Reiss sounded surprised, and Tatian hoped whatever trouble he was in wouldn't come home to the company.

"Is she any good? Good enough to work on my implants, I mean." Tatian touched his wrist. He had been complaining about the bad connection for a month now.

Reiss tilted his head to one side, an indigene's gesture. "Starli's very good, but she is local. She's not licensed to work on the full suite, just on the stuff the *kittereen* drivers carry."

"Would she work on mine?" Tatian asked. They all knew, and Reiss better than most, as involved as he was in the jet-car races, how expensive it could be to get the necessary certifications. A lot of indigene techs just didn't bother to get the higher-level, more costly papers, but still had the necessary skills to handle the implants. The trick was finding the ones who were genuinely competent.

"She might," Reiss said. "She doesn't have a lot of use for off-worlders. But if she agreed, she'd do a good job. Where'd you hear about her, anyway?"

"I ran into someone at the courthouse," Tatian answered. "Literally. We ended up talking, and I mentioned I needed some work done. And 3e mentioned Starli."

"Did you get a name? It might be somebody I know."

"Warreven. 3e's a Stiller."

Reiss grinned. "I know Raven. He's a big *kittereen* fan—I was surprised I didn't see him up at Irenfot, but I guess if he was in court, that explains it."

"What's 3e do?" Tatian asked. He still hadn't gotten used to Reiss's habit of translating the indigenes' two genders into normal speech.

"He—sorry, 3e's an Important Man." Reiss used the *franca* words, switched back to creole. "3e and a couple of 3er cousins, they're advocates. They specialize in trade cases, defending prostitutes, *marijaks*, you know. Lately, I heard they were taking on a couple of labor brokers for fraudulent hiring."

"That's going to win 3im friends," Tatian said. The labor brokers were under Temelathe's direct protection—were licensed by him personally—and were one of the more lucrative parts of the Most Important Man's private empire. Temelathe's power might technically be based on his position as Speaker of the Watch Council, and indirectly on his status as the direct heir of Captain Stane, but the money that supported all that came from off-world sources.

"Oh, yeah," Reiss said, "and that's not the best of it, either. You know who one of 3er partners is?"

Tatian shook his head.

"Haliday Stiller."

Tatian shook his head again. The name was vaguely familiar, but he couldn't place it.

"You remember," Reiss said, with a hint of impatience. "3e took the clan to court, all the way to the Watch Council, over whether 3e could register as a herm."

"That was before my time," Tatian said. But he did remember the talk; the case had been only a few years old when he first came to Hara. Haliday Stiller had demanded the right to call 3imself a herm on legal documents, and the Watch Council, officially the highest indigenous authority, and Temelathe's puppet, had not only refused to allow it, but, for good measure, had reassigned Haliday's legal gender, decreeing that, since 3e wouldn't choose, the proverbial "reasonable man" would see 3im as a woman. But the person he had seen with Warreven had definitely been male— and the name was Malemayn, he remembered suddenly. "Would Starli do the work if you introduced me? I need to get it done soon."

"I can ask," Reiss said, accepting the change of subject, and looked down at his hands. He was wired, too, had gotten his suit as part of a corporate scholarship deal. "I have to go over to Kittree Row tomorrow morning anyway, I'll ask then. You free in the afternoon?"

"I can make time," Tatian said. "Thanks, Reiss."

"No problem," the younger man said, and rose easily. Tatian watched him go, and turned his attention back to the files on his desktop, trying to ignore the faint static buzz in the bones of his hand. Tomorrow, he told himself, tomorrow, he would find out whether or not he'd have to go to the port for the repairs.

seraaliste, seraalistes:
    (Hara) the man or woman within each clan who is primarily responsible
    for negotiating with the off-world buyers; he or she is also responsible
    for mediating among his or her clan's *mesnies.* This is an elective office.

WARREVEN

They took their time walking back from lunch, savoring the heat
and the fitful land breeze. The streets had been dry when they left
the bar; by the time they reached the Harbor Market, the last
shreds of cloud had vanished inland, and thin white parasols blossomed like flowers in the spaces between the semi-permanent
stalls. Warreven paused at the edge of the embankment, leaned on
the hot stones of the wall to look along the length of the massive
quay that divided the main harbor from the smaller Sail Harbor.
This close to Midsummer, all the berths were filled with slab-
sided, broad-beamed coasters, and the quay swarmed with dockers and their machines, unloading the first of the summer's
harvest. From the embankment, it was impossible to see even the
nearest ship's cargo, but Warreven could fill in the details from
almost thirty summers' experience: there would be crates of
broadleaf kelp, the fronds packed damp, and bales of cutgrass
gathered from the shallows along the Stiller Peninsula. There
would be smaller boxes of wide-web nodes, crumb-coral, and
false-kelp fronds and bladders and even, if someone was very
lucky, a few of the deep-growing false-kelp's knotty holdfasts.
From the Stanelands to the north, there would be ships loaded
down with raw sweetsap and thornberry, branch and fruit alike,
and baskets of creeping star. And it was all going to feed the off-
world economy. He smiled without humor and shaded his eyes to
pick out the off-worlders' runabouts drawn up in the reserved
slots behind the factors' sheds, company marks bright on doors

and engine cowlings. The off-worlders were easy to pick out in the crowd of dockers and sailors, too: pale figures, draped in white or tan against the heat and sun, ghostly against the bright colors around them.

A horn sounded, and the day-ferry appeared beyond the tip of the quay, shouldering its way through the crowd of smaller boats to its anchorage below the Ferryhead. A wedding band was playing on the top deck, the pulse of the drums carrying across the water, and Warreven could just pick out the bride and her attendants, a knot of stark white silk and silver among the holiday colors.

"Anyone we know?" Malemayn asked, and Warreven turned back to face him.

"Not as far as I know."

Malemayn nodded, shading his eyes to look out over the harbor. "I'd hate to miss an obligation."

"Don't worry about that," Warreven said. "Anyone you owe a present will be sure to let you know."

Malemayn grinned, acknowledging the truth of the comment. Warreven looked past him, up the hill to the bars of Dock Row and Harborside. Most of the *wrangwys* houses, the bar and dance houses that catered to trade, off-world players, and Hara's odd-bodied were closed now; most wouldn't open until sundown, but a few were already doing business. He picked out the doors, the sun-faded bars of neon light surrounding them, wondering if any of his friends or clients were there already. Shinbone on the Embankment was open, its double doors wide to the afternoon sun, the bouncer Brisban stretching luxuriously in the warmth; a little farther along the street, a couple of off-worlders were standing outside Hogeye's, nudging each other as they scanned the showcards and dared each other to go in. Warreven made a face at that and turned away.

"We should be getting back."

Malemayn looked at him, startled, then looked up the hill toward the bars. "There's nothing we can do, Raven. Not about them."

"I know. And we should still get back to work." Warreven

pushed himself away from the Embankment wall, headed down the first set of stairs to cut through the Market, drowning his anger in the familiar noise and smells. The Harbor Market was the largest of Bonemarche's three market squares—the others were the Glass Market, on the north side of town by the railroad terminus, and the off-worlders' Souk on the edge of the Startown district—and it was always crowded, even on the edges, the stalls and stone-marked pitches gaudy with goods. Most were local products, foodstuffs, and glass, and silk in skeins and tufts of floss and bolts of dyed and painted cloth; there were a few machine-dealers as well, offering cheap off-world disk-readers and music boxes and card-comps, all at ridiculous prices. The noise of drums cut through the noise of bargaining, and he looked toward the sound to see a woman dancing on the platform where the land-spiders were auctioned at the Quarter-days. It was a good omen, a change of mood, and he started toward it, following the heavy heartbeat of the *tonnere-bas* and the intricate higher double beat of the counterpoint. He stopped at the edge of the crowd surrounding the platform, looking up at the dancer. Malemayn trailed cheerfully enough in his wake, and said, sounding almost surprised, "She's good."

Warreven nodded. The woman—she was definitely a woman—spun and stopped on the raised stage, sunlight flashing from the glass bangles that covered her arms from wrist to elbow. There were glass beads braided into her hair, seemingly thousands of them, in every color; they sparked in the sunlight, and clashed like cymbals as she bent nearly double, hair flying. Her tiered skirts, their hems sewn with still more beads and the occasional bright disk of a metal coin, stood out from her waist as she spun, then collapsed to a twisted cylinder that briefly outlined the long shape of her legs and drew cheers from some of the watching men. The platform at her feet was already littered with flowers and a few coins; the *shaal* spread out between the two drummers in front of the platform held maybe a fivemeg more in small change. There were a few off-world coins among the scattered seaglass, and more flowers. He cocked his head, seeing the latter, and then the dancer straightened again, and he saw the three parallel lines drawn in white across her cheek. Not just a dancer, then, but a *vieuvant*, one of the old souls who served God and the spirits, and this was not just a performance, but an *offetre*, a service to the spirits: she danced for, danced as, the Heart-breaker, the spirit who was spring and lust and all the unruly powers of procreation. The counterpoint drummer wore the same marks on his beardless face.

"She's very good," Malemayn said again, and reached into his pocket. He came up with a handful of coins and tossed half a dozen onto the *shaal* with the rest.

"She is," Warreven agreed, and looked around for a flower seller. He spotted one almost at once—they knew enough to congregate when a *vieuvant* danced, seemed to come from nowhere— and held up a black quarter-meg. The boy came over eagerly, basket held out in front of him.

"I have ruby-drop, mir, and rosas, and dragon-cor, the Lady likes those—"

Warreven nodded, not really listening, and picked up a spray of the horn-shaped ruby-drops. "How much?"

"A quarter-meg, mir, any coin," the boy answered promptly. "Picked fresh this morning."

"Fine." Warreven handed him the stamped glass disk and turned back to the platform. Above him, the *vieuvant* was spinning down to the end of this part of the dance, her skirts flaring out into a perfect bell of silk. He tossed the flowers onto the *shaal*—he had been fond of the Heart-breaker as a child—and followed it with a couple of long-bits and quarter-megs. Malemayn smiled.

"You always get cheated, Raven."

Warreven returned the smile. It was true enough; he was no hand at haggling. "Only in the market, cousin."

Malemayn shook his head, still smiling. "It's a good thing we can afford it. And, speaking of affording things, I thought you wanted to get back to work."

"I did, I do," Warreven answered. "I'm coming."

They threaded their way through the crowds to Harborside where it skirted the Market's edge. Just beyond the Market it narrowed, becoming little more than an access road for the warehouses that stood along the waterfront. Warreven wrinkled his nose at the acrid smell of split power cells that seeped from the nearest building and turned up the first side street, into the shade of the low houses. They had been built for the construction crews building the railroad terminus and hadn't been meant to last much beyond its completion; thirty years later, the poured sandstone walls were crumbling, but the neighborhood was more crowded than ever.

It wasn't a long walk to the base of Blind Point, where the partnership rented space for their *mesnie*. It wasn't a real *mesnie*, of course—there were only three of them, and none of them was married to any of the others, and besides, Haliday, the third partner, lived two buildings away—but it was easier to call it one than to explain it to the traditional indigenes among their clients. Traditional people had enough trouble sometimes understanding the rules of trade; it was easier to explain if the general setting was at least a little familiar. The building was tall for Blind Point, where the original settlers had built close and low, but relatively narrow; its brick frontage was eroding at the corners, and the door was set into the right-hand corner, to make the inside rooms as large as possible. Warreven scuffed his feet on the stone of the sill and kicked his sandals into the mud tray, no longer aware of the narrowness of the hall. Sunlight was streaming in through the one hand-span window at the far end of the building, throwing a wedge of light across the painted plaster wall. The design of twined doutfire and creeping stars had faded there; the colors were still true by the door, where the light never reached. Warreven made another mental note to find a painter, and pushed open the door to the main room.

It was empty, all the lights switched off to save on power fees, and Malemayn said, from behind him, "Where's Chattan, then?"

"I thought he'd be waiting," Warreven answered.

"Raven?" Haliday's voice came from the inner room. "What the hell is going on?"

Warreven frowned, wondering what ȝe was talking about this time, and Malemayn chuckled.

"What have you done now?"

"I don't know," Warreven said, quite seriously, and went into the offices.

It was bright, all the lamps lit and the heavy curtains drawn tight against the contrast-destroying sun. They had divided the space into three cubicles when they formed the partnership and moved in, but the gray foam-core walls barely reached Malemayn's shoulders, so that anyone could see in to the clutter and the bulky computers with their illuminated screens. Haliday stood in the center space, hands on hips, glaring down at one of the three screens that was linked to Bonemarche's narrowcast networks. 3e was wearing off-world clothes, as usual, and as always it gave Warreven a small shock to see the anomaly of 3er body revealed so clearly by the close-fitting fabric. But then, Haliday had always been stubborn that way: 3e had insisted from childhood that 3e was herm, not the boy 3e had seemed to be then, and even now, after 3e had lost 3er case, and been declared legally a woman, 3e refused to answer any pronoun but 3er own.

"What's Raven done this time?" Malemayn asked, and dropped the wallet that held the court disks on the nearest desk.

"Since when did you get into politics?" Haliday demanded, 3er eyes still fixed on Warreven.

"Æ?" Warreven said.

"Politics. You know what that is, though you always say you won't play—except when Temelathe calls, of course." Haliday touched the top of the display. "Why'd you wait to put your name on the list, Raven, were you afraid I'd talk you out of it? Or were you afraid I wouldn't?"

"What are you talking about?" Warreven asked, and came around the cubicle wall to get a look at the screen.

Haliday stepped out of his way, pressing 3er hips against the edge of the desk platform. "I'm talking about the election lists, that's what."

Warreven scanned the screen without answering. It was less than a week to the two-day Midsummer holiday, and most *mesnies* and clans and the five overarching Watches that governed them held their elections then, but what that had to do with him . . . ?

And then, in the center of the screen, he saw his own name, set opposite the post of Stiller *seraaliste*. He stared at it for a moment, feeling remarkably stupid, and Malemayn said behind him, "I wonder who put your name in."

"You're telling me you didn't," Haliday said to Warreven, but 3er voice had lost some of its anger.

"Yes," Warreven said, still staring at the screen. There was only one other candidate, the minimum required by clan law, and the name was all too familiar. Daithef Stiller was a perennial candidate, and more than a little mad; he had never yet been elected to anything. "I mean, yes, I didn't do it," he said, and wondered if he sounded as foolish as he felt.

"Who sponsored him?" Malemayn said.

"The nominating officer was Waterson, who's speaker for the Haefeld *mesnie*." Haliday made a face. "That's over on the sunset coast. Seconding was someone called Tortisen, of Luccem. I don't know either of them, and I can't find a directory listing, electronic or paper, for either one."

"Well, there's a simple solution," Warreven said, and reached for the ancient monophone that stood beside the computer. Parts of the system had come to Hara on the settlement ship five hundred years before—and it had been seventy years out of date on the day of landing—but it was still the only system that was certain to reach all the outlying *mesnies*. Down in the Equatoriale and along the sunset coasts, there were still small *mesnies*, mostly household size, that had evaded Temelathe's order to accept a network terminal; a larger number of others had simply refused to assign anyone to answer the system's mail. He punched code numbers from memory, lifted the headset, and waited until the tinkle of routing codes was finally replaced by a human voice.

"Black Watch House," the voice—a man's—said in *franca*, and then repeated the words in creole.

"Who's the Stiller electing officer?" Warreven asked. "There seems to have been an error in the list."

There was a little silence, and then the voice answered, "That's Brunwyf, out of the Luccem *mesnie*—it's a woman's post this year. She's away up north now, though. Can I take a message?"

"Is she on the system?" Warreven asked, without much hope. "Or the phone?"

"I'm sorry, mir. I don't know if the line's been patched yet. Can I take a message?"

And if Luccem is as traditional as I remember, Warreven thought, there's no point in even trying the network. "Yes," he said aloud. "You can tell her Warreven called, of the Ambreslight *mesnie*. Someone's put my name on the list by mistake, and I'm not a candidate."

"Warreven," the voice repeated, and there was another little silence. "I'll give her that message, mir."

"Thank you," Warreven said, but the connection was already broken. He set the headset back in its place, an unpleasant suspicion forming. Brunwyf was a nobody, just as Luccem was one of the minor *mesnies*, but it was matrilineal, and her father and husband were both Maychilders, part of the string of Maychilder marriages that Temelathe had sponsored over the last thirty years. Which meant—or could well mean—that Brunwyf was part of the faction that was aligned with the Most Important Man. "What do you know about Brunwyf, of Luccem?"

Malemayn shook his head. "Absolutely nothing."

"Isn't she married to a Maychilder?" Haliday asked. "That's one of the matri-*mesnies*, anyway, and they're Traditionalists, that I do know."

"And Traditionalists in Haefeld," Warreven agreed. "So why in all hells would they nominate me?"

"You're hardly a Traditional candidate," Malemayn said, with a grin.

"So they must've been doing someone a favor," Haliday said. "Your would-be father-in-law, Raven?"

Warreven gave 3im a sour look. "It's possible. In fact, I can't think of anyone else who'd bother. But I can't think why."

"Nor can I," Haliday said.

"Well, it's hardly important," Malemayn said. "They can't

make you run if you don't want to, Raven—not even Temelathe can manage that without it looking really bad. So as soon as what's-her-name gets back from Luccem, you can pull your name off the list."

"Do you really want to bet against Temelathe?" Warreven asked, and Malemayn shook his head.

"Not iron, no. But this would be hard even for him."

"I can think of three ways he could force it," Haliday said, 3er voice gone suddenly cold. "But the simplest—well, look who the other candidate is. If Temelathe really wants you to be *seraaliste*, Raven, all he'd have to do is rule that we can't add late candidates. He's head of the Watch Council, he can do it. And then we get Daithef as our *seraaliste*." 3e smiled, not pleasantly. "I think you'd run, Raven, don't you?"

"I'm not going to run for anything," Warreven said.

Malemayn said, "Still, the idea of Daithef as *seraaliste* is enough to give me chills. I hope they're still able to nominate someone else."

"They'd better," Warreven said. "Besides, why would Temelathe want to see me Stiller's *seraaliste*? We've been butting heads with the White Stanes since we opened the office. He knows we don't agree with his policies."

"You've done him favors before," Haliday said.

"Not like this," Warreven answered.

"It doesn't make a lot of sense," Malemayn said.

Warreven shook his head. "It doesn't make any sense at all."

The monophone chimed twice, then twice again. Malemayn made a face and reached for it, flipping the switch to accept the connection. "Malemayn Stiller." His eyebrows rose, and he touched the mute button at the base of the junction box. He held out the handset to Warreven. "It's for you. The Most Important Man."

Warreven reached for it automatically, then shook his head. "Patch it to my console, will you? I think I need to sit down for this one."

Malemayn gave a snort of laughter, and Warreven slipped past him into the cramped cubicle that served him in lieu of a private office. The work surfaces were drifted with papers and the shell-disks that their ancient computers used; more disks had accumulated on top of the main drive box and on the primary display as well. He moved a pile away from the monophone and reached for the handset cautiously, as if it would bite. Malemayn was watching over the low wall, and Warreven nodded.

"Putting you through," Malemayn said, and the next instant, Warreven heard the faint static of an open line.

"Warreven Stiller."

"Raven." There was no mistaking Temelathe's voice, low and mellow as tempered chocolate. "How are you these days?"

"Well, thank you, mir," Warreven answered, and added, knowing it would be expected, "I trust you're the same?"

"Well enough, my son."

Warreven made a face at the old endearment. It was traditional, meaningless, but it also held echoes of Temelathe's comment at Aldess's reinstatement—and was that what he wanted, introducing me to what's-his-name, Kolbjorn, from Kerendach? Warreven wondered suddenly. And referring to me as his might-have-been daughter-in-law would be just one more way of reminding me of old obligations. Of course, if it hadn't been me who would become the wife, I might've been tempted, and Temelathe won't have forgotten that, either. Temelathe never forgot anything, to the smallest detail, and Warreven was uneasily aware of memories, the child, the adolescent he had been, waiting to be invoked.

"But I'll get to the point," Temelathe went on, "and I do apologize for the haste of it. I'm told you want to withdraw your name from the election list."

"I didn't even know I was on it," Warreven said, but Temelathe was still speaking, riding over his words.

"I know it's not strictly speaking my affair, but with Brunwyf away in Luccem for the holiday, I thought I might be able to clear up the problem before it officially became one."

"That's kind of you, my father," Warreven murmured, without the pretense of conviction.

"I'm not in fact clear what the problem is." Temelathe's tone sharpened suddenly, and Warreven imagined the full force of his glare directed at the monophone. "Your clan has seen fit to nominate you; it's your obligation to serve."

"I'm not qualified to be the *seraaliste*," Warreven said, with perfect truth. The clan *seraaliste* handled the sale of all harvested and gathered crops to the off-world brokers, and a man who notoriously couldn't bargain in the markets was hardly an ideal candidate for the job. "Besides, there's another nominee."

"Œ, Raven, Daithef hardly counts as a candidate. Though I admit he'd suit me better than you in some ways."

That was true enough: Daithef could be relied on to make a bad bargain, if only out of spite. "So why, my father, are you trying to talk me into running?"

There was a chuckle at the other end of the line. "Because what's good for Stane isn't necessarily good for Hara. And there's money enough in the off-worlders that we can all share the profits."

"True," Warreven said dubiously; this was not the usual White Stane attitude. "But I'm still not qualified to be the *seraaliste*."

"I think you're underestimating your talents," Temelathe said. "Ah, Raven, this is no way to talk, not through some machine. Come to the house tonight—we're having a small dinner, nothing fancy. We can talk there."

It was not really a request, and they both knew it. Warreven sighed—there had never been an easy way to refuse Temelathe Stane; once was more than most men managed—and said, "I'm honored, my father." His tone was flat, contradicting the conventional words, and Temelathe chuckled again.

"It will be worth your while, Raven, I promise you."

"But will it be worth yours, my father?" Warreven asked. "As you said, I'm not your ideal candidate."

"Nor is Daithef," Temelathe answered, voice suddenly sharpening. And then the anger was gone, smothered, and Temelathe was himself again. "I'll expect you at seven—no, six-thirty. That will give us time to talk a little."

"I'll be there, my father," Warreven said, and broke the connection. He looked up to see the others watching him over the wall of the cubicle and spread his hands in answer.

"You're going to dinner," Malemayn said.

"Of course." Warreven looked at Haliday. "I didn't want or plan this. You do believe me, Hal?"

There was a little pause, Haliday's fierce green eyes fixed on him, and then, slowly, 3e nodded. "Even for you, Raven, this would be—baroque."

Warreven smiled, reassured, and reached across to light his workstation. "Is there anything that absolutely has to be done by tomorrow?"

"Only the usual," Haliday answered, and turned back to 3er own cubicle. "I'll flip it to you. What happened with Chattan's case?"

Malemayn stretched, the metal bracelets clattering down his arms. "Flip me copies, too, will you, Hal? We got Chattan his fees back, but the lead-judge continued the case. Wakelevedy said he'd send the voucher first thing in the morning."

"And the minute Chattan gets the money, 3e'll be off home," Haliday said, bitterly. "I don't suppose there's any way we could hold onto the money until the next hearing."

"No," Warreven said, and sighed as a list of files filled his screen.

"This isn't the case, Hal," Malemayn said, not ungently.

"This is a case we could've won." Haliday glared at the screen. "Who was the lead-judge? Archer Stane?"

Malemayn nodded.

"Damn the Stanes, singly and collectively, to all seven hells in succession," Haliday said. 3e ran a hand through 3er short hair. "Even Archer would've had to give us this one. It was perfect, damn it, poor hard-working, modest-living *halving* from the Equatoriale gets tricked into whoring in Bonemarche, and by a reputable brokerage, no less—we couldn't lose. And it would have called the whole structure of the trade into question, let everybody know that the White Stanes are backing it. So of course Archer continued it."

"We won't win this kind of case until we get somebody from Bonemarche to complain," Malemayn said.

"And we won't win this kind of case if it's a Bonemarche whore complaining," Haliday retorted.

It was an old argument, and Warreven looked back to his screen, jabbed halfheartedly at the list of files to open one at random. Over the last two calendar-years, the partnership seemed to have been spending more and more of its time dealing with the fallout of the off-world sex trade, with the full-time prostitutes and the part-time *marijaks* and *marianjs* who worked the harborside, and with the off-worlders and wry-abed indigenes who patronized them. Temelathe preferred to turn a blind eye to the business—as long as he got his discreet share of the bar and dance-house profits, he didn't care who went there, or for what— but at the same time he had to stay on good terms with the Colonial Committee and the Interstellar Disease Control Agency, who existed to regulate trade. At the same time, most of the pharmaceutical companies, from the Big Six down to the smallest pony-shows, turned a blind eye to their employees' thriving sideline in the residence and travel permits that were the other side of trade. And Hara was dependent on the pharmaceuticals for all of its hard-cash income. It was not, Warreven admitted silently, an easy situation for Temelathe, but it was a lot harder on the wry-abed.

Malemayn and Haliday were still arguing, voices low enough to ignore, and Warreven fixed his attention on the open file on the screen in front of him. It was an application-to-emigrate for someone named Destany Casnot, herm passing for male—a Black Casnot rather than a Blue, which made him distant kin; Casnot, like most of the large clans, was split between two Watches—and he paged quickly through the file, looking for the inevitable problems. The partnership didn't get the easy cases; if this had been a straightforward emigration case, it would have gone to ColCom without the need for legal backing. Sure enough, the person sponsoring the application was listed as Sera Timban 'Aukai, who called herself Destany's common-law wife. He knew 'Aukai, all right: all of the wry-abed did. She had for years managed an import service just off the Soushill Road, where indigenes looking for trade could sell or pawn traditional goods and find safe introductions. And now she was ready to leave Hara and wanted to take a current lover with her.

"Who took this emigration case?" he said, cutting through the others' continuing argument.

"Æ?" That was Malemayn.

Haliday leaned over the cubicle wall. "It's not what you think, Raven."

"Oh?"

"I know you never liked 'Aukai, but she's all right. Destany hasn't done trade for ages, they've been living together for the last seven calendar-years. ColCom's kicking her out—they caught her on a technicality, selling foodstuffs, for which she isn't licensed. She's appealing that, too, but she and Destany want to stay together."

Warreven sighed, some of the irritation fading. 'Aukai had told him, years ago, when he'd first come to Bonemarche, that he wasn't suited for trade—which had turned out to be true, but it hadn't been much help at the time. Trade was the quickest way for the odd-bodied to earn a decent living in Bonemarche; the *wrangwys* bars and dance houses where trade was played were also the places where the wry-abed found each other. He had lived on the fringes of that world, a *marijak* and occasional *marianj* rather than a proper whore, for almost two years before he'd agreed to become a clan advocate. And it still pained him to admit that 'Aukai had been right. "Do we have any other support?"

"Mostly Destany's kin," Haliday answered. "But your friend Shan Reiss has offered us an affirmation. He says he'll swear Destany and 'Aukai have been monogamous for the last five years at least."

"That's something," Warreven said, and Malemayn's voice rose from the depths of his cubicle. "Isn't Reiss some sort of Casnot himself?"

"He's still an off-worlder," Haliday said. ʒe looked at Warreven. "I wanted to ask you to pull the precedents."

Warreven sighed again, and nodded. He looked down the list of files and saw another familiar name. "All right. But I want Ironroad then."

"It's all yours," Haliday answered. "If I have to see Astrede's smug face again, I'll rearrange it for him."

3e turned away, and Warreven looked back at his screen, mousing quickly through the linked files. Stiller had built the iron road, the railroad that ran from just south of Luccem town down to Bonemarche, and then from Ostferry to Irenfot and on up the coast to Gedesrede, and despite the impossible cost—a price Stiller was still paying—Harans of every clan remembered it with respect. The Ironroad Brokerage was a Stiller company, and was evoking a Stiller triumph, which made this a matter of pride as well as law, if the complaint was true. And it probably was: Astrede Stiller held the Red and Green Watch Traditionalists who applied to the brokerage in genial contempt and tolerated no deviations from his decisions. If he said they were to go to the plants that processed the harvest for the off-world pharmaceuticals, to the processing plants they went, regardless of personal preference or any objections they might raise. The ones who didn't cooperate found themselves locked out of any job Astrede controlled. Warreven scowled at the letters on the screen, caught in a mesh of symbols, and flicked the on-screen toggle to clear the overlay. *Cooperate* was hardly the word he would have chosen; *obey* seemed closer to the truth. He flipped back to the previous file, noting the complainants' names: Farenbarne Trencevent and Catness Ferane, both of the Red Watch, both giving their occupation as diver. Chauntclere might know the Ferane, he thought. In any case, it was as good an excuse as any to see him.

He reached for the monophone again, touched the keys to call the dockyards where Chauntclere kept a mailbox when he was ashore. As he'd expected, there was no human response, only the familiar too-sweet mechanical voice announcing the box number and the box-holder's name, and then silence for the message.

"Clere, it's Raven," he said, into the recorder's faint hiss. "I need to talk to you informally about a case we've got going. Can you give me some time when you're back?" There was no need to

leave codes: Chauntclere, of all people, knew where to find him.
He touched the break key and heard someone pass the cubicle's
doorway. He turned to see Haliday looking at him again over the
wall.

"It's gone five," ʒe said. "I thought you might like to know."

"Thanks." Warreven glanced back at the screen, touching
keys to begin the shut-down. "Are you leaving?"

"Yeah. Malemayn's gone."

"Give me a couple of minutes, and I'll go with you."

"Lost your keys again?"

"No, I just—" He broke off to touch a final set of codes, and
the screen went blank. "They're in my carryall somewhere, and I
don't feel like digging."

Haliday grinned, but mercifully didn't pursue the matter.
"Your dinner's at, what, seven?"

Warreven reached under the shelf desk for his bag and
straightened up carefully, reaching across to sweep an untidy
handful of disks and papers into the carryall's main compartment.
"Six-thirty. At least, I'm supposed to be there at six-thirty.
Whether I get dinner depends, I expect, on whether or not I agree
to run."

"I wish to hell I knew what he was up to." Haliday shook ʒer
head. "There's no reason in this world for him to make you *seraaliste*—"

"Unless he's counting on my apparently legendary inability to
bargain," Warreven said, a little too sharply. He stood up, sling-
ing the still-open carryall over his shoulder. "I don't know what
he wants, Hal."

"Sorry." Haliday stood aside to let him out into the entranceway, and followed him out through the reception room into the
painted hall. The sun was low on the eastern horizon, the band of
light stretching now almost to the door, falling heavily on the sandals stacked haphazardly in the mud tray. Warreven shoved his
feet into the nearest pair, the leather warm under his toes.

Behind him, Haliday turned the heavy key, then laid ʒer hand
flat on the sensor plate to set the security system. "How does
Ironroad look? Any chance of a settlement?"

"Hard to tell," Warreven answered. "I'll know better once I've had a chance to talk to the complainants—what's-it and Farenbarne."

"Catness. He's the Ferane."

Warreven pushed open the main door and held it for 3er. "Chauntclere may know him."

Haliday grinned, but said only, "He might, at that. See you in the morning, Raven."

"In the morning," Warreven echoed, and turned down the narrow alley that ran between their building and the silk-spinny next door. The sun was blinding at this time of day, the lower limb of the disk almost touching the horizon; he shaded his eyes and picked his way down the dry side, wrinkling his nose at the familiar pungent smell of the land-spiders' pellets and the soft continual purring from their pens. The spinny door banged as he reached the end of the alley, and the purring suddenly doubled in volume, nearly drowning out the voice of the child who came to feed them. Warreven went on up the outside stairs, kicked off his shoes again on the second-floor porch. The house stood at the highest part of Blind Point; only the lighthouse stood higher, marking the entrance to the Sail Harbor. The porch faced just north of west, looking out over the open water of Lethem's Bay, and he paused for a moment to scan the harbor, the vivid sails dotting the metal-bright water. The afternoon's storm was long gone, not even a shred of cloud to screen the setting sun, and he looked away again, blinking hard to clear the green streaks from his vision. If he was made *seraaliste*, most of those ships, and the dozens of motor barges and lighters and round-bottomed coasters that ran between Bonemarche and the Stiller *mesnies* along the sunset coast, would be his business, the sale of their cargoes his responsibility. And Temelathe Stane was a hard man to refuse.

He reached into the bottom of the carryall, scrabbling through the disks and folders until he found the box of keys. He pulled it out, thumb already on the selector button, and set it against the plate. The door clicked twice and sagged open, and Warreven went on into the warm dark. He had left the house system shut down to avoid having to reset everything if there was another power surge, and he didn't bother to flick on the lights until he reached the bedroom. He still had to bathe and change—Temelathe would be satisfied with nothing less than proper dress, and besides, he himself needed the reassurance of wealth and status—and then arrange for a car to get him across town to Ferryhead where the Most Important Man kept house. The last was something he should have done before he left the office. He sighed, and went back out into the main room, shedding clothes as he went, stopping only to turn both bath taps full on. The hire office was at least used to him, and Stiller had a standing contract for the Important Men and Women; he was able to order the car and driver for the full night, with only a nominal surcharge for the late notice. If everything went really well, he thought, stripping off the last of his clothes as he headed for the bath, he could maybe get together with Chauntclere, or Shan Reiss if Clere wasn't ashore, and tour the harborside clubs with him. It had been a while since he'd been out.

He stepped into the tepid water, sliding down until the ripples touched his chin. He had shaved two days ago, wouldn't need to do it again for another few days, but his hair was a mess, matted and sweaty. He ducked his head under the nearer tap, then shut off both before he overfilled the generous tub. Soap stood in a jar beside the bath, and he reached for it, freed the stopper, and dug his fingers into the soft cream. Its heavy scent filled the air—sweet musk mingling with the sharper note of the witch's-broom—and he was tempted for an instant to rub it between his legs, over cock and balls and into his cunt, and ride the drug's bright euphoria into the next morning. But it was easy enough to lose an encounter with Temelathe, even without the broom's overconfidence, and he rubbed it into his hair instead, working the soap into a heady lather. Even so, when he reluctantly hauled himself out of the now-cold water, he could feel the broom singing in his blood.

As he worked a comb through his tangled hair, he caught a glimpse of himself in the larger mirror, and stopped for a moment to stare, thinking of 'Aukai. He was still slim, was if anything going stringy, the old curves resolving into wiry muscle, breasts too small to sag, but a little incongruous above the bony rib cage.

The boyish penis was just as incongruous, and he looked back at the smaller mirror, concentrating on his hair. Whatever 'Aukai had thought, he was certainly too old now to play trade—though it had never been his looks that worried her—but not, he thought, too old to run the harborside clubs.

He went back into the bedroom and began to pull clothes out of the chest, tossing the discards onto the piled quilts that made up the bed. He settled at least for an ivory tunic-and-trousers suit, the slubbed silk cool against his skin, and rummaged through the smaller box until he found the vest he wanted. Folhare had made it for him, from the scraps left over from making the topmost bed quilt: she had liked the colors against his skin, and said she knew she wouldn't get the chance to see him displayed against the quilt itself. The closely stitched fabric glowed like sunset in the narrow room, and he wondered if Folhare would be at this party. She was a Stane, but of the Black Watch; this was probably just a White Stane event, he decided, and emptied his jewelbox onto the bed. He sorted through the heap of bracelets and earrings and chains, metal, glass, and carved wood, pulling out the pieces that had been forged from the wreck of the colony ship that had brought his ancestors to Hara. He slid the bracelets onto his wrists, circles of twisted iron that still carried the marks of the hammer and the off-world shipbuilder's tools, fastened his collar with a square of plastic from the engine room. There was only one earring left— the other sliver of gold-washed circuit board had descended in a different branch of the *mesnie*—and he paired it with a plain, heavy gold hoop. This was a night for status. He smiled at his reflection, the angular, broad-boned face not yet too worn by the sun, eyes blacker than ever from the broom, and was pleased with the result.

The coupelet was waiting by the time he'd finished dressing, the driver leaning on the steering bar with an expression of infinite patience on his sun-wrinkled face. The destination was already set; as soon as Warreven closed the door behind him, the driver eased the heavy vehicle into motion. They turned south, onto the harbor road, sounding the coupelet's whistle almost constantly as he worked his way into the slow-moving stream of traffic. This was a bad time to try to get through the harbor district—the market there was still open, the day-boats would just be docking, and the shopkeepers and brokers and the occasional pharmaceutical's factor would be crowding the quay to inspect the day's take—and Warreven leaned forward to flip the intercom switch.

"Why aren't we taking Stanehope Street?"

The driver looked up, fixing the younger man's face in his mirror. "Sorry, mir, but there's been some trouble at the Souk, *rana* dancers. The *baas* told me to come this way."

Warreven nodded, and leaned back in his seat, resigning himself to a long, slow ride. The *rana* groups were always active around the Midsummer holiday, their riot presaging the overthrow of the year; lately, the radical political groups, Modernists like himself and the fringe groups even further to the left, had taken over the *ranas'* tactics, and staged their own protests with dance and drumming. Not that the *ranas* had ever really been apolitical, of course, but the Modernists had honed and focused the protests, trying to say new things in an old voice. The Centennial Meeting would begin at Midwinter, and the Modernists had already announced that they wanted to put the question of Hara's joining the Concord to an open vote. That meant bringing a lot of other issues into the Meeting—the question of the pharmaceutical contracts, of Temelathe's control of the government, and the existence of trade and the whole question of gender law—and Tendlathe and the Traditionalists vehemently opposed the idea. A number of the old-style *ranas* supported their position, and there had already been fights between the two groups.

Traffic slowed around them, and the couplelet's engine moaned as the driver geared down yet again. Warreven leaned sideways, trying to see around the driver's head and the shays and runabouts that hemmed them in. Ahead, Consign Wharf jutted into the main harbor, and there was a crowd gathered at its foot, spilling out into the roadway, completely blocking one of the four lanes.

"Someone's made a good haul," he said, but even before he heard the driver's noncommittal grunt, he realized that he was wrong. There were too many runabouts in the knotted traffic, not enough shays and three-ups—too many people altogether, he thought, to be a buying crowd. The coupelet lurched forward, gained another fifty meters before it ground to a halt, and he could hear the noise of drums and the shrill note of a dancer's whistle even through the coupelet's heavy shell. Three people— ordinary people, sailors and dockworkers by their clothes, without the usual tattered ribbons that marked a *rana* group—were standing on a platform balanced precariously on a cluster of fuel drums, arms around one another's shoulders, chanting and swaying to the drums. He couldn't hear the words yet, or much more than the dull rhythm, but he could see the defiance in their faces, and the tension in the movements of the listening crowd. The driver reached across his pod to flip a security switch, locking the coupelet's doors.

They inched forward, into the fringes of the crowd, and Warreven leaned back in the seat, making himself as unobtrusive as possible. Most of the attention was directed toward the people— two women and a man—on the platform, but there was no point in attracting trouble. And trouble was already present: to the left of the car, on the edge of the concrete mole that marked the end of the buyers' lot, a man in a traditional vest and docker's trousers banged an ironwood wrench against a wooden pot. His hand rose and fell in an insistent counterbeat, but any sound was drowned in the noise from the platform. He knew it as well as anyone, turned his fierce scowl on the people around him, exhorting them to join in disrupting the singers' chant. He had painted red-and-white flames, the mark of the Captain, the spirit that Tendlathe was trying to make the Traditionalists' patron, across each cheek. Most of them ignored him, or stood open-mouthed and undecided, looking at him and then back to the singers. Then at last a stocky man jumped up on the wall beside him, clapping his hands and calling to the others. The coupelet slid past before Warreven could see what happened.

They were almost abreast the platform now, and a woman's clear voice—the voice of a sea chanter, someone trained to make

herself heard over a full gale and the chaos of a sinking ship—
soared over the insistent drums.

"*Shineo was the Captain's daughter,*" she began, and most of the
people answered automatically, conditioned by years of sailing.

"*Way-hey, Shineo.*"

"*I love her a little bit more than I oughter,*" the chanter sang, and
the response faltered, some voices dropping out, others coming in
full and triumphant.

"*Way-hey, Shineo!*"

"*Oh, Captain, Captain, I love your daughter.*" The chanter's
voice was full of mocking challenge, not just of the Traditionalist
with his painted face, but of everything he and the Captain stood
for. The same note was in the crowd's answer—as if, Warreven
thought, they were all twelve again, and just learning there were
real words, strong words, names for all the things they weren't
supposed to do, or be.

"*I'll carry her across the deep blue water—*"

The driver gunned the engine, and the coupelet lurched forward into a gap in the traffic, but the sudden rumble couldn't
drown either the crowd's gleeful response or the driver's curse.

"*Garce* bitch."

Warreven lifted his head, and the driver met his eyes in the
mirror, the half of his expression that Warreven could see caught
between embarrassment and mulish conviction. Everyone knew
Warreven was a *halving*, wry-abed, and a Modernist to boot, but
this, the face seemed to say, was too much. Warreven lifted an
eyebrow, and the driver's stare faltered.

"Sorry, mir," he muttered.

Warreven nodded, and looked away. A couple of Temelathe's
militia—the *mosstaas*, mustaches, technically members of the city
patrol association, were standing on the edge of the crowd, heads
turned toward the chanter. One rested his hand on his ironwood
truncheon, but they stood otherwise passive, without noticeable
expression, watching the crowd and the singer. There would be
trouble later, Warreven thought, and wondered if Chauntclere
was safe at sea.

Traffic eased as they swung away from the harbor, moving into one of the new mixed-use districts, where old warehouses and crumbling factories had been reclaimed for the workers in the newer plants south of the Goods Yard. Few people were visible in the streets, but here and there the wide doors were open to the evening, and Warreven caught a quick glimpse of a group of women, traditionally skirted, breasts pushed up and out by the tight traditional bodices, gathered around an open stove. A few children, most in ragged hand-me-downs, played on the cracked paving, under what had been a loading dock. They stopped their game to stare at the coupelet, and as it passed, the tallest threw a stone. It fell short, but Warreven saw the driver's eyes in the mirror, watching them, and heard him mutter something indecent under his breath before he looked away.

The sun was well down by the time the coupelet drew up in front of the compound that surrounded Temelathe's house, the cool twilight thickening toward dark. Lamps were lit on either side of the gate, and the taller of the *mosstaas* on duty there waved them through without hesitation. The driver maneuvered the coupelet between the pillars and slid it neatly to a stop outside the main entrance. The house itself was bigger than the clan house over by the Terminus, was easily as large as the White Watch House, and was rumored to have cost several years' of Temelathe's disposable income. Even if that weren't true, Warreven thought—and knowing Temelathe, he doubted it—it was still an impressive sight, a mute statement of all the ways that Stane outstripped its neighbors. Lights blazed through the open doors and windows, and a woman in full traditional regalia, tiered and beaded skirts and tight bodice, crown of shells and flowers on her braided hair, came hurrying to open the door.

"Makado will show you where to put the car," the woman said, to the driver. She had the high, breathless voice of the old-fashioned high-housekeepers, but only off-worlders failed to recognize its authority within its own sphere. A dark man in off-world clothes loomed silently out of the shadows, beckoning, and Warreven let the coupelet's door fall shut behind him. The heavy vehicle slid away toward the sheds at the far side of the compound.

"Mir Stane is waiting," the housekeeper said.

And standing on his dignity, too, Warreven thought. Or maybe it was just her habit to refer to Temelathe by the most exalted form of his name. He nodded, and gestured for her to precede him into the house.

The party hadn't started yet, but a few of the guests were already present, gathered in one of the anterooms outside the main hall. The housekeeper swept him quickly past the doorway, but Warreven saw Aldess Donavie standing in the center of a circle of admirers. She saw him, too, and smiled graciously, showing perfect teeth, but did not beckon him in. There was no sign of Tendlathe—which was probably just as well, Warreven admitted. After their last argument, he'd rather keep out of Tendlathe's way for a while.

The housekeeper stopped outside a familiar door and tapped lightly on the frame. "Enter," a voice said, only slightly deadened by the dense wood, and the housekeeper pushed open the door.

"Mir Warreven, Mir Stane."

Temelathe was sitting in his favorite chair, beside the massive cast-ceramic stove. It was unlit, of course, wouldn't be lit until the coldest nights of the winter, but it was more expensive evidence of the clan's power. "I'm so glad you could come," he said, and Warreven heard the housekeeper shut the door behind him. "Sit down, make yourself comfortable. *Liquertie?*"

Warreven glanced at the tray that rested on the cold stovetop. The flask was filled with indigo liquid, and a dark, twisted shape floated in its depths: not just ordinary *liquertie*, then, but black nectar, *liquertie* infused with the root pod from a vinegar tree. "Thank you. May I pour you a glass, my father?"

Temelathe nodded, a slight, slightly indulgent smile on his weathered face. He had never been handsome, had broadened with age until he looked like one of the aged wood carvings of the Captain. He cultivated that resemblance, of course, but it was still compelling, the fierce brown eyes enmeshed in the web of fine lines that covered his face. Warreven filled the delicate glasses with liquor that flowed like thick ink and handed one across with a slight, polite bow, falling into a familiar role. The dutiful son was useful, and generally safe: it gave no opportunity for criticism and rarely required one to commit oneself to anything.

"Sit," Temelathe said again impatiently, and Warreven lowered himself into the second chair.

"Now, what's all this about not wanting to be *seraaliste?* Strictly speaking, it's not an honor you can refuse."

Warreven sipped the nectar, enjoying the thick, cinnamon-lemon taste. "I didn't ask to be on the list. I didn't even know my name was on it until today—and that, my father, is hardly appropriate procedure."

"You couldn't have been nominated without some sort of permission, at least by proxy," Temelathe said.

"Nevertheless—"

"A recording error," Temelathe said, and waved the idea away with his free hand. "Something didn't reach you—the mails can be unreliable, especially this new net you like so well. That's why I wanted to keep the old systems in place."

"It's a good reason to question my candidacy," Warreven answered. "That sort of—error—could be held to contaminate the whole slate."

Temelathe frowned. "The Modernists would love to hear you say that."

"Yes. And I agree with their positions." Warreven took another sip of the nectar, and a fragment of root-pod landed, bitter and stinging, on his tongue. "Which is why, my father, I don't understand your attitude. Let's be frank, I won't do you any good as *seraaliste.*"

Temelathe regarded him over the rim of the *liquertie* glass. "Let's be frank, then, my son. You don't do me any good as an advocate, but not opposing your name for *seraaliste* does me good with your less-radical kin. So, my son, I want you to run. I don't really care whether or not you're elected—though I think you'll care, given your opponent—but I will not have you challenge the slate." He paused, and continued with a smile, "I'm sure you'll find, if you check your records, that you received word that your name would be put in nomination months ago."

Warreven allowed himself a rather bitter smile in answer. "I'm sure." *And someone will find himself a little richer at the network offices, too, for adding a backdated note to my file.* "I won't campaign," he said, and knew he sounded merely petulant.

"I wouldn't worry about it," Temelathe said.

Warreven sighed, admitting his defeat. He wouldn't need to campaign, not if Temelathe was backing him, and the threat of challenging the slate was just that, an empty threat. The Stillers would never agree to that if he invoked Modernist politics—the Modernists were too radical even for a clan known to be progressive—and without the backing of the full clan, he could never hope to overthrow the candidacy. "I hope you don't regret this, my father," he said, and Temelathe's smile widened.

"I doubt I will." He paused. "I'd like to see you and Tendlathe friends again."

Several answers rose to Warreven's lips, but he controlled himself. He said, "First, that's his problem more than mine. Second, you don't help things by reminding him of a marriage neither one of us really wanted."

"You'd've been a better wife than Aldess."

"No, I wouldn't." Warreven stood. "Good night, my father."

Temelathe shook his head. "You're making a mistake, Raven. Tendlathe's the person you need on your side. But, good night, if you want it that way."

"I do," Warreven said, and wondered, too late, if Temelathe might not be right after all.

marianj:
> (Hara) part-time or semi-professional prostitute who plays a passive or woman's part.

marijak:
> (Hara) part-time or semi-professional prostitute who plays an active or man's part.

WARREVEN

The trouble at the harbor would only be worse after full dark. Warreven sighed, mentally dismissing his earlier plan to call Chauntclere or Shan Reiss, and leaned back against the cushioned seat, resigning himself to a quiet night. As the driver swung the coupelet onto Tredhard Street, turning north to skirt the harbor area, he saw a familiar figure striding up the long hill. He leaned forward to hit the intercom and said, "Pull over."

The driver's eyebrows rose, but he did as he was told. Warreven slid back the coupelet's window. "Folhare!"

She turned, her practiced smile shifting to a more genuine expression as she recognized the face. "Oh, it's you."

"Thanks." Warreven took in her clothes at a glance, a short off-world style skirt over heavy leggings, the low-cut traditional bodice only partly concealed by a length of spangled gauze. "Working tonight?"

"Yeah, but you're not buying," Folhare answered.

"No. Were you going any place in particular?"

Folhare gave him a wary glance. "There's a club up in Startown, I was going to go there. There's a band of sorts, and they're open all night."

"Would you mind company?"

"For old time's sake, or are you really bored with Clere? 'Cause you really don't need the money." Folhare's smile was wry. They had, briefly, shared rooms above a land-chandler's shop before Warreven had become a clan advocate.

"Old time's sake, and no one's home," Warreven answered. "And there's trouble at the harbor and I want to go dancing."

"I was down there earlier myself," Folhare said, and sighed. "All right, but I really do need to make my rent."

"I won't get in your way," Warreven said. He knew better than to offer to help. He turned back to the intercom. "You can let me out here. I won't need you after all."

The driver shrugged, visibly disapproving, but wasn't too proud to accept the Blue Watch *assignats* that Warreven offered. He pulled the coupelet away decorously enough, and Warreven stood for a moment looking up the busy street. There were bars and dance houses here, mostly catering to the locals, but the doors were closed, uninviting. If you weren't known to the bouncers, you wouldn't get in—especially tonight, Warreven thought. He said, "So where is this place?"

"Just over the hill," Folhare answered. She sounded tired, and Warreven gave her a wary look.

"Business off?"

Folhare snorted and started up the long slope. "Not great. A sale I was counting on fell through, so not only am I left with a custom quilt and no idea how I can resell it, but I'm short the rent."

"Lovely." Warreven glanced sideways as he fell into step with her, unable to stop himself from making the offer. "Is there anything I can do?"

Folhare shook her head, managed a laugh. "I doubt it. But thanks, Raven."

"If I can loan you anything—"

"No." Folhare looked sideways at him, wide mouth twisted into a grimace. "I'm still enough of a Stane not to take from Stiller."

"Oh, for God's sake," Warreven began, and Folhare shook her head.

"No." After a moment, she added, "Thanks."

"Suit yourself," Warreven said. They walked in silence toward the top of the hill, Folhare stretching her long legs against the slope. He matched her step easily enough, though she was taller, watching her out of the corner of his eye. He had known Folhare since the boarding school at Riversedge, had shared rooms with her in Bonemarche for almost six local months, all one winter and half the spring, eighteen bioyears ago. She had just been kicked out of her home *mesnie* then, less because she was a fem than because she wanted to do more than just replicate the usual traditional textiles for use and the off-world trade; he had just refused to marry Tendlathe Stane and was afraid to go home to the ensuing controversy. Half the Ambreslight *mesnie* had been furious that the marriage had been proposed at all, the other half had been furious that he hadn't accepted it regardless of the gender shift, and he himself had wanted to forget it had ever happened. Neither he nor Folhare had had much money: he had worked odd jobs and played trade when the rent ran short, which was more often than not, while Folhare had worked for a sweatshop making bad copies of traditional tunics, tried to save enough to buy the good material she needed to make the quilts that were already starting to win notice, and played trade. Warreven touched the edge of the vest he was wearing, rich red silk printed with gold, scrap from a quilt she had made him then. They could have solved all their problems by marrying, founding a proper *mesnie* of their own and thus qualifying as adult members of their clan, eligible for the clan subsidies that supported most indigenes, but the option had not appealed to either of them, and had never been mentioned aloud. Besides, Folhare was a fem, as well as a Black Stane, and any one of those factors would have made a legal marriage difficult. Probably his own *mesnie* would have stretched the point, Warreven admitted silently—he had already been suspected of being wry-abed, and the *mesnie* was desperate to remedy that situation—but Folhare would never have agreed. Or would she? he wondered suddenly, looking sideways to see her strong, broad-boned face caught in the light from a street sign, the planes of cheek and jaw made harsh by the deep shadows. Neither of them were getting any younger; if they had married, she wouldn't be hustling trade to pay her rent.

She saw him looking, and lifted an eyebrow. "Problem?"

"Just thinking," Warreven answered, and Folhare gave him another smile.

"I'd be careful of that, if I were you."

"Thanks," Warreven said sourly, and they reached the top of the hill. The landward slope was gentler, and the street was quiet, empty except for a work team unloading crates outside a small chandler's. The trapdoor in the street was open, the handlers sweating even in the relative cool of the night air; both the driver, sitting with his arms folded on the steering bar, and the store owner gave them a curious glance as they went, but the clothes were enough to make sure they passed. Seeing them watching, Folhare made a face, but sensibly said nothing.

The club was a small place and very discreet, the door marked only by a faintly glowing touchpad. Folhare laid her hand against it, waiting for a signal; only as she took her palm away did Warreven see the small brass plate that gave the club's name.

"Jerona's?" he said, and Folhare shrugged again.

"She runs the place."

The peephole opened then, and a moment later the door swung back, letting a gust of sound and sweaty air out into the street. Folhare grinned with unforced delight and stepped up into the narrow entranceway. Warreven followed, grimacing as the door closed behind them, doubling the noise. The doorkeeper leaned out of his alcove.

"I know you, serram, but serray—?"

It had been a long time since anyone had given him the off-world title. Warreven drew breath to answer, and Folhare said quickly, "It's all right, he—3e's—with me."

There was a little pause, and then the doorkeeper nodded. "All right."

The entrance hall opened into a single long room, mechanical bars in the corners, the dance floor brightly lit in the center, the band platform at the far end, and tables and tabourets in the darkness along the walls. It was almost a parody of a traditional *mesnie* hall, with the band replacing the Important Men and Women and the Names of the ancestors and the carvings of the spirits, and

Warreven wondered if it had been done deliberately. Folhare leaned close, the length of gauze brushing his arm, and said in his ear, "Do you want a drink or are you just going to dance?"

"Let's get a table anyway," Warreven said, and she gave a snort of laughter.

"Sure, but which side of the hall?"

Warreven looked again. He was used to Shinbone and the other, newer clubs down by the Harbor, where the wry-abed and trade mingled easily. Here the tables were divided, the wry-abed to the left of the band platform, trade—easily distinguished by the mix of off-worlders and indigenes—to the right. He sighed—the mixed bars were easier; trade tended to want him as a herm, and the wry-abed too often wanted actual men—but there really wasn't much of a choice. "Trade, I suppose."

Folhare nodded. "You find a table, I'll get drinks."

"Let me get this round," Warreven said, and reached into his pocket. Folhare hesitated only for a moment, then took the proffered *assignats.*

"All right. But the next one's on me."

"No offense," Warreven said, "but I hope we've both found someone else before the next round."

Folhare flashed him another quick smile and turned away toward the nearest bar. Warreven made his way through the first row of tables—it wasn't that crowded, but the empty tables tended to be toward the walls, where the lights were dimmer and the customers could see each other less clearly—aware of eyes scanning and dismissing him. He was old for this, certainly, but hoped it was less that than that he wasn't dressed for trade tonight. The music was ending, the lines of dancers spinning toward the conclusion of the dance, and he picked a table quickly, seating himself with his back to the wall, so he could watch the dance floor. The dance ended with a rattle of quick, high notes from the *contre* drum, and the lines broke apart as the individual dancers began to move back toward their tables. The noise of conversation was suddenly louder. Warreven smiled at a broad-built indigene with the speckled hair of a sailor, but got only a polite smile in return. The man moved purposefully past him, seated himself at a table of off-worlders, three women and a man, all in drably expensive clothes.

"No luck?" Folhare asked, and set a bottle and a handful of cheap pottery glasses on the table in front of him. Warreven frowned—there were four glasses, not two—and then realized that the men behind her were coming to join them. "You know my clan-cousin Bonnard, I think."

Warreven nodded. He knew Bonand Stane, all right, and, despite their both being of the same Watch, had never been fully sure that he could trust the man. There was no denying that Bonand was a Modernist and wry-abed, but they hadn't had much else in common.

"This is Alex," Bonand said, and nodded to the man behind him.

Warreven nodded again, studying the stranger. He was an off-worlder, unmistakably, and as unmistakably new to the planet, fair skin not yet marred by the sun. Classic trade, he thought, and held out his hand in the off-world greeting. "I'm Warreven."

There was no need to give clan or Watch, not yet—and not ever, given that the man was from another world, no possible kin—but he saw Bonand's quick, malicious smile and wished he'd given his full name. Alex accepted the handshake with a nod and a quick, flickering glance, interest visibly flaring and then vanishing before Warreven could be quite sure what had gone wrong.

"I need to talk to you, Raven," Bonand said, and pulled one of the chairs away from the table.

"Sit down, why don't you," Warreven answered flatly, and Bonand smiled again.

"I will. I hear I should congratulate you—Stiller *seraaliste* is nothing to sneeze at."

He had spoken in *franca*, and Warreven answered in creole, earning a quick look of thanks from Alex. "Nothing's been decided yet. I may not remain on the ballot."

"Temelathe'll have something to say about that," Bonand said, switching to creole. His accent was less clear, Warreven noticed, and was meanly pleased. Alex—any trade—was fair game, and he was good-looking. Bonand grimaced, and switched back to *franca.* "You do know what's going on, don't you, Raven? He wants to keep you off his back, and he doesn't want anyone pushing trade this season. Plus he doesn't want any clan changing brokers this season. So who better to promote for *seraaliste* than a man who doesn't know how to make a bargain?"

Warreven swallowed his first, furious response. "And where'd you hear this bit of gossip?"

"I'm in the White Watch House now, for my sins," Bonand answered. "In the secretarial pool. It's not common talk, but it's what the Important Men are saying. And Temelathe is very pleased with himself for the idea."

Folhare leaned forward, planting both elbows on the table, all thought of trade, her own business, forgotten for the moment. "That's pretty baroque, Bonand."

"So's Temelathe," Bonand answered, and laughed nervously, looking over his shoulder. "Well, it explains it, doesn't it? Why else would he nominate Warreven, they're not exactly best friends anymore. But if he gets Warreven out of dealing with trade, then that just leaves Malemayn and Haliday to make trouble. And at the same time, with Warreven as *seraaliste*, he can pretty much count on Stiller staying with—who is it, Raven, Kerendach?"

Warreven nodded.

"As long as you stay with Kerendach, Temelathe gets his cut, Kerendach makes a nice profit, and nothing changes." Folhare reached for the wine bottle. "And in the meantime, you're having to play catch-up just to figure out who's who among the druggists." She glanced at Alex, made a face. "Sorry. Pharmaceutical companies. But you know what I mean."

Warreven reached for the wine himself. The Stiller contract with Kerendach had been a matter of debate for nearly seven local years. Previous *seraalistes* had proposed changing both it and the brokers, but had never been able to come up with an acceptable alternative, though the margin of the Traditionalists' victories had been getting smaller and smaller. The more radical Modernists—and the conservative Traditionalists, like the Red Watch Feranes—swore that the largest pharmaceuticals were in collusion, had banded together to make sure that each of them got its share of the twice-yearly harvests at a bargain price. Warreven himself doubted that: the way the Big Six, and the Lesser Twenty, for that matter, bickered over labor and the special individual contracts for the harvest surpluses, made him fairly confident that they wouldn't be able to work together on anything bigger. It was more likely—if Bonand was right—that Temelathe had quietly passed the word, through the Stanes in the Licensing Office and in Trade Service and Export Control, that the Most Important Man would frown on a new contract with Stiller. "Are you with a pharmaceutical?" he said, to Alex, meaning, *or are you just trade?*

The off-worlder blinked. "Well, yeah. Not Kerendach, though."

"Good," Folhare said, with a smile, and poured him a glass of wine.

"He's with DTS," Bonand said impatiently, and Alex flicked a glance at him.

"That's right."

Warreven nodded. DTS was one of the thirty-odd midsize companies that did business on Hara, specializing in the sea-harvest from Casnot and Newcomen—not a big company at all, not even one of the Lesser Twenty—but large enough to afford to pay Stiller's prices. And small enough, specialized enough, he thought, to be less dependent on the Stane and Maychilder harvests than the larger companies. Always assuming, of course, that he ended up with the job. "Do you find yourself dealing much with Temelathe and Stane?" he asked, and Alex gave him a wary look.

"Not much, really."

"Some," Bonand said in the same moment, and the off-worlder sighed.

"DTS pays its—fees—like everybody does. What do you want me to say, that I think it sucks? I'm not in marketing, I'm a tech. I'm just passing through."

Bonand lifted his eyebrows, caught between annoyance and not wanting to alienate his date, and Warreven said, "Sorry, I wasn't being clear—or meaning to insult you. It's more . . . I was curious, really. I know the Big Six have to be careful of Stane—

they get most of their goods from them, right?—but I didn't know if that was true for companies your size."

Alex looked away. Even in the dim light, Warreven could see that he was blushing. "I'm—just a technician," he said again, and Warreven felt himself blushing in turn. Alex was trade, a player, though maybe not by the off-worlder's own definition. If he was a technician, of course he wouldn't know DTS's real policies.

"Would you like to dance?"

Alex blinked again and glanced toward the dance floor. "Sorry. I've no idea how to dance to this."

"It's not that hard," Warreven began, and Bonand pushed back his chair.

"I'll dance with you, Warreven. Keep you honest."

There was no graceful way to refuse. Warreven followed him onto the worn floor, took their place in the nearer of the lines, linking arms with Bonand and a thin woman who took the place at his left. The drums were already well into the *entrait*, the twisting rhythm signaling a cross-step dance, and Warreven sighed. He was not a terribly good dancer, for all that he enjoyed it; he would have preferred not to screw up the complicated patterns in front of Bonand, or Alex. The lead drum sounded, and the line moved forward into the first figure in ragged unison, the stuttering, high-pitched *contre* calling the changes. Warreven kept his head down, concentrating on the steps, until he was sure he had settled into the pattern of the movements. The woman at his left dropped his arm and began adding the dipping spins of an expert; he spared her an admiring glance, but knew better than to try to imitate her.

At least Bonand was no better: at the first tempo change, he shook his head, and dropped back out of the line, pulling Warreven with him. Warreven went willingly enough; they stood with the others who had given up on the change, watching as the triple line swept the length of the hall and retreated again. The woman who had been next to him was very good, Warreven saw, and he watched her with remote envy. She was at the center of her line now, thin face a mask of still concentration, her skirt flying out in an almost constant circle as she added spin on spin and still kept her place with the others. The tempo changed again, slowed abruptly, and most of the dancers slowed with it, glad of the break, gliding through the basic pattern at half their previous speed. The woman kept spinning, riding the quicker beat implicit in the lead drum's call. And then the counterpoint came in again, faster still, and she flung back her head and matched it step for step.

"She is good," Warreven said, to no one in particular, and Bonand looked at him.

"Yes. Do me a favor, Raven, leave Alex alone."

"I'm not serious," Warreven answered. "And if he is, that's not my problem."

"It's not that," Bonand said. "He's gay, Warreven."

"So?" Warreven began, and only then did the foreign word, the creole word, register. "What do you mean, exactly? He's trade."

Intense distaste and a deepening anger flickered across Bonand's face, and then he had himself under control again. "Yeah, he's trade, but he does work for DTS—he really is a tech, he hasn't just bought a permit—and he's still gay. Off-world gay—that means he wants another man, not a *halving* like you."

Warreven felt a familiar fury rising in him, at the name, at the exclusion, at the whole incomprehensible system of off-world sexuality, with its finicking distinctions that were no distinctions at all as far as he himself could see. "He's still trade," he began, and the drums stopped, silencing him. He clapped automatically with the rest of the crowd, biting hard on the rest of what he would have said—*he's still trade, and what trade wants, what they come here for, is sex with us outside that system, so I've as good a chance with him as you do*—and Bonand looked aside, sorrow chasing hope across his mobile features.

"I suppose he's trade," he said softly, voice barely audible in the sudden rush of conversation. "I know he's trade. But he is gay, and he does really work for DTS—he's different, Raven."

Warreven looked at him again, the situation rearranging itself into a new pattern in his mind. Alex might not be trade after all, might just be one of the temps who came through the system and decided to try Hara's well-known delights, but Alex wasn't what mattered. Bonand was in love with him, or had convinced himself he was in love with him, and Warreven didn't need the rest of that dream spelled out for him. He'd felt it himself a few times, the heady combination of sex and desire and something like friendship that he'd allowed to grow into the hope that maybe this one off-worlder would fall in love with him and take him with him when he left Hara. It had never happened to him, almost never happened to any Harans; IDCA almost never gave emigration permits to even part-time prostitutes. He remembered the case waiting on his desk: if Destany Casnot couldn't get a permit without a fight—Destany who had half a dozen friends willing to swear he, 3e, had been out of trade and 'Aukai's lover for seven years, there was no chance that Bonand would get one. And even less chance that Alex would make the effort for him. "He's your—" he began, and broke off because *franca* didn't have an inoffensive word for what Alex was to Bonand, "—yours. I wasn't poaching, not seriously. I'll leave him alone."

Bonand nodded, visibly regretting the confidence. "Thanks," he muttered, and turned back to the table. Warreven glanced over his shoulder and saw Folhare leaning back in her chair to talk to an off-worlder who seemed to know both her and Alex. The drums were starting again, and one of the middle drummers abandoned her drum for a reed-whistle, signaling a ring-dance. Those were courting dances in the *mesnies*, served the same purpose even in the *wrangwys* bars, and Warreven took his place in the outer circle, nodding to the short, fair-skinned man opposite him. By the time he'd made his way around the circle, he should surely have found someone. . . . At the very least, Folhare would have had the chance to finalize her arrangements. As he moved through the first figure, the fair man's hands hot in his own, he caught a glimpse of the table: Folhare still laughing, practiced and easy; Bonand leaning on the back of Alex's chair, one hand draped, unobtrusively possessive, over the off-worlder's shoulder. Only Alex himself looked uncertain, as though he didn't understand the rules. Then he swept on to the next partner, and when he looked again, only Folhare and her *jackamie* were left at the table.

mairaiche:
(Hara) farm; source of cultivated crops rather than harvest.

the spirits:
(Hara) celestial beings that occupy an intermediate position between God (defined as ineffable, unknowable, and not terribly interested in human beings) and Man. The spirits intercede for and interact with human beings, and grant favors more willingly, and, as a result, their worship, through services and *offetre,* is far more important to most Harans than the distant God. Harans generally believe that a man or woman can take on some of the characteristics of a spirit, either through dance, concentration, or sheer serendipity, and when in that state, his or her acts are seen as the actions of the spirit.

MHYRE TATIAN

Reiss was late, as usual. Tatian peered over the edge of the heavy display glasses—his implants were worse than usual this morning, making it almost impossible to work on line—and out into the bright morning sun-and-shadow that filled the courtyard, wondering irritably if the younger man was ever going to show up for work. Data from Derebought's preliminary analysis of the hungry-jack he'd bought from the market woman danced just below his line of sight, the green and gold symbols forming a twisted, familiar pattern. There were a few variants, helpfully highlighted in a brighter yellow, but not many: interesting, but it was hard to tell if it would be worth pursuing the analysis. He sighed and slipped the glasses back into place, focusing on the globular shape that swam in the sudden darkness. The outer cords were mostly inert, but they seemed to bind to the same receptors used by the psychoactive harrodine that was the drug's most active compound. That might help moderate or control hungry-jack's somewhat unpredictable effects—if, of course, Derebought had added, her note flashing tart orange below the visual analysis, the inert whatever-it-was was picked up preferentially over harrodine. Further analysis would be needed to determine any possible utility, and she wasn't prepared to make a guess either way.

Tatian sighed. This morning in particular he resented having the decision handed to him, when he couldn't switch easily from system to system, but reached for the shadowscreen to bring up the financial system. Its icon was cold and hard as ice to the touch, a bit of whimsy from a previous user; he flicked it into the center of the screen, activating it, and its cold spread as the numbers spilled across his vision, overriding the chemical shapes. The controls rearranged themselves under his fingers, new spots of warmth and cold and the fugitive suggestions of shape. He adjusted them, searching for the latest budget files, then made his query. The numbers swam dizzily for a moment, then presented him with his answer. There was still money in the budget to buy time on one of the larger systems at the starport, and to buy more of the uncleaned pods, if needed. NAPD could afford to have Derebought run the more detailed analysis, which put the question squarely back on his desk: was it worth the trouble? Probably not, he admitted silently—it was unlikely to come to anything really usable—but NAPD couldn't afford to pass up the chance at something new.

He sighed again and flattened his hand against the shadowscreen, shutting down both programs, and set the glasses aside before the cascade of codes had properly begun. "Derry?" he said, to the general pickup.

"Æ?" A moment later, the botanist stuck her head around the edge of the doorway.

"Got a minute?"

"Sure." Derebought wiped her hands on the skirts of her thin jacket, and came into the office. The scent of musk and mint clung to her, to her unbound hair, and she looked tired: it was closing on Midsummer, barely a local week, six planetary days, until the holiday, and even the most assimilated indigenes had obligations to fulfill. Those obligations would culminate in the Stane *baanket* on the second day of Midsummer, when her branch of the clan, or as much of it as could possibly afford to, returned to the *gran'mesnie* at Gedesrede to feed and be fed by their patriarch. With her off-world training and a job that paid in concord dollars, Derebought was easily the richest member of her *mesnie*; it was her particular responsibility to stand in for the rest at Midsummer. Tatian glanced down at his desktop, reading the schedule displayed there. She and Mats were scheduled to fly to Gedesrede on Fives and come back three days later: not, Tatian thought, the sort of holiday schedule I'd want.

"What's up?" she said, and lowered herself into the client's chair.

"I want your advice," Tatian said.

"If it's the analysis," Derebought answered, "I already gave you my best guess."

"Which is, you don't know whether it's worth it."

Derebought nodded. "That's the shape of it. I ran—well, you saw the results. I honestly can't say if it'll go any further."

"I think it's worth one more round," Tatian said.

Derebought sighed, and shrugged, turning both palms to the light. Both her palms and the backs of her hands were streaked with faint lines and symbols—marks of the spirits, Tatian knew, but he had forgotten which ones. "I'm inclined to do another set, yes, but if that doesn't get results, I wouldn't pursue it. Always assuming, of course, there's money left in the budget."

"I checked. There's enough—go to Buram-Hattrich or Seals, they owe us a favor."

Derebought nodded, and in the same moment, a shadow crossed the courtyard window. She looked up sharply, and Tatian was startled by the relief he glimpsed in her eyes. The main door opened and closed again with a thud. She pushed herself out of her chair and went to the office doorway. "Reiss? Is that you?"

"Yeah, sorry." Reiss peered around the door frame, doing his best to look contrite. His dark hair stood up in tufts, uncombed, and he was wearing a Haran tunic Tatian had never seen before. "I—there was some trouble at the Harbor Market last night, and I had to help some friends with bail. Then I overslept. I'm sorry, Tatian."

"What kind of trouble?" Tatian asked, and didn't bother to hide his skepticism. He had seen the news that morning—the local narrowcasts as well as the main feed from the port—and there had been no mention of any trouble. There had been talk about the harvest, and contract speculations, and how much the Stillers were spending on their *baanket*, which would be held in Bonemarche as usual. . . . "It didn't make the news."

"I'm not surprised," Reiss said sourly. "It wasn't anything serious, just some *rana* bands, but the *mosstaas* cracked down. And a bunch of people got arrested."

"And one of them called you to post bail," Derebought said.

Reiss gave her a wary smile, half embarrassed, half ingratiating. "Actually, a friend of a friend called, to see if I'd contribute to the bail, and maybe help get people home from the ironhouse. It was more of a bribe, anyway, and I had the car last night. But the judge let most of them off without charges."

"Did you have to give your name?" Tatian asked.

Reiss shook his head. "Renai knows a bondsman, ʒe handled it."

"Good."

"What was it all about, anyway?" Derebought asked. "I heard at the ceremony that there'd been something at the Souk, but nothing about the harbor."

Reiss shrugged. "Some ultra-Modernists were dancing for the Meeting—to bring local law into line with the Concord—and some of the Traditionalists got pissy. The *mosstaas* stepped in, arrested the *ranas* before a fight started."

Which meant, Tatian translated, that the issue was gender law again. The Centennial Meeting would open after the new year, its ceremonies marking the five-hundredth anniversary of Hara's settlement. It was as close to a universal forum as Hara had, the only possible counterbalance to Temelathe's control of the traditional mechanisms of *mesnie*, clan, and Watch. It didn't seem like much of an adversary, not when one looked at the power Temelathe held, but the Most Important Man was taking it very seriously indeed. And maybe he was right to do so: with the Meeting due to open in about eight local months, about six thousand hours by the more conventional reckoning, every political group on Hara was doing its best to get its issues put before the Meeting. And right now, the question of gender law—of whether or not Haran law would acknowledge the existence of mems, fems, and herms—was becoming a major issue. Temelathe Stane was doing his best to keep it from reaching the agenda, or so rumor said, not least because of the various ways he profited from trade. Tatian wasn't fully sure he believed the talk—after all, there were five sexes, no matter what local law said about it; he couldn't help thinking that Tendlathe's well-publicized opposition to off-world influence and trade was just another way to raise prices—but he wasn't surprised that Temelathe would prefer to see the debate center on gender rather than on his own domination of Haran politics. The Meeting would be an acrimonious one, whatever happened. He said, "Do you still have your meeting on Kittree Row?"

"Yeah, I called. It wasn't until noon anyway."

"I suppose it was too much trouble to call here?"

"I only had local access," Reiss said. "I am sorry."

Tatian glanced down at the desktop, tacitly accepting both the apology and the excuse. Still, it was half an hour to noon, which left only half an hour to negotiate the worst traffic in Bonemarche.

"That's why I came straight in," Reiss said. "We'll make it."

Tatian looked at him warily. Now that it actually came to dealing with an unlicensed indigene, he was nervous, which was not entirely unreasonable, either. But then, her rates had to be better than the prices the port technicians could charge. And if he didn't get the system fixed before the Midsummer bargaining began, he would be worse than useless. "Right. Let's go." He touched the shadowscreen as he spoke, securing the desktop and telling the system when he would be back.

"I'll get that analysis started," Derebought said, and Tatian nodded.

"Great."

Reiss had left his battered jigg outside the office's back entrance, as usual. Tatian followed him out into the rutted alley, wrinkling his nose at the smell of rotting seaweed, and lowered himself into the open passenger seat. Reiss kicked the motor to life and brought the jigg out into the main street at a relatively decorous pace. Traffic was heavy, as always, heavier as they reached the warren of alleys and narrow lanes that led into the Souk, until the jigg was barely moving as fast as a person could walk. He could feel Reiss's weight tipping the jigg from side to side as he scanned the passing shays, and he braced himself against the edge of the car as the jigg accelerated suddenly, darting through the gap between a three-up and a shay piled high with bales of fonori. Reiss steadied the machine almost absently—he was, Tatian reminded himself, a very good driver—and swung out and around a slow-moving caleche before the driver could do more than open his mouth to shout. And then they had made the turn onto Kittree Row, the traffic vanishing almost magically.

The buildings were low and long, like most of the buildings in Bonemarche, but instead of the usual open bay at street level, most of them showed blank faces, closed off from the street by gray-painted doors. They looked almost metallic, but Tatian knew they would be wood or cast clay. Each one was marked with a house mark like a sign—a wave, a crudely drawn crescent moon, a top-hatted skeleton—and most had a bar of black paint running horizontally across the door. Stiller was a Black Watch clan, and most of Bonemarche's population were at least nominally Stillers.

The jigg slowed, pulled sideways into the shadow of a building distinguished by a painted star and a wide band of green paint. Massingberd was a Green Watch clan, Tatian remembered, and loosely allied with Stiller against Stane. The door was propped up on a balk of wood, raised maybe a meter to let the breeze in, and Reiss leaned out of the jigg to touch a button on the wall beside the doorway. For a long moment, nothing happened, and then the door began to rise, jerking along its tracks. Reiss ducked forward slightly and brought the jigg into the bay. The engine was very loud in the confined space.

"Æ," he called, and flicked the engine off completely. "Starli, are you there?"

There was a little silence. As Tatian's eyes adjusted to the light—the bay was well lit, but seemed dim after the brilliance of the street—he could make out a knot of mostly men, gathered around a stand-alone diagnostic unit. They said nothing, watching the jigg, and then a woman pushed her way through the group, wiping her hands on a bright blue rag. One of the men switched off the diagnostic unit, and another reached halfheartedly for a tool kit that stood open beside a disassembled jet-car frame.

"So what's up, Reiss?" The woman—Starli, she must be—came fully into the light, stopped perhaps three meters away, her arms folded across her breasts. She was tall, even by Haran standards, her long hair tied up in a square of blue-and-green-and-pink print fabric, and Tatian caught himself looking again to see if she was really a fem.

Reiss said, "You remember the other day I asked if you still did work on off-world implants? My boss is having problems with a connection, and I wondered if you could help." He nodded sideways. "Ser Mhyre Tatian." The off-world names sounded harsh amid the flow of *franca*.

Starli nodded, some of the tension easing from her stance. "Mir Tatian. I'm Starli Massingberd."

"Honored, mirrim," Tatian said, and knew better than to offer his hand. "Reiss tells me you repair implants."

"For *kittereen* racers, yes." Starli tipped her head to the side, the wrinkles at the corners of her eyes tightening either in contemplation or the beginnings of laughter. "And you should know I'm not licensed."

"Reiss told me. He also said you were good."

Starli smiled then, a quick baring of teeth. Tatian was suddenly aware again of the hovering technicians, pretending to work while they listened. "He's right, mir, and good costs money. But I give discounts for metal, and I'm willing to make terms."

"And I," Tatian said, "would like to hear what you can do for me before we start talking prices."

Starli's smile widened, became for a fleeting instant genuinely amused. "Fair enough. Will you step into my office, mir?"

Tatian looked at Reiss, who said quickly, "I'll wait here." Tatian nodded, and the younger man moved to join the technicians, who relaxed at his approach.

The office was tucked into a corner, a square room that had obviously been an afterthought. The walls were glass brick, the cheapest of Hara's building materials, half clear, half translucent, and in the instant before Tatian followed her into the milk-white room, he could see how the interior lights glowed through the walls, like radiant ice. It was an odd image, on a planet as warm as Hara, and he was smiling as she shut the door behind them. Starli gave him a curious look, as though she wondered what had amused him, but said only, "What's your system, then?"

Tatian shrugged out of his suncheater, laid his arm on the battered desktop, turning his wrist to expose the control plate on the inside of his right forearm. "Inomata Cie., parts and bioware." Their implants were the standard throughout the Concord Worlds; if you didn't wear Inomata's implants, you wore their clones.

Starli grunted, switching on a powerful viewlens, and tugged it down toward his arm. She turned away and rummaged on shelves crowded with bits of equipment to produce a black-foam cradle and a set of multicolored cables. "Have a seat and let me run a few quick tests. No charge."

Tatian nodded, and pulled a stool close to the desk, sat down opposite her. He placed his arm in the cradle, plate uppermost, and Starli pulled the viewlens closer still, its thick edge blocking his view. He could feel the heat of the lights, and then, more distantly, the click of the plate release. He tilted his head slightly, wanting to see what she was doing, but the viewlens was still in his way. Starli saw the movement, however, and glanced up, a quizzical expression on her face.

"Do you want to watch?" *Most people don't,* her tone implied.

Tatian said, "Yes. If you don't mind."

She shook her head. "No problem." She pulled the viewlens down and slightly to one side. "How's that, can you see all right now?"

"Thanks."

Starli mumbled an absent acknowledgment and leaned close over the lens. Now that the flesh-toned plate was removed, Tatian could see the shallow cavity, and the gray, faintly spongy surface of the interface box, with its remote reader, circular i/o port and the quintet of smaller needleports surrounding it. Flesh welds bound it into place, the ridged scars normally concealed by the protective plate: Frankenstein welding, the cheapest kind of implant surgery. Starli fanned a handful of fine wires and plugged them deftly into the needleports; watching her certainty, Tatian began to relax. She was more like a mem than most women, certainly more so than the fem he had briefly suspected she might be, stolid and quietly competent in her work—but that was an old stereotype, and just as untrue as all the less flattering ones. Prane Am had been a technician, too, and a good one, and there was no mistaking her for a mem.

"All right," Starli said, and plugged a jack into the main port. "Tell me when it hurts."

"Right now," Tatian said, and winced as more static sang along his nerves.

Starli murmured something, squinting through the viewlens. Tatian could see blue lines and pale pink shapes drifting in the glass, but it was impossible to read their message at this angle. Static ebbed and flowed along his arm, was replaced briefly by numbing cold, and then the sensations vanished.

"Well, you're in luck, mir," Starli said. "It's the port, that's all."

"All" was a relative term, Tatian thought, but he understood her point. "Which one?"

Starli pushed the viewlens to one side, met his eyes for the first time across the desktop. "I can run some more tests and tell you for sure—at a price—or you can replace the box altogether. Frankly, I'd recommend the latter."

Tatian waited and, after an instant, tilted his head to one side. Starli sighed and folded the viewlens back down to the desktop, then tugged the cables one by one from the needleports.

"You can get a better deal at the port yourself, and you're likely to have better luck getting it officially imported—or whatever—than I would."

That was also true, and Tatian nodded slowly, thinking of Prane Am. If he wanted a good deal, he would have to go to her, which was not a pleasant thought—or maybe Reiss had connections there as well. He said, "Probably. Do you do installation?"

"Yes. But—" Starli showed her teeth again. "I'd want to be paid in metal."

"And I'd want to see your medical set-up," Tatian said, and matched her tooth for tooth.

"Fair enough," Starli said. She pushed herself up from her chair, went to a cabinet built into the wall, and tugged open the double doors. The first layer of the interior folded down automatically into an operating table, the clean-field lighting automatically; the multicolored telltales of the monitoring system glowed in the space behind it. Tatian scanned it quickly, recognizing the bulk of a doc-in-a-box and the familiar stacks of test equipment, and only then saw the twined KJ etched into the edge of the table. It was an older system, but it had been top of the line once: it was certainly good enough to replace an interface box.

"Okay," he said aloud. "What are you asking?"

"Fifty kilos of hard steel," Starli answered promptly.

"Try reality."

"That's two starcrates," Starli said. "NAPD must be able to spare that much—especially compared to what it'd cost you to get this done in the port."

She certainly bargained like a fem. Tatian said, "I still have to buy the box. You're not saving me anything there. Besides, starcrates aren't cheap, and they come out of my budget. Twenty thousand meg." That was eighty percent of what he'd pay in the port, but she wanted metal: she would take less in cash, if she could get a starcrate or two with it. He ran the company inventory rapidly through his head, enjoying the game. He knew they couldn't spare any of the working crates—they were too expensive, nearly a thousand concord dollars apiece—but most of the value was in the electronics package. If there were any damaged crates, he might be able to use the metal shell to buy her services.

"I'll take a crate instead," Starli said, as though she'd read his thought. "Or just the metal. Forty kilos hard steel."

"I can get you ten," Tatian said. "And five thousand meg in cash."

"Thirty kilos, and no cash needed," Starli answered.

"Twenty and six thousand," Tatian said. "I—even the com-

pany doesn't have that much metal to spare. And you're not sup-
plying the parts."

There was a little silence, and then Starli sighed and touched
the latch plate to refold the operating theater into its cabinet. "All
right. Twenty kilos hard steel, and six thousand meg, White or
Red cash. Agreed?"

The currencies issued by the White and Red Watches were
the most stable, had the best rate of exchange against the concord
dollar, though most Harans didn't bother with those considera-
tions. But then, Tatian thought, Starli would be buying metal, or
metal parts, with a good bit of her fee, and that meant dealing
with the port technicians. "Agreed."

Starli bowed, touching lips and forehead. "Then it can be
done at your convenience, mir. Whenever you get the box, give
me an hour's warning, and I can put it in."

"Good enough," Tatian said. "Thanks, mirrim."

They went back out into the bay. Reiss was sitting with the
technicians, passing a bottle of something from hand to hand. He
rose hurriedly at Tatian's approach, but not so quickly that Tatian
couldn't recognize the familiar squat brown jar of quarta. He
lifted an eyebrow at that, but said only, "I need you to run me out
to the port."

Reiss nodded. "No problem."

"It had better not be," Tatian said, and Reiss had the grace to
look abashed. He looked at Starli. "I'll contact you then, mirrim,
about the scheduling."

"As I said, give me warning," Starli answered. "I'll be ready."

Tatian nodded, and swung himself into the jigg's passenger
seat. Reiss kicked the starter twice, and the engine caught with a
roar that was almost deafening in the confined space. He twisted
the throttle, muting the sound, and backed decorously out into
the hot street.

Traffic was heavier than ever, and Reiss took an indirect route
through the city, skirting the Souk and the congested streets that
led into Startown. Even so, progress was slow, and he glanced
over his shoulder in apology.

"Sorry—" His eyes slid sideways then, fixing on something in the crowd behind the jigg, and he swerved abruptly, pulling the jigg into a partially cleared space between a four-up and an unloading shay.

"Reiss?" Tatian looked over his shoulder, scanning the crowd, but saw nothing immediately out of the ordinary. Then Reiss was wresting himself free of the safety webbing. "Hey—"

"Æ, *mosstaas*," Reiss called, and levered himself out of the jigg before Tatian could even think of stopping him. The crowd parted for him, and Tatian swore under his breath. In the center of the square they had just skirted, by the dry fountain, two of the city militia had stopped a woman—were questioning her, by their stance and her gestures. Reiss shoved his way through the crowd, which melted around him: *not a good sign at all,* Tatian thought, and freed himself from the jigg. *Why the hell does he have to do this?* He started after the younger man, hoping that their off-world clothes, and the pharmaceutical mark on the nose of the jigg would keep them out of trouble.

"—mistake," Reiss was saying, as Tatian came into earshot. "Astfer works with me."

"So the *wyfie's* yours?" one of the *mosstaas* demanded, smirking, and Tatian bit back another curse. Reiss was getting them involved in trade, despite his—despite Masani's—explicit prohibitions.

"We work together," Reiss said again.

The woman looked warily from him to the *mosstaas* and back again. Or, rather, the fem: this close, Tatian could see the height, the full breasts and narrow hips, the typical build that ðer off-world shirt and trousers did nothing to conceal. The other militiaman gave a snort of laughter, and the first one said, "I just bet the *wyfie* gives excellent—service."

He wore a pin at his collar, not a rank marking, but an anchor on a bed of red and white flames. Both were symbols of the Captain, Tatian knew, and then remembered someone saying that Tendlathe's party had adopted the combined signs as their badge. So this was trade again, Tatian thought. And more than that, the damned two-sex model. He said, "Is there a problem, officer?" He spoke in *franca:* it was unlikely either of the *mosstaas* understood creole, but more than that, the reminder of off-world power could only make the situation worse.

"Œ," one of the *mosstaas* began, and Reiss cut in quickly, in creole.

"Ser, I told them Astfer works for us, for NAPD. She's a good friend, they say she was throwing rocks at one of the *ranas* last night—inciting trouble."

"Which I was not," the fem said, in *franca*. ðe sounded more annoyed than anything, but Tatian could see ðer hands trembling. ðe seemed to realize it ðerself, and shoved them into ðer pockets.

Tatian took a deep breath. One way or another, this was likely to be expensive—and could be very expensive, if the Old Dame found out and didn't believe his explanation—but he'd taken a dislike to the *mosstaas* the minute they called ðer *"wyfie." "*What's the problem, miri?" he said, in *franca*.

The militiamen exchanged glances, and then the taller of the two, a bulky man with a ragged mustache and beard, said, "Mir, this—woman—was seen throwing rocks at a *rana* band last night. There have been a number of complaints filed against the *wrangwys* lately, and they have to be investigated."

"Last night?" Tatian said, and kept his tone remote. "Our people were working late last night, getting ready for the harvest." He slipped his hand into his pocket as he spoke, a familiar, ostentatious movement. The taller man's eyes followed the gesture, but his partner was looking at the fem.

"We've got witnesses, and a complaint from someone who matters—"

"Witnesses who could be mistaken," the first *mosstaas* said firmly. "With people like her—hells, they look alike."

"I'm sure there's been a mistake," Tatian said, and took his hand out of his pocket. He kept a wad of White Watch bills folded there, for emergencies, and let the corner of the folded packet show as he extended his hand. "Let me recoup your losses."

"She works for you," the shorter man said flatly, not bothering to hide his disbelief.

People were watching them, Tatian realized suddenly, watching from a distance, kept at bay by the *mosstaas'* truncheons and the certainty of a holstered pistol, but watching nonetheless. He allowed his eyes to slide sideways, scanning the faces, but couldn't read the expressions. Some would be disgusted, certainly, seeing this as trade, one more sexual transaction; maybe a few would be radicals, glad to see the *mosstaas* humiliated, but most of them were silent, wary, and he didn't know what they thought. And it didn't matter, not at the moment, so long as no one else interfered: Reiss had started this, it was up to him to get them both, all, out of it. "That's right," he said. "Works for our botanist, Derebought Stane." *And I must remember to tell Derry that, when we get home.* "Is there a problem?" He gave the words bite, let his hand, still holding the money, sink a little, and the taller militiaman reached hastily for it.

"Not at all, mir, I apologize for the inconvenience. I'm sure there's been some mistake—but she'd better be more careful next time."

"I'll see to it," Tatian said, grim-voiced, and the *mosstaas* turned away. He looked at the fem, then at Reiss. Reiss gave him his best smile.

"Thanks, *baas*—"

Tatian shook his head. "Later. I have an appointment at the port. Bring your friend—charmed to meet you, serram—and you can take her home on your way back to the office. We'll discuss it when you get back."

5

straight:
(Hara) one of the nine sexual preferences generally recognized by Concord culture; denotes a person who prefers to be intimate with persons of one of the two "opposite" genders.

MHYRE TATIAN

The fem was very quiet on the ride to the starport, perched uncomfortably in the space meant for cargo, but Tatian was very aware of ðer presence. ðe meant trouble, ðer very presence meant trouble, both with the Old Dame, if—when—ðe heard about it, and quite possibly with the local authorities. If Reiss had just looked the other way. . . . It was hard to think that with the fem ðerself sitting behind him—the *mosstaas* were notorious for the efficiency of their confessional techniques—and he sighed and looked sideways out the jigg's scratched windscreen.

They had passed the city limits—unofficial, marked only by the way the buildings stopped—and the land had gone from the low scrub of the coastline to the long hills of the high plains. He had seen the transition a hundred times before, but he caught his breath yet again as the jigg topped the first big rise, and he could look out across the green-and-gold land. It was mostly flaxen and flowergrass, the flaxen distinguishable by the larger seedheads that bowed the heavy stalks into graceful arcs, but here and there he could see the bright blue patches that were daybeans in flower, or the low, dark green clumps of blue pomme bushes. This close to Bonemarche, the land was flagged for the local gatherers, the bright pennants, each one marked with the name and symbol of a Stiller *mesnie*, flickering in the steady breeze. Hara's crops could not, generally speaking, be cultivated successfully—they seemed interdependent in ways the indigenes had never had the population nor the need to determine—but the *mesnies* were careful of their land and jealous of their privileges. There were well-worn paths through the best acreage, and as the jigg topped the next rise, Tatian could see a gathering party clustered around a wood-bodied draisine, sorting blue pomme for the markets. Redbirds, Hara's largest land animal, circled overhead, and he was not surprised to see that netting had been spread over some of the best-looking bushes. The Traditionalists argued against the practice, saying that netted bushes had a poorer crop the following year, but most *mesnies* did it anyway, rotating from stand to stand. Blue pomme was too much of a staple crop, salable to other indigenes as well as off-world, not to take the chance.

"Did you get what you needed?" Reiss asked at last, raising his voice to carry over the whine of the jigg's motor and the rush of the transports in the fast lane.

"Partly."

"Starli's good people."

"I still need parts," Tatian said. "Anyone you'd recommend at the port?"

Reiss shrugged, not taking his hands from the steering bar. "You're better connected there than I am. I usually end up buying from Guinard's."

Guinard's boasted of being the only tech supply house on Hara with multiple licenses; it was correspondingly expensive. Tatian sighed again. That meant he had the choice of paying Guinard's prices or talking to Prane Am, and neither was particularly appealing. For a moment, he wondered if there was any point in talking to Eshe Isabon or Shraga Arsidy, but dismissed the thought almost as soon as it had formed. All off-worlders guarded their sources of supply jealously; even his closest friends would be reluctant to reveal their company's secrets to an outsider. Am, at least, was her own agent.

The starport itself lay on the flat land of the first great plateau: barren land, by Haran standard, good for nothing but the ubiquitous drift-grass. The indigenes mixed its fibers into their bricks, strengthening the coarse clay. Stiller was rich in drift-grass, if nothing else. They had easily been able to spare the land for the port, and in any case, Tatian thought, they had been well paid. He could see the towers of the docking cradles over the roofs of the support buildings, top lights blazing red and white even in the daytime. He counted the reds as the jigg turned onto the approach lane: seven shuttles loading, which meant at least seven bulk carriers in orbit overhead. It was definitely getting close to Midsummer, and the first big deliveries from the *mesnies;* he only hoped he hadn't left his repair too long.

Reiss pulled the jigg to a stop in the shade of the Central Administration building. "Do you want me to wait?" he asked.

Tatian shook his head. "No. Take your friend home, and then tell Derry what's happened. Tell her to put some sort of plausible excuse on record, just in case someone decides to check up on us."

"But you already paid the *mosstaas,*" the fem said, sounding startled, and then looked as though ðe wished ðe hadn't spoken.

"I'm more concerned about IDCA," Tatian said, still looking at Reiss. The younger man nodded, his expression for once somewhat chastened. "I want it taken care of, Reiss."

"I will, *baas,*" the younger man said. At his gesture, the fem scrambled forward into the passenger seat, and he touched the throttle again. The jigg pulled decorously away from the curb, and Tatian stepped into the sudden cool of the Administration building.

Prane Am worked for the Port Authority itself, in the larger of the two repair facilities. Rather than use the maze of tunnels that connected the buildings, Tatian cut across the almost empty staging lot, blinking again at the heat and the gathering clouds. In a few weeks, this lot and the dozen loading bays it serviced would be filled to capacity, and draisines and shays would be backed up on the access roads, waiting their turn to unload. At the moment, though, only about half the bays were open; shays were drawn up to the platforms where off-worlders and indigenes directed the machines that moved the cargo. He surveyed them with a professional eye—Kerendach had been doing a steady out-of-season business for a while now, so their presence was to be expected, but what DTS was doing with a cargo that size this time of year was beyond him, and he made a mental note to check up on them once he got back to the office.

He was sweating freely by the time he reached Repair One, and he thought he heard a distant rumble of thunder: the afternoon storms were arriving as usual. He ducked through the narrow doorway, pushing hard against the stiff seal, and stopped just inside to get his bearings. For once, all the internal partitions had been folded back, opening up the full central volume. In that space, a shuttle hung, suspended from a metal cradle, dwarfing even the biggest cargo movers, its one extended wing almost touching the wall above his head. The exoskeletons that crawled across its surfaces and along the cradles looked almost human-sized by comparison. There were three of them in use, clustered around the shuttle's steering jets. He stared up at them, shading his eyes against the cold glare of the working lights, and wondered which was Am. Before he could find an internal systems port, however, a speaker crackled on the wall behind him.

"Tatian? Is that you?"

"Hello, Am." He waited, not quite sure of his welcome. She had sounded cheerful enough, but the speaker distorted emotion.

"Hang on a minute, I'm due break. I'll be right down."

Tatian allowed himself a small sigh of relief and waited while one of the exoskeletons withdrew itself along a support beam. It clicked into a port at the top of a main pillar, and a small figure emerged from its center. She climbed down the long ladder and came to join him, stopping only to enter a code in the shop computer.

"It's good to see you again," she said, and jerked her head toward the side door. "Let's go out."

Tatian followed her through the smaller door into the alley that ran between Repair One and the technician's shed next door. It was shaded but still hot, the air heavy with the oncoming rain. The dirt-drifted paving was spotted with stains of spilled coffee and *aram* cuds, and the air smelled of ozone and fuel cells and the heady spice of the drift-grass.

"I haven't seen you in ages," she said. "How're things?"

Tatian shrugged, but couldn't repress a smile. He had half-forgotten, in the unpleasantness of their last quarrel, just how attractive she was. The close-fitting worksuit outlined the ample curves of hips and breasts; the tool belt just accentuated her tiny waist. She saw him looking and smiled back, appreciative and rueful all at once.

"Busy," he said. "Things have been busy. And I hope I'm not taking you away from anything."

"Nothing important," Am answered, and looked back at the half-open door. "They had a couple jets jam when they were coming in, and the owner's freaking. But, hey, it pays the rent."

"Freelance job?" Tatian asked. Am, like most of the port technicians, rented time on the company equipment to do outside jobs, jobs that would otherwise be at the bottom of the company priority lists.

Am made a rocking gesture with one hand, and Tatian nodded. So-so, sort-of, the motion said, and that just meant that the job had been placed through the port's gray market. Someone offered someone extra overtime, or a favor, or something—he himself had made that bargain often enough—and the job queue got rearranged.

"Speaking of which," Am said, and smiled. "No offense, Tatian, but what brings you out here?"

Tatian laughed. "I need to buy parts. I've got a problem with the interface box, and it looks like it'll be easier just to replace it."

Am nodded again, her mobile face abruptly remote and serious. It was the look she always had when she was working, or thinking about work, and it had never failed to evoke an odd mix of lust and jealousy. It figured she had taken up with a mem, he thought bitterly. They would at least share that obsession.

"I can get you a box," Am said, after a moment. "But—you have Inomatas, right?"

"Yes."

"That I can't do, at least not if I'm remembering your prejudices right. I can get you something secondhand, I heard there's a Mark Three Inomata available right now, or I can get you a new, up-to-the-minute clone. Take your pick."

"That's not much of a choice," Tatian said.

Am shrugged. "I know you hate clones. At least there're no HIVs on Hara."

"There are plenty in the port," Tatian answered. That was another reason the pharmaceuticals spent so much time and effort on Hara: Hara was the only human-settled world that had no native HIV strain, and the off-world strains seemed to find no toehold in the indigenous population. Unfortunately, whatever it was that protected the indigenes—and no one had isolated it yet—had absolutely no effect on the resident off-worlders.

"For a druggist, you're pretty phobic about used parts," Am said.

"That's not the issue," Tatian said, and bit off what could easily escalate into a too-familiar quarrel. Am had a technician's contempt for the softer sciences. "You said there was a Mark Three, a real Inomata. How would it work with the system I've got? And how much are they asking for it?"

"I can get it for about two-fifty, three hundred cd," Am answered. "But that doesn't include installation."

"I've got someone who'll take care of that."

Am nodded. "There shouldn't be any problem tying it into your present system—you were running the Three-Eight, right?"

"Right." Trust her to remember that, if nothing else, Tatian thought.

"You may find it a little slower, but you'll get used to that."

"How much slower?" Tatian asked.

"The difference is in nanoseconds, but sometimes it feels perceptibly different, mainly when large blocks of data are involved." Am shrugged again. "I think a lot of it's psychological."

Tatian sighed. He didn't like secondhand bioware, less from any rational fears—risk of infection or rejection—than a childhood terror of bodysnatchers, the killers who had roamed the cities of Dodona, murdering for the expensive implants people wore beneath their skin. The worst of the gangs had been broken before he was born, but they had remained part of Dodonan folklore. But the alternative was a clone, and even with Am's help and advice, there was simply too much risk of getting a defective part. "I'd rather get the real Inomata," he said, and Am nodded.

"That's what I'd do."

"Will you broker for me? I'd take it as a favor, Am."

"All right." She glanced sideways, consulting internal systems. "It'll be three hundred—and I don't suppose you have it with you?"

Tatian shook his head. "I can wire it."

"All right—" She broke off as a door opened in the technician's shed, mobile face drawing into a sudden frown. Tatian glanced over his shoulder, curious, to see a tall mem in a sleeveless overall and a worn-looking worksuit standing in the doorway.

"I thought we were taking break together, Am," þe said. The accent was Haran, unmistakably, and the jealous note was equally clear.

Tatian scowled, and Am said hastily, "This is business, Mous. I'll be over in a minute."

"Æ?" the Haran said, with patent disbelief, and Am's frown deepened.

"Don't give me this shit, Mous. I'll be in in a minute, okay?"

"Oh, yes," the Haran said bitterly, and closed the door with a thump.

"Going native," Tatian quoted, with equal bitterness, and Am glared at him.

"Don't you start."

"I thought you were straight, *straight* as in liking men," Tatian said.

"I am straight," Am said, but the words lacked conviction. "Mous, he . . ."

"þe is a mem," Tatian said. "I don't care what þe calls þimself, þe's a mem, and that makes you at the very least differently straight from when you were sleeping with me."

"And what the hell business is it of yours?" Am demanded. "You and I were pillow-friends, and that's all. If I want something different, that's my affair."

"You gave me a hard time about going native," Tatian said. "Just because I have to deal with the indigenes based on what they tell me they are. But I'm not the one who's changed my tastes and not bothered to tell anyone."

Am glared at him for a moment. "All right, I'm di, I guess. Are you happy now? It's not exactly what I expected either."

"I—" Tatian stopped, shaking his head. *Adults don't change their minds*, he wanted to say, *not about something as important as this. And if they do, they* tell *people, and then they apologize. And most of all, they don't harass me for doing exactly what you're already thinking about doing. I don't do trade, never have, it's not fair*— He took a deep breath. "All right. I suppose it's none of my business. But I've never played trade, and you know it."

"I know," Am agreed, looking away, and there was a little silence. "I'm sorry," she said, after a moment, and looked back with a smile that was more of a grimace. "I shouldn't've said that. It's this fucking planet. Mixes everything up."

And that, Tatian knew, was as close to an apology as he was going to get. "I'll wire you the money," he said, and immediately wondered if he should have said more.

Am nodded, her eyes already drifting to the door. "I'll tell Cesar to hold the box for me."

"Thanks," Tatian said, and she gestured vaguely.

"No problem. I'll see you around."

There was no alternative but to take the monorail back to Bonemarche. He stood on the high, bare platform, wishing that the knot of indigenes in janitorial coveralls hadn't taken up all the narrow band of shade, wishing that he had a parasol like the old woman in traditional dress who waiting in solitary splendor at the far end of the platform. The sun was veiled by high, thin clouds, but the heat was fierce in the damp air; toward Bonemarche, the horizon was purple with the promise of the afternoon storms. As the notice board began to flash, signaling the approaching train, he thought he saw Eshe Isabon hurrying up the ramp to the platform, but he wasn't in the mood for company. He stepped back, putting a pillar between them, and was glad when ðe didn't seem to notice his presence.

Not for the first time since he'd come to Hara, he found himself wondering why he'd accepted this assignment. He could have stayed on Joshua, stayed with Mali Kaysa—sane, sensible, man-straight Kaysa, complicated in ways he understood. He closed his eyes, shutting out the white sky, the dark horizon, remembering instead the lights of Helensport and the cool nights when they'd walked home together from one of the clubs or a show or even just from working late. He could almost feel her hand cool in his, hear her laughter and the cheerful voice of the demi couple, a woman and a fem, who shared the narrow garden between their rented houses. They had thrown good parties, that pair, and he remembered an image from one with special clarity: Kaysa with her mahogony hair straight as rain, for once freed from its braid to flow almost to her waist, standing in the blued light of the door lantern. She had been watching a man and a woman, friends of hers from the translators' office where she worked, going through the first almost ritual questions, each trying to signal sexual interest without going too far, just in case the other wasn't interested.

"You could've told him she was man-straight," Tatian had said, and put his arm around her waist.

"I'm not a matchmaker," Kaysa had answered, and leaned companionably against him. "Besides, this is more fun."

That memory had an ironic feeling to it now, on Hara, where there weren't any rules, or at least not ones that he could accept as normal, or even reasonable. That party had been one of the last ordinary nights before he'd been offered the Haran assignment— which paid too well, offered too much chance of promotion, to refuse—and he clung to the memory. The people had been sane, reasonable, ordinary, had known who and what they were: it was something to hold to on Hara.

He found a seat in the corner of the poorly cooled car away from the fading sunlight and settled in for the ride back to Bonemarche, listening with half an ear to the chatter of the half-dozen or so indigenes who shared the car. Outside the window, the thick grasses rose and fell in the rising breeze, the half-open seedheads of the flaxen tossing like foam. The sky over Bonemarche was dark with clouds, and he saw the first bolts of lightning streak from cloud to sea. The monorail track was the highest thing on the upper plain, always vulnerable, and he was relieved when the train negotiated the curves of the descent without incident and passed between the first buildings, following the Portroad into the city. By the time the train pulled into the station at Harbor-look, the first drops of rain were falling, leaving damp patches ten centimeters wide in the dust of the platform.

He shared a ride back to the Estrange with a pair of techni-cians, from WestSiCo, who spent most of the ride mumbling ar-cane shipping formulae. They reached Drapdevel Court just as the rain was ending. The court was mostly dry, for once, just a few puddles starting to steam as the clouds broke, and he pushed open the office door without bothering to take off his shoes. To his surprise, Derebought was sitting at the lobby console, the privacy screen unfolded along the desktop edge.

"I'm glad you're back, Tatian, these—people—have been waiting to see you."

Tatian looked sideways into the little waiting area, wondering what else would go wrong today, and sighed deeply, recognizing the IDCA agents sitting on the padded bench. "What do you want?"

Stevins Jhirad grinned, and unfolded þimself from the bench. þe was tall for a mem—wasn't much like the stereotype of a mem at all, Tatian thought, not for the first time. þe was too tall, too thin, most of all too quick of tongue and hand, more like a herm than a mem.

"To talk to you, what else?" þe said, still smiling.

"Talk away," Tatian answered. NAPD's dealings with the In-terstellar Disease Control Agency were infrequent, but had rarely been profitable or pleasant.

"In private, if you don't mind, Tatian." That was Kassa Valmy, rising easily to stand by her partner. She smiled then, as though to rob the words of any threat, but Tatian didn't feel par-ticularly reassured.

"Is there a problem?" he asked, and waved them ahead of him into his office. If there was a problem, it wouldn't come from business, he added silently, was more likely to be something per-sonal—either his encounter with the *mosstaas* this morning, though that seemed unlikely, or Reiss. Probably Reiss, he thought, and closed the door carefully behind him, gesturing for the others to take a seat.

Jhirad settled þimself comfortably in the nicer of the client's chairs, cocking one long leg across the other, but Valmy shook her head. "I'll stand, thanks. I've been sitting all day."

"Suit yourself." Tatian sat down at the desk and touched the spot that lit the desktop screens. Nothing popped to the surface, neither urgent mail nor internal files requiring instant attention, and he ran his hand across the shadowscreen, transforming the display to meaningless geometric patterns. "So what can I do for you?"

"I hear you had a busy day," Jhirad said.

Tatian glanced at þim: the *mosstaas*, then. "I suppose."

"Bribing the *mosstaas* in broad daylight right in the middle of the Souk," Valmy said, and gave another broad grin. "Even for Hara, that's ballsy."

"I don't see any Harans objecting," Tatian said, after a moment. "Or are you here on the chief's behalf?"

Jhirad snorted. "Godchep Stiller wouldn't care if you paid off a murder in his office, as long as he got his cut."

"True," Tatian said. "So . . ."

"A friendly warning," Valmy said, and Jhirad frowned.

"Not even that. Call it advice, Tatian—and friendly advice, too."

Tatian said nothing, waiting, watching them across the desktop that ran with color. Jhirad and Valmy had been on Hara for nearly two hundred kilohours—better than sixteen local years, four standard contracts—and in that time they had gotten a reputation as tough but honest. If they were offering a warning, or advice, whatever they wanted to call it, he would be a fool not to listen to them.

Jhirad seemed to take his silence for consent. "Local politics are going to be complicated this year. You don't want—none of us off-worlders want to get involved in it. You can't win friends, not this time."

"Call off Shan Reiss," Valmy said, and didn't bother to smile this time.

"What's your problem with Reiss?" Tatian asked. "It was me who paid off the *mosstaas* today."

Jhirad gave þis partner an irritated glance. "Reiss was, is already involved, and not just in politics. He's speaking for a man who wants to emigrate, he's one of the witnesses who'll swear that Destany hasn't done trade for the required twenty kilohours."

"That would be Reiss's business," Tatian said. "And yours. And it's all legal. I never knew you two to be so concerned with one emigration case before. So tell me what's really going on."

Valmy laughed softly. "Your point."

"Thanks," Tatian said, and waited.

"What's going on is, the local authorities have asked that we intervene," Jhirad said. "The request comes from the highest level."

Tatian stared at þim for a long moment, unable to believe what he'd heard. Temelathe Stane was notorious for keeping the Concord authorities at arms' length, for insisting on the absolute independence of the indigenous institutions. For him to ask for help—to request that the IDCA intervene in an emigration case—was almost unimaginable.

"Our bosses," Valmy said, "would like to establish the precedent."

"I bet they would," Tatian said.

"What they—what we want," Jhirad said, "is for Reiss to withdraw his statement."

Tatian's eyebrows rose in spite of himself. That was the last thing he had expected from these two; Valmy and Jhirad had always treated trade cases fairly, within the Concord's laws, and they didn't usually back down if they thought their superiors were making a mistake. On the other hand, Temelathe had never asked for help before. "Why?"

"Shan Reiss has more friends among the Modernists, and in the Black Watch, Stiller and Black Casnot, than anyone needs right now," Jhirad said. "And the case is sensitive. Destany Casnot is being sponsored by Timban 'Aukai, who's heavily into trade."

Tatian nodded. "I've heard of her."

"Who hasn't?" Valmy murmured.

"Tendlathe is really opposed to trade," Jhirad went on,

"which would be more useful if he wasn't also opposed to us—off-worlders in general, I mean, not just the IDCA."

"That's nothing new," Tatian said.

"No. The problem is, they—Destany and 'Aukai—are going to be represented by local advocates, and they've picked a group that's downright notorious for defending people in trade. The word on the street is that one of the three—"

"Haliday Stiller, if you know that name," Valmy interjected.

"I do." The herm who tried to challenge gender law, Tatian thought, and lost. Warreven's partner.

"—is just looking for a case that will let ʒim challenge the whole gender system." Jhirad smiled again, the expression wry. "You may begin to see our problem."

Tatian nodded again. Under other circumstances, the IDCA would be glad to see the legality of the Haran sex trade questioned in the local courts, but not when it meant questioning the off-world presence as well. Tendlathe could get entirely too much power out of this case; better to get concessions from Temelathe instead, do him a favor, and wait for a more propitious moment to attack trade.

"On top of all that, or as a result of it, Temelathe has been screwing around with the Stiller election lists," Jhirad said, and Tatian frowned at the apparent inconsequence. "Bear with me, Tatian, it all fits."

"Go ahead," Tatian said, and leaned back in his chair. He heard himself doubtful and knew the others did, too.

"He's taking a hell of a chance," Valmy said, almost to herself. "There are a lot of people pissed off about it."

Jhirad nodded. "Basically, he's arranged for Stiller to nominate two unsuitable candidates for *seraaliste*. One is a man named Daithef, who's considered pretty much a joke, and the other is Warreven, who is one of the advocates involved in this case. We think he's trying to get Warreven out of the courts and is either trying to bribe ʒim—*seraaliste* is a powerful position, the person who holds it is one of the more important Important Men—or at least get ʒim out of the way, keep ʒim away from trade cases for the next calendar year. It's also possible he's trying to bring ʒim back into his party. You know—no, you probably don't know, it was before your time—Temelathe wanted 3im to marry Tendlathe, and I think he, Temelathe, would still like to have Warreven on his side."

"Warreven said no to that," Valmy said, "and rumor says 3e's saying no to the nomination, too."

Tatian blinked, trying to imagine the person he'd seen—long hair and pointed chin, strong bones beneath skin like silk, loose vest and trousers and the clashing metal bracelets, casually kind and as casually sexual, like and not like any indigene he'd met before—married to Tendlathe Stane. The idea, the casual switch of legal gender, was too alien, and he shied away from it. It was just as strange to think of Warreven as Stiller *seraaliste*: it was odd to think that he might be negotiating with 3im next year.

"You know 3im?" Valmy asked.

The words were casual, but the look that accompanied them was not. Tatian smiled ruefully. "I literally ran into 3im yesterday at the Courthouse. We talked—3e gave me the name of a technician who might be able to work on my implants."

"You've been—running into—a lot of awkward people lately," Valmy said. "All of them in trade."

Tatian sighed. "So tell me about the fem."

"ðer name's Astfer Stiller," Jhirad began, and Valmy made an irritated noise.

"þe'll give you clan and kin before þe answers your questions. You've been on Hara too long, Stevi."

"ðe's a paralegal—an advocate of sorts, but trained to handle Concord law, too," Jhirad went on, as though þe'd never been interrupted. "ðe's a known member of the New Agenda movement, and ðe's been doing work for Haliday on trade cases."

"Which one is New Agenda?" Tatian asked.

"They propose that the Centennial Meeting be asked if Hara should rejoin the Concord as a full member world," Valmy said. "And they really don't like Tendlathe. It was New Agenda members who stood up in the Watch Council and said he shouldn't be confirmed as Temelathe's heir."

Tatian whistled softly. That had taken courage, and it hadn't done any good: Tendlathe's status had been officially acknowledged the year he himself came to Hara.

"You begin to see how it all fits," Jhirad said. "This may be about trade, about one emigration case, but there's a whole lot of other things connected to it. And because of that, we—the IDCA, and through us, Customs and maybe even ColCom—have a chance to get some real influence on the government here. I'm asking you to ask Reiss to withdraw his statement."

Damn. Tatian shook his head slowly, knowing only too well how Reiss would respond to that request. *I'm going to murder the little bastard for getting me, the company, mixed up in this . . .* "And what happens to what's-his-name, the guy who wants to emigrate, if Reiss agrees? It's going to matter to him."

Jhirad looked away. Valmy said, "I don't know. I can't promise anything, Tatian. But if it comes up now, with Reiss's name on it, our bosses are going to push for a trade investigation of NAPD."

"And that's blackmail," Tatian said.

"I suppose," Valmy answered. "But that's how it's been put to me."

"This is not a good time to play politics," Jhirad said, and pushed þimself slowly to þis feet. "Unless, of course, you're us. Talk to Reiss, Tatian. The worst of the pressure should be off by Midsummer. That's not long."

"I'll talk to him," Tatian said. "But I don't make any promises."

"Fair enough," Jhirad said equably, and slid open the door. Valmy followed him out, letting the door slide closed again behind her.

Tatian sat for a long moment, staring at the pale cream fiber that covered the walls. What Jhirad and Valmy were asking was technically illegal; more than that, it would be hard to get Reiss to go along with it, even if he were given a direct order to withdraw his statement. He, Tatian, would have to invoke Masani's rules against trade, the threat of firing, and he hated to do that when he knew perfectly well that Reiss wasn't profiting from his games. On the other hand, he understood the temptation IDCA was facing. To have the chance to intervene in Hara's government, not just legally but actually at the Most Important Man's personal request, was too good a chance to pass up. He sighed, ran his hand, flat-palmed, across the shadowscreen to wake the desktop. The IDCA agents were right when they said this was politically a difficult time, and more than that, they were also right when they hinted that NAPD was being dragged into trade. And that, the Old Dame had made very clear, was not to happen. He would do what the IDCA agents wanted, ask—no, *tell*—Reiss to take back his statement, but he would do it because he could not risk NAPD's becoming involved in trade.

---

wry-abed:
> (Hara) the politest colloquial term for men who prefer to have sex with men and women who prefer to have sex with women.

WARREVEN

The cellar room was cool, pleasantly dim, the pinlights arranged across the ceiling in patterns to mimic the stars. It wasn't much of an illusion—the heavy beams that supported the dance floor broke the pattern, distorted it into odd geometry—but the steady pounding of drums and feet made the lights tremble like stars seen through atmosphere. Warreven grinned at the thought and earned a glare from Haliday, sitting across from him in the other corner of the private cubby.

"Relax, Hal," Malemayn said, and reached for the jug of nightwake that stood in the center of the table. He refilled the five cups, leaving the sixth still empty, and looked at Warreven.

Before he could say anything, however, the off-world woman at his left said, "Damn Shan Reiss anyway. There isn't time for this."

The man beside her growled agreement, and then looked embarrassed, picked up his cup and drank to hide his uncertainty. Warreven watched him, still not certain what to make of him. Destany Casnot seemed very ordinary to be the cause of all this trouble, a big, light-skinned herm, who had once been flashily handsome but had settled into the thick-bodied Casnot middle age. It was hard to imagine that he had done trade; harder still to imagine what 'Aukai saw in him that made her want to bring him with her into her exile. Warreven glanced at his hands, folded on the tabletop, in the overlapping circles of light, seeing dirt under the broken fingernails. Reiss had said that Destany had a *mairaiche*, a truck garden, of his own in the scrub outside the city, between the Bounder Road and the hills; why anyone would give that up, the rare security of cultivation, was more than Warreven could understand. And to give it up for Timban 'Aukai—

"We know," Haliday said, and managed to sound almost convincingly soothing. "He'll be here." 3e looked at Warreven then, too, and he sighed.

"I talked to him this afternoon. He said he'd come." *After I invoked his clan, our shared Watch, and a few summers screwing around with him in Irenfot,* he added silently, *but he did say he'd meet with us.* Haliday was looking at him as though 3e'd read his thoughts, and Warreven looked hastily at the time display over the street-side door. "It's only just time."

Haliday made a face, and the woman said again, "I don't have time for this."

Warreven glanced at her. The years had not been particularly kind to Timban 'Aukai, and she had not been beautiful to start with, a rangy, raw-boned woman who wore exaggeratedly tight-waisted clothes to keep from being mistaken for a mem. She was still wearing the clothes, a wide belt cinched painfully tight over a flowing shirt that seemed meant to add bulk at the hips, but her once-fine skin had been coarsened by the Haran sun, and there was a scar along her jaw where a sun-tumor had been removed. 'Aukai looked back at him, her pale eyes—an odd, off-world color, gray like winter clouds—flicking up and down in automatic assessment. It was an expression Warreven remembered all too well—he was probably meant to remember, he told himself, and met her stare without flinching.

The music, drums and whistle, was suddenly louder, and Warreven twisted in his chair to see Reiss coming down the stairs from the dance house overhead. One of the servers intercepted him, saying something in a voice too low to be heard over the drumming, but Reiss shook his head, gesturing to the table. Malemayn lifted a hand, and the off-worlder came to join them, dropping into the remaining chair.

"Sorry I'm late," he said cheerfully. "Hope you haven't been waiting long." He poured himself a glass of nightwake without waiting for an invitation and smiled guilelessly around the table, not quite meeting anyone's eyes. Haliday's frown deepened, and Malemayn laid a hand on ʒer elbow, signaling silence.

Destany said, "You know the situation, Reiss. How can you back out now?" *On me, your clan-cousin—your adopted clan, that took you in:* he didn't have to say any of that, and even in the dim light, Warreven could see the color rising in Reiss's cheeks.

"I don't have a choice," Reiss said, still in that too-bright tone that masked embarrassment, and Warreven leaned forward before anyone else could speak.

"'Aukai's right, we don't have time for this. Tell them what you told me, Reiss."

Reiss glanced at him, the blue eyes, foreign eyes, like 'Aukai's conspicuous even in the relatively low light. When he spoke, the false brightness had utterly vanished. "I don't have a choice, not if I want to keep my job. IDCA came down hard on my boss, and he told me flat out, withdraw the statement, or I don't work for him anymore. I'm sorry, Destany—" For the first time, he looked at him directly, Casnot to Casnot. "—but I'm not risking my residency."

"You were born here," Destany said.

"I was born in Irenfot," Reiss said. "You know that. No offense, Stany, but I don't want to go back there. If I lose my job, that's the only place I've got legitimate rights."

"They can't hold you to that," Haliday began, and Reiss laughed.

"Can't they? I'll have pissed off IDCA, and they have final say here."

"Or if they do," Haliday said, with dignity, as though ʒe hadn't been interrupted, "you can fight it."

Reiss shook his head again. "They're making this into a question of trade. I can't fight that—I've played around too much, they make an issue of it, they can get me for that. I'm sorry."

"Why in all hells are they so concerned about trade now?" Malemayn said, then made a face and answered his own question. "Because it's us, and everybody knows we're looking for a case to challenge the trade system."

"This wasn't it," Haliday muttered. 3e sighed, and looked at 'Aukai. "Maybe you'd—Destany'd—be better off with another set of advocates."

"Do you think it would help?" 'Aukai asked, and Malemayn shook his head.

"Probably not, unless you can get another off-worlder to swear for you. Or if Reiss changes his mind."

"Reiss is kin," Destany said flatly. "I don't know off-worlders anymore."

"All I ever wanted was for Stany to be with me," 'Aukai said quietly. "Either for me to stay, or him to come with me. You wouldn't think it'd be that complicated."

Well, yes, I would, Warreven thought. *You've run trade out of your shop for close to a local decade, you can't expect IDCA to do you any favors now.* He said nothing, however, leaning back in his chair as Malemayn turned to Reiss.

"Do you think it would make a difference to your boss, to IDCA, if we weren't involved?"

Reiss shrugged. "I have no idea. Look, I don't know what's really going on, anymore than you do."

"If it did, would you make your statement again?" Malemayn asked.

"Absolutely," Reiss said, and glanced at Destany. "I don't want to back out on you, on my obligations. I know what I owe Casnot, it's just—I don't have any choice."

"We could ask Langbarn to take over," Malemayn said, and Haliday snorted.

"He's—þe's still a mem, no matter what þe calls himself. The courts won't like it."

Warreven looked at 'Aukai, shutting out the conversation. It didn't really matter, not unless they could find some way to persuade Reiss's boss—Mhyre Tatian, he reminded himself, with an odd thrill that he wouldn't admit was pleasure—to let Reiss make his statement. Beyond 'Aukai, a frieze of the spirits danced along the wall, Captain and Madansa and Agede the Doorkeeper with his eyepatch and bottle of sweetrum; the painted Captain, broad-shouldered, broad-bearded, reminded him of the feel of Tatian's body against his own as they stood for an instant in unintended embrace. He dismissed that thought before it was fully formed: that was not the way to persuade a man who opposed trade so vehemently.

"What's NAPD's problem with trade?" he said aloud, and Malemayn glared at him.

"What in all hells does that have to do with anything?"

"I don't know, exactly. Bear with me, would you?"

Haliday grinned, showing sharp, feral teeth. "Raven's the only one with an idea so far, Mal."

Malemayn threw up his hands. "Fine."

"I'm sorry, I didn't mean to interrupt," Warreven began, then shook his head. "Have a drink, Mal. I think I have an idea."

Malemayn made a face, but the anger was fading. He reached for the nightwake pitcher, gesturing with his other hand for Reiss to proceed.

"The Old Dame—Lolya Masani, ðe owns the company—doesn't approve," Reiss said. "Partly it's ðe doesn't want us getting in bad with either Customs or IDCA—there's some stuff, semi-recreational, that we export that's strictly controlled in the Concord, and Customs could make life very hard for us if they wanted—and partly ðe just doesn't like the idea." He grinned suddenly. "ðe's got this tape ðe gives to every newcomer, where ðe lays down the law to them. No new drugs unless ðe clears them, and absolutely no trade. ðe'll fire anyone who sells a permit or a residency. And ðe's done it, too."

"So Tatian isn't opposed to trade per se," Warreven said slowly. "He just has to make it look good for Masani?"

"I don't know about that," Reiss said. "I mean, he doesn't approve of the players—I don't think he'd sell permits even if the Old Dame didn't say he couldn't."

Warreven waved that away. "But a case like this, where the trade was well in the past, and it's just two people who love each other and want to be together—if we offered him some incentive, some reason to change his mind, do you think he would?"

"He wasn't exactly happy when he told me I had to pull out," Reiss said. "Basically, IDCA made him do it."

Malemayn said, "We don't have anything to offer."

"Besides money, of course," Haliday said, "and that would be a little crude, for dealing with an off-worlder."

Warreven smiled. "But in four days, assuming the elections go the way Temelathe wants them, I'm the Stiller *seraaliste*. I control the sea-harvest, the land-harvest, and everything that's surplus to the present contracts is mine to sell where I please. Would that be sufficient incentive, do you think?"

"It's pretty crude," Malemayn said. "You won't be part of the group legally, but still . . ."

"I think it's clean enough," Haliday said. "But would this Tatian buy it?"

"I don't know," Reiss said, sounding dubious. "IDCA won't be pleased."

"I would imagine it would depend on what you offered him," 'Aukai said. For the first time since they'd come to the dance house, she sounded like the woman Warreven remembered, strong, decisive, and just a little contemptuous of the world around her. "Make the price high enough, and any druggist will stand up to the IDCA."

"We can't do anything until after the elections," Malemayn said thoughtfully, and looked at Warreven. "But that still leaves us time. I think this'll work, Raven. I think it will."

Warreven grinned, enjoying the praise. If he had to leave the courts, he could at least use his new position to benefit his partners. Temelathe would expect no less—and besides, he admitted silently, it would be a pleasure to annoy the Most Important Man.

omni:
> (Concord) one of the nine sexual preferences generally recognized by Concord culture; denotes a person who prefers to be intimate with persons of all genders. Considered somewhat disreputable, or at best indecisive.

WARREVEN

The room was cold, the cooling unit turned to its highest power, rattling in its corner. Warreven shivered and reached for a corner of the topmost quilt, pulling it half over his naked body. Behind him, Reiss stirred, shifted so that he was free of the quilts. Warreven could feel him sweating still, not just from the exertion of sex, and wondered again if all of the Concord Worlds were cold planets. It had seemed the thing to do, to invite Reiss home with him, when they were both flushed with the power of Warreven's idea, but now, lying in the cold bedroom, the moonlight through the thin fabric of the shutters warring with the fitful light of the *luciole* in the corner, he wondered if he'd made a mistake after all. It had been months since he'd even seen Reiss, longer since he'd slept with him; the sex had been good—Reiss was always good—but it had somehow reminded him of his days as trade.

"The light," Reiss said sleepily, and Warreven rolled to look at him.

"You want it off?"

"No, I'm going to have to go home in a while," Reiss answered, sounding a little more awake. "I was wondering, is that one of the bug lights?"

They had been speaking *franca*, and Warreven blinked at the unfamiliar term. "The *luciole?*"

"Yeah. It doesn't still have the bugs in it, does it?"

Warreven grinned. "Not in the city, it doesn't. It was my grandfather's, my mother had it fitted for grid power a few years before she died." He looked at the softly flickering lamp, a cèramic sphere shaped like a knot of *arbre* vines, standing in a base like a shallow bowl. None of the holes was bigger than his thumb:

the light had originally been the home of a colony of *luci*, the luminescent sea-flies of the peninsular coast. In the old days, before Rediscovery, you made a lamp like that by digging up a colony of *luci*. The queens would be confined to the center of the sphere, while the drones roamed freely, feeding them; each new generation added new light. "I've never seen a real *luciole* myself, not one that wasn't converted. One of my great-aunts said they were noisy, always buzzing, the drones all over the place, and the shelf would get all sticky from the sugar water they used to feed them."

"Sounds disgusting," Reiss said, and ran a hand along Warreven's side. His hand slipped further, cupped Warreven's breast, and Warreven turned away, shrugging his shoulder to dislodge him. There was an instant of tension, a stillness between them like a silence, and then Reiss stroked the other's back instead, running his fingers along Warreven's spine in mute apology. Warreven relaxed into that touch and, after a moment, pulled his hair forward over his shoulder, out of the way.

"I should go," Reiss said, but made no move.

"Suit yourself," Warreven answered. "You're welcome to stay." The neighbors would talk, of course—they always did; he sometimes wondered what they had gossiped about before the advocacy group had bought the building—but then, they would talk anyway, once he brought the quilts to the laundress.

"Thanks," Reiss said, and sighed, rolling onto his back. "No, I have to be in early tomorrow—I'm driving Tatian to Lissom to look at a possible surplus contract—and I don't really want to show up in the same clothes I wore yesterday."

He kicked himself free of the last top quilt and sat up, the sweat still a faint sheen on his back. Warreven rolled over to watch him dress, drawing the quilt up over his shoulders, glad of its warmth. Reiss was surprisingly fair where his clothes protected him from the sun; the hair of his chest and groin was unexpectedly dark against that pallor. Tatian was even paler skinned, and golden-haired, Warreven thought, like a spirit in a *babee*-story, and he wondered suddenly if that meant Tatian would be blond all over. It was an arresting thought; he caught himself smiling and shook the image away. It was a mistake to let himself think of the off-worlder in those terms, no matter how handsome he was, or how good his body had felt in that momentary contact. Tatian was just the man he had to bargain with for Reiss's statement, and Destany's freedom—nothing more, not even an object of fantasy, not if he, Warreven, wanted to win.

6

rana, ranas, also *rana* band, *rana* dancers:
> (Hara) a group of men and women who use traditional drum-dances to express a political opinion; *rana* performances are traditionally protected by the Trickster, and by custom cannot be stopped unless the *ranas* make an explicit request for their audience to take political action. *Ranas* traditionally wear multicolored ribbons, a mark of the Trickster, as a sign of their special status.

WARREVEN

Warreven had been drinking since the polls opened at noon—sweetrum and water, cut one-and-two so that he could barely taste the alcohol—but even so, he'd nearly finished the bottle. He glanced again at the media screen, lit but with sound muted, and turned away as soon as the count for *seraaliste* crawled along the bottom of the display. He was still winning—had already won, if he was honest with himself, and that meant that the clan's profits were his responsibility for the next year, until Midsummer came round again. One local year, twelve kilohours by the off-worlders' reckoning—twelve thousand and ninety-seven hours, to be precise—before he would be free again. But the harvest surplus was squarely in his hands, to sell where he pleased. Daithef wouldn't approve of that, anymore than he'd approved of Warreven's candidacy, and had spent the last few days of the campaign telling anyone who would listen that it would be a full year before Stiller's profits would be safe again.

Warreven made a face—he wasn't that incompetent, and in any case a barrel-back clam would do a better job than Daithef—but admitted that any deal with NAPD would have to be handled cautiously. The price would have to be to NAPD's advantage if there was any hope of using the sale to force Tatian to allow Reiss to bear witness, but it couldn't be too good, or he himself would lose credibility with the Stiller *mesnies*. His plan was beginning to seem more complicated than he'd anticipated; he grimaced again, putting the worry aside, and poured the last of the sweetrum into his cup. There wasn't much left, and he added water to bring the mixed liquid almost to the rim of the cup.

In the screen, the image shifted, showing the Glassmarket cleared for the first night of the Stiller *baanket*. The major celebrations would take place tomorrow and the next day, over the two days of the Midsummer holiday, but tonight Stiller would welcome the clan and introduce the new officers to their people. He would have to attend, of course, but not for the full night. Once he had shown himself on the platform, along with the other officials, he would be free to do as he pleased, to celebrate like any other Stiller. *And what I please . . . not Reiss's company, this time, but someone like me, another indigene.* He reached for the monophone and punched in the codes before he could change his mind.

The routing codes jingled past, and then there was dead air while the last tone pulsed steadily. Warreven waited, counting, and was about to break the connection when a voice answered.

"Æ?"

The secondary screen lit, tardy, the image streaked with static. Warreven stared at it, at the visual pickup behind it, and said, "Hello, Chauntclere."

"Raven." Neither the tone nor the expression were welcoming. "I suppose I should congratulate you."

"If you must," Warreven answered. Chauntclere Ferane stared back at him from the viewscreen, patently skeptical. His hair and short beard were streaked with salt stains, patches of odd, paler color, rust and amber and straw-gold, from a season spent aboard his tender. His crew, and the divers in particular, would be piebald from the mix of coral salts, wind, and the kelps they harvested. "It wasn't my idea, Clere."

"I believe you."

"God and the spirits!" Warreven glared at the screen, and after a moment, Chauntclere looked away.

"Anyway, congratulations. It says a lot for Stiller that they elected a Modernist."

It was a peace offering of sorts, though not strictly true—Warreven was more of a moderate, if not by Ferane then by Stiller standards—and Warreven nodded, accepting it as meant. "Thanks. And, speaking of celebrations, how would you like to go to the first-night's *baanket* with me? We wouldn't have to stay long, and I thought we could hit some of the harbor bars, maybe a dance house or something, afterward."

There was a little silence, and then Chauntclere shook his head, mouth twisting in a grimace that was intended to be a smile. "I don't think that's a good idea."

"It doesn't mean anything, I just wanted company."

"And to hit the bars, and screw around afterward," Chauntclere said. He shook his head again. "I don't think so."

Don't flatter yourself, Warreven thought, but knew better than to say it. It would take months to talk Chauntclere out of his anger—*and besides, that was exactly what I meant. I can't slap at him for getting it right and saying no.* He said, "Clere—"

"Some other time," Chauntclere said. "You know that, you know I want to see you. Just—not tonight, not at the *baanket*. It wouldn't look right, not for you, not for me."

"Would you meet me after?"

"I—don't know," Chauntclere said. "Where are you going?"

"The Embankment, probably, probably to Shinbone," Warreven answered.

Chauntclere made a face and looked away. "If I'm there, I'm there, but don't expect me. I've got the boat to think about."

Warreven sighed, acknowledging a half truth: sailors did care, not what their captains did, but that certain proprieties were observed. And two of the most important rules were no trade, and sleep wry-abed in foreign ports, not at home. "All right. Did you hear anything about Catness? That was the other reason I called."

Chauntclere answered the lie with a quick grin, but said only, "I told you, I don't know him. And I haven't run into anyone else who does—I doubt he's a diver, no matter what he says, or not a very good one. I'll let you know, though, if I hear anything."

"Tell Malemayn," Warreven said. "I'm not handling the case anymore."

"All right."

"Thanks," Warreven said, and broke the connection.

In the main screen, a team of *faitous* were stacking the last cord of wood into the main balefire; a second group, supervised by a *vieuvant* in black and someone in traditional dress who had to be part of the outgoing clan administration, were draping the smaller fires with braids of feelgood as thick as a man's arm. Behind them, women in traditional dress were loading clay kettles with mealie-fruit and gollies the size of a man's fist, while other women, more practically dressed, fed the cooking fires and the stone grills set up behind the serving table. Warreven wondered what the fatuous commentators were saying, how they were explaining the quaint indigenous customs for the off-world audiences, but didn't bother to turn up the sound. Instead, he touched keys again, typing in another mailcode, and waited while the system routed his call. The holding tone sounded twice, and then the secondary screen lit again.

"Yes?" Folhare's face in the screen was dark, hawk-nosed, strong in its cold beauty.

"Hello, Folhare," Warreven said, and felt the old familiar fondness steal over him. If she had been a man, or he a woman—and as always put aside the knowledge that the latter, at least, was a kind of possibility, that his calculations were based on unreal gender—he, at least, would have pursued. "How'd you like to come to tonight's *baanket* with me?"

Folhare blinked once, still smiling, and cocked her head to one side. "This is sudden, *coy*, what's brought this on?"

"I don't want to go by myself," Warreven answered.

"So who turned you down?" Folhare's smile turned wry.

"Is that fair?" Warreven demanded, and made himself sound more indignant because it was true.

"I suppose not. Are you—I can't imagine this would be entirely smart, Raven."

"I wish everyone would stop minding my business," Warreven said.

"So someone did turn you down," Folhare said, with mild satisfaction. "Clere?"

"Does it really matter?" Warreven forced a smile. She was

right, of course: bringing her as his guest would be deliberate provocation, but in his present mood, it seemed the thing to do. "I would like your company, Folhare."

There was a little silence, Folhare still with her head tilted to one side in question, and then she sighed, straightening. "I shouldn't tell you this, but you might want to know there's going to be a *presance* at the *baanket.*"

"Ah." *Presance* was a new word, a Modernist word; it meant the sort of performances the *ranas* had always given, drums and dancers and singing, but the songs of a *presance* generally had a more focused sting in their lyrics. "How—?" Warreven began, and then shook his head. "You made the dance-cloth."

"I painted the banner, actually."

"Well, then." Warreven spread his hands, nearly knocking over the now-empty cup. "Don't you want to see what happens?"

Folhare grinned. "I do, but I don't want to cause you trouble. Or me, for that matter."

"It's over for both of us," Warreven said. "No one would expect any of the makers to show up—except the dancers, that is— and I could use female company."

"As if I count."

"The law says," Warreven began, and Folhare made a sound of contempt, as though she would have spat.

"The law, as you've quoted me more than once, is an ass. Oh, hells, yes, I'll come. When do you want me?"

"We hired a coupelet to take us to the market," Warreven said. "Malemayn, Haliday, and anybody they invite, and me. I'll pick you up at eighteen-thirty, if that's all right. We should miss the worst of the crowds."

"And still get the best of the *baanket,*" Folhare said. "I'll be ready."

"Thanks, Folhare," Warreven said. "I'll be glad of your company."

"Say that again when this is over," Folhare said, and broke the connection.

Warreven replaced the monophone's handset, wondering if he was making a mistake. The other Important Men and Women of Stiller would be there, and he would be compared to them, not just by the Stillers in Bonemarche, but by the rest of the clan in the *mesnies* north of the city. But then, they would probably be delighted to see him with any woman, even one as unlikely as Folhare Stane, he told himself, and went into the bedroom to change for the *baanket*.

He shared the coupelet with Haliday, Malemayn, and a dark, lively woman who was introduced as Lyliwane. She was well named: even with her hair piled into festival braids, she was still a hand's width shorter than Malemayn's shoulder. Warreven, who was no better than average height, felt suddenly tall and gangling next to her. Both she and Malemayn were elegant in holiday finery; Haliday wore off-world clothes as usual, 3er only concession to the occasion a bright embroidered *shaal* wrapped man-style around 3er hair. The driver took them wide around the Harbor Market, and swung down the main street of Startown—uncrowded, for once; most of the off-worlders were either home, or already at the Glassmarket—heading for the row of former warehouses that had been converted to housing along the southern edge of the district.

Folhare was waiting in the opening of what had been the loading bay, tall and elegant in a tight bodice and a tiered skirt, the traditional clothes and the profusion of cheap dower jewels—earrings, necklaces, a dozen glass bracelets—incongruous coupled with her close-cut hair. An old woman sat at the other side of the open bay, dividing her attention between the street and the cone of silk and the netting hook in her lap. Children were playing somewhere back in the shadows, their voices clear and distinct as Malemayn opened the coupelet's door, but the sunlit forebay was empty except for the old woman. Folhare gathered her skirts around her and stepped carefully down the stairs to the street. Warreven, leaning past Haliday to greet her, saw the old woman frowning, her hands for once still on the hook.

"Who's she?" he asked.

Folhare lifted her skirts to mid-thigh, freeing her legs to climb into the coupelet's crowded compartment. "A sort-of cousin, or maybe an aunt. Her name's Savvil, she wants to be mother to us all."

"And she doesn't approve of Stiller?" Warreven asked, and edged over to make room for her.

"She doesn't approve of me," Folhare answered. "Celebrating Stiller's *baanket* is about the least of my sins."

There was no need for introductions: Bonemarche's active Modernists were still a small enough group that most people who were involved in politics had met all the others at one point or another. Warreven leaned back against the padded seat as the driver kicked the coupelet into motion, and Malemayn touched his shoulder.

"Want some?" He held out a bright green paper cone filled with a mix of poppinberries and creeping stars and the hot red seeds of the vinegar tree.

"Thanks," Warreven said, and took a handful of the roasted berries, crunching them one by one to release the drop of painfully sweet dew concentrated at the center. Folhare waved away the cone, but Lyliwane took a larger helping, began eating them in order, berries first, then the seeds, and finally the creeping stars.

"As if we're not going to get enough at the *baanket*," Haliday said, but 3e, too, took a few of the berries.

As they got closer to the Glassmarket, the streets became more crowded, and normal traffic, shays and three-ups and draisines, vanished, leaving only jiggs and the occasional coupelet to compete with the pedestrians. Nearly everyone was heading in toward the marketplace; Warreven saw a single shay, marked with the glyph of one of the lesser pharmaceuticals, stranded at a corner, trapped by the pressure of bodies and the steady movement. The driver, an indigene, leaned forward to rest both arms on the steering bar, obviously prepared to wait it out. His passenger's face was in shadow, almost invisible, but a hand tapped impatiently against the shay's body. Their own coupelet slowed, gears grating, and Malemayn winced.

"Maybe we should walk from here."

"Whatever." Warreven looked at the others, and Haliday shrugged. Lyliwane extended one tiny foot to reveal high-soled summer clogs.

"Believe it or not, I can walk in these."

"Let's," Malemayn said, and hit the intercom button without waiting for an answer. "You can let us out here, the traffic's getting too bad. After that—enjoy the *baanket*, we won't be needing you to get home."

"Thank you, mir. At your pleasure, miri." The driver's voice crackled back through the tinny intercom, and a moment later, the coupelet ground to a halt. He didn't bother pulling to the side of the road; there were no other vehicles to worry about, and the crowd flowed past it like water around a rock. Malemayn popped the side door, levering himself out into the crowd, and turned with forgetful courtesy to offer his hand to Haliday. 3e ignored him, but both Folhare and Lyliwane accepted the help in struggling out of the low compartment. Warreven followed them, slamming the door behind him. The taste of the creeping stars was strong on his tongue, bitter and sweet, like burned sugars. The afterimage was there, too, a faint haze of color around the stores' lights, and he watched his feet for a minute, until he was sure he'd adjusted to its effects.

They left the coupelet behind them quickly, walking with the flow of the crowd toward the Glassmarket's open hexagonal plaza. Six blocks away, Warreven could hear the beat of the drums and the shrill two-toned call of flat-whistles; as they got closer, it was all he could do to keep from dancing with them. Ahead of him, a woman—no, he thought, a fem—in tunic and trousers broke into a quick skipping step, and the men with her laughed and applauded. She bowed, too deeply, and her *shaal* slipped, so that she had to snatch it up from the dust, and nearly overbalanced in the process. One of the men caught her, still laughing, and as she spun in his arms, Warreven saw her eyes white and staring, and the mark of Genevoe on her face. She was already flying, high on hungry-jack or sundew, the Trickster's own drugs, and Warreven glanced curiously at Folhare, wondering if this was part of the planned *presance*.

Folhare saw the look and leaned close, her words all but drowned in the genial noise of the people around them. "No, she's not, and I don't thank you for thinking it. Ours is to be done stone sober, or—certain people—will know why."

Easier said than done, Warreven thought, but they had reached the edge of the Glassmarket, and he caught his breath in startled delight. Even expecting it, even having seen it before, the sight of the Glassmarket filled with Stillers—all his kin, in some way, all somehow family—was enough to make him momentarily glad of his allegiance, and for an instant he could almost look forward to his time as *seraaliste*. Normally, the sunken floor of the market was filled with *vendee*, marketfolk who had held their spots for generations. Some still sold glass, though not as many as before, and on a clear day the center of the market glittered like flame, sunlight sparking from finished goods and the rods and spheres of raw glass sold to other craftsmen. The Madansa, the spirit of the markets, painted on the wall of the warehouses overlooking the marketplace carried spheres of glass in each hand and wore a glass crown on her braided hair. There had been a field of glass under her feet, but sun and hands, touching the images for luck, had worn away the paint.

The character of the market had changed, anyway. The lesser *vendee*—the majority, now—sold fabrics, clothes, and quilted coverlets to a mix of indigenes and off-worlders. A few, the upstarts who held spaces along the perimeter, sold off-world goods, but most of that trade was confined to the Harbor Market and the Souk. Tonight, however, and for the next two days, the stalls and carts had been hauled away, and the plaza was filled with people instead. Their silks glowed under the massive lights, haloed and refracted by the creeping star's effects; the same light glittered from glass and shell jewelry, and gleamed from the ribbons that tied the wreaths of flowers. Beyond the crowd stood the platform where the Important Men and Women, clan officers and heads-of-*mesnie*, would stand for the announcements, and below them, mostly hidden by the mass of people, were the tables of the *baanket* itself. The cooks and tenders—there would easily be a hundred of them, probably more—were invisible, too, but the smell of the food proved their presence. The weight platform, where bulk goods were sold under the eyes of city and clan officials, had been covered over by a temporary staging, and the first of the bands was playing, their music lost except for the drumbeat and the occasional shrilling of the whistles.

"Here," Malemayn said, and Warreven turned, startled, to see the other holding out a wreath of catseyes. Lyliwane, laughing at his side, wore two great sprays of the flowers tucked into her crown of braids.

"Æ?"

"For you," Malemayn said, and set it precariously on Warreven's head.

"I don't need flowers," Warreven said, adjusting it anyway. Looking around, he could see half a dozen other couples wearing them, all officially, passing for men and women, though he thought he saw at least one other herm, and maybe a plump mem, among the group. He scowled, reaching for the wreath, and Malemayn shook his head.

"You're our *seraaliste* now, Raven, our very own Important Man. You should be wearing." He turned to Folhare. "And for you, mirrim."

Folhare took the wreath he held out to her, slung the bright blue flowers like a necklace across her shoulders. "Where'd you get it? It's lovely."

"There was a boy selling them," Malemayn said, and gestured vaguely toward the crowd behind him. Warreven looked and saw a thin herm holding a basket piled high with greenery. *Boy, indeed,* he thought, and the flower seller winked at him. He smiled back, temper somewhat restored, and looked away again.

"You're taking this a little seriously," Haliday said, but 3e was smiling. 3e, too, wore a crown of catseyes, the vivid yellow bright against 3er black hair. "And, speaking of Important Men, you, Raven, should be getting to the platform, I think."

Warreven made a face, but had to admit 3e was right. The platform was filling up with dignitaries; it was time, he supposed, to take his place with them. He looked to his right, over the heads of the crowd, and saw the windows and narrow balconies of the

White Watch House crammed with bright-clad figures: Stanes and their Maychilder kin-by-marriage and the occasional Landeriche or Delacoste, come to watch the Stiller display from an appropriate distance and to judge its probable cost and the clan's generosity. There were a few duller figures, too, drab among the locals: off-worlders, almost certainly pharmaceuticals, who were Temelathe's guests. Tendlathe would be there, too. "I hope they enjoy the show," he said, and held out his hand to Folhare, less as a courtesy than to keep from getting separated in the crowd.

Folhare took it, her fingers cool in his, leaned close again as they started toward the platform. "I guarantee they'll be—impressed."

---

woman:
    (Concord) human being possessing ovaries, XX chromosomes, and some aspects of female genitalia; she, her, her, herself.

MHYRE TATIAN

Tatian stood on one of the narrow balconies of the White Watch House, his shoulder jammed painfully against the coarse brick of the building shell, and wondered if carved ironwood was really strong enough to hold the seven adults who filled its platform. The single child, no older than sixty-nine or seventy kilohours, hardly seemed large enough to count. He pressed himself harder against the bricks as the child wriggled past, disappearing back into the main room, and waved away a *faitou* offering a tray of feelgood wrapped for stick smoking. The other people crowding the window greeted her gladly, and he winced at the acrid cloud that cloaked the balcony for an instant before the wind carried it away.

"So, Mir Tatian," a familiar voice said, and Tatian turned awkwardly to face Wiidfare Stane, a glass beaker of *liquertie* in his hand. "I'm glad you could make it this year."

"My pleasure," Tatian answered, and hoped the Licensing

Officer couldn't hear the insincerity in his voice. Wiidfare had invited him every year before, as he invited all the off-world heads-of-station, and every year Tatian had refused—until now. *And I wouldn't be here this time if Reiss hadn't managed to piss off Stane and involve me in it.* The party was a blatant display of Stane's power—Stanes and off-worlders standing together to look down on the celebration of a lesser clan—and Tatian, who did a great deal of business with Stiller *mesnies*, had never felt it was entirely wise to attend.

"But you're not drinking," Wiidfare said. "Let me get you something."

From most other Harans, Tatian thought, regarding the other man with detached dislike, that would be mere forgetfulness, an inappropriate courtesy that he wouldn't mind declining. But from Wiidfare, it was always a challenge. "I'm fine, thanks," he said, and met Wiidfare's ill-concealed sneer with a bland smile.

"Surely a little sweetrum-and-water won't hurt."

The voice was unfamiliar, but the face was not. Tatian nodded warily to Temelathe's son, said, "Mir Tendlathe."

Tendlathe lifted a hand, summoning one of the hovering *faitous*. He was a slender man, willowy where his father was solid, and Tatian had to make an effort not to glance down, looking for a herm's breasts and hips. In any case, Tendlathe wore a narrow, neatly trimmed beard and moustache: it wasn't an infallible indicator, but it was a sure guarantee of legal gender. A *bonne-faitou* came scurrying, ironwood tray held at waist height, and Tendlathe gestured expansively. "Do try some, ser Mhyre, I think you'll find it to your liking."

"Since you insist," Tatian said, in his most colorless voice, and lifted the jug that stood in the center of the tray. He sniffed it—odorless, and probably just water, though one could never be entirely sure on Hara—and then added it to one of the glasses, cutting the sweetrum even more. He set the jug back, murmuring his thanks to the *bonne*, and smiled at Tendlathe. "Your health, mir."

The Haran tipped his head in graceful acknowledgment. Tatian sipped carefully, barely letting the liquor past his lips, and was glad to see that Tendlathe, at least, had told the truth. With the additional water, the sweetrum was tolerable even to an off-world metabolism.

He looked away from Tendlathe and Wiidfare, back out over the crowds filling the Glassmarket. He had been unable to pick out Warreven among the candidates presented; there had been several people, all passable men, who wore their hair loose and ragged as Warreven had done, and it had been impossible to recognize anyone's face at this distance. The speeches—which had been inaudible, anyway—seemed to be over now, and the action was divided between the tables where the food was served and the side platform where the band was playing. Just the drums were audible, their rhythm vying with the inchoate noise of a thousand voices.

"Impressive, isn't it, mir?" Tendlathe said.

Tatian made a noncommittal noise, a Haran proverb dancing in his brain: *never praise Stane to Stiller, or Stiller to Stane.*

"It's nothing to Gedesrede, of course," Wiidfare said, "but it's nice enough."

"I've heard quite a lot about the Gedesrede *baanket,*" Tatian said. He judged it was time to establish some sort of common ground. "Our—NAPD's—chief botanist is a Stane."

"I assume she's on her way home now, then," Wiidfare said.

Tendlathe said, as if he hadn't spoken, "Which *mesnie?*"

"Riversedge," Tatian answered. "And yes, Mir Wiidfare, she and Mats are heading up there in the next few days."

Wiidfare started to sneer, but Tendlathe silenced him with a quick look. "That makes us kin," he said, and grinned at Tatian's quickly suppressed look of disbelief. "Closer than just Stane and Stane, I mean. My mother was from Riversedge, and I was practically fostered there. What's her name? I'll look for her."

"Derebought Stane." There was no point in using her compound name, Stane-Lanhos; Harans didn't recognize the form— one more thing they didn't admit to—and the reminder of her off-world marriage might undo all the good this conversation had done.

"Derebought," Tendlathe repeated. "I'll certainly look for her."

Tatian nodded, not knowing quite what to say, not sure why Tendlathe was going out of his way to speak to him, and glanced out over the Glassmarket again. Something was moving on the fringes of the crowd, by the band platforms. He frowned, trying to make out what was happening, and saw movement among the drummers on the platform. Someone—the figure was totally indistinct at this distance—climbed or was lifted up to join them. There was a moment of confusion, and then the newcomer lifted a bright white-and-yellow disk drum over his or her head, began beating out a new, insistent rhythm. A banner rose at the back of the platform, nearly toppling a drummer, and unfolded on multiple supports to reveal painted shapes maybe twice lifesize. Tatian squinted at them, trying to read their elliptical message—they looked like yet more representations of the ubiquitous spirits, the interpreters to humans of Hara's distant God—and heard Wiidfare mutter something.

"—fucking Modernists."

Tatian glanced over his shoulder, startled by the vehemence of his tone, and saw Tendlathe's hand close on the other indigene's arm. His expression didn't change, handsome face still smiling faintly, but Wiidfare winced, and Tatian saw Tendlathe's knuckles pale as his grip tightened further.

"This is Bonemarche," he said, and his voice sounded strangely tight, only a ghost of its earlier ease remaining. "Things are different in the *mesnies*. They wouldn't stand for this there."

Tatian looked back toward the banner, now fully opened, five figures—*not the spirits after all*, he thought, *but more like caricatures of the five sexes, a Concord motif given a new, uniquely Haran shape*—stood hand-in-hand against a stylized background of sea and sky. More figures, most in traditional dress, a couple in dull gray that might have been meant to stand for off-worlders, posed in front of the banner, but he was too far away to understand their mime. Uniformed *mosstaas* started to shove their way into the crowd, but the Stillers blocked their way: the protesters had chosen their moment well. He heard a laugh behind him, hearty, and sounding genuinely amused.

"They've got heart, the Stillers," Temelathe said, "and brains. Not a milligram of common sense in the entire clan, but kilograms of brains." He edged out on the balcony, distance glasses in hand, and the other Stanes scrambled to give him room. Tatian found himself pushed back against the doorway, the edge of the bricks digging painfully into his spine.

"It shouldn't be allowed, my father," Tendlathe said. He was still smiling, as though he'd forgotten to let his lips move; the expression looked ghastly against his sudden pallor, brown skin drained of blood. "It's disrespectful to you, and to Stane. The *mosstaas*—"

Temelathe laughed again, as though his son had never spoken. "God and the spirits, that's clever. And the one doing me's very good." He lowered the glasses, looked behind him, shrewd eyes—eyes that weren't laughing at all, Tatian noticed—sweeping across the mixed crowd of Stanes and Maychilders and off-worlders. "Take a look, ser Mhyre, it's almost a shame you're missing the performance. Not that we aren't delighted to have you here, of course."

He thrust the glasses almost into Tatian's face, and the younger man took them mechanically. He couldn't refuse; it was less an offer than an order, and he thumbed the tuning wheel, buying the seconds he needed to get his own expression under control. Any pharmaceutical, any off-worlder, would have done anything for this display of Temelathe's magnanimity, he thought. Why the hell did it have to be me? He raised the glasses, focusing the double lenses on the banner, and the scene beneath it leaped into sharp focus. A group dressed as men and women, though their bodies very obviously didn't match their clothes, clustered in the center, watched by the two "off-worlders." A man in overdone jewelry—and he was obviously meant to be Temelathe, from the padded shoulders and chest and coarse black and gray wig to the tricks of stance and gesture—was sorting the people in traditional clothes into pairs, matching "male" to "female" regardless of real gender or the mimed wishes of the people. Before he'd finished sorting, however, one of the "off-worlders" tapped him on the shoulder, pointed to a "man" who had been padded to resemble a herm. "Temelathe" shook his head, and the "off-worlder" offered something that looked like a purse. "Temelathe" took it, nodding vigorously, and shoved the "herm" toward the "off-worlder." It was the most blatant representation of trade, and Temelathe's connections to trade, that Tatian had ever seen on Hara.

"You see," Temelathe said. "They are good, aren't they?"

"They seem—talented," Tatian answered, and handed back the glasses, wondering what he should have said. The Old Dame would have known, but ðe was on New Antioch, and he was responsible for ðer business here.

Temelathe laughed, throwing his head back, and a few of the other Stanes managed to laugh with him. Tendlathe lifted both eyebrows in disbelieving disdain. His color was coming back a little, but his mouth was still set in that faint, unreal smile.

"They are talented," Temelathe said, still grinning hugely. "Clever and talented, that's Stiller for you. No sense, but clever as monkeys. Of course, good mimics don't make good actors, do they, ser Mhyre? And Lammasin Stiller's a really talented mimic."

"I wouldn't know," Tatian said, stiff-lipped. He felt a chill run through the room.

Tendlathe said, "The *mosstaas* should clear the market."

Temelathe shook his head. "Nonsense. Let Stiller—let the Modernists, it's not even all of Stiller, though it will be if I turned the *mosstaas* on them—let them have their day. It won't matter."

"This is what happens when you let people like Warreven have their say. Yes, it matters," Tendlathe said, and his father took him firmly by the arm. Tatian saw the younger man flinch before he had himself under control again.

"It doesn't, and it won't," Temelathe said firmly. "Let it be." He looked around the room, visibly gathering his people. "Come, come, the first remove must be ready. Time and past for us to be fed."

Most of the Stanes trailed obediently after him. Tatian waited in the doorway until the people on the balcony had filed past him and followed more slowly.

"Christ." The voice and the curse were off-world, and Tatian turned to find Chavvin Annek at his elbow. She was the head of operations at the port, one of the most important off-worlders on Hara, someone whom even Temelathe would not want wantonly to offend; even so, Tatian wished she would keep her voice down.

"That's a nasty thing to do to Lammasin," she went on. "That was meant to travel, that little verdict. He'll have a hard time finding work now. Or worse."

Tatian stared at her, unable quite for an instant to believe what she was saying. But this was Hara, and Temelathe did have that kind of power—and there was nothing at all that he or Annek could do about it. He touched her arm gently, turned her toward the dining room. "Dinner, Annek."

"He's a friend. Lammasin, I mean. Oh, damn it, I've got to get word to him."

"He's bound to hear soon enough," Tatian said.

"Not necessarily." Annek shook her head. "This could mean real trouble for him."

"I take it he's not on the net?"

"No." Annek lowered her voice. "Tatian, I need to ask a favor. I'll owe you for it, I promise."

Tatian looked warily at her. Having the port's head of operations owe him a favor could be a very useful thing, certainly, but he'd already been warned away from Haran politics. "If I can, I will," he said, and hoped it would be something reasonable.

"When we're done here, and it can't be soon enough, I've got to find Lammasin, warn him, before that bastard Tendlathe sets the *mosstaas* on him," Annek said. "I don't want to run the Dock Row bars alone. Will you come with me?"

Tatian hesitated. He could escort her safely enough—and it wouldn't do him any harm to be seen to be a friend of Chavvin Annek's this time of year, a voice whispered at the back of his mind. "All right," he said. "Now, dinner. Before someone wonders where we are."

Annek sighed, forced a smile. "You're right, and thank you. But I can't say I'm very hungry."

"Nor am I," Tatian answered, and they went on together into the brightly lit dining room.

---

herm:
: (Concord) human being possessing testes and ovaries and some aspects of male and female genitalia; 3e, 3er, 3im, 3imself.

WARREVEN

For once, the sky had stayed clear for most of the *baanket*. As he and Folhare crested the hill above the Harbor Market, he could look across the lights of the harbor and see the brightest stars vivid against the seaward horizon. Only a few wisps of night haze obscured the familiar patterns; the moon was almost down, its thin crescent blurred by a thicker streak of cloud.

"A gorgeous night," he said, and Folhare grinned.

"In more ways than one."

Warreven smiled in response, and the land breeze strengthened, bringing with it the sound of drumming from the Glassmarket. A whistle shrieked, shrill and raucous, but then the wind eased, and the drums faded again. "Do you think the *presance* did any good?"

"It certainly got people's attention," Folhare said lightly.

"Seriously, Folhare."

She didn't answer for a moment, the only noise the click of her shoes against the paving. They were still a hundred meters above the Embankment, where the bars and dance houses stayed open all night, farther still from Dockside and the Gran'quai, where ships loaded and off-loaded cargo without regard to the clock. Warreven was suddenly aware of the empty street, the dark side alleys, and glanced reflexively behind him—but the night of the *baanket* was usually fairly quiet. Even so, he wasn't sorry to see the blue glow of a police light on the side of a building a few meters farther along, marking an emergency summons box. Not that the *mosstaas* would be much help—it was always anyone's guess if they would actually respond to a call, though the better districts paid a service fee to make sure of it—but the automatic alarm would wake anyone sleeping in the apartments above the shops and warehouses, and people were usually quick to keep the peace in their own neighborhoods.

"I hope so," Folhare said at last. "I do think so. It made the issue pretty clear—and if nothing else, it got them laughing at Temelathe. That's something, anyway."

Warreven nodded. That had been impressive, the crowd's gasps and the startled, not-quite-approving murmurs as people realized who the *presance*'s central figure was meant to represent, and then the spreading laughter, shock giving way to titillated amusement when the absurdity of the presentation struck home. Not everyone would believe it, of course, but for a few minutes, the Most Important Man had been reduced to a bumbling pimp. "He's going to be furious. Your people had better keep their heads down for a while. Was that Lammasin who was doing Temelathe?"

"Yes." Folhare gave a rueful smile. "He was supposed to be better masked than that. Oh, well, he's scheduled to do some work in Irenfot after the holiday, so that ought to keep him out of trouble."

"I hope so," Warreven said. They had reached the Embankment then, and he turned right onto the broad walkway. The streetlights were brighter, more closely spaced, and most of the buildings were also lit, lights around a doorway or tracing a stylized, three-armed tree to indicate an open bar. Drumming and voices spilled out into the street as a door opened, were cut off again, and two mems left arm in arm, the same *shaal* thrown defiantly around their shoulders. Warreven watched them go, idly curious, and was not surprised to see them draw apart before they'd reached the first streetlight, the taller mem wrapping the *shaal* around his head to pass for male.

"Shall we try Shinbone?" Folhare asked, and Warreven nodded. That was his favorite among the dance houses; they hired decent drummers and kept the peace among the mix of clients.

Its doorway was brighter lit than most, surrounded by a double band of light, gold and green, and there were two trees outlined in lights to either side of the entrance. As usual, a slumped figure, so wrapped in layers of *shaals* and tunics as to be little more than a dark lump, sat just outside the pool of light, and extended a bowl marked with the Cripple's crutch as they passed: Aldinogh, who owned Shinbone and three other houses along Harborside, was careful to propitiate the spirits, and anyone living who might be jealous of his prosperity. Warreven reached into his pocket, came up with a handful of small change, and dropped it into the bowl, saying, "From the lady, too." He jerked his head toward Folhare.

The lurking figure didn't answer, but Folhare gave him a grateful glance. Warreven hid a twisted smile. She might claim to be fully assimilated, a true Modernist, but she, none of them, could quite free themselves of the teachings of childhood. Oh, it was easy to explain why the customs had developed the way they did—Hara's population was relatively small, but there were always people who ended up outside the *mesnie* system, either by choice or accident, and the tradition that said you could not safely refuse anyone who asked help in Caritan the Cripple's name had obviously grown up to protect that minority—but, even knowing that, it was almost impossible to break those old habits.

The hulking doorkeeper nodded to them as they passed— from him, a major concession—and they went on into the single long room. Like every other dance house in the city, Shinbone had mechanical bars in each of the four corners, and a band platform at the far end of the hall, but at least here the tables surrounding the dance floor weren't strictly divided between trade and the wry-abed. The groups crowding the tables were fairly well mixed—*or at least*, Warreven amended, *the ones in the light were mixed.* There was no way to know if the people groping in the dark at the edges of the room had stuck to the more usual divisions. "Do you want a drink?" he said, to Folhare, but she was looking past him into the shadows by the closest bar.

"I—there's someone I need to see first, thanks."

Warreven glanced sideways, to see a group sitting around one of the larger tables. A tiny *luciole* glowed on the center of the table, between bottles of sweetrum and a smoking pot, but it had been turned low, so that its light barely reached the faces. Even so, he recognized one of them—Lammasin, without the makeup and the padding that had made him look so much like Temelathe—and that meant that the rest of the group would be the other actors from the *presance.* "Do you think it's smart?"

"Æ?"

"Do you want to be seen talking to them right now, for your sake or theirs?"

"It's a *wrangwys* house," Folhare said, impatiently. "Who's going to talk to the *mosstaas?*"

That was sheer bravado, and they both knew it: the *mosstaas* had a network of informers that ran throughout the Dockside houses. But there was no arguing with her in her present mood, Warreven thought. He looked back at the table, ignoring the sound of the drums calling the next dance, and saw a stranger, a woman in the full skirt and shaped, peplumed jacket marked with the silver rings of the port administration, leaning over Lammasin's shoulder. She said something, her face shielded by the fall of her chin-length hair; Lammasin waved her words away, then, changing his mind, beckoned for her to sit beside him.

"If it'll be a problem for you, of course," Folhare said, and made the words a dare.

Warreven barely heard her, seeing a second figure emerge from the shadowed corner where the bar stood. Mhyre Tatian, his blond hair and beard unmistakable, handed the off-world woman a bottle of something Warreven didn't recognize, then stopped behind her chair. He looked almost protective of her, as though he were guarding her, Warreven thought, though she hardly seemed aware of his presence as she leaned toward Lammasin, her bottle already pushed aside. He realized that Folhare was looking curiously at him, and said, "No, not a problem."

Folhare's eyebrows rose in patent disbelief, but Warreven ignored her, heading for the table.

"Mir Tatian, I didn't expect to see you here."

Tatian looked at him over the neck of his bottle, one corner of his mouth curving up into a sardonic half smile. "Mir Warreven. Congratulations on the election."

He hadn't spoken loudly, but a couple of the people at Lammasin's table heard and looked up. Warreven took a step away, deeper into the shadows—no need to be overheard as well as seen—and saw Folhare touch Lammasin's shoulder, whisper something in his ear. "Thank you. I think we have some unfinished business, you and I."

"If you mean Shan Reiss's statement," Tatian answered, "it's finished business. Sorry."

Warreven blinked, startled by the refusal even to discuss it, and said, "Feeling that way about trade, I'm surprised to find you here." He waved his hand toward the dance floor, and the mix of off-worlders and indigenes watching from the side tables.

Tatian made a face. "I came with Annek." He looked at the table, where the off-world woman was still talking earnestly. Lammasin hardly seemed to be listening; seemed more intent on the smoke now rising from the pot in front of him. "Is that guy, what's-his-name, Lammasin, a friend of yours?"

"A friend of a friend," Warreven answered cautiously.

"We, Annek and I, were at the Stane party at the White Watch House tonight," Tatian said. "Mir Temelathe was not at all happy with that parody your friends put on. He threatened to keep him from working, and Annek thinks he can do it."

"Of course he can," Warreven said. "He recognized Lammasin, then?"

"Yes."

"Damn." Warreven looked back at the table, at Folhare still hovering, an expression of faint disgust shadowing her face as she watched Annek talking to Lammasin. If Temelathe had recognized the actor, then Lammasin would indeed need to lie low for a while—it wouldn't be a bad time to visit his home *mesnie*, wherever that was, as long as it was out of Bonemarche. Irenfot wouldn't be far enough away, was too much under the influence of the Stanes, like all the cities on the Westaern, to be truly safe. And besides, he added silently, the job that was supposed to take him to Irenfot would almost certainly vanish, if the Most Important Man was angry.

"Tendlathe was very upset, too," Tatian said. "You might also tell your friends he wanted to set the *mosstaas* on them."

"So what else is new," Warreven said sourly. He remembered Tendlathe in the library at White Stane House, hand clenched on the arm of his chair. "He doesn't like off-worlders, he doesn't like Modernists, he doesn't like trade, and most of all he doesn't like being reminded that there really are five sexes. Facts like that confuse him. But I appreciate the warning."

"It was Annek's idea. I can't take credit. But if you can convince him it's serious—"

"Maybe Folhare can," Warreven answered, and knew he sounded dubious.

At the table, Annek shook her head, and pushed herself up out of the chair, leaving her drink untouched on the table. "Let's go, Tatian. I'm not doing any good here."

Tatian nodded, looking around for a place to leave his own drink, and Warreven said, "Wait."

Tatian set the bottle on an unoccupied table and looked back at him.

"I do have other business with you," Warreven said, "in my new job. I'd like to discuss the surplus with you."

Even in the uncertain light, he saw the flicker of interest cross Tatian's face, quickly muted. "Our office is in the Estrange, Drapdevel Court. You're welcome to come by."

"I will," Warreven answered, and the off-worlder nodded and turned away. Warreven watched them go, Tatian looming over the smaller woman, a protective presence at her side, and wondered if they were lovers. He didn't think they were, but couldn't give a real reason—something in Tatian's voice when he'd said it had been Annek's idea to come to Shinbone, maybe, or just something in his stance, too casual, almost automatic, to be more than courtesy. And those reasons were nothing more than wishful thinking; they were hardly relevant to the job at hand.

ser, serrem, serray, serram, sera:
> (Concord) honorifics placed before the surname to indicate the gender
> of the person (man, mem, herm, fem, woman), considered in Concord
> usage to be part of the person's full name; the generic plural is sersi.

MHYRE TATIAN

The bad connection in his wrist was getting worse. Tatian tried to ignore it, to concentrate on the desktop display, on the patterns of rough and smooth on the shadowscreen, instead, but the sensation was too irritating. He rubbed his wrist gently, barely touching the protective plate, and winced at the sudden rush of pain. The pressure set off a feedback loop—as he had known it would, as it had done every time he had touched his arm—and the stinging, pins-and-needles sensation shot up his arm and across his chest like the precursor of a heart attack. He swore under his breath and grabbed the edge of the desktop with his good hand, squeezing his fingers into the wood until the pain and tingling had eased again.

He took a careful breath and touched the main control switch, turning off the implanted system. The itching, like the fizz of bubbles under his skin, stopped instantly, and the figures for the newly drafted contract vanished from in front of his eyes. He muttered another curse and worked the shadowscreen, projecting the same numbers onto a secondary screen. It was hard, slow, and clumsy, working without the implants, but the system was getting bad enough that he couldn't afford to work with them, either. If Am would just hurry up and confirm that she'd bought the box— his eyes strayed to the message screen, obstinately dark despite the golem he'd set to forward him any incoming messages from the port—then he could get the surgery done and get back to normal. If Am was still angry—

He shoved that thought away and touched the shadowscreen to transfer the new numbers from the secondary to the main screen, filling in the blanks in the draft of the new contract with the Liassan *mesnie*. The numbers looked good, and he'd only had to deviate from NAPD's preferred standard contract in a couple of places. Even with those changes, and even factoring in the worst possible weather and harvest conditions, the company should show an acceptable profit. And if the weather followed the predicted patterns . . . He ran his hand over the shadowscreen again, fingers pressing hot and cold spots that changed and shifted under his touch. If the weather stayed within the meteorologists' predicted limits, NAPD would increase its revenue by a little under seventeen percent. That wasn't just Liassan, of course, and it didn't account for fee increases from the various Stane offices—and there would be increases, once Temelathe's people realized that NAPD's profits were up—but there wasn't anything he could do about that. Temelathe's share was like an act of God: one paid and was grateful it was no worse.

It was still hard to be philosophical about it, especially after Wiidfare's latest attempt to drag NAPD into permit trading, and Tatian found his thoughts drifting away from the contract details, wondered instead if there was any way to avoid Temelathe's levies. There was plenty of opposition to the Most Important Man, the *presance* at the Stiller *baanket* had been ample proof of that; maybe there was a way the pharmaceuticals could use that opposition to force Temelathe to take less. He shook himself then, scowling at the screens. First, the pharmaceuticals wouldn't cooperate if it affected their profits, and, second, the Modernists made no particular distinction between one company and another. All he would do is get himself kicked off the planet, and NAPD either banned entirely or at best severely restricted. He thumbed the selection menu and called up the file of contracts waiting for renewal. Without the implants, checking them would be a tedious business. Tatian eyed the first screen without eagerness and was grateful when the intercom buzzed.

"Yes?"

"Ser Mhyre." It was Derebought's voice and the formal tone

and title she used to warn him of something out of the ordinary. "There's someone to see you, if you're free. Mir Warreven—the Stiller *seraaliste.*"

Tatian stared at his desktop without seeing the open screens, mind racing. Warreven had mentioned the Stiller surplus—which rumor said was considerable—at the dance house, Shinbone; unfortunately, any offer was almost certain to come with strings attached, strings that led directly to Shan Reiss and his withdrawn statement. Tatian suppressed the memory of Reiss's face when he'd heard the ultimatum, the expression of frantic guilt, and touched the intercom. He would be foolish not to listen to what Warreven had to say—and beside, he admitted, silently, I'm curious. "I'm free. Show 3im in, Derry, please."

"Right away."

Tatian blanked his screens—though there wasn't much point; copies of the same documents would be sitting on Warreven's desk already—and the door opened. Derebought said, "Mir Warreven."

Warreven nodded 3er thanks and stepped past her into the office, holding out 3er hand in off-world greeting. Tatian leaned across the desk to take it and was aware again of the jewelry, thick hoop earrings, half a dozen metal bracelets, and even the long necklace was more metal than glass. Warreven was, at a conservative guess, wearing half an ordinary indigene's yearly income: it was a sobering reminder of 3er importance, and Tatian guessed, a deliberate one.

"Shall I make up a tray?" Derebought asked, and Tatian looked past Warreven to see the botanist frowning slightly. Her message was clear: this was an important person and an important meeting; the traditional amenities should be observed.

"Please," Tatian answered, though he doubted someone as assimilated as Warreven would be unduly impressed by anything NAPD could provide, and gestured for the indigene to take the visitor's chair.

"Thanks," Warreven said, with a glance over 3er shoulder that included Derebought, and sat down opposite Tatian.

Tatian reseated himself at the desk, glancing again at Warreven. The *seraaliste* was dressed much as 3e had been at the dance house, a soft silk tunic over soft trousers, all expensively casual, and 3er thick hair had been pulled back into a single braid. The planes of 3er face looked harder without the mane of hair; Tatian was suddenly aware of the shadows under 3er eyes, and the lines just beginning at the corners of 3er mouth. 3e was unexpectedly attractive—handsome rather than beautiful, but still the classic herm looks—not to his usual taste, and Tatian looked down at the empty desktop to break his stare. This had happened before, and not just on Hara, would happen again. Herms and women shared some physical attributes; it was easy to be attracted to the "feminine" aspects of a herm, and ridiculous to think of acting on that attraction. "What can I do for you, Mir Warreven?"

"I hope quite a lot," Warreven answered, "as I hope I can do something for you. I understand you've already been buying from Stiller?"

"*Mesnie* contracts only."

"I wonder if you're still interested—or able—to buy?" Warreven tilted 3er head to one side, wide-set eyes narrowed slightly, as though 3e might smile. The door opened then, and Derebought came in, carrying a tray laden with imported coffee and a triple jug of *liquertie*. Tatian's eyes narrowed for an instant, inspecting the offering. Derebought knew the traditional proprieties better than anyone else on NAPD's staff—that was the reason she was responsible for these social duties, though it always gave Tatian an odd feeling to see the botanist handling protocol—and she was saying, as clearly as if she had spoken aloud, that Warreven was very important indeed.

"*Liquertie*, mir?" Derebought said, to Warreven. "Or perhaps coffee?"

Tatian let the ritual wash over him, wondering just what Warreven wanted. *No, that's obvious, 3e wants Reiss's statement; the real question is what 3e'll offer to get it. Or maybe I'm misreading the whole situation, and 3e's just here for the harvest. Derebought wouldn't have brought out coffee if she didn't think a deal was a solid possibility.* He accepted a cup of the coffee—the real thing, imported from Atalanta, too expensive to drink more than once a week—and waited until the door had closed again behind Derebought. "NAPD is usually able to acquire worthwhile items, either craft or harvest. Do you—does Stiller, forgive me—have something on offer?"

Warreven smiled. "The harvest has been good this year generally, which you know, and the Westaern sea-harvest particularly so. Which you also know. Stiller has significant surplus, and the *mesnies* have agreed that it should be placed on offer in a single lot, to be handled by the *seraaliste*. I wondered if NAPD would be interested."

Tatian blinked. The sea-harvest had been unusually good; if Stiller was offering the entire surplus as a single block, the harvest was likely to be extraordinary. Reiss's statement wouldn't be an unreasonable payment, for such an unheard-of offer. He put that thought aside and said cautiously, "We're interested, of course. But I understood your contract was with Kerendach."

"The *mesnies* have voted me full bargaining rights," Warreven answered. "In effect, it's mine to do with as I please, and I'm not fully satisfied with Kerendach right now."

Plus you want something from me, Tatian thought. He said, "As I said, we're always interested. I'd like to see some details first, of course. Then I can make a rough offer."

Warreven set an old-style disk on the desktop and slid it past the tray of *liquerties*. "I think everything you'll want is there. I'll be frank with you, I would go to one of the Big Six, but they tend to stick together. I doubt they'd offer me much more than Kerendach would, and that hasn't been adequate for less." 3e hesitated, as though 3e would say more, then leaned back in 3er chair.

Tatian took the disk, then ran his hand over the shadowscreen to activate the multiformat reader. He slipped the disk into the cradle, and there was a pause while the system sorted through competing formats. Then the first of the summaries flipped into view. It was enough to make him catch his breath—that block alone would increase NAPD's potential income by about a tenth of the current total—and he paged quickly through the file, dizzying himself with the possibilities. Warreven was offering broadleaf kelp, and cutgrass and wideweb, the staples of the Haran sea-harvest, but 3e was also offering crumbling coral, coral fish, and even half a dozen false-kelp holdfasts. Those were worth over a thousand concord dollars apiece, more if they were close to whole: the false-kelp grew too deep for Haran divers easily to reach its base, and in any case, harvesting the holdfast killed the plant. Most of the holdfasts that reached the off-world markets came from storm wrack, and the Big Six bought and sold most of them; for Warreven to be able to offer six as surplus was extraordinary—and a tribute to the negotiating skills of the previous year's *seraaliste*, who had set the contract quotas with Kerendach. It also made it easier to contemplate giving Warreven the extras 3e was sure to want. Tatian paged slowly back to the top of the file, imagining the Old Dame's response to this bounty, and said, "Has Kerendach made an offer, or are we getting first chance?"

"They have a standing offer for surplus," Warreven said. "It's in the secondary file."

Tatian flipped that open, eyebrows rising. "It seems—less than generous," he said at last. In point of fact, it was ridiculously low for the surplus of an excellent harvest, and he wondered who at Kerendach had made the tactical error. If it had been his business, he would have doubled the standing offer sight unseen—but somebody had been operating on the assumption that Warreven's inexperience amounted to stupidity. "I think we could—would—better it."

Warreven smiled again. "There is another matter, of course."

Tatian matched the smile. "Of course." *And here we go*, he thought. *Shan Reiss's statement for the chance to bid on the surplus, which is one of the best block offers I've ever seen—except that I've been told explicitly, by the Concord agency, that letting Reiss testify can do most to ruin my company, that I cannot not let Reiss get involved in this case.* "Reiss?"

"Reiss." Warreven looked at him, suddenly serious, face gone from exotic beauty to sudden stony gravity in one of the instant changes so typical of a herm. "I owe my partners this one last thing. It seems a fair trade, the statement for your chance at our surplus."

Tatian didn't answer for a moment, marshalling his own arguments. "I'm not autonomous, you know. And my ultimate boss has made it very clear that none of us on Hara are to get involved in trade. That includes Reiss."

"So Reiss said," Warreven answered. "But this needn't be a question of trade. Reiss is a Black Casnot by courtesy and custom, and so is Destany—the person in question. It's Reiss's obligation to speak for him, since he can give testimony that would be useful, not a matter of trade at all, since Destany hasn't done trade for seven, eight years—local years, too. I don't know how many kilohours. I'm sure NAPD is quick enough to make use of Reiss's kinship when it's convenient; this is the other side of that obligation."

That was accurate enough, Tatian admitted, he had made good use of Reiss's myriad connections, friends and relatives and clan-cousins all up and down the Main Continent, but kept his face without expression. "It's not just my boss. The IDCA will see this as trade, and they've already said they'll put a stop to it."

"IDCA profits from trade themselves," Warreven said, with the hint of an old bitterness. "They're not going to give that up without a fight."

"That's not true," Tatian said involuntarily, and wanted to take back the words as soon as they were spoken. That was an old charge among the indigenes; nothing any off-worlder said to contradict it seemed to convince them, and there was no point in antagonizing 3im over such an ancient grievance.

Warreven said, "IDCA does profit from trade, or do only direct payments count? It's trade that makes all the permits so profitable, that lets them keep, what, over two hundred people on planet, on their payroll; if it wasn't for trade, they'd be the same size as Customs, what's that, fifty people? And don't tell me that some of that two hundred don't take payments to look the other way, pass questionable documents, little things like that. Why shouldn't they, when their bosses play trade with Temelathe to justify their existence?"

"The IDCA is here to protect all of us, you as well as us," Tatian said, goaded. "You may not have HIVs now, but let one person in with just the right strain, and your immunity may not last."

"It hasn't happened yet," Warreven answered, but ʒer anger was fading as quickly as it had flared. "No, I understand how the mutations work, I understand that whatever it is that's keeping us safe may not always work, but at the same time, IDCA is using that excuse to keep us trapped here. We can't win. Anyone who wants to go off-world, unless they're connected to one of the corporations, they're assumed to have done trade, and so there's a forty kilohour waiting period, that's over three years, before they'll even consider the application, which they can enforce because we're not fully of the Concord and the Colonial Committee agrees with IDCA. And all the while, trade goes on. And there still aren't any HIVs on Hara."

It was obviously an argument ʒe'd made many times before. Tatian stared at ʒim, admitting the justice of the argument—though he doubted the IDCA was doing it deliberately. Or not fully so: their mandate was to control the spread of infectious disease between star systems, the HIVs primarily, but all the lesser plagues as well, and their people could be blind to other issues in that all-consuming pursuit. "Which is why the Modernists want Hara to join the Concord," he said aloud, and Warreven gave a flickering grin.

"Well, it's why I support the Modernists," ʒe said.

"And why Temelathe opposes them?" Tatian asked.

"Oh, nothing so subtle," Warreven answered. "No one ever gives up power willingly, not power like his."

"And Tendlathe?"

Warreven hesitated. "Tendlathe is subtler," ʒe said, after a moment. "Sometimes, in some ways, or maybe he's just more convoluted. But the main thing is, he doesn't like change. And this, you must admit, would be a big change."

"It's Tendlathe the IDCA are worried about," Tatian said bluntly. He hadn't meant to tell the other that, still wasn't sure it was smart—but he was sure that they would be better off dealing honestly.

Warreven tilted ʒer head to one side. "How? I mean, Temelathe is the Speaker, Ten—Tendlathe won't have real power until he dies."

"They—the IDCA—think that if you push this case, Tendlathe will be able use it to whip up feeling against us. And, frankly, we don't need that. I don't need that."

Warreven made a soft hissing sound through 3er teeth. "Ten doesn't have that much support—most people know where the metal comes from, and it's not from Tendlathe. And besides—" 3e broke off, shrugging, looked vaguely uncomfortable. "I'm not fond of 'Aukai, and I don't know Destany, but it's not right, what IDCA's doing to them."

That last was true enough, Tatian thought, but he wasn't so sure about the former. He had seen Tendlathe's face when the dancers had unfurled their banner, seen the tight fury, barely contained. Even without broad-based support, that anger could be dangerous, and he wondered if Warreven wasn't underestimating the other man's power, or at least his willingness to use it. Or maybe not: if Jhirad had þis story right, and þe usually did, Warreven knew Tendlathe very well indeed. He looked back at the desktop screen, at the open files that showed the list of the Stiller summer surplus. He hadn't liked the IDCA's interference, not in pharmaceutical business—not in Reiss's business, not something that was so blatantly political, the IDCA reaching for more control over the indigenes who played trade—and the numbers and symbols that danced on his screen were more than enough to make it worth pursuing at least a little further. "Given the issues," he said, "I'll have to confirm any offer with my boss. I can say that we're very interested."

Warreven nodded. "I can accept that, certainly. I'm not—unaware—of the potential awkwardness of your position. But I'll need to know something soon."

"How soon?"

"Within the week," Warreven answered. "Or I will need to explain why I'm not taking the block elsewhere."

"That's acceptable."

"Good." Warreven pushed 3imself up out of the chair. Tatian copied him and leaned across the desk to offer his hand. Warreven's fingers were almost cold, startling in the Haran warmth. "I'll look forward to hearing from you."

Tatian remained standing as the door closed behind 3im, still unable quite to believe in what he'd been offered. The best of the end-of-season, more and better than anything NAPD had been able to find on its own, more than they'd ever been offered by anyone—but at a price that might well prove impossible. He heard the outer door close and saw, through the half-closed sun shutters, Warreven walking away across the courtyard, the thick braid of 3er hair swaying against the rich green silk like the tail of a stalking cat. *And I wish I knew for certain*, Tatian thought, *that what 3e was hunting wasn't us.*

He looked back at the files on the desktop and reached for the intercom button. "Derry? Mats? Come in here a minute, please."

The door slid open almost at once, as though they had been waiting for the summons—*which*, Tatian added silently, *they probably had.*

"Do we have an offer, then?" Derebought asked, and at Tatian's gestured invitation, seated herself in the client's chair. Lanhoss Mats leaned over her shoulder, long boned and loose jointed, the skin of his hands and face marked with faint scars where incipient sun-tumors had been cut away.

"We have an offer," Tatian said, and knew he sounded less than enthusiastic. He touched the shadowscreen, created a copy of Warreven's file, and dumped it to the free drive. "It's a very good offer, in fact. Stiller's selling the end-of-season surplus as a single block." He pulled the button with its embedded copy out of the drive and tossed it to Derebought, who caught it by reflex. "Take a look at this, see what you think. Give everything a tentative grade and a going price, and get back to me. As soon as you can, please."

Derebought nodded. "I didn't think they could make bulk offers, I thought the Big Six wrote their contracts to prevent it."

"That's not our problem," Tatian answered. "If Warreven says 3e can sell, we can buy."

"Kerendach won't like it," Mats said.

"If this flies," Tatian said, "we won't have to worry about Kerendach." *Kerendach is the least of our worries*, he added silently. *Just the IDCA and Tendlathe—which ought to be enough for anyone.*

"I'm going to want a direct line to the home office, and an appointment with Masani ðerself," he went on. "As soon as we're in alignment."

Mats glanced at the floor, and then at the wall, calling up internal systems. "Depends on the port queue, of course. But there's a forty-hour window opening at midnight."

"Better than I expected," Tatian said.

"So what's the catch?" Derebought said.

"Derry," Mats said, protesting.

Tatian smiled. "Politics, what else?"

"Reiss's—" Derebought began, and Tatian shook his head.

"I don't want to go into details, not yet, maybe not ever. This could be very sticky, people. For now, I'm taking full responsibility."

That was enough to make even Mats raise his eyebrows. Derebought said slowly, "If you're sure. . . ."

Tatian nodded. "I'm sure. Mats, we'll need to talk to shipping."

"I'll get started on the analysis right away," Derebought said, and went out, closing the door again behind her.

Mats lowered himself into the chair she had just left. "If you want estimates, Tatian, you'll have to tell me how much stuff we're talking about."

Tatian reseated himself, and fingered the shadowscreen until he found the conversion program. "Very roughly, one hundred twenty-five to one hundred fifty mass units. Not all of that will need starcrates, of course."

Mats sighed noisily. "You don't ask for much, do you? Okay." He looked sideways again, fingers curling around his left wrist to work the input pad buried beneath the skin. "Okay. I've got enough crates to handle about eighty, maybe ninety-five mu. Maybe as much as a hundred if I can get some of the bad ones back in service. Normally, I'd borrow, but . . ." He let his voice trail off, and Tatian nodded, not needing to have the sentence finished for him. Under most circumstances, the other pharmaceuticals would be willing to lend spare equipment, but not when so much money was at stake.

"What can we ship bare?"

"I'd rather not ship any," Mats said. "It depends on what we're getting, of course."

"Generally speaking."

Mats shrugged. "Cutgrass usually travels well, and wideweb if it's been rough-processed. Buyers tend to assume damage, though."

"I'll make you a copy of the list," Tatian said, hand busy on the shadowscreen. "See what we can do if we get everything."

"You're optimistic," Mats said.

"We might as well look at the best case," Tatian answered, and flipped the data button across the desk to the other man.

Mats nodded, stuffing it into his pocket. "I'll ask around, too, see if I can line up a few more crates before anyone hears about the deal. I can probably arrange to get another two or three."

"That sounds good," Tatian said. "Thanks."

"No problem," Mats answered, and levered himself up out of the chair.

---

mem:
> (Concord) human being possessing ovaries, XX chromosomes, some aspects of male genitalia but not posessing testes; þe, þis, þim, þimself.

WARREVEN

Warreven took the long way back to the Black Watch House and the *seraaliste*'s office, over the hills of the mixed neighborhoods between the Estrange and the Glassmarket rather than along the Embankment and Harborside, not wanting to run the risk of meeting either Destany or 'Aukai. The discussion with Tatian had gone well, he thought—the off-worlder had seemed willing at least to consult with his superiors, and he'd certainly been interested in the surplus—but he knew 'Aukai would expect instant results, and he didn't look forward to explaining that she'd have to wait a little longer. With any luck, he could avoid her completely, leave explanations to Haliday or Malemayn. . . . He sighed then. It didn't feel right, supporting them in what was nothing more than longterm trade—but then, it was their business, their choice, and they had a right to it. IDCA was treating them badly: that was the truth, not just a convenient way to get Tatian's sympathy. It didn't matter that he didn't like or trust 'Aukai; she was in the right, this time, and he—or Haliday and Malemayn, since he'd been forced to resign the partnership—had an obligation to her.

It was a longish walk, through streets that were alternately prosperous and poor, shops and houses mixed with manufactories. Heat radiated from the open doors of the glassmaker's sheds, and he could hear the dull rush of the fires inside. Most of them were using imported fuel now, and the emptied plastic cylinders clogged the alleys, waiting for the salvagers' trucks. The air smelled of glass and spilled oil, and he had to step carefully around puddles where the chemicals that colored the glass had run into the street. On Grantpas Street, half a dozen women—no, he realized, with a sudden shock, at least three of them were herms, and the rest looked more like fems, long-legged and narrow-hipped, all in a mix of traditional or off-world clothes that made no pretense of concealing their anomalous bodies—sat or stood along the back wall of the Blue Watch House. Their goods, quilts and clothes and bright coarsely knotted caps, spread out on the paving in front of them. There were no children in sight—unusually; the *vendee* generally brought their offspring with them and let them earn their keep—but then he saw a single light-haired toddler clinging to the leg of one of the herms. The sunlight shone on the piled silks, tunics and trousers, and vests in all the colors of the rainbow, and from the bed quilts hung against the blond brick wall behind them, but no one stopped to buy. On the wall above their heads, a painted Madansa spread her hands, displaying painted bounty: this was a recognized market, then, but one without customers.

That was almost unprecedented, and he looked around, curious and wary. The short street that led into Swetewater Square where the Blue Watch's main market was held was clear; nothing blocked passage between the two areas, but there were *mosstaas* by the barred side door of a spicery. One of the pair held a camera conspicuously in his hands, trained on the marketwomen. Warreven slowed his pace, pretending to examine the nearest quilt— blue and gray and gold, the sort of colors that Folhare loved to play with—and saw the cameraman work his controls, recording him. He looked back at the quilt and saw the nearest woman look- ing at him, a sour expression on her face.

"What's all this, then?" he asked, and tilted his head toward the cameraman.

The woman—herm, really, the shape confirmed by the off- world clothes—stared back at him, her expression unchanging. *"Mosstaas*, serray. Do you want to buy?"

The off-world term was a small shock. Warreven blinked, and a second woman—a fem, this time, traditional skirts falling lank from her waist—stepped hastily forward.

"Mir Warreven, isn't it? You spoke for me in small-court last year. Secontane—Casnot, of the Barres *mesnie*. Black Casnot."

Warreven nodded. He remembered the case, though he wouldn't have recognized her out of the off-world clothes she had been affecting then. "What's going on?"

"We—we're all part of the Newfolk Cooperative—we got kicked out of the Swetewater market because we wouldn't dress appropriately—"

"Wear traditional clothes," the first woman interjected. Face and voice were bitter.

"—and then the *mosstaas* showed up," Secontane continued, with a minatory look at her friend. "They started taking pictures, and of course no one wants to buy under those circumstances. Not even the off-worlders are interested now."

"Who sent them?" Warreven asked. "The marketkeeper?"

"Probably," the first woman muttered.

Secontane shook her head. "I don't think so. We worked hard to get this space—I thought, we all thought, it was a good com- promise. The Watch gets a traditional market, and we still get a space. They just showed up."

Warreven sighed, squinted at the pair still lurking in the shad- ows of the doorway. It was not, strictly speaking, his business—

but she's of my Watch, and I will be damned before I let them get away with this. "Let me see what I can do," he said, and started toward the *mosstaas* without waiting for an answer.

"Spirits go with you," someone—not Secontane, and not her friend—murmured after him.

The *mosstaas* with the camera lifted it even higher as he approached, training the round dark eye of the lens on him. A targeting light glowed red in its depths, signaling that the machine was on and recording. Warreven smiled cheerfully into it. "Who's in charge here?"

"I am." That was the man without the camera.

At his words, the cameraman lowered his machine, and the light flicked off behind the lens. Warreven looked at them—back-country boys from the Peninsular *mesnies*, by the look of them, unhappy and out of place in the big city—and said, "What's your authority for this?" He pointed to the camera.

The cameraman glanced warily at his senior, a single betraying glance, and the other man cleared his throat. Warreven could see his eyes move, flicking across the metal bracelets and necklaces as well as the body beneath the loose clothes, and was glad he had worn his full regalia. "My own authority, mir." The honorific came reluctantly, but it was there. "We're encouraged to use our initiative."

"The marketkeepers have agreed these women can use this space," Warreven said. "By law and custom, you have no right to interfere."

"These—people—are potentially troublemakers," the *mosstaas* answered. "It's my responsibility to keep the peace."

"No one's causing any trouble here," Warreven said. "Except you for them."

"We're protecting the market," the cameraman said. "Keeping a record. If people are ashamed to be seen—"

"It's our responsibility to keep the peace," the other *mosstaas* said again.

Warreven looked at them, seeing for the first time the badge, the Captain's anchor awash in a sea of red and white flames: Tendlathe's followers, ultra-Traditionalists. "The marketkeepers authorized this," he said again, and reached out to touch the carved and painted circle with one fingertip. The *mosstaas* didn't flinch, but his eyes were wary. "Their right supersedes yours—the Captain has no rights in the marketplace, that's Madansa's domain." Warreven tilted his head toward the painted figure, her broad face impassive, hands outstretched over a frieze of food and cloth and glass. "I'm prepare to take this to the marketkeepers, and your superiors."

"They'll approve it," the cameraman muttered.

The other *mosstaas* nodded. "Our superiors will back us in this, mir."

"But they haven't yet," Warreven said. "Until then—and only if they agree—you have no right to be here."

The cameraman glanced again at his superior, who hesitated, then nodded once, jerkily. "All right. But we'll be back, and with all the authority you, mir, could want. We have friends higher than you."

Warreven nodded back. "Tell Tendlathe that I—that Warreven—want to talk to him."

"I'll tell him that," the senior *mosstaas* said, and managed to sound menacing. At his gesture, the cameraman tucked his machine under his arm, and the two walked away across the market, disappeared down a side street toward the local headquarters. Warreven watched them go, wondering if he'd done the right thing when he reassured Tatian that Tendlathe's power was limited. For the *mosstaas* to act like this—interfering in trade had always been Temelathe's one great taboo—they had to be very sure, both of Tendlathe's approval and his ability to protect them. He walked back toward the line of marketwomen, who offered scattered applause, softly, to keep it from carrying beyond the confines of the market.

"Thanks, mir," Secontane said, and Warreven shrugged.

"Thank me if it works. They say they've gone to get written authority."

"The marketkeepers will support us," Secontane said, and beckoned to another fem. "Bet, go tell Farelok what's happened, and tell him a marketmaster would help us a lot."

"Right, *baas*," the woman—she was the most traditionally dressed of the group—answered, and started away, hoisting her skirts to her knees to move more quickly.

Warreven nodded, hoping she knew what she was talking about. "Good luck," he said, and started back toward his own Watch House.

Important Man, Important Woman:
> a man or woman who has, by virtue either of a job or by election, been accepted as someone who can represent or speak for the clan.

MHYRE TATIAN

Voska's was crowded, as usual. Tatian paused just inside the door, grateful for the cool air that washed over him, let his eyes roam across the crowd. He recognized most of the people—fellow pharmaceuticals, staffers from ColCom and the IDCA and Customs, neighbors from EHB Three, a couple of port techs he'd played racquets with—and it took him only a few seconds to spot Arsidy Shraga and Eshe Isabon. They were sitting at their usual table, about equidistant between the live bar and the kitchen hatch, an empty platter between them. Isabon looked up then and lifted a hand to wave him over. Tatian waved back, but pointed to the bar. ðe nodded, but Shraga lifted his empty bottle and mimed pouring another drink. Tatian sighed, and nodded: he would buy this round.

He crossed to the stationary bar and fed *assignats* into the automat, waiting for the locks to release. When the off-world section came around, he collected three double-serving bottles of wine, and then threaded his way through the tables to join his friends.

"Very generous," Shraga said, and reached up to snare a bottle.

Tatian set the remaining bottles on the table and seated himself between them. Isabon tilted a bottle to the light to read the label and lifted an eyebrow.

"Very generous indeed."

Tatian ignored the implied question, busied himself opening his own bottle.

"It's good to see you again, Tatya," Shraga said. From the sound of his voice, he'd been drinking for some time already. "I propose a toast. To home. Where they have five sexes, one calendar—"

"And everything isn't spiked with a restricted substance," Tatian said, and lifted his own glass in answer.

Isabon grinned. "And the only thing that jumps into your lap and purrs has four legs, not six, right, Shraga?"

Shraga shuddered ostentatiously, and Isabon went on, "Shraga just spent a week in the Estaern, and his hosts at the last *mesnie* raised land-spiders."

"And gave them the run of the compound," Shraga said.

Tatian gave the other man a sympathetic look. Haran land-spiders weren't really spiders, of course; they were a species of crustacean, averaging thirty centimeters across the body, not counting the extravagant legs. They were friendly, docile, and spun the silk that clothed the wealthier half of Hara's population, as well as provided a tidy export income for the Stillers, Feranes, and Delacostes—and they undeniably did purr—but he had never quite felt comfortable with the creatures. Of course, NAPD dealt in flora, not silk, so he'd never had to learn to like them.

"It did something interesting to the silk, letting them run loose like that," Shraga went on. "You might want to check it out, Isa."

Isabon nodded, looked at Tatian. "So what did you want, buying a nice drink like this?"

"To talk," Tatian answered, and took a sip of the wine. It was good, chilled and not too sweet, and free of the underlying clove-tingle of Haran drugs. The music had started, off-world music with the bass tuned unnaturally loud, and he was grateful for the cover it provided. Isabon waited, a smile just touching ðer thin lips, and Shraga made a face.

"Oh, my god, politics."

"What else?" Tatian said. "The IDCA. And maybe Tendlathe Stane."

"That's a match made in hell," Isabon said. "But hardly likely."

Tatian said, "The IDCA have asked me—unofficially but firmly—not to do something, because it would give Tendlathe an excuse to act against trade and against them."

"All at the same time?" Shraga asked, and Isabon hushed him.

"At the same time," Tatian agreed. "And I'm under—shall we say considerable economic pressure?—to do exactly that. I'm wondering what you two know about Tendlathe's status."

"He has a lot of power," Isabon said, ðer voice without noticeable inflection. "So do the IDCA."

Tatian waited.

"I heard," ðe went on, "that they're being asked to step in on an emigration case. Trade matters."

Shraga waved that away. "It'll never happen. Not in Temelathe's lifetime—and not in Tendlathe's, he hates all of us. He'd like nothing better than for us all to pack up and go home."

Isabon's eyes flicked sideways. "Well, Shraga's right there. Tendlathe really wants the Concord to go away."

"How the hell would they manage without us?" Shraga demanded. "No metal, no tech of their own—"

"They did all right after the First Wave ended," Isabon said impatiently. "He figures they can do it again." ðe fixed ðer eyes on Tatian. "He's very sensitive to issues of gender, it seems. And to trade. He seems to think that if they could just get rid of trade, all the herms, mems, and fems would just—disappear."

"That's crazy," Tatian said.

"No crazier than anything else on this planet," Isabon answered. "And he's got support, Tatian. I had to send one of my assistants to Redlands last month because they were so uncomfortable dealing with me. I hate to say it, but the IDCA might be right. This is not the time to give him any excuses."

Tatian sat silent for a moment. He still had trouble understanding how Harans could deny the existence of three of the sexes, when mems, fems, and herms walked past them every day, a full quarter of the population. But then, he'd once had a polite, slightly mad conversation with an old *vieuvant*, who had told him quite sincerely that the story about the five sexes being the result of hyperlumin-induced mutation was a lie, or at best a misperception, and that all that was really required to bring humanity back to its proper two-gendered state was to stop coddling these people and force them to make up their minds what they really were.

"Redlands must've loved dealing with an assistant," he said aloud.

Isabon smiled, showing teeth. "I told them, they could deal with me directly, or with my assistant, who would not have the authority to offer more than the preset contract. They took the assistant and the contract. I can live with the insult when it saves me that much money."

"Idiots," Shraga said. He would have said more, but Isabon leaned forward.

"So, Tatya, what do you hear about labor trouble in Pensemare?"

"We don't do business on the Westland," Tatian answered, with perfect truth. "All I've heard is that the Donavie are going to file a protest."

"Like it would do them any good," Shraga said.

Tatian poured himself a second cup of wine, letting the gossip wash over him. He had gotten what he had come for—was willing to pay for the information with whatever he could contribute to the conversation. His heart wasn't really in it, however, his mind occupied with the upcoming conversation with the Old Dame. If Isabon said he should do what the IDCA wanted, he should probably listen to ðer—but Warreven's opinion had to carry some weight, too, maybe more weight than ðers. He would put both opinions to the Old Dame, he thought, let ðer make the final decision, but he wanted this contract.

By the time he left Voska's, it was late enough that he called a rover to drive him back to the office in the Estrange. He paid the driver, a skinny man in cheap flaxen gauze, fifteen grams in metal to wait in the parking alley behind NAPD's section of the building, and went inside, feeling slightly guilty. It was uncomfortable being this much richer than the general population; even on Antigone, his last station before Hara, he hadn't felt so out of sync with the rest of the world.

Derebought had left the databutton on his desk, along with a print of her first-run results. Even allowing for error and misunderstanding, and the inevitable shifts in demand and price, the total was enormous. Tatian refolded the papers and set them aside as carefully as if they held the harvest itself. He had underestimated by almost two million. If they took the contract, NAPD would nearly double its profits. Or more.

He flicked the external switch to restart his system, waiting in the silence of the empty building while the machines whirred to life. When the desktop screen lit, a bright orange message reminded him that it was less than an hour to his scheduled conference with Masani, and he fiddled with the shadowscreen to invoke the comm management program. He checked the parameters—all as they should be, just the same as they had been the last time—and flipped the program to standby while he went over Derebought's figures a final time. Even at their most conservative—*improbably, impossibly conservative*, he thought, though superstitiously he would never have said that aloud—the profits remained worth the risk. He would warn Masani of Valmy's and Jhirad's visit, of course, and their threat—and Isabon's warning, ðer suspicion that they might be right—but he couldn't imagine turning down this chance. And the Old Dame had never refused a challenge in ðer life.

The system chimed then, signaling the preliminary signals from the port. Tatian recalled the communications program and waited while it matched channels and input/output checks. Finally, the screen cleared, displaying the familiar codes of a transsystem link, and the wallscreen opened. Masani looked out at him, expressionless, a tall fem, raw-boned, with harsh lines from the hard weather on a dozen different planets and dark, farsighted eyes. The visuals were only fair, static hazing the edges of the screen, haloing the central images with little rainbows, but the audio was much better, Masani's voice nearly as clear as on a transcontinental linkup. ðe listened to his summary, demanded a copy of the preliminary assessment and whatever else Derebought came up with on later runs, and then fixed him with ðer fierce stare.

"So everything's wonderful, except that the new *seraaliste* wants Reiss to make a report, sorry, a court statement, that the IDCA has explicitly told you to kill."

"Yes." Tatian watched the image warily, ðer face and moving hands haloed by rainbow static. He wanted this contract, he realized suddenly, wanted it more than was entirely reasonable—but enthusiasm was appropriate, he told himself, when there was this much money involved.

"And the IDCA wants to kill Reiss's statement because Temelathe asked them to get involved, and Temelathe wants it killed—why?"

"I don't know for certain. My best guess—" Tatian spread his own hands, deliberately scaling the gesture to the limits of the comm package, repeated what he'd said before. "From what Valmy and Jhirad said, I think Warreven's partners want to use this case to force a general discussion of trade. And that means gender law as well, how many sexes there actually are. None of the *mesnies* are real comfortable with that, and Tendlathe, who's a bit of a nut case, as far as I can tell, is working on them to keep things just the way they are."

Masani's mouth twisted. "And Tendlathe is confirmed as Temelathe's heir?"

"Yes," Tatian said again.

ðe snorted. "But Warreven thinks he doesn't really have the support." ðe looked away then, expression suddenly sad. "I remember when I first came to Hara, everyone assumed I'd do trade, because I'm a fem and I had my own company. Then the indigenes decided I was a woman, so I spent about ninety-seven kilohours, eight local years, having to explain myself to everyone." ðe shook ðer head, shook ðerself back to the matter at hand. "All right, I don't like trade, and I don't have a problem with NAPD being known to be involved in this case if it's meant to break trade. Temelathe knows where I stand on that. But I especially don't like the IDCA telling me what I can and can't do when I'm not breaking any laws. So. Does this Warreven really have this much to offer?"

"The sea-harvest has been very, very good this year," Tatian answered. "There may be—hell, there will be some exaggeration, either in the grade or in the total quantity available, but we've already factored that into the estimates. The *seraalistes* don't dare play too fast and loose with the numbers, not if they expect to keep doing business with us."

"Certainly," Masani agreed, with a slight, unpleasant smile, and Tatian remembered too late that ðe had traded on Hara for ten years. "But does your Warreven know this?"

That could give me nightmares if I let it, Tatian thought. He said, "Yes. I think ʒe's more knowledgeable than ʒe lets on."

"Not too much more, I hope," the Old Dame said, and Tatian smiled dutifully. ðe sighed, looked down at ðer own screen, ðer blunt-fingered hands sprawling across ðer desktop. Every movement sparked a rainbow, so that ðe moved in a cloud of refracted light. "So you think it's worth fighting the IDCA on this one."

"I do," Tatian answered. "We're well within the law—hell, what they're asking is illegal, not anything we're doing. And I don't think we're going to see another surplus like this for another forty-three, forty-four kilohours."

"All right," Masani said. "We'll do it. I'll warn the accountants to expect the buy. Get me the final figures as soon as you have them, and I'll sign the drafts. I assume ʒe'll want a metal payment?"

"Not decided yet," Tatian said, and ðe grunted.

"There usually is. Remember, we need at least five hundred hours lead time for that, and seven fifty would be better."

"I will."

"Good. And, Tatian. Nice work."

ðe cut the transmission, leaving the screen streaming with multicolored static, before he could respond to the unexpected praise. He touched the shadowscreen and watched the shutdown procedures flicker across his desktop, wincing at the charges that appeared in the accounting screen. Interplanetary communication was painfully expensive; at this rate, he thought, he had maybe three calls left for this budget year. He entered the codes that accepted the charges and authorized payment, then made a note in his private file to recheck the communications budget, just to see where the money had gone. There had been two calls when Derebought isolated the guafesi, and— He deliberately shut off those thoughts. It was late, and he was tired; better to deal with that in the morning, he thought, and flattened his hand against the shadowscreen. The machine flashed a last quick series of queries, but he kept his hand flat until the last light had winked out. He flipped on the main security systems, with their seventy-second delay, and walked out the back door to the parking alley.

The rover was still there, the driver curled in his compartment like a mouse in its nest. Tatian tapped gently on the window, and the thin man woke instantly. He came upright in the same moment, eyes focusing first on his board, and then on Tatian himself. Seeing him, the driver relaxed, and reached across to open the passenger door.

"All done, mir?"

"All done," Tatian answered, and climbed into the passenger compartment.

"Where to, then? Going dancing? I know some good places, even for an off-worlder." The driver looked at him in his mirror, his grin showing badly patched teeth.

Tatian shook his head. "Not tonight. Just home—EHB Three."

Everyone knew the compounds where the majority of the off-worlders lived. The driver nodded, and slipped the rover into gear. Tatian leaned back in his seat, aware for the first time of just how tired he was. Not that it was that late, really—barely past two—but it had been an active day. And, he admitted, with a quiet smile, an exhilarating one. If everything worked out, if he could keep the IDCA at arm's length and trade Reiss's statement for the surplus contract—well, at the least, he would certainly earn one of the Old Dame's generous bonuses, not to mention put himself well ahead in the promotions stakes.

The rover slid out of the alley, turned onto the ring-road that carried traffic around the maze of linked courtyards that made up the Estrange. From the top of the slight hill, he could see between the buildings to the harbor; the lights seemed brighter than usual there, and he wondered if some of the harvest was in. Then he realized that the light wasn't steady and was much too orange for the usual working lights.

"Fire?" he said, and the driver slowed.

"I heard sirens earlier, mir," he volunteered. "They were heading toward the docks—toward Dock Row, the north end. Do you want to take a look?"

Tatian shook his head, though he was tempted. "Just home," he said again, and thought the driver looked disappointed.

"Right, mir, EHB Three it is."

"Thanks."

There was more traffic on Tredhard Street, most of it going away from the harbor. Tatian squinted through the doubled glass of passenger compartment and driver's screen and thought he saw barriers pulled across the road at the base of the hill, barring traffic from the Harbor Market. People in uniform were standing there, not firefighters in their silver, but the dull black of the *mosstaas*; he imagined he could smell smoke in spite of the rover's filter, but couldn't see the flames.

"Something's burning for sure," the driver said. "In Dock Row, it looks like."

Tatian nodded, still staring down the badly lit street. If it was in Dock Row proper, the off-world warehouses should be safe enough, since they stood at the north end of the street, clear of the Market. Dock Row itself was mostly bars and dance houses—the center of trade, he realized suddenly, and shivered in spite of the warm evening. If someone was striking back at trade, Dock Row and its bars were a good place to begin. He shoved the thought away. There was no point in speculating until he knew what had actually happened—for all he knew, someone had been careless with a stove, or lightning had struck, some natural disaster. In the mirror, he saw the driver shake his head.

"I'm going to have to go the narrow way, mir, by the Soushill Road."

"Fine," Tatian answered, and a moment later they were in shadow again as the rover turned onto the smaller street. Soushill Road was mostly small shops, chandlerys and hardware, and the occasional software broker or satellite tracker, all closed down against the night. Even the streetlights were out; only the occasional dot of an alarm system glowed in the corner of a doorway. The driver muttered something and switched his lights to high.

Then, from nowhere, came the snarl of an engine. A massive shay shot from an alley and swung skidding into Soushill Road. The driver swore, jamming on his brakes, and Tatian caught himself stiff-armed against the partition separating him from the driver's compartment. Pain flared in his arm, along the lines of the faulty implant. He caught a glimpse of the shay's open body, of the dozen figures in it, black-robed, black-hooded, faces hidden by blank white masks like the faces of unfinished dolls. One of them lifted an empty ring, also white, white as bone, lifted a white feather-tipped stick and mimed striking the empty air, as though he—she? þe? ðe? ʒe?—beat an invisible drum. He was still drumming, white-gloved hands holding the empty drum frame over head, as the shay skidded around another corner and vanished completely.

"What the hell was that?" he demanded, and cradled his arm against his chest, trying not to jar the implant box.

"I—don't know, mir. Never seen anything like it." The driver's voice was frightened, and the eyes that met his in the mirror were wide and staring. "Never at all."

You're lying, Tatian thought, and could not have said what made him so sure of it. *But whatever they were*—he conjured the black-robed shapes again, the white masks and gloves and the invisible, frantic drum—*whatever they were, whoever they were, you knew them. You knew what they meant.* "Take me home," he said aloud, knowing better than to press the issue, and leaned back against the padding. Reiss would know, or Warreven; he would ask one of them in the morning.

odd-bodied:
> (Hara) colloquial generic term for herms, mems, and fems.

MHYRE TATIAN

The fire on Dock Row made the narrowcast news on both the port and the local channels. Tatian set the system to search-store-and-replay and watched the stories as he dressed, but there was no mention of the black-robed figures. The local channels displayed vivid pictures of silver-suited firefighters, bright against the flames, but said little about damage or causes, noting only that two bars had burned and no one had been reported killed. The port system named the bars—Tatian didn't recognize either of the names—and estimated that the damage would force them out of business. The newsreader, a plump, pretty woman with an expressive voice, carefully controlled, added that the *mosstaas* was looking into the cause of the fire. Which means, Tatian thought, that it was arson. He saw again the figures in the back of the shay, the white hands and the white drum, and wondered if they'd had anything to do with it. They had certainly looked menacing enough, but on Hara, who could tell?

He rode the EHB shuttle into Bonemarche and got off at the Estrange with perhaps a dozen other people who worked for the companies there. The largest group, junior botanists and lab techs from NuGen, were talking loudly about some new plant they were working on—*which couldn't be that promising,* Tatian thought, *or they'd be keeping it more of a secret*—while a couple of hard-muscled secretaries were discussing the ranking system for the Nest's full-contact *mattata* tournament. Tatian had dated one of them, briefly, smiled as he drew even with her, and received a pleasant smile in response. It seemed suddenly strange that no one was talking about the destruction of the bars, and he said, on impulse, "Did you see the fire on the news this morning?"

"Fire?" The woman looked blank, shook her head.

"Oh, I saw that," the other secretary said. "The one by the harbor, right? It's a good thing it wasn't by the warehouses." He looked at the first woman. "Some bars burned down, on Dock Row. If it'd been a little farther north, it would've taken out the Starsys warehouse."

"That would have been bad," the woman said, and stopped at the entrance to the arcade, where a gray-haired indigene in off-world clothes sold bread and local honey from a folding cart. "We were lucky."

The bar owners weren't, Tatian thought, but their attention was already on the breads spread out for sale. *Or the people who went there.* He remembered the crowd at Shinbone: not what he'd expected, less trade, or less obviously trade, than what the indigenes called odd-bodied and the wry-abed, mems, fems, and herms, and anyone whose sexual tastes didn't match the indigenes' simple male/female model. It had been one of the few places on Hara not run by off-worlders where he'd felt things were—almost—normal, and he wondered suddenly if that was what the indigenes were looking for when they did trade. And the money was good, too, he reminded himself, striving for his usual detachment, and went through the arcade into Drapdevel Court.

For once, Reiss was there before him, perched on the edge of the secretarial desk in the outer office, a chunk of spicebread in one hand and a stylus in the other. He looked up as Tatian entered and hastily blanked his screen. Tatian sighed, wondering what he was doing this time—*probably more work on his jet cars, using our design systems*—but said only, "I need to talk to you, Reiss. When you've got a minute."

"Any time," Reiss said, and used the stylus to flick virtual switches. "Now?"

"That would be good," Tatian said, and the younger man followed him into the office.

Tatian touched his wrist, then winced, hit the override a fraction of a second too late to stop the cascade of static. He touched the shadowscreen instead, lighting the desktop, and glanced quickly at the update screen. It showed nothing of immediate importance, and he looked back at Reiss. He hated having to reverse himself, the more so because he had known he was wrong, and said, "It's about that case you were involved in, Destany Casnot's."

"So Raven came through," Reiss said.

"You knew about this," Tatian said, and controlled his anger with an effort. "You work for NAPD, Reiss, whatever your clan affiliations are. I can't afford divided loyalties, especially right now."

"No, it's not like that." Reiss shook his head. "I had to tell them, tell Raven and Haliday, and Destany, for that matter, and when we met to talk it over, Raven said something about offering part of the surplus. I didn't know if 3e could, much less whether it'd be worth it. That's all I knew."

Tatian stared at him for a moment. It was plausible enough—if nothing else, Reiss wasn't the sort of person one trusted with a complicated plan—and he nodded slowly. "All right—"

"One thing," Reiss said. "Okay, maybe I should've told you, even if I didn't know what Raven was going to be able to do, but what you were asking wasn't right. I owe Destany—more than that, 3e's got rights, even if 3e is an indigene."

Tatian took a deep breath, biting back an instinctive, angry answer. Reiss was right, and more than that, he knew that NAPD was wrong. "You've lived on Hara all your life," he said, after a moment. "You know who has power—you know how much power the IDCA has, particularly if they can connect a company to trade. To fight that, you need solid backing, and for the Old Dame to give us that, well, we need a solid reason, something the Board and the shareholders can appreciate. Yeah, maybe I should've told you—like you maybe should have told me—when I got the offer. In retrospect, I'm sorry I didn't. But right now, we have Masani's support—you have Masani's support, to make this statement. Let's go from there."

"Would you have done it without the—offer?" Reiss asked.

I don't know. Tatian said, "I couldn't have. It's that simple, Reiss."

There was a little silence, and then Reiss looked away. "All right," he said, almost inaudibly, then shook himself. "I'll talk to Haliday—Destany will be pleased."

Tatian nodded and looked back at the blinking desktop as the door closed behind the other. *Would I have done this without Warreven's offer, without the lure, the bribe, of the surplus? Well, I told the truth when I said I couldn't have risked it, couldn't have taken the chance of getting the IDCA down on us—but it's also the truth that it wouldn't have occurred to me to take the chance without Warreven.* He sighed, and reached for the shadowscreen, trailing his fingers through the virtual controls until he could call up the communications system. The mail screen was almost empty, only a few general circulars, and nothing from Prane Am or the port. He swore under his breath at that and switched to the general monophone system, punched in the numbers Warreven had left on file. At least he could let Warreven know that they were prepared to do business.

The communications screen stayed empty for several seconds, then flashed a single word—FORWARDING—and a second string of codes. Tatian raised an eyebrow at that, raised both eyebrows as the CONNECT notice appeared followed by the message VIDEO N/A.

"Æ?" a voice said, from the wall speaker.

"I'm looking for Warreven," Tatian said, in *franca*. There was a little silence, and Tatian made a face at the blank screen, anticipating another routing error.

"I'll see if he's available," the voice said, and was replaced by the hiss of a holding signal.

Tatian sighed again, and settled himself to wait, reaching for the shadowscreen to call up another set of files. To his surprise, however, the holding signal vanished within a minute, and Warreven's voice spoke from the wall.

"Yes?"

"Mhyre Tatian here. I wondered if we could meet."

"Ah." There was another little silence, live silence this time, and Tatian could imagine Warreven's brows drawn together in thought. He missed the video image, wondered where Warreven was that lacked such basic capacity. . . .

"I assume you have good news," Warreven said, and Tatian dragged his attention back to the matter at hand.

"Yes. At least, we're prepared to talk."

"That is good," Warreven said. "I'm—I have some business to finish here, I'm at the Harbor, Barbedor's club on the Embankment. Can you meet me here, say, at noon?"

Tatian nodded, then remembered the missing video. "All right. Does this club have an address?"

There was a pause, and Warreven's voice, when it came, sounded grimly amused. "No. But you can't miss it. It's the one on the south side of the missing buildings."

"I'll be there," Tatian said, and flattened his hand against the shadowscreen.

A new file had appeared in the working window: Derebought had arrived and was passing on the latest assessment of the Stiller surplus. Tatian paged through it quickly, noting where she had been able to confirm the prices, then filed back to the beginning and began to go through it item by item. He wasn't quite finished by noon, but saved it and his rough notes for her, and headed for the Harbor Market.

It wasn't a long walk, across to Tredhard Street and then straight down the long hill, and for once the sea breeze was relatively cool. He looked to the horizon, flecked with sails, but there was no sign of the usual afternoon storms. The year had turned already, he thought, and saw, all around him, indigenes wrapped in *shaals* and jackets against the cooler air. The wind brought the sour smell of cold ash as well, and he saw a few flakes of soot the size of a man's hand blown against the corners of the buildings. More ash was streaked in the gutter, carried by the overnight rain.

The *mosstaas* had set up a blockade at the end of Dock Row, bright orange wooden barriers pulled haphazardly across the traffic way. A four-up was parked beside it, but only a couple of troopers were in sight, leaning bored against the nearest barrier. Tatian approached them cautiously, aware of their holstered pellet guns and the heavy fibreplast paneling along the four-up's sides and lining the driver's cab. He was aware, too, of the weight of metal in his pocket, good for bribes, but they paid no particular attention to him. Or to anyone else, for that matter, Tatian thought. Pedestrians were moving freely along the length of the street. The smell of smoke was stronger here, and as he got closer, he could see the gap in the roofline, and the charred beams that spanned it, all that remained of the clubs. There were more *mosstaas* on duty there and more bright-orange barriers; he looked for the investigators the news reports had mentioned, but saw only the black-clad troopers standing in twos and threes.

As Warreven had promised, Barbedor's was hard to miss. It stood next to the remains of its neighbor, little more than firescarred brick walls and the shattered remains of the roof tumbled in on itself. The same flames had seared Barbedor's bricks, turning them from ochre to red streaked with black. The fire had knocked out the sign lights as well; Barbedor's name was a ghost of empty tubing over the doorway, and one side of the stylized tree that labeled it as a bar had cracked in the flames' heat, spilling chemicals down the brick facing. The main door was open, though, and he could hear voices from inside, and the low, insistent beat of a drum.

He stepped through the open doorway, paused for a moment to get his bearings, wrinkling his nose at the sudden stench of smoke. The band platform was empty, as were most of the tables; the drumming came from the speakers that hung above the dance floor. He looked around, not seeing anyone he recognized in the shadows, and the bartender called from the bar, in accented creole, "Sorry, ser, we're not serving."

"It's all right." Warreven's voice came from the side of the room, where a door had suddenly opened, spilling yellow light into the bar. "He's with me."

A big man, hair and beard bleached a startling orange, followed ʒim out, scowling, and Warreven said, to him, "I told you I had another appointment, Barbe. Hal or Malemayn will get back to you."

"Like it'll do any good," the big man growled, and turned back into his inner room.

Warreven looked at Tatian. "I'm glad you could meet me

here. Have you eaten? I'm starving—my day started a little earlier than I'd planned."

"I can eat," Tatian said, with less than perfect truth. There were too many foods on Hara that no off-worlder dared eat.

Warreven smiled. "There's a place on the Embankment that serves off-world food. We can go there, if you'd like."

"It suits me," Tatian answered, and followed the herm out of Barbedor's. Warreven turned left, just skirting the barricades and the watching *mosstaas;* following 3im, Tatian could feel heat still radiating from the ruins, like the warmth from an oven.

"I'm amazed nobody was killed," he said aloud, looking at the charred beams, the fallen walls, and Warreven snorted.

"Nobody was killed because the fires started small, there was plenty of time to get out. It's just the firefighters didn't show up for an hour or two, and by that time, it was too late."

3e hadn't spoken loudly, but 3e hadn't lowered 3er voice, either, and Tatian saw the nearest *mosstaas* give them a hard stare. The noise of an engine came from behind him, and he glanced over his shoulder, grateful for the interruption, to see a big shay, its ironwood body painted in the firefighters' yellow and silver, edging past the *mosstaas'* barricade. Warreven looked, too, and made another face.

"So the promised investigators finally make their appearance."

Tatian looked back—saw that they were out of earshot of the nearest *mosstaas.* "Aren't they a little late?"

"Only if they actually want to catch who did it," Warreven answered. 3e shook 3er head. "I'm sorry, I'm not fit company. I've been up since about four when Barbedor called. He's an old friend."

"I take it your group is representing him?" Tatian asked, and they turned onto one of the short stair streets that led down to the Embankment.

Warreven nodded. "He wants us to, anyway. Just in case there's something he can do. He had a part interest in the Starlik, that was the smaller club."

The Embankment was crowded in the good weather, indigenes and a fair number of off-worlders alike enjoying the cool breeze. Warreven led him to a cookstall on the Harbor side of the Embankment—it was little more than a three-sided shack with a row of grills along the back, and Tatian hesitated until he saw the empty boxes labeled *Surya's Samosaas* stacked along the wall by the power hookup. That was an off-world brand, and safe; he bought two of the heavy pastries and waited while Warreven picked out a thick yellow stew served in a hollowed-out melon. They found a place in the sun along the broad wall and sat, shielding their food from the wind. From this angle, looking back up the hill, the burned-out buildings were very visible, a break in the neat line of the street fronts. He could see the marks of the fire on the building to the north, as well as on the front and side of Barbedor's, and a scorched patch on the roof of the building next to it, could see, too, three figures in silver protective suits poking idly in the wreckage.

Warreven saw the direction of his gaze and smiled, jabbing a wooden spoon savagely into the stew. "From this distance, you might almost think they wanted to catch the bastards who did it."

Tatian looked at 3im, wondering what was in the stew that smelled of woodsmoke, and then realized that the scent was clinging to Warreven's hair and clothes. "Then it's true the fire was set," he said aloud.

"I'm sure of it," Warreven answered. "Not that it'll ever be proved, of course. But it started in the back, where the alley doors are—were—and those are the two houses where most of the radicals hung out. They did some trade, sure, but they were mostly for the wry-abed. If it wasn't set, well, you'd have to think the spirits took a personal hand."

"I worked late last night," Tatian said, balancing the hot, crumbling pastry in the palm of his hand. "As I was going home, I saw the fire, and then I nearly got run down by a shay that was full of—well, I don't know what they were. They were wearing masks, white masks, no paint, not much feature, and then white gloves and bulky black—like a cape, I guess, or a really full tunic." He could see them in his imagination, the silent drummer and his followers, started to say more, but stopped, not wanting to reveal how much they had disturbed him.

"Ghost *ranas*," Warreven said, and shivered. "God and the spirits."

"What are they?" Tatian asked, after a moment.

"Nothing good," Warreven answered grimly. "They—you know what *ranas* are, right?"

"Sanctioned protesters, I thought? They have something to do with your spirits."

Warreven nodded. "They're under Genevoe's—the Trickster's—protection, they can say anything as long as they stay within the form." 3e grinned suddenly. "You saw the *presance* at our *baanket*, that's the sort of thing the *ranas* do. And as long as it stays a dance, a mime, a song, even Temelathe has to put up with it, by custom and by law." The smile vanished as quickly as it had appeared. "But the ghost *ranas* . . . They don't just protest, they'll take action. They say they're enforcing tradition, custom, whatever, but they'll hurt you if you don't agree with them. They killed a man eight years ago; that was the last time they were active here in the city. There are more of them in the *mesnies*, especially down in the Equatoriale." 3e turned sideways then on the broad, sun-warmed stones of the wall, fixed Tatian with a sudden fierce glare. "And you say you saw them last night, near the fire?"

"I saw a shay full of them, maybe twelve, fifteen of them, driving up one of those side streets onto Soushill Road," Tatian answered. "One of them had an empty drum frame, was pretending to play it." He imitated the movement, half embarrassed, and swore when the gesture dislodged a piece of pastry. "They turned up another street—they were going uphill, away from the fire—and that was all I saw."

"What time was it?" Warreven demanded.

"I could see firefighters already there," Tatian answered. "If you're thinking they started it, I don't know. All I could say was that I saw them. My driver might be able to tell you more—"

"Not if it means speaking against the ghost *ranas*," Warreven said. The eagerness had vanished from 3er voice again. "It could well have been them, but we'll never get anyone to testify."

Tatian stooped to pick up the broken bit of pastry and tossed it into the nearest trash can. Hara had no scavengers, none of the usual city birds that swooped and fought for crumbs; anything that spilled would lie where it fell until it rotted. "I have to say, if they started it, and if it took the firefighters that long to get to the bars, they waited a long time to run away. And they were in a hurry."

"I suppose you're right," Warreven said. "I—" 3e broke off, staring up the hill. Tatian followed the direction of 3er gaze, saw a sudden bustle of activity around the fire site. There were more firefighters now, not all of them in silver suits, and more *mosstaas*, and a crowd had gathered on the street to either side, pushed back by the black-suited troopers. As he watched, a white-painted ambulance turned onto the street, began making its way slowly through the crowd.

"Oh, Christ," he said, a sick certainty settling over him, and Warreven stood up quickly, leaving 3er stew on the wall beside 3im.

"Come on."

Tatian followed 3er toward the nearest stair. Other people on the Embankment had seen the same thing, the gathering audience and the ambulance, and were heading for the stairs themselves. The two moved along with the steady stream of people. Halfway up the stairs, Tatian looked up and saw Barbedor fighting his way down toward them, the orange hair and beard conspicuous in the mostly Haran crowd.

"Warreven! Raven, wait."

"What is it?" Warreven asked, and stopped, bracing 3imself against the rail. Tatian stopped, too, and grunted as someone elbowed him; then the people behind him sorted themselves out and flowed past up the stairs.

"Raven, it's Lammasin, I saw him—" Barbedor broke off on an intake of breath that was almost a sob.

"Lammasin's dead," Warreven said, and took a deep breath.

Tatian, pressed close to 3im by the crowd, felt the breath catch in 3er chest, then steady again with an effort.

Barbedor nodded. "They found the body under the wall, I knew him by the chain he wears, the metal one."

"How did he die?" Warreven's voice was still unnaturally calm.

"In the fire, they say, but I'd stake my life he wasn't at the club, either one of them, last night." Barbedor's face twisted. "Lammasin is—was arrogant, but he wasn't stupid, he knew he was in trouble."

Another elbow caught Tatian in the ribs, and he felt a brief, unfriendly pressure at the small of his back. "Warreven," he said. "Let's move."

Warreven shook 3imself, nodded, and took a single step. Barbedor struggled for a moment to turn around, and then they were all moving with the crowd back up the stairs to Dock Row. There were too many people in the street to see what was happening in the fire site; an ambulance attendant stood by the closed rear compartment of þis machine, bored, mask hanging loose around þis neck, but that was all.

"God and the spirits," Warreven said quietly. "You're sure it was Lammasin?"

"The necklace," Barbedor began, and broke off, nodding. "I'm sure."

"Right." Warreven looked at Tatian, managed a small, apologetic smile. "I'm sorry, Tatian, we won't be able to discuss our business after all. I'm going to be needed here, I think."

"All I needed was to confirm our interest in your offer," Tatian said. "Is there anything I can do to help?"

"I appreciate that," Warreven said, and looked toward the burned-out buildings. "I don't know what—wait, that woman the other night, your friend—"

"Chavvin Annek," Tatian said. *Oh, my God*, he thought, *she was a friend of Lammasin's. Somebody should tell her—I should tell her, warn her what's happened—*

"Was she close to Lammasin?" Warreven went on.

"I don't know," Tatian said. "I think—she knew him well enough to go looking for him after the *baanket.*" He took a deep breath, conscious again of the heavy smell of cold ash. "I can tell her, if you'd like."

"He had a wife and kids," Barbedor said.

Tatian frowned, annoyed by the assumption of trade, and Warreven said, "Let me find out for certain what's happened, then I'll let you know. And, yes, if you'd tell her, that would be a help. I don't know who his off-world friends would have been."

"I can talk to her," Tatian said again. "Warreven, I—I'm sorry."

"Thanks." Warreven took another deep breath, and turned toward the ambulance. "I'll let you know what's happened," ʒe said, over ʒer shoulder, and disappeared into the crowd, Barbedor at ʒer heels. Tatian stood for a moment, staring after them, then turned his back on the crowd, on the burned shells of the buildings, heading back toward Tredhard Street and the familiar confines of the Estrange.

---

vieuvant:
> (Hara) an "old soul," a man or woman who is recognized as a reliable and accurate conduit for the will of one or more of the spirits; some *vieuvants* speak only for one spirit, others for more than one.

WARREVEN

The *memore* for Lammasin was held in Haliday's flat, nearly forty people crowded into the four rooms and the open porch. The air was thick with the smoke of feelgood and powdered sundew and the sweat of too many people in too small a space. Warreven struggled into the main room to pay his respects, stopped in front of the memorial tablet to draw Agede's mark on his forehead with the ash that lay in the dish in front of the freshly painted tablet. Given the way Lammasin had died, the ash was a gruesome reminder, and he wasn't surprised to see that the widow was sitting well away from the tablet, white mourning *shaal*—probably her bride-clothes reused—drawn over her head to shadow her face. Another woman stood at her side, one hand resting lightly, protectively, on her shoulder, while a child, also in white, sat cross-legged at her feet. He—she? the clothes and the thick chin-length hair could have belonged to either—sat hunched over, scowling as though daring anyone to comment on his reddened eyes. Warreven nodded to the guardian, but came no closer: he hadn't known Lammasin well, he was here more as Haliday's partner.

It was hot in the flat, despite the cooling system pushed to its highest setting, and voices rose and fell in argument in the back room. Warreven made a face, and worked his way back out onto the balcony. To his surprise, Mhyre Tatian was leaning against the corner railing, as far from the brazier and its smoldering braid of feelgood as he could get. Warreven glanced over his shoulder, looking for the off-world woman who had been Lammasin's friend, and, when he didn't see her, pushed through the crowd to join the off-worlder.

Tatian nodded a greeting, both hands braced lightly against the wood of the rail. Despite the breeze, he was sweating; Warreven could see the lights of the spinny yard beyond him, their output almost tangible in the heavy air.

"I didn't expect to see you here," he said.

"I came with Annek," Tatian answered, and for an instant, Warreven thought he heard impatience in the other man's voice. Then it was gone, and the off-worlder went on, "She didn't want to come alone, given the trouble recently."

"The ghost *ranas* won't touch off-worlders," Warreven answered, and then sighed. "Or at least they haven't yet. She's probably smart, at that."

"How are things?" Tatian asked. "Have they got any leads?"

Warreven glanced over his shoulder again, making sure none of the dead man's kin were in earshot. "They don't even know for sure how he died. The *mosstaas* say he was caught in the fire, but no one who was at either club says they saw him there. It's a mess."

Tatian nodded. "A lot of our people—off-worlders in general, I mean, not NAPD—are worried. Having protests at the harbor every day hasn't helped."

Warreven leaned on the balcony beside him, looking down into the spinny yard. The land-spiders hopped and scuttled in the lamplight, casting a web of shadows; on the wall above the pens, newly reeled silk hung to dry, heavy and unmoving in the light wind. A door banged, and one of the boys from the spinny came down the steps into the yard, began dividing them by size and weight into the appropriate feeding pens. His soft voice blended with their trilling purrs as he cooed and called them by their names, oblivious to the people on the balcony next door. Warreven took a deep breath as the breeze surrounded him with smoke, tasting its musk on the back of his tongue, and looked out over the harbor. The light at the tip of the market mole flashed twice and was echoed by the South Harbor Light on the horizon; he knew that the Blind Point Light would follow, a short flash and then a long beam sweeping across the seaward horizon, but that light was behind them. He heard Tatian cough and shift, moving out of the smoke that was already drifting away again, and turned back to face him.

"Like I said, those *ranas* aren't supposed to do more than make fun, and the ghost *ranas* have never attacked off-worlders. You should be all right."

"Mm." Tatian did not sound particularly convinced, and Warreven had to admit that he could understand the other man's uncertainty. Tendlathe's supporters had been increasingly vocal over the last few days—he had seen one of their *ranas* near the Souk, red and white ribbons weighted with the Captain's anchor, singing against the odd-bodied. Another had gone through the market by the Blue Watch House, overturning the women's makeshift stalls, and the *mosstaas* had done nothing. Folhare said their own *ranas* would dance there, try to protect them, but their presence wouldn't do much for sales.

"I don't suppose the *mosstaas* will make any effort to suppress them."

"The Most Important Man didn't like Lammasin's performance, did he?" Warreven answered. "I can't imagine he's grieving much—or going to put his weight behind any investigation. And of course Tendlathe has a lot of influence with the *mosstaas*."

"That's a really stupid statement," Haliday said. "And I'd appreciate you not making it in my house."

Warreven looked over his shoulder to see Haliday standing against the nearest pillar. 3e was scowling, and Warreven sighed. "Sorry, Hal, you're right."

"Show some sense for once," Haliday went on, and jammed 3er hands into the pockets of 3er trousers. "Anyway, you're wanted, *coy*. The Most Important Man would like to talk to you— nicely phrased, he just wants to talk, but he took the trouble to track you down here."

"Who was it who called?" Warreven asked. If it was one of Temelathe's functionaries, he might be able to get out of the meeting, arrange to do it later—

Haliday shook 3er head, as though 3e'd read the thought. "Not one of the secretaries. A woman, I think, might have been Aldess, but I couldn't be sure." 3e paused. "It probably wasn't Aldess, I think she'd still speak to me. If she recognized my voice, of course."

Warreven nodded, already wondering if he could get a rover. With the ghost *ranas* active again, he would rather not walk to and from the trolley stations. Haliday smiled again.

"And I called the service. No cars available tonight."

"Damn." Warreven looked back toward the harbor. The light was fading fast now, the rising moon barely more than a hazy patch of silver, its shape diffused and distorted by the layers of cloud. The streetlights beyond the next line of houses seemed unusually dim, muted by the weight of the evening air.

"I can give you a ride there," Tatian offered. "You'll have to find your own way back, though."

"Thanks," Warreven said. Temelathe would probably offer him a ride home, or, at worst, he should be able to find a rover.

He followed Tatian down the long stairs to the street, passing still more people coming to pay their respects, and was glad to see that the jigg waiting under the streetlight did not have pharmaceutical markings.

"The security's on," Tatian said, and Warreven froze without touching the fibreplast body. He could feel the field's edge only a few centimeters away, lifting the hairs on his arms. "Okay, you're clear."

The field vanished in the same instant, and Warreven gingerly opened the passenger door. He settled himself in the passenger seat and watched in fascination as displays sprang to life along the edge of the windscreen. Tatian glanced at them casually and kicked the engine to life.

"What's the best way to get there?"

"The easiest way is along Harborside," Warreven began, and Tatian laughed.

"Under the circumstances, maybe there's another way?"

Warreven paused, considering. He rarely had to find his way around in Bonemarche, relied always on the network of hired rovers and coupelets or on the trolleys and his own feet. . . . "Take a right at the end of the street," he said at last, "and follow that around onto Crossey."

Tatian nodded, and put the jigg into gear. He was a good driver, Warreven realized, with some surprise—he had thought that was Reiss's job, to ferry the company's important people from place to place—and managed the narrow streets with ease. Even the pack of children playing in the circle of a houselight didn't seem to bother him. He sounded the whistle, but softly, more a warning than a demand, and kept the jigg moving at a steady, inexorable pace, so that even the oldest boys thought twice about playing chicken. Only when they were past did he look into the mirror, face thoughtful, and Warreven cocked his head to one side, watching him curiously.

"Problem?" he said, after a moment, and Tatian shook himself.

"No, not at all, just something I hadn't realized. There aren't that many kids in the Nest—the housing block where I live."

It didn't seem that strange, and Warreven shrugged. "I wouldn't think you'd want to uproot your family for, what's the norm, a four-year contract?"

"Maybe not," Tatian answered, and didn't sound convinced.

"Usually there are more, that's all. At least there were on all the other planets."

They crossed Tredhard Street just above Soushill Road—Warreven was careful to keep them away from that street, just in case the ghost *ranas* were active again—and the sound of drums was suddenly loud. Warreven looked toward the Harbor, felt his own pulse quicken, seeing Tatian's sudden frown, relaxed as he saw the people gathered in the circle of lights just inside the Market square. "It's all right," he said aloud, "it's just a regular *rana.*"

Tatian allowed himself a sigh of relief, and eased the jigg across the traffic. "How can one tell?"

Warreven looked back, seeing the drummers facing each other, lifted above the group around them by a makeshift platform, a sheet of fibreplast balanced on fuel cells, and the dancers with their clusters and knots of multicolored ribbon. "*Ranas*—real *ranas*—will always have drums or a singer, that's what makes them legitimate, not political."

"Not political?" Tatian said, in spite of himself, and Warreven grinned.

"Political according to the law, anyway. The way things have always been done, political gatherings can be suppressed—that's supposed to be reserved to the *mesnies*—but political gets defined as 'getting together to talk about issues.' If you dance and sing—particularly if you're clever—it can't be politics."

"Oh, right," Tatian said. "Like having dinner regularly with the Most Important Man is neither politics nor business."

Warreven laughed. "Exactly like. Turn left here."

Tatian swung the jigg onto the broad street that ran parallel to Harborside. "I bet it works, though," he said, after a moment. "If you can't say anything directly, but have to make it a song—no, you make it a symbol, don't you? you have to talk in symbols—then you can't ever move from opposition into the system. At least not without losing the power you had before."

Warreven looked sideways at him, not liking what he'd heard. The *ranas* had real power, effective power—the very existence of the ghost *ranas* proved that; they wouldn't take on the distorted image of true *ranas* if true *ranas* weren't real— But it was true that it was hard to go from protest to holding office in the clans and Watches: the Modernists had been trying for years and still didn't win the elections. Still, you won elections through compromise, through consensus, not debate, and the *ranas*, true *ranas*, were a powerful tool there. "You can tell real *ranas* by the ribbons, too," he said. "*Ranas* are supposed to wear lots of colors—all the colors of the spectrum, supposedly, it's to prove they're not political—and they usually use ribbons. These days, nobody wears black, either."

"I'll remember that," Tatian said. "I can't say it was hard to recognize the ghost *ranas* when I saw them." He paused. "None of this is making me feel any too happy with our agreement, Warreven. Tendlathe's people are looking a lot more powerful than I thought."

Warreven hesitated, debating a lie, then made a face. "More powerful than I'd thought, too. He's got more support among the *mosstaas* than I'd realized."

"Not good."

That was, Warreven admitted, an understatement. He slanted another glance at the off-worlder, the strong planes of his face briefly highlighted as they passed a door lamp. "Killing Lammasin—that's got to be too much, even for his people. And I—I don't intend to be driven off, yet."

Tatian nodded. "I figured. This is personal, right?"

Warreven blinked, startled, then shrugged. "In a way, certainly. But I'm not like Haliday. I—I'm sure you've heard the story, I could've married Tendlathe—"

"Lucky you," Tatian said, under his breath, and Warreven grinned.

"—but I didn't want to change gender. I'm perfectly happy as a man."

"But—" Tatian broke off, shaking his head.

But you're not a man. The words seemed to hang between them, and Warreven sighed. He had forgotten, for a moment, that he was talking to an off-worlder, who couldn't see beyond the physical body. "Legally and by choice, I am. That's what matters."

"I know." Tatian took his eyes off the road long enough to offer an apologetic grimace. "I do know. I'm sorry."

Warreven nodded. "But you're right, the situation's more complicated than I thought. I'll be very interested in what Temelathe has to say to me."

"So would I be," Tatian said. "If you can tell me."

"I'll do what I can," Warreven answered.

They reached the Stane compound at last, and without being asked Tatian pulled up well outside the light from the gate. "I doubt it would do you any good to be seen with me, just at the moment," he said, and Warreven nodded.

"Probably not. I appreciate the ride, very much."

"Not a problem," Tatian said, and shrugged. "I'm sorry I can't stay. Do you want me to try to come back for you?"

Warreven shook his head, but he was obscurely pleased by the offer. "No, but thanks. I can get a ride from here." He climbed out of the jigg before he could change his mind and stood for a moment leaning in the open door. "Be careful."

Tatian nodded. "You, too."

Warreven straightened, letting the door fall closed again behind him, and started toward the compound gate. He heard the whine of the engine as the jigg pulled away, but did not look back. There were four *mosstaas* guarding the gate, not the usual two—at least one of them armed, pellet gun and ironwood truncheon—and Warreven was careful to move slowly as he came into the light.

"I'm here to see Mir Temelathe," he said. "My name's Warreven."

The leader of the *mosstaas* looked less than pleased, and Warreven resigned himself to the tedious ritual of identifying himself to their satisfaction. They let him through after a dozen questions and two calls to the house while he stood under the lights for the imported security cameras, and Warreven walked up the long curve of the drive, deliberately slow to give himself time to control his temper.

The housekeeper, the same woman Warreven had seen the last time, was waiting again on the steps, but this time Aldess Donavie was waiting with her. She looked completely recovered, very elegant in the off-world style that was just becoming fashionable in the Stanelands *mesnies*, narrow trousers and vest under a heavily beaded *shaal*-coat. It looked like one of Folhare's designs, Warreven thought, irrelevantly, and the housekeeper stepped back to hold the door open. Aldess came to meet him, holding out both hands. She knew her status—Tendlathe's wife, Temelathe's daughter-in-law, blood daughter of Bradfot Donavie, the richest man on the Westland—and knew, too, that it would be acknowledged.

"Raven. It was good to see you at the reinstatement. I appreciated your coming."

Warreven took her hands, aware of metal rings, a broad metal bracelet, bigger and heavier than his own, and they mimed a kiss. "Not at all. I was sorry to hear of your loss."

Aldess waved that away. "I wish we'd seen you the other night. I know Tendlathe was disappointed."

I bet, Warreven thought. In the hallway lights, her coat glowed the deep blood scarlet of ruby melons, its subtle woven floral outlined in glittering flecks of red glass. Not Folhare's work—she was never so restrained in her designs, and besides, Aldess would never buy from her—but probably much more expensive. He said, "I was on business, and I didn't want to interrupt the party."

"You should have done," Aldess said. "We would have been glad to see you, and I know Tendlathe would like to congratulate you on becoming *seraaliste*. You must be very proud."

"I'm—enjoying the work," Warreven said, with perfect truth. He didn't trust Aldess, anymore than he trusted any Stane, and he was doubly wary when she was sent to meet him, doing what was properly a servant's job. Temelathe wanted something badly, to offer such an acknowledgment of status.

Aldess smiled, showing perfect teeth. Once, Warreven remembered, the front teeth had had a fractional gap between them; it had vanished within a year of her marriage. She tapped gently on the door of Temelathe's study, pushed it open without waiting for a response. "Warreven, father," she said, and Warreven walked past her into the little room.

Temelathe was sitting in his chair beside the stove, feet resting on a low stool of carved ironwood. The designs were worn away in places, the rounded shapes blurred, and Warreven wondered just how old the piece was. Ironwood was almost as hard as its namesake; it would have taken generations of use to blunt its glossy finish. The air smelled of *donettoil*, and looking closer, he could see the rough-cast bowl resting in the chamber of the stove, piled embers showing gray and orange. There was a wheel of milkcheese on the table, the hard brick-brown sailors' version, and a basket of flat sailors' bread, too: all the trappings of a casual visit, Warreven thought, but none of the reality.

"My father," he said, and knew he sounded as wary as he felt.

Temelathe waved toward the guest's chair. "Sit. No, wait, throw some more *donettoil* on the fire. This is almost gone."

The basket was sitting on top of the stove. Warreven filled the shallow scoop with the coarse, red-black grains—they were about the size of sea salt, the freshly dried kind that the old people preferred, before the mills had crushed it—then opened the stove door and sprinkled them cautiously over the embers. The first few flashed like lightning as they hit the coals, and then the rest stabilized, sending a fresh cloud of smoke into the room. Warreven inhaled its fragrance—sharp and almost oily, the various seeds and leaves that went into the compound blending into a bitter, complicated smoke, dominated by the chimetree resin—and turned back to the guest chair without taking any more. Temelathe watched him morosely, and Warreven could see that his eyes were subtly reddened by the smoke. How long have you been sitting here, my father, with only the stove for company? he wondered, but that was not the sort of question one could ask Temelathe. He said, "You asked to see me, and I'm here."

Temelathe nodded. "Which is something, I suppose. You're making my life very difficult, my son, I hope you know that."

Warreven said nothing. This was not what he'd expected when he'd received this summons, and he didn't know how to handle Temelathe in this mood.

"You're very good," Temelathe said, after a moment. "I'm almost sorry I ever encouraged you to take up the law."

He had used the creole term, not the traditional word that

meant both Haran statute law and the web of custom that gave it context. Warreven said, "Yes, I'm good at it. I warned you, my father."

Tatian grunted something, said, more clearly, "I could make life extremely difficult for NAPD. They'll have other contracts, you know, and not just with Stiller."

"We've—discussed—this before," Warreven said. *Though not so openly—what in all hells is he up to?* "The Big Six make all their contracts this way, favors done here and there, and they wouldn't thank you for throwing their usual methods into question."

"So you bring the whole question of trade into the courts," Temelathe said, "and you and your partners can posture to your hearts' content, and all the while we—my people, your people, the odd-bodied are my responsibility, too—lose their one decent source of income."

"Decent?" Warreven laughed.

"Are you ashamed of what you did, my son?" Temelathe asked.

His voice was deceptively mild, and he was not, Warreven thought, as drunk as he'd appeared. "No," he said, "of course not."

Temelathe tilted his head in unspoken question, and Warreven shook his head, managed a smile that was genuinely amused. "No, you won't bait me, my father. I didn't particularly enjoy it—I wasn't even particularly good at it—but, no, I'm not ashamed."

"Then why do you want to close down the trade? It's a safe space—this is a delicate balance, my son, the Six and I and IDCA and the Watch Council and now Tendlathe and his people. If trade ends, your kind will have no place left to go, and if you and Haliday keep pushing, I'm going to have to give you an answer, and there aren't any good ones. If I say yes, we'll follow the Concord, follow their laws, then IDCA will step in to regulate prostitution, and people like you, my son, will be whores all their lives. The *mesnies* will drop you from the rolls, the clans will pretend you don't exist, and you certainly would be neither *seraaliste* nor advocate. If I say no, we stand by our laws and custom, then Tend-lathe wins. I have to close the dance houses and the *wrangwys* bars and he and his have an excuse to go hunting you out. If I ignore the whole issue—if you and Haliday and the rest of you let me ignore it—then you all stay safe."

Warreven stared at him, knowing that everything he said was true, and not nearly enough of the truth. "The fact is, the odd-bodied exist. Sooner or later, my father, we—you, the Watch Council, the *mesnies*, even Tendlathe—are going to have to admit it. Better now, when you're running things, than when Ten takes over. We need names of our own."

"If you meant that, my son," Temelathe said, "you'd call yourself a herm, 3e, 3im—like Haliday."

That stung, especially since Tatian had said very nearly the same thing. Warreven said, "I call myself a man because you only allow two choices, and this was the closest fit. I call myself a man because I'm better at that than at being a woman—and certainly better at that than being Ten's wife." He stopped abruptly, tipped his head to one side in sudden question. "I've played by your rules, my father. I made my choice, I lived with it, but it won't ever be good enough, will it? I'm only a man as long as it's conve-nient for you."

Temelathe smiled, but said nothing.

"And if the bars are safe," Warreven went on, "how did Lam-masin die, my father?" He touched the mark on his forehead. "I came from his *memore.*"

Temelathe's smile vanished. "That was none of my doing, Warreven, I give you my word on that." Warreven said nothing, and the older man sighed. "The trouble with you, my son, is that you've always been able to figure out just about anything, but you've never had a grain of common sense with it. I've no use for those people myself. I wanted Lammasin out of work for a few months, not dead. Not a martyr. But now that they've tasted blood, it's going to be harder to keep them in line."

"In Bonemarche, they say that someone in the White Stane House paid off the *mosstaas* not to find the killers," Warreven said. *Which leaves Tendlathe, if it isn't you.* He left the words unsaid—he didn't need to say them; Temelathe would know as well as he what was meant—and Temelathe leaned back in his chair.

"Tendlathe and his friends are frightened. They don't like change, my son."

Which was as close to an admission as he was likely to get. Warreven took a deep breath, inhaling the smoke from the brazier, and felt the first familiar touch of the drug's lassitude. *Donettoil* had been a good choice, better than feelgood or dreamsafe; it relaxed without offering visions, made one less cautious, and less argumentative, too. He thought Temelathe was telling the truth, at least about Lammasin's death, stared at the glowing embers in the center of the stove. He said at last, "I know what I should say, that I'm not afraid of the ghost *ranas*, but I'm not that stupid. And I know Tendlathe's temper hasn't gotten any better. But people are angry. Lammasin was a good man."

"I know that," Temelathe answered, and visibly bit back something more. After a moment, he said, "I'm not happy with this contract, my son. Not at the price you're getting for it. I can't afford it. I'm not going to make it easy for you."

"I didn't expect you would," Warreven said. "With your permission, my father?"

Temelathe waved a hand. "Put another scoop on the fire, my son, as a favor, and you're free to go."

Warreven did as the older man asked, ladling out another measure of the *donettoil* and pouring it carefully onto the embers. Smoke billowed out more vigorously this time; he left Temelathe sitting in its cloud and made his way back out into the hallway.

It was quiet, quieter than he'd expected, no noises, none of the household *faitous* anywhere in sight, and he hesitated, startled by the silence. The air smelled of the night breeze, sea and salt and the night-blooming starshade; he looked around for the open window and instead saw the curtains that hid the garden doors moving in the fragrant air.

"Raven?" Tendlathe pushed the curtain aside, stood framed in the doorway. "Aldess said you were here. I'm glad I caught you."

Warreven hesitated again, searching hastily for an excuse—he was hardly in the mood for a conversation with Tendlathe—and the other managed a rueful smile.

"Look, I'm sorry about last time. I got carried away—it's something I feel strongly about."

"So do I," Warreven said. "I—feel strongly—about a lot of things, too."

"I know." Tendlathe glanced over his shoulder. "I got your message, and—look, we can't talk here. Come out in the garden with me?"

"Ten—" Warreven broke off, shaking his head. I don't want to talk to you because I think you caused a man's death, and I've just come from his *memore:* it was not a tactful comment, and at the best of times Tendlathe wasn't likely to respond well. And this was hardly the best of times.

"It's important," Tendlathe said. "Please?"

Warreven sighed. If Tendlathe was in a conciliatory mood— and he had to be, or he wouldn't bother being polite—it was worth swallowing his own anger to meet him halfway. "All right," he said aloud, and Tendlathe held aside the curtain. Warreven stopped under the hanging fabric, the silk gauze just brushing his head, and only then thought to wonder at the gesture. It was courtesy, certainly, but from a man to a woman, not between two men. He was being oversensitive—not surprising, after the events of the evening, but hardly useful. He shook himself, walked on down the path that curved away from the house. The light dimmed a little as Tendlathe came to join him, letting the curtain fall back into place. The low hedge that separated the upper terrace from the flower walk below was wound with starshade, the white flowers, large as a man's hand, almost luminous in the darkness. Their scent was heavy in the air, the honeyed sweetness almost drowning the smell of the sea.

"I know what you're thinking, Raven," Tendlathe said, "but I didn't do it."

Warreven glanced back at him, eyebrows rising in unspoken question, and Tendlathe made a face.

"I didn't kill Lammasin. I swear to you by the Captain, by the Watch and the clan, I didn't do it."

"I never thought you did it," Warreven said, after a moment, and saw something, relief, maybe, or possibly contempt, start to cross the other's face. "I never thought you stabbed him, or knocked him over the head, we don't know which yet, and then set the fire. Not personally. But I do think you know who did it, and I think you're responsible."

"That's not fair."

"Isn't it?" The light from the house was falling across Tendlathe's face, throwing half of it into shadow, striking a fugitive spark from the pin, anchor and flames, that closed his plain collar. Warreven watched him, an odd, clinical anger filling him. It was the same anger that sometimes consumed him in the courts, giving passion to his arguments, and he welcomed it, welcomed the power, the strength it brought him. "And would you swear to that, by the Captain, on Watch and clan, that you had no idea this would happen?"

Tendlathe opened his mouth, closed it again, and said at last, "Someone overstepped himself."

"What'd you have in mind, just beat him up, teach him a lesson?"

"Not exactly." Tendlathe glared at him. "But people are angry, Raven, angry and scared, and you might've known something like this would happen if you kept pushing things."

"Me?"

"You, Haliday, the rest of the Modernists."

Warreven laughed.

"God and the spirits!" Tendlathe reached out blindly, snatched a flower and a spray of leaves from the hedge, let them fall, crumpled, to the stones of the terrace.

"Oh, that's very helpful," Warreven said. He didn't think to be afraid until he saw Tendlathe's fist rise. He ducked, the reflexes honed in a dozen bar fights taking over, caught the other's wrist, forcing his hand down. He could feel the bones shift under his fingers, saw Tendlathe flinch, rage vanishing as quickly as it had appeared, didn't release his grasp until he felt the tension disappear from the other's arm. Tendlathe jerked himself free, swearing, and they stood facing each other in the dark, each a mirror image of the other. They had fought like this once before, years ago, over the marriage. Warreven remembered with painful, physical clarity how it had ended, himself finally astride Tendlathe, pinning him down, one hand in the tangle of his hair. They had lain there for a long instant, anger warring with unexpected, unwelcome desire, and then Warreven had pulled free and stalked away. He had thought he had won, until he felt the next morning's bruises and started to face the consequences of his decision.

He could see the same memory in Tendlathe's face, the color high on his cheeks, visible even in the dim light. Warreven took a deep breath, not wanting this to end the same way, and said flatly, "So what did you want, Tendlathe?"

Tendlathe blinked, head lifting, a little movement, but it was as if he'd been slapped. Something, regret, shame, anger, was briefly visible in his face, and then it was gone, his expression controlled again, shuttered, all emotion suppressed. "I was going to offer you a deal. Drop this case—I don't want Father to bring in the off-worlders, let them get their hands in our government—drop this case, and I'll see that those women of yours are left alone."

"Women?" For a moment, Warreven didn't understand, then remembered the marketwomen outside the Blue Watch House. If the ghost *ranas* or even the *mosstaas* turned on them, they would have no way of defending themselves. Even if Folhare and Haliday had managed to talk their *ranas*, the Modernist *ranas*, into offering protection, it might not be enough, not against the ghost *ranas*— And then they would have to wait for another case, another chance, to question Hara's laws, to bring them into line with the Concord—with reality—never mind what it would do to Destany and 'Aukai. "You bastard," he said, almost conversationally, and turned, and walked back up the path toward the house.

"You'll regret this, Raven. I promise you."

Warreven lifted a hand, jerked it upward, an ageless, universal gesture, but kept walking. He might have won—though, like the last time, he'd have to wait until morning to be sure—but he didn't like the potential cost.

9

wrangwys:
  (Hara) literally, "wrong way," generally used to refer to herms, mems,
  and fems, and anyone whose sexual preferences don't match the male/
  female model; has been adopted by that group as a self-referential term,
  and is not insulting within the group.

WARREVEN

The housekeeper was able to find a rover for hire—and a good thing, too, Warreven thought; he had no desire to see anything more of the Stanes—and he waited on the steps while the driver maneuvered the awkward vehicle up the long drive. The driver was stocky and good-looking, with a beardless face and a line like a scar at the corner of his mouth that deepened when he smiled. He held the door politely as Warreven climbed into the passenger compartment, then returned to his place behind the steering bar. He wasn't too proud to take the tip the housekeeper discreetly offered, palming the *assignats* with the ease of long practice. Or maybe þe was a mem, Warreven thought suddenly, looking at the other's body, the straight, blocky lines, a solid cylinder from shoulders to hips. Certainly he was dressed as a man—almost aggressively so, if he was passing, trousers and tunic cut on exaggerated lines. But then, the odd-bodied had to pass, no matter what Temelathe said. Even Haliday passed at times, either as man or woman.

The driver edged the rover through the compound gates, past the *mosstaas*—a different foursome—lounging against the columns. The driver kept his head down as they slid past, eyes fixed on the road; Warreven nodded and smiled, enjoying the play of status. Then the rover had turned down the first main street, and Warreven saw the driver's shoulders relax a little.

"Where to now, mir?"

Warreven sighed. Under other circumstances, he would head
for Harborside, but tonight it seemed wiser to avoid the district.
"Blind Point," he said. "Just north of the light—I'll direct you
when we get there."

The driver nodded. "No problem, mir."

The rover turned again, onto the winding street that led down
from Ferryhead to the edge of the Harbor. It was well lit, and
lights showed in the upper windows and in the courtyard entrances; there were people visible as well through those openings,
men and women silhouetted against the lights. Things looked almost normal—but of course they could, in Ferryhead, Warreven
thought. Ferryhead was where the Stanes—the White Stanes—
and their allies lived, and all the rest of the clan officers who made
their very good livings dealing with the off-worlders. Of course
things would look—would be—normal: they paid the *mosstaas*
very well to make sure it was true. Despite the almost reflexive
bitterness of the thought, he was relaxing, the tension easing from
his back and shoulders. There would be things he could do to
counter Tendlathe, or, if he couldn't, Haliday or Folhare would
know who could.

Harborside itself seemed busier than ever, lights blazing on
the docks, and on the bars and dance houses rising up the side of
the hill. From this angle, the burned-out bars on Dock Row were
invisible; there were just the lights, vivid and inviting. Even
through the rover's filters, the air smelled hot, heavy with feelgood and a dozen other compounds, and the sound of drums came
with them. Warreven sighed, and saw the driver glance up into his
mirror. "Sure you don't want to stop, mir?"

Warreven smiled, meeting the dark eyes. "All my—friends—
are at sea. I'd hate to be alone."

The driver shrugged, one-shouldered, still looking in the mirror. "That could be fixed pretty easily."

"I appreciate that," Warreven said, and matched the faint,
rueful smile he could see reflected. "But it was a hard meeting, I
doubt I'd be good for much of anything."

The driver shrugged again, both shoulders this time. "Blind
Point, then, mir."

They turned onto Tredhard Street, the rover's engine groaning as it matched the incline. Warreven looked back, to see the *ranas* still drumming on their makeshift stage. The listening crowd seemed larger, too, and the *mosstaas* were nowhere to be seen.

"They've been at it all night," the driver volunteered.

Warreven nodded again, settling himself against the padded seat. They had reached the intersection of Dock Row, and for a moment he imagined he could smell the ashes, the remains of the fire. The street's power hadn't been fully restored, either; there were gaps in the lines of light, and a number of the signs flickered and fizzed, throwing erratic shadows. The driver turned down the next street, heading north toward Blind Point, and Warreven was suddenly aware of gaps in the line of houselights, of glass shattered in front of every other house.

"What the hell—?" he began, and the shadows seemed abruptly thicker, shapes moving against the motion of the rover.

"Shit," the driver said, and slammed the throttle forward. The engine snarled in protest, choking as the system tried to handle the rush of fuel, and then the *ranas* were all around them, tattered black robes dull in the uncertain light. One of them held a drum hoop—white as bone, white as fire, empty—while another held the white-painted frame for a ceramic gong. They stood frozen, a ring of white-faced, white-handed ghosts surrounding the rover, and then the drummer lifted a white-painted stick and began to mime a steady beat. One of the others swooped close and peered in the window by the driver's face. The one carrying the gong frame gestured as though to strike it, and the *ranas* froze again.

A couple of them carried clubs held loose at their sides; at least two more carried the jointed lengths of ironwood that trail walkers used against unfriendly mountain spiders. They were blocking the street ahead of the rover; Warreven didn't dare move to look back, but guessed that there would be as many behind the car. Then the one carrying the gong frame struck again, and the drummer took up the beat. The *rana* closest to the rover leaned toward the passenger compartment, and Warreven met the white-masked stare. The eyeholes were covered with tinted glass;

he caught only the faintest sense of movement, of the shift of human eyes behind the dark lenses.

"Drive," he said, and leaned forward to punch the driver's shoulder.

The driver shot him a frightened glance—there were *ranas* in front of the rover, and behind it, no place to go without running them over—and the *rana* pushed himself back from the rover's side, reaching for something he'd held concealed in his ragged robe. Warreven caught a single glimpse of the length of chain—metal chain, stolen surely from the starport, five eight-centimeter-long links of polished metal—and punched the driver's shoulder again.

"Drive, damn it!"

The driver hit the throttle again, and the rover lurched forward. In the same moment, the length of chain swept down, shattering the long side window. Warreven ducked away from the rain of glass, saw the driver duck, too, but the rover kept moving forward, picking up speed. The *ranas* dodged back, scattering in confusion, and the driver swayed upright again, sent the rover skidding down the narrow street. Warreven looked back, ready to duck again, and saw the ghost *ranas* standing in the roadway, miming laughter. Then the rover had turned the first corner, heading back toward the relative safety of Dock Row, and he straightened cautiously. He was shaking—he'd been lucky, the glass had missed him, but it had been close, too close—and leaned forward to touch the driver's shoulder.

"Are you all right?"

"Yeah, no," the driver said, his voice shaken. "Maybe—I will be."

Warreven looked into the mirror, saw the driver's face reflected, marked with a line of blood. The rover swung around the next corner and turned onto Dock Row, into the flickering lights of the dance houses. "Pull over, let me see."

The driver eased the rover into the curb, into the relatively steady light of a houselamp. Rather than risk the shattered glass that covered half the passenger seat, Warreven climbed out through the street-side door and came around the rover's nose to peer in the driver's half of what had been the window. Behind him, a few of the people who had been waiting in the doors of the bars and the dance houses moved a few steps closer, not knowing whether or not they would need to intervene. Warreven ignored them, stooped to lean into the empty window. "Let me see," he said again.

The driver turned to face him. The breaking glass had scored a long cut from cheekbone to jawline, and the blood was still welling sluggishly from it; there was more blood on his shoulder, staining the pale fabric of his shirt. "It's not so bad," he said, and fumbled for something in one of the storage compartments. "I'll be all right."

Warreven eyed him uncertainly, and a voice said, behind him, "Is everything all right?"

He turned to face a big man, the sort of ex-docker the rowdier *wrangwys* houses hired to keep the peace. He was staring at the rover with a kind of detached curiosity, as though he were wondering if they were going to bleed on his employer's property, or if they could safely be sent elsewhere. Warreven took a deep breath, wondering how to explain, and the driver leaned past him, putting his head out the smashed window.

"Belbarb. Thank the spirits it's you."

"Trouble?" the big man asked, looking at Warreven, and his hand went to the docker's hook stuffed into his belt beneath the loose fabric of his vest.

The driver nodded. "Yeah, but not with him. We ran into a ghost *rana*, the bastards—they smashed the window into me." He started to say more, winced, and pressed his shirt fabric against the cut. "Bastards."

Belbarb nodded, looked from him to Warreven. "Are you all right, mir?"

"Fine," Warreven answered, and shook his head, looking at the driver's face in the light from the houselamp. "That looks like it could use a weld."

The driver started to shake his head, but Belbarb said, "He's right, Fisk, that does need some work. I think Marrin's upstairs— you can leave the rover here, I'll square the *mosstaas.*"

Warreven took a step back as the driver opened his door, wondering what to do. He wanted to get home, he had work to do in the morning, but he had no desire to brave the *ranas* again, at least not yet— Fisk stumbled, and Warreven caught his arm, steadying him. "Are you sure you don't want to go to a clinic?"

"Marrin's all right," Fisk said, and Belbarb nodded.

"He's an off-worlder, a medic, he—rents here. He knows what he's doing." His eyes swept over Warreven, across his chest and hips, came to rest on the metal bracelets. "You'll be wanting a drink, mir."

Warreven nodded. "Thanks. I'm Warreven. Stiller, of the Ambreslight *mesnie.*"

"Belbarb Stiller." The big man nodded again, this time with approval, and stooped to take half of Fisk's weight. "Come on, Fiskie, let's get you inside. Illewedyr, go get Marrin, will you?"

Warreven followed them into the unexpected quiet of the bar. The music had stopped, drummers and a flute player standing idle beside the little dance floor, and the rest of the customers had gathered in fours and fives, muttering angrily. They were a mix of off-worlders and indigenes: another trade bar, Warreven thought, and leaned heavily against the bar. A thin, pale man with sun-darkened hands and face—Marrin, certainly—shoved his way through the groups to drop a medikit on one of the tables. The flute player did something with a control board, and one of the spotlights turned and tilted, catching the table in its light. Fisk sank into the waiting chair, and Marrin bent over him, muttering to himself. The noise rose in the bar again, angry voices tumbling over each other, and the bartender moved toward Warreven, her eyes still sliding to the table where the medic worked.

"What can I get you?" she asked, and seemed to catch some message from Belbarb. "It's on the house."

"Thanks," Warreven answered. "Bingo, if you have it."

Bingo was the strongest of the Haran liquors. The woman nodded and came back in a few seconds with a narrow glass half filled with the faintly cloudy liquid. Warreven drank half of it in a gulp, the stuff searing his throat, and took another, more cautious sip. "I suppose the *mosstaas* should be called."

"Oh, æ," Belbarb said, and lowered his bulk onto the stool beside Warreven. "We can call, but if they'll come—or if they'd do anything once they got here—well, that's the question, isn't it? Fisk's a *dandi*, and wry-abed to boot. Do you think they'll work on this one? Would you pay for it, mir?"

Warreven flicked a glance at him. So Fisk was a mem, and even the protection of the bars, the safety Temelathe had been preaching, didn't extend to calling in the law. But of course Belbarb was right, too: it was unlikely the *mosstaas* would do much for þim. "I will. I doubt it'll do any good, but I will. And put my name to the complaint, if that'll help."

"I doubt it," Belbarb said. "No offense, mir, but you're one of us."

Warreven sighed. "I agree, I doubt it'll help. But I think you ought to get it on record."

Belbarb glanced at the clock above the door, its round display showing the moon almost down, and the time floating above the star pattern. It was less than an hour to legal closing. "Let's wait until Marrin's finished, æ? Better all around."

"All right," Warreven said. The bar would be closing by the time the medic had finished welding the cut closed, and Fisk had had a drink or two to kill the pain and settle his nerves. Belbarb couldn't risk calling the *mosstaas* without driving off the off-worlders who didn't want to be known as players. Nothing would be gained by calling them earlier, anyway: if the rumors were true—and after tonight, he had no doubt that they were—Tendlathe was protecting the ghost *ranas*, and the *mosstaas* wouldn't argue with him. I wonder if he's doing more than protecting them? he thought suddenly. Ten could have set this up, set me up. . . . It wasn't a pleasant thought, and he was glad to push it away. The timing was wrong, and he couldn't have known the rover's route. He and Fisk had just been unlucky, and there was enough of that in Bonemarche to go around.

clan-cousin:
> (Hara) technically, a man or woman within one's own age cohort in the shared clan who is not otherwise related; in common usage, a man or woman of one's clan to whom one feels some tie or obligation, but to whom one is not more closely related; the use of the term generally expresses a sense of affection and kinship between the people concerned.

MHYRE TATIAN

Warreven was late that afternoon, arriving with the end of the early rain, an insulated jug in one hand, disks and link-board in the other. 3e was still dressed in the clothes 3e had worn at the *memore*, a dull bronze silk tunic with a faint, geometric pattern woven into its surface, and 3er usual loose trousers. 3er hair was pulled back in an untidy braid, and Tatian wondered—not without some envy—where 3e had spent the night. Warreven smiled as though 3e'd read the thought and set the jug on Tatian's desk.

"Help yourself, it's *wiidwayk.*"

"No, thanks." To Tatian, the herbal brew tasted like sugared turpentine, though the indigenes seemed to drink it by the gallon.

"Suit yourself," Warreven said. 3e unstoppered the jug and drank, then set it aside, saying, "I'm sorry I'm late. I had—kind of a busy night and slept in."

Tatian wrinkled his nose as the smell of the *wiidwayk* drifted toward him. It seemed as though it had been months since he'd had a "busy night" of his own, since he'd broken with Prane Am, who still hadn't gotten back to him about the interface box. "No problem. I'm glad you're here, though. We need to get these papers signed." He was pleased with the speed with which the terms had fallen into place, once he'd confirmed his interest.

"I know." Warreven wrapped his hands around the jug, looked at it for a long moment. "The ghost *ranas*—on the way back from seeing Temelathe last night, a band of them broke in the window of my rover. Fisk—the man driving—got a nasty cut from the glass, and I ended up spending the night in a Harborside bar. And then I had to go to the *mosstaas* with him—no luck there, of course, but at least the complaint was filed."

"Jesus," Tatian said. "Are you all right?"

Warreven smiled again. "Fine—tired, but fine. And Fisk is all right, too. There was a medic there, an off-worlder, who took care of him."

"Glad to hear it," Tatian said. A player, he added mentally, automatically, but that doesn't make him any less competent.

"There is something you should know," Warreven said. "Before we sign, I mean. The Most Important Man wants me to, well, I suppose *revise* is the word, our contract, and he's prepared to make it as hard as possible for you to go on doing business here if I, if you, don't."

Tatian looked down at his desktop, at the screens scattered beneath the opaque surface. The profit projections lay on top, Mats' shipping report beside it—they had export permits and starcrates for the most valuable goods, and Mats was reporting that the indigenous Export Control Office was asking only a few hundred concord dollars in extra "fees" to process the remaining permits—and he shook his head slowly. "So far, we haven't had any trouble. And we always pay our way. What's the problem?"

"Reiss," Warreven said. "Or, more precisely, this case of ours, Destany and 'Aukai."

Tatian snorted. After all the effort he'd gone to—after the chances he was taking, standing up to the IDCA, risking NAPD's hard-won position on Hara—to be told that Warreven was backing out was too much. Warreven tilted 3er head to one side.

"I don't intend to change my position," 3e said. 3e laughed then, sounding genuinely amused. "I don't like being threatened, and anyway, it's not like I had any desire to run for *seraaliste* next year. I still want Reiss's statement, and as far as I'm concerned it's still part of the price. But I thought I owed you the warning."

"Why?"

Warreven blinked. "I prefer to do business when people understand all the risks. Besides, I like you."

"Thanks. But I meant, why stand up to Temelathe, especially now? Why does this case matter so much?" Tatian shrugged.

"Look, I don't want to be rude, but there are a couple of cases like this every year. Can't you wait for the next one, if you want to make a point?"

Warreven looked away. The thick braid of 3er hair fell forward over 3er shoulder, and 3e worried at its end, twisting it between long fingers. The gesture seemed strangely familiar, and then Tatian remembered the woman he had been involved with on Joshua, long-limbed, long-haired Kaysa, who had done just that whenever she was nervous about something. It was no wonder he found Warreven attractive; 3e shared some of her tricks of movement and gesture.

"The truth?" 3e said, and let 3er braid fall back into place. "A lot of reasons, I suppose. I'm tired of waiting—after all, there's never going to be a good time, by definition, right? And it's not right. All Destany wants is to be with zher lover, that shouldn't be this difficult."

Tatian blinked, startled to hear the off-world pronoun, however badly pronounced, and Warreven sighed again.

"And on top of that, I don't like 'Aukai. I've never liked 'Aukai. So I don't want to give up on her case. And Tendlathe isn't Speaker yet, no matter what he thinks he is. So, I'm telling you now, Reiss's statement stays part of the bargain. If you don't want to take the risk—if you can't afford to stay in the game—" 3e spread 3er hands. "That's your choice, of course."

But you lose the harvest surplus. Tatian looked down at his screens again, at the numbers spread across the multiple files. Masani had already given ðer opinion; the final choice was, as always, up to him. *The numbers are too good, the profit's too high to lose,* he thought. *If it's a real problem, ðe can transfer me next year, that ought to satisfy Temelathe—and I can't say I'd be that sorry to get off this crazy planet. . . .* He stopped then, remembering Masani's words: '*I spent eight local years explaining myself,*' ðe had said, but it was more than that, more that no one, not the IDCA and ColCom, not the indigenes, had been able to see ðer as ðerself. That was the other factor in the equation, the joker in the pack. The system, trade, the whole bizarre two-gendered Haran worldview, was simply wrong; Warreven was right, the IDCA spent too much time trying to manage trade, and not enough time facing the implications of the system they were trying to control. If they really wanted to deal with HIVs, they could spend more of their time and effort looking for whatever it was that gave Harans their immunity. "I don't see any reason to change my plans," he said. "Reiss has said he wants to testify. As long as that holds true, I'll back him."

"Thanks," Warreven said softly, and then straightened, pushing the disks across the desktop. "Shall we get on with it, then?"

Tatian nodded, and ran his hand over the shadowscreen to bring the proper window to the surface. At the same time, the blockwriter whined to life, and he slipped the first disk into the reader's slot. There were no changes to the contracts—they had been straightforward enough; it had only been Reiss's testimony that made things complicated—but Warreven read through the last drafts a final time, head bowed over 3er screen. Then 3e nodded, and scrawled 3er name across the touchscreen, then added the codes that confirmed both 3er identity and 3er authority as *seraaliste.* The blockwriter whined again, copying the file and then sealing the disk, and Tatian allowed himself a sigh of relief. It was good to have them signed—good not to have to keep making and unmaking his decisions, good to be committed to this one. He said aloud, "I understand some of your offering is already in port?"

Warreven nodded, tipped 3er head to one side, the corners of 3er mouth turning up in 3er familiar almost smile. "I suppose you'd like to look at samples."

"I would."

"I thought you might," Warreven said. "I spoke to our captain, he'll be expecting us."

They took the company rover over to Harborside, left it parked on Dock Row in an empty lot beside one of the bars. It was open, and Warreven spoke briefly to the manager, a thin, worried-looking woman, before coming back to join Tatian. "She says it should be safe there, even with a company mark."

Warreven sounded less than certain, and Tatian sighed, thinking of his budget if he had to get the rover repaired. Still, his predecessor had bought the rover on-planet; it wouldn't be impossible to replace, he thought, and turned to look across the roofs of the Embankment to the docks below. The clouds had burned off, and the afternoon was unusually clear. Sea and sky were blue, flecked here and there with white, and the pale wood and stone of the Gran'quai itself seemed to glow in the harsh sunlight. The market in the foreground was almost empty, only the food sellers and a few vendors with carts snugged up to the power points on the southern perimeter; the rest of the stalls were empty, just painted white lines marking their divisions. The *rana* band was still there, though, still dancing on its makeshift stage—only two drummers now, and a woman who held a flute—as was the audience. That was larger than Tatian had remembered, maybe fifty or sixty people, most of them wearing the bright ribbons that Warreven had said meant they were members of the band. There were dockworkers on the edge of the group, conspicuous in their faded, practical clothes, and more were watching from the Gran'quai itself.

"I don't see the *mosstaas*," he said aloud, and Warreven glanced back at him. A few strands of hair had worked free of 3er braid and clung damply to 3er forehead.

"Over there," 3e said, and pointed. "By the Customs House."

Tatian looked again and saw three people—all men, by the look of them—standing in the arched doorway. They didn't seem to be doing anything, but people were giving them a wide berth, and then, there was the empty Market. "Trouble?" he asked, and Warreven shrugged.

"I don't think so. Come on."

3e led the way down a narrow street—no stairs this time, but the pitch was still steep enough that Tatian wished there had been steps. They crossed the open Market, the drumming, a steady, even beat that kept the dancers moving in easy patterns, loud enough to drown conversation. Tatian felt the looks as they passed, the shifts of expression that registered an off-world presence, and for the first time, he was aware of the weight of the ironwood dockers' hooks that hung at people's belts. More people carried the tall sticks, ordinary wood rather than the fire-tempered ironwood, wound with multicolored ribbons: *Not as deadly as the hooks*, Tatian thought, *but effective enough in a brawl.* They seemed peaceful enough, however, mostly caught up in the rhythm of the drums, but he was still glad when they crossed the wide stone ledge that marked the edge of the Market and came out onto the wood of the Gran'quai.

The dock was crowded, the usual mix of sailors and dockers and factors, but not as busy, most of the dockers standing idle, clustered around their machines or beside the heaps of cargo. Halfway down the dock, hot air shimmered over a crane's engine compartment, and a little further half a dozen men and women wrestled a gangplank into place while the ship's captain watched from the stern rail, dividing her attention between the dockers and the *ranas* in the Market.

"We're down here," Warreven said. "Berth seven."

Tatian nodded, squinted through the sun along the row of ships. In the strong light, the colors bled together; it was hard to tell where one ship ended and the next began. He shaded his eyes with one hand, picked out a shore barge, broader beamed than the rest, riding high and so nearly empty, and then a snub-nosed coaster, its wheelhouse painted with a crowing cock. The image was startling, on Hara, and then he remembered that one of the Captain's symbols was the rooster.

Suddenly, someone shouted behind them, a high, wordless cry of anger, and Tatian swung to see a fibreplast-walled cargo shay turning into the open space of the Market. A second shay followed, pulling to a stop a dozen meters from the first. Their cargo spaces were filled with dark-helmeted *mosstaas*, maybe twenty men in each; the sun glinted dully from their fibreplast riot shields. Tatian caught his breath—there weren't enough of them to take on that crowd, not easily; people were going to get hurt—and then a single man, shoulders badged with the five-feathers badge of a commander, swung himself down out of the lead shay. He started for the makeshift stage, striding without haste across the Market, and the crowd made way for him, sullen, conscious of the other *mosstaas* waiting in the shays behind him.

"God and the spirits," Warreven said. "He's brave enough."

"Stupid," Tatian said, and heard his voice tight and frightened. They were trapped on the Gran'quai; if the *mosstaas* charged the crowd, they would have nowhere to run, except back onto the quay itself. He heard engines behind him, glanced over his shoulder, and saw smoke belching from the engine compartment of the nearest coaster. Clearly, its captain had come to the same conclusion, and was ready to cut and run. Another engine burped to life, and then a third.

The *mosstaas* commander had reached the platform and swung himself up easily. The drummers stopped, their song petering out into a last ragged flurry of notes. The flute player stepped back a meter, giving him room, but made no other move.

"You're in violation of the laws governing political assemblies." The *mosstaas* commander's voice carried clearly: either the platform was miked, Tatian thought, or he had brought his own loudhailer.

"We're not political." That was the flute player, her voice as clear as the commander's. "We're a *rana*, nothing more."

"I know her," Warreven said. "That's Faireigh—she's a chanter, one of the important ones."

The *mosstaas* commander shook his head. "I don't see a singer. This is no *rana*, people, either you go home quietly, or we'll disperse you ourselves."

There were shouts from the crowd, quickly quelled, the first instinct for defiance hushed by more sensible neighbors. Faireigh glared at the *mosstaas*, hands on hips, a big gesture, nicely calculated. Then, slowly, she turned back to the microphone. "You hear the man, we're not a *rana*—we're violating the assembly laws." There was a shout of protest at that, and she lifted her hands, quieting the crowd with a gesture. "I won't say you don't have a point, but we're not the violent ones here. We don't want to see the innocent hurt, or even threatened. We're willing to go—but since the man wants a song, I'll sing us out, this time." She took a deep breath, began before the *mosstaas* commander could protest, her clear voice cutting easily through the confused noise.

"*Our boots and shoes are all in pawn—*"

The crowd caught up the next line, a ragged, angry chorus. *"Go down, you blood-red roses, go down."*

Tatian caught his breath. He had heard the song before—it was a long-haul *chaunt*, something the sailors used raising anchor or hauling lighters along the coastal canals—but he'd never heard that note of snarling fury before. Warreven threw back 3er head and laughed aloud, the long braid dancing across 3er back. "Oh, she's good, Faireigh is, there's nothing they can to do stop her."

"You hope," Tatian said.

"Not a thing," Warreven said, and bared teeth in a suddenly feral grin. "It's an old song, old as Earth, everybody knows it doesn't have anything to do with politics."

"The foreman says, before I'm through," Faireigh sang, and the crowd answered instantly.

"Go down, you blood-red roses, go down."
"You'll hate your mother for having you."

Behind her on the platform, the *mosstaas* commander stood with his arms crossed, trying to look as though he was in control of the situation. Warreven opened 3er mouth and added 3er clear contralto, slightly off-key, to the chorus.

"Oh, you pinks and posies.
Go down, you blood-red roses, go down."

Tatian glanced warily at 3im, then back at the stage as Faireigh lifted her hands to encompass the singers.

"It's growl you may but go you must.
Go down, you snow-white roses, go down."

The crowd staggered in its echo as people realized belatedly what she'd said, and Faireigh swept on.

"If you growl too loud, your head they'll bust."

This time, the chorus came clear, all the pent-up anger displaced into the changed words. *"Go down, you snow-white roses, go down."*

"Oh, how stones are roses," Faireigh sang—as if anyone needed it made any clearer, Tatian thought, and glanced quickly sideways. The *mosstaas* still stood unmoving, penned in their shays.

The chorus was a savage affirmation. *"Go down, you snow-white roses, go down."*

Faireigh waited for the last voice to die away, then bowed to the *mosstaas* commander—the irony was visible even from Tatian's distance—and climbed down off the platform. The drummers followed her, instruments tucked awkwardly under arms, and the crowd made way for them as though they were royalty. Already, the people on the fringes, on the Market side and by the makeshift stage, were starting to edge away; the crowd was dispersing, as ordered, but on its own terms. Tatian shook his head.

"There's going to be hell to pay for this one," he said.

Warreven looked at him, still smiling. "Maybe. Probably, even. But it's been a long time coming." 3e took a deep breath, looking back at the people moving away from the stage.

"Warreven!"

"Haliday?" Warreven tilted 3er head to one side. "I might've known you'd be here."

The herm grinned back at 3im. "How could I miss this? Damn, Faireigh's good."

"She is," Warreven agreed, and glanced at Tatian. "I don't think you've met my partner, Haliday. Mhyre Tatian."

"Not properly," Tatian agreed.

"I saw you at the *memore*," Haliday said, and held out 3er hand. Tatian took it, studying the newcomer. 3e was rather ordinary, for the herm who had challenged Hara's gender laws in the planet's courts, a stocky, brown-skinned person with close-cut dark hair and wide, prominent cheekbones. Not as handsome as Warreven, Tatian thought, and was startled by his own response. Haliday released his hand, looked back to Warreven.

"Raven, but I need to talk to you."

"Can it wait?" Warreven tilted 3er head toward the offworlder. "We were here to look at the surplus samples."

"It's important," Haliday said. "I wouldn't interrupt if it weren't."

Warreven sighed. "I'm sorry, Tatian. The captain—Aylese, his name is—knows to expect you, he'll show you what you need."

Tatian stared back at 3im, wanting to protest, recognizing the futility of it. He would do well enough with the ship's captain, anyway, in some ways better without Warreven to explain away discrepancies between the labeling and the actual product. It was just—it was dangerous to stand up against the *mosstaas* right now, when trade was coming into question. There was too much at stake to risk everything in the streets, too much chance of losing. . . . He saw Warreven smile again, saw the same glee reflected in Haliday's plain face, and couldn't find the words that would convince either of them. "Be careful," he said at last, and wasn't surprised when Warreven looked blankly at him. "Just—be careful."

---

jackamie:
   (Hara) literally "boyfriend"; always a very casual term that can easily become an insult.

WARREVEN

He watched Tatian walk away down the length of the Gran'quai, golden hair vivid in the sunlight, looked back at Haliday with a frown. "I should be going with him. This better be important, Hal."

"It is." Haliday took his elbow, turned him toward the Market. "There's going to be a meeting of all of the Modernist groups, and all of us *wrangwys*. The way the *mosstaas* dispersed the crowd, God and the spirits, we've got our chance. That was too blatant, even for them, stopping a perfectly ordinary *rana* when they haven't made an attempt to track down the ghost *ranas*. This is something everyone can rally behind."

Warreven nodded, feeling the excitement rising in his chest. Haliday was right, this might be the thing they needed to bring the people who weren't interested in the odd-bodied's problems, who pretended trade didn't exist because it made them uncomfortable to think too much about it, onto their side. The *mosstaas* had overstepped: Faireigh's *rana* had been well within the limits of custom, if not strictly of law, and they had been silenced—but these ghost *ranas* were outside both law and custom and were allowed to act. "It could work," he said, and knew his tone belied the cautious words.

"It will work," Haliday said, fiercely. "The meeting's tonight at the twentieth, at Bon'Ador."

"Then why—" Warreven began, and Haliday waved the complaint away.

"We—you and me and Folhare and Lunebri and Illewedyr and anybody else we can find—need to start putting together some ideas for proper *ranas*. Something we can show them, give them something to start off with."

Warreven nodded. "You want me to find Folhare?" It was a good guess; everyone knew they were old friends.

"If you could, that would be great."

Warreven nodded. "I'll try. She'll be working—at the workshop, I mean, not trade."

"She's more likely to listen to you," Haliday said. "I don't think she likes me much—" 3e broke off then, eyes fixing on something, someone on the far side of the Market. Warreven followed the direction of 3er gaze and swore under his breath. The man standing between two empty stalls, just where the shadow of the Customs House touched the foot of the Embankment stairs, was unmistakable, and, as unmistakably, he had seen and recognized them, and started across the empty Market to meet them.

"What the hell is Tendlathe doing here?" he said, and Haliday spat on the stones at 3er feet.

"I can't talk to him, I can't even be civil to that bastard."

"Fine," Warreven said. "I'll talk to him. You go on, get everybody together, and I'll meet you—where?"

"My place," Haliday answered, already walking away. "Or Bon'Ador, if it gets late."

"I'll be there," Warreven said, and advanced to meet Temelathe's son.

"Warreven." Tendlathe stopped a meter from him, lifting a hand to shade his eyes. "Was that Haliday?"

"Yes." Warreven kept the sun behind him, grateful for even that petty advantage. Tendlathe looked tired, heavy shadows under his eyes, and his beard looked as though it hadn't been trimmed in days. Warreven allowed himself a moment of satisfaction—after the night before, Tendlathe had no right to look less than tired—then brought his emotions under control. He had been stupid to let Tendlathe bait him; he wouldn't let it happen again. "What brings you to the Market, Ten?"

"I might ask you the same question." Tendlathe turned so that he was out of the sun and stood beside Warreven, looking back toward the Embankment and the bars of Dock Row above it. The burned-out shells of the bars made a conspicuous gap in the orderly row, and Warreven made a face, seeing it, thinking of the ghost *ranas*.

"I had business here—I am *seraaliste* now, remember, thanks to your father."

"So you're going through with that contract?" Tendlathe asked. His voice was mild, deceptively so, and Warreven lifted an eyebrow at him.

"Yes, I'm going through with it. I told you that last night. I'm not going to change my mind."

"You're making a mistake, dealing with these people," Tendlathe said.

"It's hardly Stane business, it's our contract," Warreven said, deliberately misunderstanding, and Tendlathe scowled.

"It's Stane business, my business, because it's politics. The system works as it stands—works very well, Raven, especially for your kind. I don't know why you have to try to change it now."

Warreven looked at him, silhouetted against the stage platform. The *mosstaas* commander was crouched on one corner, talking to a pair of troopers. "But it doesn't work, Ten. You know that as well as I do."

"It works well enough," Tendlathe said, and sounded almost conciliatory. "We don't need changes, not if it brings in the offworlders."

"Are you crazy?" Warreven glared at him. "We've already changed. We've been dealing with the off-worlders for exactly a hundred years, of course we've changed, only the system hasn't caught up with us. And it's breaking down because people like you won't admit it."

Tendlathe shook his head. "No, the system's breaking down because people like you—" He waved his hand, the gesture barely indicating Warreven's body. "—*gellions, halvings*, you don't, you won't admit there's something wrong with you."

"Fine," Warreven said, through clenched teeth. His good intentions evaporated, fueled by the anger and the fear of the night before. "Treat it like it's my fault for being born. But I do exist, we exist, *halvings*—" He broke off, angry that he'd used the old word, substituted the creole terms, awkward on the tongue. "—herms, mems, fems, and we've existed since our people left Earth. You can't possibly believe it's sin, unresisted entropy, whatever the *vieuvants* are calling it these days. Hyperlumin is mutagenic, it made us—space travel made us, you can't go FTL without the drug."

"That's what the off-worlders say," Tendlathe said. His face was tight and set behind the thin beard. "It's their excuse. But we don't have to be like them. We're not the same."

"We're not that different, either," Warreven said. "You talk like they're aliens or something."

"They are," Tendlathe answered. "In every way that matters, they are aliens. That's what this is really about, Raven, don't you see? We aren't like them, and we can't become like them. We, what we are, is too important, we're all that's left of what people, human beings, are supposed to be, and if we change, that's lost forever."

Warreven stared at him for a long moment, shook his head to hide the fact that he had no idea what he should say. He could smell dried broadleaf kelp, wondered if a crate had broken open somewhere along the Gran'quai. "We've already changed. We're the same species," he said at last, and wasn't surprised when Tendlathe shook his head.

"Not anymore we're not. And I refuse to believe that they are human."

"You're fucking crazy," Warreven said.

Tendlathe laughed. "I'm right. Right for Hara, anyway, right for us. Just because I recognize the truth doesn't make me crazy."

"If they're not human," Warreven said slowly, "what does

that make me, Ten? I'm a herm, that's real, I've got tits and a cock and a cunt, and what does that make me?"

"You can pass for a man," Tendlathe said, after a moment. "You can make the effort."

"Pass for human," Warreven said bitterly. "Fuck you, Tendlathe." He turned away, blind angry even in the relative shade, started toward the stairs that led to the Embankment. Tendlathe's voice floated after him.

"I meant what I said, Warreven."

Warreven swung around, seeing the dark shape against the sunset sky. "So did I."

He took the long way to Blind Point, as much to give himself time to calm down as to avoid the streets where the ghost *ranas* had been seen. At the fountain that marked the intersection of Hauksey and Blakelams streets, he stopped and scooped water from the pool, splashing some on his face before he drank. The fountain on its raised triangle of land was quiet, as quiet as the Harbor Market, and he seated himself on its broad ledge, looking back toward the sea. Normally, the little square would be full of vendors, selling everything from sweetrum to feelgood and doutfire, but today there was only a thin herm with a half-empty basket of flowers. She was dressed like a woman in thin, clinging trousers and the traditional tight-laced bodice, carelessly stuffed to make her breasts seem larger than they were. From where he sat, Warreven could see the outline of the pads beneath the fabric. She saw him looking, and turned toward him, tucking her basket under her arm.

"Æ, brother, did you come from the Market?"

Warreven nodded, not moving.

"I have friends there," she said, "and I worry."

"They should be all right," Warreven said. "I was there. The *mosstaas* shut down the *ranas* that were there—" He bit down hard on his own anger, seeing the same shock reflected in the other's face, and continued more calmly. "Nobody was hurt, though, everyone went peaceably."

The flower seller sighed, and set her basket between them on the lip of the basin. "That's good news, brother." She reached into the water, cupping a double handful, and drank noisily. She shook her hands, water still running down her chin, and said, "I heard there was going to be trouble. But I also heard that Temelathe told the *mosstaas* hands off."

Warreven hissed between his teeth, the country sound that indicated incredulity. "I wouldn't count on it, my sister."

The flower seller shrugged, wiping her hands on her thighs. The fabric clung, sweat-damp, outlining thin legs. Warreven was suddenly aware of their shape, of the fullness in her—3er—crotch, and the breasts padded to fill the too-large bodice. It had been years, it seemed, since he had looked at another *halving*, another herm, besides Haliday, and really seen the bodies that mirrored his own. And even Haliday had always seemed more man than herm or woman, if only because they'd been boys together. . . . And Haliday was right, he realized suddenly. They couldn't pass, none of them, no matter how much they tried, at least not well enough to satisfy Tendlathe and the people like him.

"If they haven't done anything," the flower seller said, "it might be true."

"They haven't done anything yet," Warreven said, and 3e grinned, revealing a missing tooth at the side of 3er mouth.

"And I don't intend to count on that, my brother." 3e hoisted 3er basket, resting it on 3er narrow hip—a woman's gesture? a human gesture?—and stepped gracefully off the edge of the fountain. He didn't watch 3er go, suddenly, coldly, afraid.

10

jillamie:
>   (Hara) literally "girlfriend"; always very casual, and can easily become an insult.

WARREVEN

The fog had come in while they were in Bon'Ador, filling the streets that led up from Harborside. From the doorway of the club, Warreven could see the the lighthouse tower at Blind Point rising above the heavy layers of vapor, the beam of light cutting a golden wedge through the dank air. To his left, the empty street ran straight to the Glassmarket, drowned in cloud. The sunken center held the fog like a basin, only the poles of the streetlights rising out of the mass: even if it hadn't been well after hours, the merchants would have had to close. A single figure was moving on the larger sales platform—a cleaner, or maybe a late-closing merchant, *shaal*-hooded against the damp. He or she was knee-deep in fog, and more wisps curled and eddied, fine as smoke, around her/his shoulders, clearly visible in the market lights. Warreven caught his breath, admiring the image, and the door opened behind him.

"Any luck?"

Haliday stepped up beside him, shaking ʒer head. "There's not a car or rover to be had, for love or money. The service said, maybe in an hour, but Reinier wants us out of here."

"He could let us wait," Warreven said, irritated, and Haliday shrugged.

"He's got his license to think of. He said the *mosstaas* and the Service Board have been breathing down his neck."

"He could close the damn bar," Warreven said, and sighed, looking back toward Blind Point. There was no one else in sight—not surprising on a night like this—and the street seemed to vanish before it reached the top of the hill, obscured by a drift of fog. "I don't suppose we could get a trolley."

"It's a fifteen-minute walk to Harborside, or thirty to Terminus, and we'd never make that before they shut down," Haliday said. "We could make it home in that."

Warreven hesitated. He didn't want to walk, not tonight, not with the ghost *ranas* still loose, but he especially didn't want to have to cross the streets above Dock Row where they'd been most active to get to the trolley station at Harborside. "I guess we walk," he said, and Haliday nodded.

"There's two of us, and it's a nasty night. Even the ghost *ranas* have to take a night off sometime."

"You hope," Warreven said sourly, and jammed his hands into the pockets of his trousers. It was cold—he was cold, and the fog was seeping through the fabric of his tunic, damp on his skin.

Haliday made a sound that was almost laughter and started up the hill. Warreven followed, hunching his shoulders against the chill. "At least the meeting went well," he said.

Haliday nodded. "We should have a couple of good *presances* worked up, and then the *ranas*—our *ranas*—can start playing them."

"If that's enough," Warreven said. He shook his head, trying to shake away the memory of Tendlathe in the Harbor Market, denying that the off-worlders were human.

"It will be," Haliday said, and smiled, the expression wry. "It has to be. Temelathe hasn't left us any other way."

Warreven shook his head again. They reached the top of the hill and started down the other side, the fog rising to meet them, damp on their faces and necks. The streetlights seemed to make the mist more opaque than ever, so that for a moment he could barely make out the buildings on the other side of the street. Haliday's face, little more than an arm's length, was blurred, as though seen through smoke. Haliday glanced at him again.

"Pity the poor sailor," 3e said, and the words were half a prayer.

Warreven nodded, thinking of the seascape tonight: no wind, calm seas, all the familiar sea- and landmarks flattened, just the lights and mostly the bells and horns to mark the coast's worst hazards. He'd been at sea once in a similar fog, coming down from Ambreslight with Chauntclere, and Clere had made no pretense of bravado. They had dropped anchor, set all the lights blazing and rigged the boat-horns to sound steadily, and had been very glad of the dawn. He tilted his head, wondering if he could hear any of the ships that must be caught offshore, but heard only the familiar tri-toned howl from Ferryhead. It was followed a few seconds later by the louder double note of Blind Point, and then the Sail Harbor buoy.

"Do you think the off-worlders will support us?" Haliday asked.

Warreven shrugged. "Some of them, maybe. Tatian will—they, NAPD, are already sticking their necks out for us, with Reiss's statement."

"He's getting enough for it," Haliday said. "And remember, Raven, by all accounts he's so-abed."

"That's not the point," Warreven answered, all the more sharply because he'd heard the same rumors. "And this could do a lot for us. What was it Astfer said, all we need is one clear case?"

Haliday nodded. "But this isn't going to be it, that I'm sure of. Destany's hardly the perfect candidate."

"Neither's 'Aukai," Warreven muttered.

"Temelathe is being smart," Haliday said. "He's letting Tendlathe do all the dirty work, and then he goes out to the *mesnies* and wonders aloud if the pharmaceuticals will go on dealing with us if he can't keep the peace."

"There's not much the *mesnies* can do about Bonemarche," Warreven said.

"You hope," Haliday said, with another crooked smile.

The fog had thinned a little, was drifting in patches across the roadway. The buildings to either side were changing, becoming older, residential, tall narrow buildings jammed close to the street to leave room for gardens and spider pens at the back of the property. There were no streetlights here; instead, each household was responsible for a light above the main door, so that the street was lit by a line of orange globes, each a little above head height. In the fog, they looked like strands of night-pearls, the glowing spheres stretching the length of the street. They reminded Warreven vaguely of holidays, of dancing on the Irenfot beaches when the *shedi* were spawning and the strings of phosphorescent egg cases washed ashore with every wave. The last time he'd seen night-pearls had been three years ago, after the *kittereen* races, the year he'd met Reiss.

A shape loomed out of the fog bank ahead of them, the low-set lights throwing its shadow back across solid-looking mist. Warreven stepped sideways into the middle of the street, looking around for a police light, and slipped his hands out of his pockets again. Two more shapes joined the first, instantly and silently, familiar shapes in the loose black robes and hoods and the white, doll-faced masks. Warreven looked over his shoulder, ready to run. Five more *ranas* blocked the street behind them, three in the lead, two shadowy in the fog behind. He turned back to the first group, heard Haliday swear under 3er breath beside him. The *ranas* moved toward them, not hurrying, and instinctively he shifted so that he could see both groups. Haliday matched him, so that they stood back-to-back in the middle of the open road. On any other night, there would have been traffic, some chance that a rover or shay would come by, disrupt the line, give them a chance to run, but they hadn't seen a vehicle all night. He glanced quickly at the windows on the upper floors, saw a few still with lights behind them, and raised his voice to shout.

"Hey! What do you want with us? Leave us alone, or there'll be trouble."

He had pitched his voice as low as he could, but it still came out contralto, more woman than man. One of the *ranas* pointed and mimed laughter, arms crossed over its belly. Warreven felt himself flush.

"Let us past," Haliday said, in the same tone 3e would have used to a dream-drunk sailor.

The *ranas* ignored 3im, circling to surround them. There were at least a dozen of them, most of them carrying the clubs and spider-sticks Warreven had seen before. There was no drummer, this time, no bell carrier, and he tasted fear, sour at the back of his mouth.

"What have we here?" The whispering voice came from the nearest of the *ranas*, one of the three who carried a spider-stick. A man's voice, Warreven thought, but the mask seemed to have an electronic distortion unit built into it, hiding his identity completely. "A pair of titticocks—and one of them pretty, too."

Again, several of the *ranas* mimed laughter. Warreven could feel himself shaking, looked up at the windows, hoping someone would see what was going on, would help. Instead, the windows that had been lit were suddenly darkened: the neighborhood had made its decision. The *rana* leader lifted his stick, shook it so that the joints snapped suddenly into place, three sharp clicks like breaking bones, turning it into a rigid bar of ironwood.

"You, *jillamie*." He pointed the stick at Haliday. "You got a pretty face, but the body's a mess. What the hell are you?" The circle moved closer, closing in.

Warreven looked up at the darkened windows, unable quite to believe they'd been abandoned to the *ranas*. Haliday took a step toward him, so that they were almost touching, close enough that Warreven could feel the faint warmth of 3er body against his back.

"And how about you?" The stick cracked again, bending all along its length, snapped rigid pointing at Warreven's chest. "Dressed like a boy, yells like a girl. So which are you, *swete-metes?*"

Warreven took a deep breath and played the only card he had. "I'm Warreven. The Stiller *seraaliste*." To his relief, his voice sounded almost normal, deep enough to pass for male.

"Warreven. We know Warreven." Even through the distortion box, the leader's voice was rich with satisfaction. He gestured with his stick, and the nearest of the *ranas* lunged like a dancer, flourishing a docker's hook in his left hand. Warreven dodged by reflex, but the hook caught his tunic, ripped down and away, the sharp tip scoring a painful line across his chest and side. He spun

away, too afraid to cry out, turning his shoulder to catch the next
blow that never came.

"What've you got under there?" the leader asked. "Show us,
Warreven. Show us what a man you are."

"Go to hell," Warreven said, and the docker raised his hook
again.

"Show us," the leader said.

Warreven stood frozen for an instant, the fog cold on his exposed skin, burning on the long cut that ran from collarbone to
hip. He couldn't fight them, not unarmed—not even if he was
armed—and it might get them out of this alive. He'd done worse,
he told himself, and didn't believe it.

"Need some help?" the leader asked, and Warreven achieved
a sneer.

"Not from you," he said, and lifted his hands to the tunic's
neck. He pulled the torn cloth apart, baring his breasts to the fog
and the cold. The house-lights left no hope of concealment; he
stood half naked and fought to seem unashamed. The *ranas*
mimed laughter—no, he thought, they were laughing behind
their masks and knew his cheeks were burning.

The leader laughed softly and turned to Haliday. "And what
about you, *jillamie?*"

"Go to hell," Haliday said.

Behind ʒer, a window scraped up in the wall of houses. Warreven looked up, letting the torn tunic fall closed again, but saw
no one in the narrow opening. All the windows were still dark, just
the one open a handspan at the bottom. A voice came from it,
high and quavering with age or fear.

"I've called the *mosstaas*. I've called them."

There was a moment of silence, of stillness, the *ranas* for an
instant unmoving, and then the leader laughed behind his mask.
More slowly, another *rana* mimed laughter, and then a second,
and a third.

"We don't need to worry about that," the leader said, and
pointed his stick at Haliday again. The window slammed down
again behind them. "So what are you, *jillamie? We can't tell.*"

Haliday glared at him. "I'm a herm."

"No such thing, not on Hara," the leader murmured.

"I'm still a herm." Haliday stood braced and rigid, fists clenched, ready to take them all on.

Warreven recognized the blind fury, had seen it before and knew enough to fear it, to fear what 3e would say or do. "Hal—" he began, and bit off the word before it was formed.

The *rana* leader said, "We don't have herms on Hara, just titticocks who can't make up their minds. So which are you, *jillamie*, or do we have to decide for you?"

"I'm a herm," Haliday said again.

The leader shook his stick, and it bent at the three joints, cracking loudly. Three of the *ranas* lunged for Haliday, who swung to face them, one arm raised to block the first blow, the other striking for the nearest *rana*'s stomach. Warreven grabbed for another *rana*'s shoulder, pulling him partially away from Haliday, felt hands on his own shoulder and, painfully, on his hair. He drove his elbow into someone's ribs, heard a gasp of pain, but the grip on his hair didn't loosen. A fist slammed into his kidneys; something else—something harder, he caught a blurred glimpse of what might have been a knobstick or the end of one of the clubs—caught him a glancing blow along one cheekbone. Pain exploded in his head, down his neck, sharp yellow lights flowering across his vision. He tried to kick the *ranas* holding him, but his knees buckled instead, and he sagged bonelessly in their grip. He heard Haliday cry out, a short, meaningless sound, saw through a haze of tears and doubled vision 3im stumble and fall huddled to the pavement. The *ranas* moved in, but not too close, taking turns and leaving each other plenty of room to swing their clubs.

"Boy or girl?" the leader said, and laughed aloud.

"Hal!" Warreven struggled to get his feet under him, to shake himself free of the hands on him. Someone hit him again, twice, body and head; he tasted blood, and knew his legs wouldn't hold him. His sight was going, or maybe the house-lights had gone out, and then a whistle sounded, and the *ranas* abruptly let him go. He fell to his hands and knees, shook his head in a desperate attempt to clear his vision, but only set off another wave of light and pain, knifing down his neck and spine. He heard footsteps, running away, the sound flattened by the fog, and thought the street was empty again—except for Haliday.

3e lay crumpled, body drawn in on itself, arms still lifted to protect 3er head. There was blood on the pavement, smears and a spreading pool, almost black in the house-lights. Warreven dragged himself to 3im, not daring to try to stand. He heard a window open, and then another and another, but didn't bother looking—he doubted if he could have seen that far—reached awkwardly for Haliday instead. 3er face was a mess, swollen and bloodied; one arm was visibly broken, bent between wrist and elbow. He touched 3er neck, feeling for a pulse; 3er skin was cold under his fingers, and he felt nothing. He thought 3er chest was moving a little, but couldn't be sure. Please don't let 3im be dead, he thought, and heard a door open behind him. This time, he did turn, newly afraid, to see a woman standing there, poised to slam the door shut again if there was more trouble. She looked old and frail, *shaal* pulled tight around her shoulders.

"I called the Emergency," she said, and he thought she might have been the person who had called the *mosstaas* before. In the distance, he heard the sound of a siren, drawing rapidly closer; he hoped, vaguely, that they would see him and Haliday before they came too far down the street. Red lights flared through the fog, and the noise of the siren was suddenly overwhelming. He tried to turn, to call to them, but the world seemed to swing under him, and he collapsed sideways on the cold paving.

---

gay:
:   (Concord) one of the nine sexual preferences generally recognized by Concord culture; denotes a person who prefers to be intimate with others of exactly the same gender.

MHYRE TATIAN

Tatian woke to a wail of sirens and lay for a second in the red-pulsing darkness of his bedroom before he realized that the sound was coming from the communications system. He swore under his breath, and fumbled for the remote that lay beside the bed, touching the keypad to bring up the lights and accept the incoming message. He grimaced as the light hit his eyes, blinked hard, and jammed fingers into his tangled hair. The air from the environmental system was dank and smelled strongly of the sea. He heard the media center come on in the main room, and then the relay screen on the wall beside his bed lit, asking if he wanted to establish a reciprocal transmission.

"Not likely," Tatian muttered, and then, because it was an older system, jabbed blindly at the remote.

The screen blinked confirmation—I/T VIDEO AND AUDIO, O/T AUDIO ONLY—and opened like a window on bright lights and white-painted walls and a face that he didn't immediately recognize. He recognized the background first—hospitals were the same all over human space—and only then realized it was Warreven beneath the bruises.

"Tatian?" 3er voice sounded small, lighter than usual, distorted by 3er swollen mouth.

"I'm here," Tatian answered. "Jesus, what happened to you?" *Or do I need to ask? I warned you there would be trouble*— He killed the thought, startled by his own response, frightened by the ugly swellings. One eye was covered with a dark bandage, the cheekbone beneath it puffed and misshapen, 3er lower lip split and swollen into an ugly pout. 3e was standing close to the sending unit—it would be a cheap pay-as-you-go unit, and they were close-focus at the best of times, a poor substitute for real privacy—but Tatian thought he could see the iridescent shape of a neck brace below the bruised chin. "Are you all right?"

Improbably, one corner of Warreven's mouth twitched up in what might have been a smile. "Very sore. But I need your help."

"You got it," Tatian answered, and flung back the covers. "What do you need?" Only then did it occur to him to wonder what he was doing, and he shoved the thought aside, impatient with himself. Warreven was a friend as well as a business partner, and 3e was hurt. That was enough for anyone.

"It's Haliday," Warreven said. "We were together, he—3e's a

lot worse than I am. I want to get 3im into the off-world hospital, where they know how to deal with herms. I need your help, Tatian."

"You got it," Tatian said again. He was reaching for his clothes as he spoke, pulling on trousers and a shirt. He fastened his trousers and picked up the remote again, wishing he had been able to get his implants repaired. He touched the control pad, and a side screen lit, date and time prominently displayed—0358/9/ 14, nearly dawn. Beneath it, a cursor flashed its silent query. "Where are you?"

"Terminus Hospital," Warreven answered.

Tatian shifted his fingers on the remote, wishing he were at his office, with the shadowscreen and the full system at his disposal. Then, impatiently, he triggered a secondary line and watched the side screen flush red as he waited for the connection. The red faded to pink as the office systems came on line, vanished completely as the link was fully established and he touched keys to send the proper passwords. As the screen cleared, he entered more commands, calling up his annotated map of the city. It flashed into view a heartbeat later: the system was slow, its response coming through too many ports for real efficiency, but it would do. Terminus Hospital was close to the massive railroad complex just north of the city proper, maybe twenty minutes' drive from the Nest; he wondered how far Warreven had had to come to get there. "I can be there in half an hour. Do you need me to bring anything?" *Our doctor*, he added silently, and probably money.

Warreven started to shake 3er head, winced, and said, "I don't think so. I've called Malemayn, too, he's bringing me some clothes. And cash."

I'll bring metal, Tatian thought. *Just in case.* He swept a handful of coins off the shelf beside his bed, already calculating its worth and the value of the larger cache of coins in the apartment safe. He would bring those as well, he decided. It would be easy enough to repay the company. "I'll be there in half an hour. We have a doctor on retainer at the port, I'll alert her. What exactly are you concerned about?" *You mentioned clothes,* he thought suddenly. Does that mean rape? The thought was literally sickening. He swallowed bile and touched the remote to record Warreven's answer.

"Hal—he's beat up pretty bad, the bastard *ranas* kicked him in the groin a few times, and in the stomach, zhim—ȝim, I mean, ȝe's herm." Warreven stopped, took a deep breath. "Like me. I don't know how badly ȝe's hurt, but I don't know if the doctors here will treat ȝim right."

Tatian nodded again, not particularly reassured, but knowing better than to betray that. "I'll alert our doctor," he said again, "and I'll be there in thirty minutes. Are you sure you don't need anything else?"

"Sure," Warreven echoed, and managed another wincing smile. "Reasonably, anyway. Tatian—" ȝe stopped again. "Thank you."

"I'm on my way," Tatian said, and cut the connection. He touched the remote again, brought up the list of emergency codes, and scrolled down until he found the listing for the clinic that had NAPD's contract. He hesitated—neither Warreven nor Haliday could by any stretch of the imagination be considered NAPD employees—but clicked the selection switch anyway. If necessary, he would pay any costs himself, and figure out where to get the money later.

The screen lit, displayed the subtly patterned screen of an expensive answering system. "Please enter your clinic code and state the nature of your problem." The sweetly synthesized voice was echoed by icons and a string of print across the screen. "If you do not have a clinic code, please enter star nine-nine-nine for emergency access."

That, Tatian knew, would throw the call over to Bonemarche's emergency response teams. He called up his own code instead, and dispatched it; the screen went momentarily blank, and then the synthetic voice said, "Please state—"

It cut out in midword, and the holding pattern vanished to reveal a rumpled-looking woman. "Jaans Oddyny here."

"Mhyre Tatian—"

"I know." The woman scowled at him, looking from secondary screen to the communications systems. "You look all right. What's the problem?"

"It's not me," Tatian said. "A friend of mine, an indigene, is hurt—3e was attacked on the street and badly beaten. I'm concerned about 3er treatment. 3e's in the Terminus Hospital right now. Can you take an interest?"

Oddyny's eyes narrowed. "Is this trade?"

Tatian bit back an angry answer. "It is not. Those damned ghost *ranas* of theirs—"

Oddyny lifted a hand in apology. "I had to ask. And it's important, can affect treatment."

Tatian nodded slowly, admitting that she was right—but the assumption that anything between an off-worlder and an indigene had to fit into the category of trade was still infuriating, especially when it was trade that had caused the attack on Warreven. "I understand," he said. "It's still not trade. Warreven's a colleague."

"So your account pays?"

"For now—" Tatian began, but Oddyny swept on unheeding. "Sort that out later. All right. There's a small matter of professional etiquette involved, but if your friend asks—or if the people over at Terminus have the brains to ask for an outside opinion—use my name. I'll have the call patched to me directly. Good enough?"

Tatian nodded. There would be no problem getting Warreven to make the request.

"Since 3e's a herm," Oddyny went on, "I'd encourage you to get 3im to seek outside treatment. These people—" She broke off, shaking her head. "They're competent enough, but not for the intersexes. What they won't see, they can't treat."

"I'll tell 3im," Tatian said. It wasn't something he'd thought of before, but he could see it clearly once Oddyny had pointed it out to him. If Harans didn't willingly distinguish five sexes in their daily lives, saw three of them as abnormal, defective, Haran doctors would always be tempted to ignore them, concentrate on the resemblances to the "real" sexes rather than the differences among them. "Thanks, Doctor."

"I'll be waiting," Oddyny said, and broke the connection.

Tatian turned off the secondary screen, went out into the main room, and uncovered the safe to initiate the release sequence. He entered the necessary codes and waited, watching the lock-lights flicker, suppressing his uncertainty. He needed the advantage that metal could bring—Warreven needed that advantage, at any rate, and Warreven was at the very least a valued supplier. The door sagged open at last, and he reached into the narrow compartment, brought out the first of the prepared packages. It was heavy—three kilograms, according to the neat label—and the coins moved uneasily in the wrapping, shifting against the cloth. He weighed it thoughtfully, decided he didn't need more, and closed the safe again. He shoved it into a small carryall, stuffed a furoshiki on top of it to muffle the sound of the coins, and headed for the door.

The company rover was in the garage space underneath the building. He rode the elevator down to it, very aware of the silent building and the cold white light of the halls. Most of his neighbors were asleep; somewhere security was watching, cameras sweeping steadily overhead as he made his way through the maze of corridors. It should have been reassuring, usually was reassuring, but tonight he could think only of the streets outside the Nest's protective fences. He was very aware of the weight of metal at his side, the dull distinctive sound of coins in his pocket, and he paused for a moment in the garage door, scanning the well-lit space. There was no one in sight, just the double rank of rovers and triphibians, most with company marks on their noses or side walls, and he made himself move quickly toward his own vehicle. He touched the security release, laid his hand against the lock plate, and felt the confirmation pulse pour down his arm, warm honey mixed with the sharp peppery spikes of static. At least the interface was working reasonably well; he felt the data puddle briefly in his palm, and then the lock clicked open, loud in the silent space. The security lights winked out on the control panel. He levered himself into the driver's pod, locking the door behind him, and kicked the machine into motion.

The fog had dissipated. Tatian could see trash blowing in a rising breeze, and the air that came in through the ventilator smelled now of rain. There wasn't much traffic—it was too early for even the earliest morning jobs, too late for the bar and dance-house crowds—and he kept to the outer roads, the faster roads, as much to avoid the *ranas* as for speed. If they were attacking Stiller's Important Men, a company mark wasn't likely to be much protection, either. He passed a pair of shays, mud-splattered cargo platforms piled high with wooden crates, heading toward the starport, but otherwise the road was empty, the poured-stone surface dull in the headlights.

The streets were a little busier around the Terminus, small shays and three-ups competing with the occasional jigg or rover. The railroad buildings themselves were brightly lit, and he heard the moan of a railway whistle, and then the shriek and clatter as a train jerked into motion on an invisible track. The hospital was close to the freight-yard entrance, and he pulled the rover into what seemed to be a shared lot, wondering if the place had origi-nally been built to take care of the inevitable railroad injuries. If so, Warreven—and Haliday, of course, though he hardly knew 3im—would probably get competent care. Red strip-lights sur-rounded the nearest doorway, and a red-lit universal glyph shone above it, signaling the emergency entrance. There were ambu-lances parked there, too, hulking triphibians that could go just about anywhere on the planet, and, as he got closer, he could see a trio of crewmen in bright orange rescue suits, passing a smoking pot from hand to hand. Even on Hara, that was a little unnerving. He looked away and pushed through the double doors into sud-den sterile light.

Inside, the broad hallway was as empty as the streets. Colored lines—all unlit at the moment—wove a surreal braid along the stark white floor; one of them, pale mauve, turned left perhaps twenty meters down the corridor, into a door painted the same odd shade. Tatian looked around, lifted his right hand, exposing the pickup embedded in his wrist, but felt no touch of an infosys-tem. There was, however, a wall board, and he studied it doubt-fully, unable to decide if he'd find Warreven faster through Main Ward/Information or the Admitting Desk.

"Can I help you, mir—ser, I mean?"

The voice was light and cheerful—almost too cheerful, Tatian thought—and he turned to face a thin young man in disposable greens. And I hope he's on his way to dispose of them, he added silently. There was a smear of something, dark as blood, on one cuff, and another on a pocket edge, as though he'd stashed gloves or instruments there and forgotten about them. "Yes," he said. "A friend of mine was brought here tonight—Warreven Stiller. How would I find him?"

The young man's eyes widened. "The *seraaliste*, you mean. He's upstairs, treatment room C-15. You can follow the gold line."

Tatian glanced at the floor, and nodded. "Thanks."

The gold line led him up a wide, empty staircase, and down another empty corridor before bringing him into an open space delineated by an expanse of worn gold carpet. Four other carpets led off at angles, like the spokes of a wheel; the doors set into the walls between them were painted the same dull ochre. The technician on duty at the bank of monitors barely looked up to direct him to the proper corridor, and Tatian hoped his competence was in inverse proportion to his social skills.

Warreven had a room to 3imself toward the end of the hall, a small room with barely enough space for the diagnostic table and its associated machinery as well as the medic's chair and desk. 3e was sitting on the end of the table, bare feet dangling, shoes discarded in a corner. The cable of a monitor cuff trailed from under the torn sleeve of 3er tunic. The tunic had been torn down the front as well, was held together by the hunch of 3er shoulders that threw the fabric forward. 3er head was down, body bent forward from the waist, hair no longer braided falling forward to screen 3er face. The stillness, the pitch of 3er body was frightening, and Tatian hesitated in the doorway. 3e looked up then, moving gingerly, and Tatian winced at the sight of the huge bandage and the multicolored plastic collar supporting 3er neck.

"You look a mess," he said, and the less swollen corner of Warreven's mouth twitched up.

"Don't make me laugh, it hurts." 3e gathered the monitor cables in one hand and slid cautiously off the table. "I'm glad you're here."

"What happened?"

Warreven started to shrug, and grimaced. "Exactly what I said. We ran into a ghost *rana* band, and they don't like the *wrangwys*—herms." 3e made another face, as though annoyed with 3imself for using the *franca* word, and turned to face the banked monitors. The torn tunic swung open, and Tatian caught a glimpse of small high breasts and a thin line of red-orange synthiskin running diagonally across 3er body before 3e pulled the fabric closed again. "They—we got beat up. I'm all right, or at least I will be. It's Hal I'm worried about." 3e gestured to the monitors. "Do you know how to access these things?"

"You can't usually get into other people's records," Tatian answered, but examined the control pad. He laid his hand and wrist port experimentally in the access cradle, felt the confirmation pulse stab into his skin, but his sight stayed clear, free of the normal overlay. "It's either on a personal password or a palmprint scan. I can't get in."

"Damn." Warreven turned away, trailing cables, and Tatian caught the bundle before it snagged on the corner of the diagnostic table.

"Careful."

3e ignored him, lifting a hand to tug at the iridescent collar. "3e should have an off-world doctor, someone we can trust. Not these people."

"Don't touch it," Tatian said, automatically—he recognized the system, one of the deep-muscle repair techniques, knew it shouldn't be removed until the doctors agreed—and then, "Trust them to what?"

Warreven turned to face him, leaned 3er weight against the end of the table. The cables dragged across 3er body, pulling the tunic open again. Tatian caught another glimpse of gold-brown skin and the long line of the bandage before Warreven dragged the torn edges back together. The fabric was filthy, as though 3e'd rolled in the gutters—which 3e probably has, Tatian added, silently. God, 3e doesn't sound good— He glanced again at the bank of monitors and found the bright red button that would summon help, reassuringly prominent among the array of smaller screens and touchpads.

"Trust them not to alter 3im," Warreven said. "If 3e's really hurt, if there's serious damage, they're more likely just to cut him—3im—than try to save him."

Tatian blinked. It was one thing not to know how to treat herms' complex bodies, entirely another to surgically alter them to conform to Haran prejudice—but then, on a world that didn't admit herms existed, there would always be the temptation to "correct" the "defect" rather than go to the effort to restore Haliday to 3er natural condition. He suppressed a shudder, and said, "I've already spoken to Jaans Oddyny. She's with our contract clinic. She's willing to step in the minute she gets a request."

"I want 3im moved to the off-world hospital," Warreven said. "The one out at the port."

Tatian eyed 3im warily. "That's going to depend on how 3e is, right? Whether or not 3e can be moved."

Warreven took a deep breath. "Yeah, I suppose—I know. I'm just worried, that's all. They haven't told me anything about how 3e is yet, just that 3e's stable."

Tatian looked back at the displays. "Want me to call a tech? They might be able to tell you something now."

Warreven started to shake 3er head, stopped. "No—I don't know. They're supposed to be getting rid of this thing soon, I thought." 3e touched the collar.

Before Tatian could say anything, a technician—not the man who had been watching the monitors—tapped on the door frame. Tatian moved aside, and the woman stepped past him with a murmured apology to lay her arm in the access cradle below the monitors. The multiple screens lit instantly, filled with data from the cuff and collar. Tatian thought he recognized a skull shape among the numbers and unfamiliar shapes, but the image rotated away before he could be sure. The technician nodded to herself and ran her free hand over the nearest shadowscreen before she detached herself from the cradle. The screens stayed lit, numbers shifting as Warreven breathed.

"Your neck's looking much better, mir, you can take the collar off now."

Warreven lifted both hands tentatively to the catch, and Tatian said, "Let me." He worked the release mechanism, felt the machine go loose and flaccid in his hands, and unwound it and the cable from Warreven's neck. 3e lifted 3er head, and 3er hair spilled down for an instant over his hands, as coarse and fluid as the land-spiders' raw silk. Now that the collar was gone, the bandage covering Warreven's left eye looked worse than before, blue-black synthiskin bulging over swollen skin and presumably a medipack.

The technician ran her hands over the shadowscreen again, studying the numbers in her multiple screens, then turned to Warreven. "Your neck will still be sore, but there's no serious damage—nothing broken, and no muscles torn."

"Wonderful," Warreven said, without enthusiasm.

"What we're worried about," the technician went on, and laid a probe gently against the conductive bandage, "is the eye. The system would prefer to keep you here through tomorrow—"

"No," Warreven said.

"—but we think you'll rest better in familiar surroundings. And that's the main thing: you need to rest your eyes as completely as possible, give that one a chance to heal on its own." She removed the probe, looked back at the screen. "It should recover fully, but the bruising is severe, and another shock could do permanent harm. That's why we have it packed so thoroughly, and we'll want to check it again in twenty-six hours. We can prescribe painkillers, something to help you sleep, which is the best thing for you, or you can just take deepdream."

"I'll do that," Warreven said. "How's Haliday?"

The technician touched her screen again, and the displays went abruptly blank. She frowned to herself, laid her arm back in the cradle, the fingers of her free hand working on invisible controls, and a voice from the doorway said, "Raven? God and the spirits, you look awful."

"Thanks," Warreven said sourly.

"How's Haliday?" The newcomer held out a bundle of clothes, and Warreven took it gratefully.

"She's finding out."

"Ah." The newcomer looked at Tatian, tilted his head to one side. "I'm Malemayn, I don't know if you remember."

"I remember." Tatian held out his hand, deliberately foreign, and Malemayn took it warily. He was a tall man, perhaps a finger's width taller than Tatian himself, and his face was bonier than Tatian had remembered from their earlier brief meeting. Or maybe it was just the hour and the circumstances, he admitted. There weren't many people who looked their best in a hospital setting.

"Tatian's talked to his doctor," Warreven said. "If Hal needs it."

"Thank you," Malemayn said.

"I've got the records now," the technician said. "Sorry about the delay, I was waiting for the update."

"How is 3e?" Warreven asked.

"She's stable," the technician said, "and still unconscious. The doctors have decided to keep her under until they can get the first repairs completed. There were a number of broken bones—femur, both bones in the right forearm, three ribs—but her skull is intact. The internal injuries are controlled and under treatment." She freed herself from the contact. "I'd say she's out of danger—she'll have to spend a few weeks in Recovery, but she should be fine."

Tatian heard Malemayn give a sigh of relief. Warreven said, "3e."

"Æ?" The technician looked confused for a moment, then blushed. "I'm sorry."

"Which is why," Warreven said, looking at Malemayn, "we need an off-world doctor."

The technician bridled, and Malemayn said quickly, "We'll see—I'll see to it, Raven, you're in no shape to deal with this."

"I mean it," Warreven said, and reached for the bundle of clothes. 3e fumbled it open, dropping the shirt, and stooped to pick them up, wincing, before Tatian could do it for 3im. "Can you get me out of this thing?"

The technician, her face still with disapproval, moved to release the monitor cuff. Over her shoulder, Malemayn gave Tatian a speaking look; responding to that appeal, the off-worlder said, "Look, she said you need to rest, Warreven. Let me take you home."

"I can stay and look after Haliday," Malemayn said. "I'll get the doctor's name from Mir Tatian, talk to the doctors here, see what—if anything, you don't know anything's wrong, Raven—see what needs to be done."

Warreven turned 3er back to them all, shrugged off the torn tunic. The end of the bandage was just visible where it crossed 3er hipbone and vanished beneath the waistband of 3er trousers. There was blood on them, a little darker than the fabric itself. The technician made a clucking noise, half sympathy, half embarrassment, and reached for the clean shirt, deftly easing it up over 3er arms and shoulders. "Thanks," Warreven said. "Sorry—"

The woman waved away the apology and turned back to her machines.

Tatian looked from 3im to Malemayn, frowning. He didn't like the position the other advocate was putting him in, the tacit invitation to side with him against Warreven, to brush away Warreven's real fears. "I think Warreven's right, Mir Malemayn. No reflection on the staff here, but Mir Haliday is a herm, and our doctor has more experience treating them."

Malemayn's mouth twisted, but then he had himself under control. "I agree that a second opinion would be a good thing—"

"The doctor's name is Jaans," Warreven said. 3e jammed 3er feet into 3er shoes.

"Jaans Oddyny," Tatian said, and reached into his pocket for the thin disk. "These are her codes."

Malemayn took it, and Warreven said, "Give me your word, Mal, that you'll call her."

"I'll call her," Malemayn said grimly. "I promise, Warreven."

Warreven sighed, and relaxed slightly. Tatian said, "Let me take you home. Can you walk, or do you want a floater?"

"I can walk," Warreven began, and the technician shook her head.

"I've called for a wheelchair."

The chair, when it came, was exactly what she had called it, a chair with wheels instead of legs. Tatian walked beside it to the entrance and bribed a waiting *faitou* to bring the rover around to the entrance. Warreven got 3imself into the passenger compartment without much help and leaned back cautiously against the padding.

"Do you know how to get to my place from here?"

"I'm assuming you can tell me," Tatian answered, and Warreven nodded. Tatian looked sideways at 3im, thin face outlined in the light from the hospital entrance, and was privately less sure. 3e roused 3imself enough to give directions, however, and guided him competently enough through the maze of narrow streets that lay between the Terminus and Blind Point. Tatian wedged the rover up against the side of the building, leaving enough room for a shay to squeeze past, if its side wheels bumped up onto the opposite walkway, and came around the rover's nose to help Warreven climb out of the low-slung compartment. The indigene was already out, leaning against the rover's roof. 3e saw Tatian looking, straightened painfully, and led the way down the narrow passage between the buildings. Tatian followed closely, grateful for the first pale light of dawn, wondering if he should offer his hand, but Warreven seemed determined to make it on 3er own. 3e stumbled once, halfway up the stairs, and Tatian steadied 3im, bracing himself to offer whatever help the other would accept, but then 3e rallied and climbed the last half dozen steps without help. 3e fumbled with the key for a few moments, bending close to the lock, but then the door opened and Tatian followed 3im inside.

As the lights came on, he looked around with unabashed curiosity. There wasn't much furniture—a carved, heavy-looking bench padded with bright cushions, a cast ceramic stool painted to look like a drum, a length of polished wood propped on glass bricks that served as a table, more cushions piled on the floor beside the bench, media center wedged into a corner—but one short wall was lined with storage shelves filled with stacked disks and hardcopy. A cheap reader lay on the floor in front of the media center, and there was another on the floor beside the bench, a crumpled tunic half covering it.

"God and the spirits, I want a bath," Warreven said.

"You sure?" He looked sideways, winced at the rush of static that blurred his vision, looked at the media center instead. The time display was dark; he said instead, "It's almost dawn."

"I know," Warreven said. "But I'll be glad I did later."

3e disappeared down a short hallway. After a moment, Tatian followed, not fully certain he'd been invited, but very certain the other shouldn't be left on 3er own. The hall led to a dark bedroom, the piled quilts of the bed just visible in the rising light, and the bathroom and kitchen opened to either side. Water was running in the bathroom, and he tapped on the half-closed door.

"Need a hand with anything?"

The door opened at his touch, and Warreven looked out at him. "Actually, yes, if you don't mind. I'm really sore."

"I don't mind," Tatian said, and stepped into the sudden warmth. The tub was enormous, nearly long enough for him to lie with arms outstretched, and deep, the edges rising well above his knees. Both taps were turned full on, and the air was thick with steam.

"It's the shirt," Warreven said. "I can't get it off." 3e had loosened the neck, and Tatian stepped forward, lifted it carefully off over 3er head. Warreven murmured a thank you, turning 3er back to step awkwardly out of 3er trousers. 3e lowered 3imself into the steaming water, leaned back stiffly to hold 3er head under the still-running tap. At that angle, 3er body was fully exposed, bruises dark on 3er ribs and one thigh; the synthiskin bandage ran from 3er left collarbone all the way to 3er right hip, slicing across the shallow curve of one breast, ended in a broader patch of synthiskin that covered the hipbone and a deeper cut. He was on Warreven's blind side, a third of 3er face covered by the lump of dark bandage, and he suspected they were both glad of the illusion of privacy. Warreven shifted then, penis bobbing in the moving water, started to reach over 3er head, and stopped, muttering a curse.

"Could you—" 3e stopped, though whether it was embarrassment or pain Tatian couldn't be sure. It didn't matter; 3e looked miserable, the bruises on 3er face and shoulders and across 3er unexpectedly muscled stomach darkening rapidly, and Tatian took a step forward.

"What do you need?"

"My hair," Warreven said. "I need—I want to wash my hair, and I can't."

Tatian lifted an eyebrow—it didn't seem like a good idea—but on second thought it was probably better not to argue with 3im. "No problem," he said, shoving his sleeves back above his elbow, and knelt cautiously beside the tub. A squat pottery jar stood on the tiles in the corner, and he loosened its stiff lid. It was filled with a pale green cream that smelled strongly of catseyes and, more faintly, of witches'-broom. Tatian eyed it warily—would even Harans put hallucinogens into soap?—and said, "Is this it?"

"Yes." Warreven seemed to have learned better than to nod. 3e leaned back again, bending from the hips only, dipping 3er head into the stream of water from the tap. Tatian suppressed the desire to look for a pair of gloves—the witches'-broom was topically active—and dipped two fingers gingerly into the jar. The musky smell of the catseyes made him sneeze; Warreven blinked and shifted so that he could reach 3er hair.

"What happened to your chest?" Tatian asked, and smeared the cream onto 3er hair. His fingers were tingling already, but he told himself that was purely psychological.

Warreven looked embarrassed again. "A *rana* with a cargo hook," 3e said, after a moment.

"He could've killed you," Tatian said.

"He wasn't trying to," Warreven answered. "They, their leader, was trying to make a point about herms. Or about me, that I was one. Cutting me was actually incidental."

Tatian shuddered, unable to suppress the vivid image, began

to rub the soap into 3er hair, cautiously working up a lather.
"What did the *mosstaas* say?"

"Æ?" Warreven's good eye blinked.

"You didn't call the *mosstaas*?"

3e made a noise that might have been laughter. "They
wouldn't've come. Tendlathe's paid them off."

"Bastards." Tatian looked away from the bruised face and
body, the massive bandage covering 3er injured eye, the thinner
strip running from shoulder to hip, made himself concentrate on
the mass of hair under his hands. Even tangled as it was, it felt like
silk, heavy and so smooth that the strands seemed to catch on the
calloused skin of his fingers. He winced, thinking of the pressure
on Warreven's neck, and carefully freed himself. Warreven
sighed, suddenly and deeply, and let 3imself relax, so that 3er head
lay heavy in Tatian's hands.

"That feels better." 3er voice was slurring—a combination of
the broom and whatever else they'd given 3im at the hospital, Tatian thought, and probably a very good thing.

"Good," he said aloud, and took 3er shoulders, guiding 3im
back under the stream of water again. Warreven let 3imself be
moved, the visible eye closed now. Tatian was reminded again of
Kaysa, she of the long mahogony braid, and the long, graceful
limbs. Not that 3e was particularly feminine, anymore than 3e was
masculine—3er body beneath the water drew his eyes, long legs,
long, clearly defined muscles, cock and the swell of the cleft scro-
tum behind it. 3e had forgotten to hunch 3er shoulder, and 3er
breasts, herm's breasts, small and definite against the bony ribs,
were fully exposed. A perfect herm's body, Tatian thought, and
felt himself flushing, embarrassment as much as desire, well aware
that he was responding as much to the memories of Kaysa as to
Warreven's presence. The broom sang in his blood, Warreven lay
passive in his hands, and he made himself look away, feeling de-
pressingly adolescent, concentrated on rinsing the last of the soap
from 3er hair until his erection subsided.

"All done," he said, and Warreven nodded and sat up slowly.
Tatian stepped back, but stayed close enough to steady 3im as 3e

climbed carefully out of the tub. He handed 3er a towel before 3e could ask and looked away while 3e dried 3imself, moving as slowly as an ancient.

"Do you want me to comb out your hair?" he asked, and Warreven wound the towel awkwardly around 3er waist, wincing as the coarse fabric touched bruises and the bandaged cut.

"I'd appreciate it," 3e said, and lowered 3imself carefully onto a padded stool. "I don't think I could manage on my own."

A wooden comb lay on the edge of the tub. Tatian picked it up and began to work out the snarls. Kaysa had taught him how to do this—her hair had been one of the pleasures of the relationship—and he worked slowly, careful not to put too much pressure on Warreven's neck. The bandage hid most of 3er expression, but when Tatian looked more closely, 3er good eye was closed again, and he thought 3e might be falling asleep under his hands.

"That's finished," he said at last.

Warreven sighed, straightened slowly, and turned to face him, drawing the towel up over 3er chest. "Thanks. God and the spirits, I hurt."

"Did you get anything from the hospital for it?"

"No." Warreven moved 3er shoulders experimentally, grimaced, and stopped. "I have deepdream, and doutfire; one of those'll be fine."

"Where are they, in the kitchen?"

"Yes." Warreven roused 3imself with an effort. "The blue cabinet."

"Go to bed," Tatian said. "I'll get them."

"What about you?" The towel slipped; Warreven started to reach for it and let it slide back down to 3er waist, held it there. "You're welcome to stay."

"If you don't mind," Tatian said, "I'd be glad of a bed. It's almost morning, and I'd like some sleep."

Warreven started to nod, checked 3imself instantly. "There are quilts in the chest—the one under the media center—and the couch isn't too bad. I'll—"

"I'll find them," Tatian said, startled by the rush of protectiveness—more of the broom, he thought. "Go to bed, Warreven."

ʒe gave him a wincing smile and turned away, dropping the towel on the floor behind ʒim. Tatian picked it up, folded it automatically, and set it back on the rack, then went into the kitchen to find the drugs.

There were several boxes and canisters, jumbled into the cabinet with pottery dishes and half-empty boxes of food, and he pried open lids until he found a jar with dried doutfire. He shook out four of the thin cylinders of bark—paper-thin, fragile in his clumsy fingers—and brought them into the bedroom. Warreven was already in bed, the top quilt drawn up to ʒer shoulders, but ʒe roused ʒimself enough to chew and swallow the doutfire. Tatian hesitated, wanting to do more, not knowing what more he could do, then switched out the light and went back into the main room.

The sky was pale beyond the windows, and he studied the controls of the media center for a moment before he found the time display. If there was a remote, it was nowhere in sight; he fiddled with the rudimentary keypad instead until he'd located the local communications system. The smaller screen lit, offering him options, and he scrolled through the unfamiliar menus until he found the way into the secondary system that most off-worlders used. Then he punched in Derebought's codes—audio only, no visual at this hour—and waited while the call went through. The screen flashed white, and Mats' voice said, "Yeah?"

He sounded both sleepy and annoyed; Tatian allowed himself a smile, knowing the cameras were off, and said, "It's Mhyre Tatian. Sorry to wake you, but it's important."

"Hang on," Mats said, but he already sounded more awake. "All right. What's up?"

"I'm not going to be in today at all, and maybe not tomorrow," Tatian said. "Warreven's been attacked by the ghost *ranas*, and I'm at ʒer place—ʒe called me from the hospital, asked me to get an off-world doctor for ʒim and the herm ʒe was with."

"God and the spirits." That was Derebought's voice, quickly smothered.

Mats said, "Derry's right, boss, we've already been warned off local politics."

"I know." Tatian bit back his own annoyance. "That's why

I'm calling you. I'm on leave, as of yesterday. Fix it in the records, will you? I don't have access from here. You don't know where I am, or what my plans were. You don't know anything about me playing politics, or anything about me and Warreven."

"All right," Mats said, and Derebought broke in.

"Do you want me to let Serram Masani know what's happened?"

Tatian hesitated, then nodded, forgetting for an instant that the screen was blank both ways. "Yes," he said, "but as discreetly as you can. Don't use the port lines unless you have to."

"All right." He heard Derebought's intake of breath as she considered her next words. "Are you sure this is . . ." Her voice trailed off again as she failed to find suitably diplomatic phrasing.

Tatian finished it for her. "Smart? No. That's why I'm clearing out of day-to-day business for now. I want NAPD to have deniability."

"You think it's that bad?" Derebought asked, and he could almost hear the shake of her head. "Sorry, you wouldn't be doing this if you didn't."

"No." Tatian took a deep breath.

"How can we contact you?" Mats asked. "This number?"

"Try it," Tatian said. "This is Warreven's residence, so I don't know how long I'll be here. But I'll keep in touch myself. Go ahead and get as much of the surplus in from the *mesnies* as you can—you can handle payments, Derry—and by the time you're ready to ship, this should have blown over."

"All right," Derebought said. "Be careful."

"I will be," Tatian answered, and cut the connection. He stood for a moment, staring at the screen without really seeing the shut-down codes. This wasn't smart, that he did know; he was getting much too deeply involved in Hara's politics, and if he had any sense at all, he'd leave Warreven asleep, tell Jaans Oddyny he wouldn't take care of anymore payments, and pull himself and NAPD well clear of the whole situation. He had the contracts in hand, signed and sealed, and Stiller was bound to honor them. That should be enough for anyone. He shook his head then, turned away from the now-dark center—just the time display glowing green in the upper corner of the multiple displays. It was too late for that now, he was already committed—and besides, he admitted silently, he didn't want to abandon Warreven. 3e was the only reasonable person—reasonable indigene, anyway—he'd met on this unreasonable planet. He owed 3im what support he could give.

11

Agede, the Doorkeeper:
(Hara) one of the seven spirits who mediates between God and Man; Agede's domain is change, death, birth, and healing.

WARREVEN

When he woke again, it was afternoon, the light that filtered in through the shutters cool and indirect. He lay still for a few minutes, hoping that if he didn't move he could drop back into sleep, but the pain in his neck and down his chest and ribs was too much to be ignored. He had a headache, too, radiating from the bruised eye and socket to stab both temples and down to the point of his jaw. Turning his head to check the chronometer sent weird streaks of light across his vision, pain flaring with them, and he rolled instead onto his side—setting off more aches, but not as sharply painful—so that he faced the glowing box. It read eighteen-ten; he swore, thinking of Haliday, and crawled out of bed.

He was able to dress himself, barely, struggled into loose trousers and a tunic that opened from neck to hem, but his hair defeated him. It still hurt too much to raise his arms above his head, hurt even worse when he tried to twist the long strands into a braid, and in the end he left the mass of it loose and stumbled toward the kitchen to get more doutfire. Tatian had left the box open on the counter, and Warreven carefully extracted four more of the fragile rolls. Two shattered under his touch; he sighed and licked his finger, dabbed up the shards, letting the thin, bitter fragments dissolve on his tongue.

"How are you feeling?" Tatian was standing in the doorway, arms braced against the walls to either side.

"Like somebody hit me," Warreven answered, and was rewarded by one of Tatian's quick grins.

"I wonder why?"

Warreven smiled back, cautiously, newly aware of bruises, and reached into another cabinet for a bottle of sweetrum. He uncorked it, drank, flinching as the liquor hit the cuts on his lip. The raw sugar taste of it seemed to cling to his back teeth, but it took away the bitterness of the doutfire. "Maybe because somebody did. Has Malemayn called, have you heard anything about Hal?"

"He called around noon," Tatian answered. "Oddyny'd been over to look at ʒim. He said there hadn't been any change, that he'd call if there was. He left a number at the hospital, though, if you want to try that."

Warreven took another swallow of the sweetrum, started to nod, and felt the muscles of his neck tighten painfully. "Yes—it's not that I don't trust you, I just want to talk to him myself."

"I figured," Tatian said, and stepped back out of the doorway.

Warreven slipped past him, still carrying the bottle of sweetrum, vaguely surprised that the off-worlder's presence was so reassuring. Maybe it was the very matter-of-fact way that he'd stepped in, the ordinary, reasonable common sense of it all—which hardly seemed to be common anymore. The media center was lit, both screens turned to news channels, and Tatian cleared his throat.

"You seem to have made the narrowcasts."

"Me?" Warreven looked at the screens. Both showed the Harbor Market, crowded not with merchants but with the same sort of crowd that had been dispersed the day before. Even the *rana* band was back, half a dozen drummers now, and a pair of flute players, perched on a platform that looked higher and less stable than the previous day's stage. People were dancing—any time there was drumming, people would dance—but beyond them crates and spent fuel cells and all the other debris that collected on the docks had been dragged into a crude barricade. Tough-looking dockers—and not just dockers, Warreven realized, but men and women in ordinary clothes, with only the multicolored *rana* ribbons to mark them as something different—leaned against it, blocking all access to the Gran'quai.

"Officially," Tatian said, "they're continuing yesterday's protest against the ghost *ranas*. But the main thrust of what they're saying is, if you and Haliday aren't safe, no one is."

"Wonderful," Warreven said, and took another swallow of the sweetrum. The pain was starting to ease, even the headache, and the lights were beginning to show faint, rainbowed haloes. It was going to be difficult to balance comfort and sobriety.

"The code's there," Tatian said, and pointed to the table beside the media center. He had found the remote as well, Warreven saw, and stopped to collect it, then turned to the couch, shoving aside the quilts Tatian had left neatly piled there. He sat down, setting the bottle beside him, and ran stiff fingers over the remote's control surfaces, bringing up the main screen and then the new codes. The menus flickered past, a montage of text and symbol, bringing him first into the hospital's main system, and then into a secondary paging system. He entered the last segment of Malemayn's codes, and waited. The communications screen went blank, except for a time display; in the screen beside it, the drummers moved in frantic rhythm, following a chanter's gestures. His shadow fell across the heads of the dancing crowd, stretched to the edge of the empty Market. As he turned, jeering, to the camera, Warreven could see the Trickster's mark vivid on his cheek.

"Raven?" The communications screen cleared with the word, and Malemayn's face appeared at its center. Warreven could see white walls behind him, and the occasional out-of-focus figure of a nurse or doctor, elongated shapes in pale green: still calling from a public cubicle, he thought, which meant Haliday wasn't well enough to have a private room. Malemayn sounded worn out, and the stubble was dark on his cheeks. Warreven touched his own face, feeling the coarse hairs starting, and wondered if he would be able to shave himself in a few days, once the swelling went down.

"How's Hal?" he asked.

"Stable," Malemayn answered. "No change from what I told Tatian. That off-world doctor, Oddyny, she was here again, and she says he, ʒe should be moved over to the Starport as soon as ʒe's able, which should be in a day or two. ʒe's still unconscious, but Oddyny says not to worry. They're keeping ʒim under to let the treatments work."

Warreven allowed himself a long sigh of relief. He hadn't realized, until that instant, just how frightened he had been. "So ʒe'll be all right?"

Malemayn nodded. "Oddyny says it's going to take a month or so, but ʒe'll be fine. How are you?"

"Sore," Warreven said, and Malemayn laughed.

"You look like death. No, you look like the Doorkeeper."

Warreven looked sideways, found his reflection in the glass of the nearest window. With the black bandage covering one eye, he did look a little like the popular drawings of Agede the Doorkeeper, the spirit of death and birth and change. "Thanks," he said sourly, and did not reach for the sweetrum. Agede was always drawn with a cane and a bottle; there was no need to complete the resemblance.

"The tech said you should be sure and reschedule your appointment, have your eye looked at sometime tomorrow."

"Reschedule?" Warreven scowled at the invisible camera.

"They wanted to see you this afternoon," Malemayn said. "I mentioned it to Tatian, but he thought—we both thought—it was better to let you sleep. The tech said you should be sure and come in tomorrow, though."

Warreven nodded, not looking at the off-worlder. He wasn't entirely sure he liked Tatian's looking after him, wasn't sure he entirely disliked it, either. But then, it had been Malemayn's decision, too.

"I'm going to stay for another hour or so," Malemayn went on. "Oddyny said she'd be back to take another look at Hal, and she said she'd have time to give me an update then. And then I'm going home and get some sleep."

"What about Hal?" Warreven asked, a little too sharply. The old fears rose in his mind: Haliday left alone, unconscious, the doctors deciding to castrate, or simply not to save, ʒer ambiguous body, all because there was no one there to protest—

"Relax," Malemayn said. "I made it very clear, and Dr. Jaans was with me, that Hal's to be treated like they'd treat an off-worlder. I left a couple hundred megs with the ward nurse, too."

Warreven nodded, appeased. "That ought to be enough."

"I'll pay more if I have to," Malemayn said.

"Let me know what I can put into the pot," Warreven said.

Malemayn shook his head. "We'll adjust this through the partnership. Once this is all over. Æ, Raven, I don't know how we're going to keep working, with Hal in the hospital and you supposed to be being *seraaliste*—"

He broke off, shaking his head again, this time in apology, and Warreven looked away, embarrassed. "I know, Mal, I'm sorry. For what it's worth, it wasn't my idea."

"And this wasn't Haliday's either," Malemayn said. "I know." He sighed, looked down at something beneath the camera's line of sight. "Look, I've got to go. I'll call you if there's any change, any news at all, but if you don't hear from me, everything's fine."

Warreven nodded again. "Give Hal my love," he said, softly, even though he knew Haliday couldn't hear the message yet. Malemayn nodded, and broke the connection.

"I hope you don't mind my not waking you," Tatian said, after a moment. "I went in and looked, but you were pretty well out of it."

In the main screen, a shay filled with *mosstaas* pulled into the Market, and Warreven caught his breath before he realized it was a clip from the day before. "It's all right," he said, still watching the screen. "I think sleep was probably the best thing for me."

"That's what I thought," Tatian agreed.

The image in the screen changed again, returning to the live feed. Warreven frowned, trying to figure out where the cameras were stationed—on the Embankment, maybe, or on the Customs House balcony—and the off-worlder cleared his throat.

"Look, it's maybe none of my business, but you might want to think of moving Haliday now. If 3e's well enough, of course."

"Æ?" Warreven tipped his head to one side, felt the muscles tighten, but the pain was distant now, deadened by the sweetrum and the doutfire.

"You know your planet better than I do," Tatian said, his

voice abruptly formal. "I'm not presuming to tell you your business. But this doesn't look good to me." He gestured to the screen.

Warreven looked again, seeing the line of dockers and *ranas* mixed together, the crude barricade—and also the drums and dancers, a pair of flute players now leading the performance. "It's still a *rana*, still within the law," he began, and broke off, hearing the absurdity of his own words.

"So was yesterday," Tatian muttered.

"I know." Warreven stared at the screen, seeing not these dancers but Faireigh, hearing her voice soaring easily above the other voices. *Go down, you snow-white roses,* she had sung, and Tendlathe would never forget that, any more than he had forgotten Lammasin's insult. Or Warreven's own, the insult of his existence. Warreven suppressed a shiver, looked away from the screen. "What have they been saying, what's the Most Important Man doing about this?"

"Staying clear," Tatian answered. "Oh, they said about an hour ago that he's meeting with the harbormasters and the head of the *mosstaas*, supposed to be deciding if this is interfering with trade, but as best I can tell, he's waiting for it to die down on its own."

"That's smart."

"Not necessarily." Tatian glared at the screen, and the image shifted to a pan along the length of the Gran'quai and the boats tied up there. "See there? It is interfering with commerce, and the pharmaceuticals aren't going to put up with that for long."

Warreven frowned, for a moment not seeing anything different, and then realized that the usual traffic of dockers' drags and devils was completely absent. No one was off-loading; the ships' crews were idle, or with the dockers at the barricades. "It's only been one day," he said. "Does that make enough of a difference?"

"Not one day," Tatian said, grimly. "But if this isn't settled—well, I already spoke to my people. They said the Big Six are starting to get a little nervous. They're shipping a good million a day right now, and they can't risk losing the harvest."

Neither could the *mesnies*, Warreven thought. They would be putting pressure on Temelathe to end this, too, especially the conservative *mesnies* of the Equatoriale—and with the pharmaceuticals and Tendlathe also pushing to close down the protest, Temelathe would have a hard time balancing all those demands. And if there was more trouble—if Temelathe tried to send the *mosstaas* in again, tried to disperse a legitimate *rana* after they'd singularly failed to stop the ghost *ranas* and their violence. . . . The people at the Harbor wouldn't stand for it two days in a row. They would fight, and then Temelathe would have no choice but to turn the *mosstaas* loose on them. And that would give Tendlathe the excuse he needed to act.

"What about Tendlathe?" he said aloud. "Where's he supposed to be?"

"With his father, I guess." Tatian looked at him, his expression very serious. "Look, did you mean what you said—God, was it only the day before yesterday? That Tendlathe was behind the ghost *ranas*, and Lammasin's murder?"

Warreven laughed. "Despite what Hal thinks, I don't say things like that lightly. Yes, I think he's responsible—and I told him so to his face—which didn't exactly endear me to him, I suppose. But we'll never prove it."

"So he's responsible for this, too?" Tatian waved his free hand, the gesture taking in the bandaged eye, the second bandage hidden under Warreven's tunic. "Beating up you and Haliday?"

"Probably," Warreven answered. It hurt more than he'd expected, admitting that, acknowledging that the man he'd grown up with had almost certainly arranged the attack, was the person who'd planned not just the beating but the ritual humiliation. "He—Tendlathe thinks that we—the *wrangwys*, and you offworlders, too—aren't really human anymore."

Tatian made a small, mirthless noise. "Funny. There're people in the Nest—other off-worlders—who think the same about Harans."

Warreven smiled in spite of himself. "God and the spirits, I'd like to see Ten's face if you told him that." This was hardly to the point, and he forced his mind back to Haliday. On the screen, the dancers were twisting themselves into a long spiral, a country dance that wound into a tight knot and then usually dissolved into laughter and cheerful chaos before it could unwind again. The dockers on the barricade were watching, but distantly, their attention on the roads that led down from the Embankment. "You may be right about moving Hal," he said, and reached for the remote. "I'm assuming the port is defended?"

"Of course." Tatian looked back at him steadily, defying him to be insulted. "Nobody spends this much money on a backward planet without making sure they can protect the investment."

"Under the circumstances," Warreven said, "I find that reassuring." Under other circumstances, it would be less so, but he put that thought aside for later consideration. He touched the keypad, recalling the codes Malemayn had left.

"I'm relieved," Tatian said. He paused. "What's Tendlathe's problem with herms anyway? I—well, I was at the *baanket*, remember. The *presance* really bothered him."

Warreven shrugged, watching codes shift on the communications screen. "I don't know," he began, then shook his head, ignoring the faint thrust of pain. He owed Tatian more than that, after all the off-worlder had done for him. "That's not strictly true. We're built a lot alike, look alike—you've seen him—and everybody knew I was a herm, so he got teased a lot. And then the marriage didn't help." Because he did want me, at least a little, Warreven realized suddenly, but it wasn't something he could say, sounded too conceited, too much like a cheap romance.

Tatian was nodding thoughtfully. "There was always a lot of gossip in the Nest about him. A lot of people think he's a herm."

"I'm glad he doesn't know that—" Warreven broke off as the screen changed, displaying Malemayn's image. "Mal, I'm glad I caught you before you left."

"So am I," Malemayn answered. "I was going to call you."

"Is—" Warreven broke off, suddenly afraid, and Malemayn shook his head.

"No, Hal's fine. But Dr. Jaans says things are strange in the city; she wants to move ȝim tonight."

"Trust Oddyny to have her finger on the pulse," Tatian muttered.

Warreven said, "That's what I was calling you about, actually. I—we've been watching the news channel, and I thought Hal might be better off at the port if anything goes wrong."

Malemayn nodded. "That's what Oddyny said. I wanted to tell you first, though, see what you thought."

Warreven shivered. "I think too many people are saying it's the right thing for us not to do it."

"I've seen some of it," Malemayn said. "Everybody's watching it here, too. Have the *mosstaas* moved in at all?"

"I haven't seen them," Warreven answered, and glanced at Tatian.

"The last I heard, Temelathe was supposed to be holding them off."

"Well, that would be the first good news in all of this," Malemayn said sourly. "I'll tell Oddyny we agree."

Warreven nodded. "Thanks."

"Not a problem," Malemayn said, and the screen went blank.

Warreven sighed, touched the keypad to shut down the communications system. "Are you hungry?" he asked, and was surprised to find that he himself was.

They ate in near silence, just the occasional words from the media center to break the stillness, watching the light fade over the Harbor Market and outside the flat's windows. Warreven listened for a while to the newsreaders' chatter—nothing new, still no word from Temelathe or Tendlathe or the *mosstaas*, though the Big Six were rumored to have asked for a meeting with Temelathe the next morning—and then pushed himself up off the couch and went out onto his porch, taking the bottle of sweetrum with him. It was almost empty, and he could feel it slurring his movements, but at least the pain had receded. He leaned against the railing, the land breeze eddying past, warm against his shoulders, looked through the deepening twilight toward the Harbor Market. In the pens next door, the land-spiders trilled and purred, disjointed bits of sound, but no one came to comfort them. That was unusual—the spinners were always very conscientious—but then, this night was hardly ordinary.

It was still hard to believe that Tendlathe was doing this—that

Tendlathe, whom he'd known, man and boy, for almost twenty-five years, had put him and Haliday and everyone like them, firmly outside the human race. But that was the problem, of course: he himself had never been boy nor man, except perhaps in law, and that had meant that Tendlathe had always had forbidden possibilities—impossibilities, by his definition—dangling before his eyes. And it hadn't helped, Warreven admitted silently, that he'd enjoyed teasing Tendlathe, had made no secret of the fact that he would sleep with him, as long as no change of gender, of identity, had been required. And I would have done it, too, and cheerfully, up until a week ago.

He heard the chime of an incoming call from the media center, but didn't turn his head. Something wasn't right, something more than the restless spiders next door. The air was damp and heavy, a haze of light hanging over the Gran'quai, but that was nothing unusual. He tilted his head carefully to one side, listening, and then realized what it was. The streets were silent, none of the usual murmur of traffic on the ring roads or down by the harbor. It was as if Bonemarche was waiting, everyone either already at the harbor, with the *ranas*, or hiding in the safety of their houses—

"Warreven?" Tatian was standing in the doorway, hair and beard turned brighter gold by the lights behind him. "There's a call."

Warreven made a face, pushed himself away from the rail. His bruises had stiffened while he stood there, and he had to catch himself against the door frame. Tatian stood watchful, not offering help, but within reach, and Warreven had to admit it was gracefully done. "Who is it?"

Tatian shrugged, and Warreven looked at the screen. Chauntclere Ferane looked back at him, broad face and salt-stained beard framed by the darkness of a dockside office. The windows were closed behind him, light glinting from the narrow panes, but the noise of the drums was still loud, doubling the sound from the news channel.

"Raven, it's me."

Warreven looked around for the remote, and Tatian handed it

to him. Warreven nodded his thanks and hit the button that activated his own camera. An icon lit, warning him that the transmission was now reciprocal, and Chauntclere flinched visibly.

"God and the spirits, you look a mess."

"I'm getting tired of hearing that," Warreven said, and immediately wished he hadn't. "I'm all right. It looks worse than it is."

"It looks bad enough," Chauntclere said. The sun-carved lines at the corners of his eyes and between his eyebrows were suddenly prominent. "I thought—they said the ghost *ranas* had nearly killed you, but I didn't believe it."

Believe it, Warreven thought. And a lot worse for Haliday. He said, "I'm—I will be all right. Hal was hurt a lot worse than me."

"I'm sorry. Is she—?" Chauntclere stopped, as though he didn't know how to ask.

"ʒe's going to be all right," Warreven said. He saw Chauntclere's eyes flicker at the creole word and used it again deliberately. "That's why they attacked us, Clere, because ʒe and I are herms."

"And because of who you are," Chauntclere said automatically. "I mean, you're the *seraaliste*, and everybody knows Haliday—"

"Everybody knows Haliday because ʒe went to the Council to get the legal right to call ʒimself a herm," Warreven said. "And they know me because I handle trade cases. The other herm who works with Haliday." Out of the corner of his good eye, he saw Tatian shift as though he were uncomfortable and made a face. "I'm sorry, Clere, it's been a bitch of a day."

"Yeah." Chauntclere gave a slight, embarrassed shrug, one shoulder moving under the faded cloth of his working vest. "But Hal is going to be all right, isn't she—zhe?"

Warreven nodded, and Chauntclere sighed with what looked like genuine relief.

"I'm glad."

And to be fair, Warreven thought, he probably was. There was nothing mean about Clere. He said, "Are you at the Harbor? What's going on down there?"

Chauntclere glanced over his shoulder, turned back to the camera. "Oh, yes, I'm still on the 'quai. I can't get off, the *ranas* won't let me past—won't let any of us past, they say they won't let us off-load cargo until Temelathe agrees to the *mosstaas* hunting the ghost *ranas*. I heard about an hour ago that Temelathe was supposed to come down here himself to talk to the leaders, but I don't know if it's true."

"Wonderful," Warreven muttered. Still, it might do some good: Temelathe knew how to balance the various factions; he had been doing it better than anyone else for almost thirty years.

Chauntclere looked over his shoulder again and shook his head. "I've got to go, this is the only working line on the 'quai, and I can't hog it. But I'm glad you're all right."

"I will be," Warreven said. "I'm glad you called, Clere—" The screen went dark before he could be sure the other had heard. He let himself sink back onto the couch, wondering how he'd fallen into the middle of all of this. Part of him wanted to be at the Harbor—he had earned that much, to see this through—but another part cringed at the thought of facing the darkened streets again. The memory of the ghost *ranas* returned, black robes and white faces, so that for an instant he could almost taste the fog and the shame and the fear. He made a face, as though that could erase the memory, and saw Tatian looking at him curiously. "I half-wish I was down there," he said defiantly, and Tatian gave a lopsided smile.

"I bet. I think I'd rather watch the narrowcast, myself."

"The other half is perfectly happy to," Warreven said. He looked at the screen again. "I wonder if Temelathe is going to try to negotiate with them?"

"He'd be smart to, I think," Tatian said, pushing himself away from the wall and coming to collect the dishes that remained on the table. "Do you want anything?"

Warreven started to shake his head, said instead, "No, thanks."

Tatian nodded vaguely, and started for the kitchen. Warreven leaned back against the cushions, grateful for their softness, and watched the rainbows gather around the lights. The doutfire would be wearing off soon; he thought about asking Tatian to bring him some, but couldn't muster the energy.

The media center buzzed again, startling him fully awake. He touched keys automatically, accepting the call, and frowned as a string of codes flashed across the base of the screen. The forming image split, dividing in half and then in thirds, and steadied. Three faces looked out of the screen, slightly elongated despite the system's attempt to keep the pictures proportional. Folhare he recognized at once; the other two, both men, were less familiar. He frowned, and then recognized the darker of the two. Losson Trencevent was one of the Modernists' regular speakers, one of the people who were usually seen on the narrowcasts and quoted in the broadsheets. He had never much liked Losson and didn't bother to hide his annoyance.

"Folhare? What is it?"

"Trouble," Folhare answered. At least, Warreven thought, she didn't start by telling him how bad he looked. "I—we need your help."

Warreven looked from her to the others. Losson was looking at something out of sight, while the second man—Dismars May-childer, he remembered suddenly, the Modernists' nominal leader, and their perennial candidate—was frowning impatiently. "What for?"

"You know Losson—" Folhare began, looking sideways, and Dismars cut her off.

"Temelathe is willing to negotiate. You—he likes you, and you're one of the Important Men. We need your voice as well, if we're going to get concessions on the Meeting."

Warreven stared at the screen, looking past him at pale green walls with a delicate stenciled tracery of flowering vines. "I'm not exactly an Important Man," he said, and stressed the final word. "Does this include the *wrangwys?*"

Losson drew an angry breath, and Dismars said quickly, "We've got a chance to get concessions on a lot of things, War-reven. There's no one issue. We should be able to get the big things through, that's the important thing."

Which doesn't include me, Warreven thought. I should have guessed—should have known. "Folhare?"

"What?" Her head lifted warily.

"You're a fem, *coy*, as *wrangwys* as me. What do you say to me?"

In the other two screens, he saw Losson start to roll his eyes, and as quickly suppress the movement. Dismars, more controlled, looked sideways as though he wanted to dictate Folhare's answer. And that, Warreven thought, was the real problem. If you weren't a man, you were a woman, and neither of the roles fit a herm. Neither role fit 3im—Haliday had known that for years, that was why 3e had gone before the Council. "Well, Folhare?" 3e said, and didn't bother to hide the cold anger that filled 3im.

"I—" Folhare stopped, made a face. "No, I'm not completely happy, Raven. But this is the only chance we're going to get."

And that was true, Warreven acknowledged, but it wasn't good enough. 3e tilted 3er head to the side, ignoring the streak of yellow light that shot across his vision, fixed his good eye on the split screen. "All right," 3e said. "I'll come down with you. I'll talk to Temelathe with you—not for you, you've been warned, but I will talk to him."

"We need to present a united front," Losson said, and Dismars waved a hand at him.

"I understand what you're saying. And I'm not ignoring your concerns, I promise. But Folhare's right, this is our best, maybe our only chance, to get to speak at the Meeting."

"I'm on my way," Warreven said, and jammed 3er thumb down on the remote, switching off the machine. 3e pushed 3imself to 3er feet, still furious, and saw Tatian standing in the doorway, frowning. "Don't tell me I shouldn't do this—"

The off-worlder shook his head. "Do you want me to drive you? I've still got the rover."

Warreven took a deep breath, silenced in the middle of 3er anger, and opened 3er mouth to say one thing, then shook 3er head, said simply, "Why?" Tatian blinked, looked almost hurt, and Warreven made a face, felt the anger rising again. "It's not that I don't trust you, it's just—I'm not sure I understand. And I'll be damned if I'll accept it if it's pity, or you presuming to take care of me—"

Tatian shook his head. "You're right. It's not that simple. The Concord went through this I don't know how long ago, and we've forgotten what it was like. But those people, they've missed what's really wrong here, and you're the only person I've met who does see it—well, you and Haliday. So I want to help." He shrugged, looked almost embarrassed by the sentiment. "And I doubt you could get a car tonight, even if you paid metal."

Warreven nodded, appeased. It had never occurred to ʒim that the Concord Worlds must have once faced the same issues, the same questions, what was and wasn't human, but it was reassuring to hear it said and to know what their decision had been. "Thanks. Yes, I'd like—I'd be grateful if you'd drive me. I just have to get some things."

ʒe pushed past Tatian into the hall and went into the kitchen to get more doutfire. ʒer hands were clumsy on the lid, and it took ʒim several seconds to shake loose another curl of the bark. ʒe pocketed the rest of the box and turned back toward the door. The bathroom door was open, and ʒe caught a glimpse of ʒimself in the mirror above the tub: a thin person—herm—in black, one eye hidden by the black bandage. It was Agede's image, Agede the Doorkeeper, and ʒe lifted a fresh bottle of sweetrum in salute. Agede looked back at ʒim, Agede with his bottle and his cane, and Warreven smiled fiercely, knowing what ʒe was going to do. ʒe collected a walking stick from the bedroom—red, not black, but it would do—and went back to the main room, lifted ʒer bottle to ʒer reflection as ʒe passed. Tatian, blond hair and beard golden in the light from the media center, looked at ʒim uncertainly, and Warreven grinned.

"I'm ready when you are."

Tatian steered the rover through the darkened streets, empty except for the occasional—very occasional—hurrying figure. They ducked into doorways or side streets as the rover passed, and Tatian shook his head.

"I don't like this. Are you sure—" He broke off then, shook

away whatever else he would have said, but Warreven gave a rueful smile.

"Am I sure it's smart, or am I sure I know what I'm doing?"

"Either." Tatian negotiated the turn onto a narrow street, easing the rover around a shay drawn up to shield someone's main doorway.

"I know what I'm doing," Warreven answered, and hoped it was true. At least, he thought, I know what I'm planning.

Tatian nodded. "I don't want to try to get too close to the Harbor Market. Is there someplace we can stash the rover—someplace we can get to, and get away from, fast, if we have to?"

Warreven frowned, then nodded. "Take the next left."

Tatian turned obediently, and the rover slid down a suddenly brightly lit street between rows of brick-fronted warehouses. The heavy doors—ironwood, rather than true steel, but strong enough to keep out all but the most determined looters—were barred, security lights flickering their warning above the lock plates. At the end of the street, however, a space opened abruptly, shallow, but wide enough to keep the rover off the main traffic way. A pair of shays, one with company marks, the other without, were already parked there, and Warreven nodded to them.

"Good enough?" 3e asked.

"How far are we from the Market?" Tatian asked, but he was already easing the rover into the space between the shays.

"There's a stair-street right there," Warreven answered. "It leads down directly to the Market, comes out behind the auction platform—where the stage is now. Now a lot of people use it."

Tatian nodded again. "All right. If we get separated, or if there's trouble, we get away and meet back here. With any luck, everybody will take other streets." He popped the rover's doors and levered himself out of the compartment.

"You sound like you've done this before," Warreven said, and followed.

Tatian sighed. "I got caught in a riot on Hermione when I was just starting out. It's not something I particularly want to repeat."

"Who does?" Warreven said, pleased with the lightness of 3er voice, and led the way down the half-lit stairway.

There was a shantytown at its foot, a cluster of maybe half a dozen shacks built with the cast-off wood of shipping crates and the occasional bright-blue sheet of plastic, tucked into the dubious shelter of a disused factory outbuilding. Warreven hesitated, but there was no easier way—and no time to turn back, 3e told 3imself, not if 3e wanted to get to the Market in time to deal with Temelathe. Behind 3im, 3e heard Tatian mutter a curse and ignored him, kept walking, setting an easy pace, down the last steps and out onto the paving.

A low fire was burning on the patch of bare ground between two of the huts. The sound of the drums came clearly from the Market, and someone, no more than a slim shape behind the fire, was tapping out a counterpoint on a hand drum. Another figure—male, or maybe mem—stood silhouetted against the flames, bottle in hand. Warreven ignored them and kept walking, aware of Tatian at 3er back, all the muscles in 3er back and sides protesting the sudden knotted tension. 3e was expecting catcalls, or worse, but heard nothing except the stutter of the drum, and then even that fell away, so that 3e was moving in step to the drums at the Market alone. At the edge of the Market, 3e could stand it no longer and looked back, to see the shanty folk standing silent, the man and the drummer joined now by a woman, child on hip, and then another and another, gender blurred by the shadows. Not knowing certainly why 3e did it, Warreven lifted 3er bottle in salute and turned back to the Market. The murmur of a name followed, not his own, and 3e heard Tatian swear again.

The Harbor Market was bright and abruptly crowded, light and shadow jagged against a sky black and emptied of stars. The crowd in front of the band platform was mixed, looked like a holiday crowd more than a protest, sailors and dockers in rough work trousers, wrap-shirts thrown on against the cool night air, dancing with ordinary people in rough-spun silks and *shaals*. There were people from the *wrangwys* houses in a mix of ordinary and off-world clothes, and even a few genuine off-worlders, caught between curiosity and fear. Maybe a third of them—and every one

of the odd-bodied, Warreven realized with a thrill of pleasure—
wore the *ranas'* multicolored ribbons, every color, any shade of
every color, but not black or white. The air was thick with smoke,
smelled of charcoal and feelgood and spilled *liquertie;* at the foot
of the Gran'quai, in front of the barricade, a bonfire was lit. The
smoke of it rolled off toward Ferryhead, carried by the fitful wind,
almost white against the dark sky.

The band was drumming on the makeshift stage, playing a
cheerful rhythm, a song 3e had danced to in the *wrangwys* houses.
It still sounded festive, more of a celebration, Midsummer or
Springtide rather than a *rana* protest, but then 3e saw the line of
people between the bonfire and the barricade. They stood shoulder to shoulder across the end of the Gran'quai, and even at this
distance 3e could see the firelight reflecting from metal—more
metal than he had imagined the docks might possess, metal in
chains, in bars, maybe even in the barrels of guns. The dull sheen
reminded 3im of the ghost *ranas,* emphasized the defiant solidity
of their stance, and 3e shivered, suddenly afraid again.

"Are you all right?" Tatian asked quietly, and Warreven nodded.

"Give me a minute," 3e said, and sank down on the nearest of
the fused-stone bollards that marked the first ring of stalls. 3er eye
was aching again, streaks of light searing 3er sight; 3er neck
throbbed, a dull pain that promised worse to come, and the cut
was burning where 3er clothes had rubbed the bandage. 3e
grimaced, tugging at the waist of 3er trousers, and lifted the
sweetrum bottle to 3er lips. It was almost empty already, and 3e
caught a crazed glimpse of the sky, a single pinpoint of light—a
pharmaceutical satellite, almost certainly, not a star—blazing in a
rainbow halo before 3e lowered the bottle. There was a flower
lying at 3er feet.

3e looked at it, startled, and looked up to see a woman standing a meter or so away, two fingers to her lips in conventional
acknowledgment of the spirits. For an instant, the gesture was
shocking—3e had meant it, had courted that identification, but it
had been a long time, a decade, maybe two since 3e had worn the
mask of any spirit—and then training reasserted itself. 3e lifted

the bottle in salute, and another flower, this one blue with a gold heart, landed beside the first. 3e nodded to that giver as well—a pot-bellied, well-dressed man in company badges, who should probably have known better—and pushed 3imself to 3er feet.

"What's this all about?" Tatian demanded, but quietly, his voice pitched to carry only to Warreven's ears.

Warreven glanced back at him, couldn't restrain a sudden wild smile. "They see Agede—the Doorkeeper, one of the spirits, one of the powerful spirits—not just me, and they see Agede is a herm, I'm a herm, and that, Tatian, is how I'm going to win."

"Oh, my God," the off-worlder muttered, and the words were more than half a prayer.

"Something like that," Warreven agreed, and started toward the bonfire. 3e could feel people watching, more and more of them turning to watch their progress through the glare of the lights; 3e could see, quite clearly, how the crowd parted for them.

The sound of the band was louder than ever by the bonfire, more than one drum calling the various lines of the song, flute soaring above to carry the melody. People, men and women and the *wrangwys*, were dancing in the firelight, maybe half-following the orderly patterns of a traditional dance, the rest improvising in the confined space. Warreven smiled again, feeling the drums in 3er bones, feet automatically picking up the pattern, and a boy swung toward 3im, hands out to invite the dance. He was young, maybe fifteen or sixteen, thin and hungry-looking, dark hair cut close to his skull. Seeing Warreven, his steps faltered, and Warreven held out 3er hands in answer, took the boy's cold fingers, and twirled him gently away. 3e caught a quick glimpse of the boy's face, open-mouthed, blank with shocked surprise, realized that he, too, was a herm. 3e smiled, and held out the almost-empty sweetrum bottle, tossed it toward 3er erstwhile partner. The boy—herm—caught it awkwardly, two-handed, and Warreven turned away, skirting the bonfire.

Ahead, the firelight rose and fell on the faces of the people who blocked access to the Gran'quai, reddening the colors of their ribbons, gleaming from the metal of the chains and the pry bars in their hands. At the center of the line, blocking the single opening in the barricade, was a group all in single colors, red and purple and orange and yellow and green and blue, all the colors of the spectrum; their hair was bound up under turbans of the same color, lips and eyes painted to match, hands gloved. Warreven suppressed a shudder at that reminder, but they were clearly the leaders of this part of the protest, and 3e made 3imself walk steadily toward them.

"Don't look back," Tatian said, "but you've acquired a following."

Warreven felt 3er shoulders twitch, painfully, but managed not to turn. "I'm here to see Dismars," 3e said, to the *rana* dressed in orange, and saw the woman shiver.

The man next to her, all in green, said, "It's Warreven. He's expected."

He spoke loudly enough to be heard over the sound of the drums, but Warreven, glancing down, saw the orange woman's free hand curved in a propitiating sign. She stepped aside, letting through the line, but the green man said, "Wait. The off-worlder—"

"You're not closing doors to me?" Warreven asked, gently, and the green man fell silent. 3e stepped through the line, and Tatian followed.

Behind the barricade, on the Gran'quai itself, everything was different. The drums were softer, muffled by the stacked crates, and there were no dancers. Instead, a gang of dockers was busy with haul bars and an antigrav, adding a final load of crates and balks of ballast wood to the barricade. A devil, one of the portable engines that powered the cranes, chugged softly itself in the background, throttled down, but ready. They were lling to keep things peaceful: that was the message of the ban he bonfire and the dancers, the carnival in the Market, but the re equally prepared to fight. Warreven wondered how m more guns were hidden on the dock, how many tool la had already been dragged up out of workshops and ship ids, and started as someone shoved something into 3er ha d not to drop it, see-
It was a bottle, nearly full, and 3e two fingers to her lips ing a woman sailor backing away,

before she turned back to the barricade. The cork was off, and 3e could smell sweetrum. 3e sipped it, not knowing what else would be mixed in it, and tasted starfire bitter beneath the sweet. 3e took a deeper swallow then, grateful for the drugs to numb the rising pain behind his eye, and saw the leaders of the Modernists gathered beneath one of the working lights, a noteboard propped up on a bollard.

"I'll wait here," Tatian said, and stopped just outside the range of the light.

Warreven nodded, and stepped forward. "I'm here."

3e saw one of them—a younger man, someone 3e didn't know—touch his lips, saw Folhare's sudden grin and Losson's angry stare. Dismars said, "Warreven." He, too, had pitched his voice to carry beyond the little group, to identify 3im, take away the mask of the spirit. Which isn't possible, Warreven thought, not tonight, not this time, you called me, and here I am, not what you expected and not what you can use. 3e spread 3er hands, and smiled.

"Is Temelathe really coming, then?"

"He's on his way," Dismars said, grimly, and Losson broke in.

"And we need to be sure we're all after the same things."

"You wanted me here," Warreven said. "Here I am."

3e saw Dismars and Losson exchange quick glances, and then Dismars said, "And we're glad of it. I appreciate your help, Warreven."

Wait until it's over, Warreven thought. 3e said nothing, however, just waited, and Dismars looked back at the noteboard.

"All right," he said. "We've made a list of our demands— you're welcome to take a look, Warreven—but the main thing is, we want to speak at the Meeting."

Warreven accepted the noteboard that Folhare held out to 3im, worked the controls to glance quickly down the list. Gender law—described "trade and related questions"—was there all right, but looking the faces surrounding 3im, 3e couldn't muster much confidence their willingness to press the question.

"Without that," Dismars went on, his eyes fixed on Warreven's face, "without we can't hope to achieve anything."

"And we can't get anything if there's a riot," Losson growled.

"We can't stand up to the *mosstaas*," a younger man corrected, frowning.

"And we lose any hope of getting support from the *mesnies*," Losson said.

"All right," Dismars said sharply. "Are you willing to talk to Temelathe with us, Warreven?"

"I'll talk to him," Warreven said.

Dismars opened his mouth to say something more, but a woman's voice from the barricade interrupted him.

"Æ, miri, the Most Important's here."

"How many?" Dismars called back.

"One caleche," the woman answered. "And three, no, four big shays. All *mosstaas*." Behind her, the band's steady beat faltered, and then the leaders had it under control again. "They're stopping at the Embankment, though."

"Right." Dismars took a deep breath, looked around the circle of faces, including even Warreven in his intent stare. "Let's go."

He led the way out through the opening in the barricade, the rainbow-dressed line parting to let them through. Warreven, following at the back of the group, was aware of Tatian behind 3im, sliding through the barricade unchallenged. In the Market, the crowd was silent, no one dancing now, despite the continued music of the *rana* band on the platform; there was a smaller crowd—the people who had followed 3im to the barricade, Warreven realized, with a sudden thrill—to the left of the bonfire, mostly the odd-bodied, their attention swiveling between the barricade and the approaching *mosstaas*. The shays had stopped at the edge of the Market, and *mosstaas*, dozens of them, armed with riot guns and cast-ceramic breastplates, spilled from the open bodies, formed up neatly on the worn stones. Warreven looked toward the platform, toward the stairway that led back up to the warehouse street where the rover was waiting, saw yet another group, not part of the *rana*, not yet, but from the shanty, watching just outside the market lights. A few of the people who had been dancing slipped away as 3e watched, but the shanty dwellers remained.

Something moved in the darkness beyond the shays, and a

heavy caleche slid past them into the light. The crowd parted for it, reluctant but wary, closed in again as it ground to a stop just beyond the bonfire. The passenger door opened, and Temelathe stepped out. A *mosstaas* followed, pellet gun at the ready, and then Tendlathe, slim in the firelight. He looked over his shoulder at the shays, but made no gesture. He started to follow his father, the trooper instantly at his shoulder, but Temelathe waved them back, and they stopped a meter or so from the caleche. Temelathe looked almost incongruously ordinary as he crossed the open space between the two groups, a bulky, gray-haired, gray-bearded man in plain trousers and an old-fashioned vest over a new-style shirt, his hair still knotted at the nape of his neck. Warreven felt old loyalties tugging at 3er heart, looked deliberately past him to Tendlathe, standing a little ahead of the *mosstaas* now, both hands deep in the pockets of his trousers.

"Miri, mirrimi," Temelathe said, and though he didn't seem to raise his voice, it was pitched to carry easily through the crowd, and along the line of people in front of the barricade. "This is outside of enough. I understand your complaints, and I agree, this lawlessness, these ghost *ranas*, have to be stopped, but this is no way to get anything done. Disperse now, and we can meet properly in the morning."

There was a murmur, half angry, half uncertain, and Dismars shook his head. His voice wasn't as clear as Temelathe's, but it would carry to at least the nearer of the crowd. "Tomorrow isn't soon enough, mir. We need to talk now."

"I agree that we need to talk," Temelathe said, "but not like this." He gestured, the broad sweep of his hand taking in the bonfire and the *ranas* as well as the barricade and its guardians. "There's a lot that needs to be said, to be discussed, but not like this. We need to sit down together, without any lives at stake. This, this is an illegal gathering, and I can't permit it to go on. Disperse now, peacefully, and we can talk tomorrow."

"This is legal," Losson said.

Dismars said, "Mir, yesterday's *rana* was dispersed, when it was well within the bounds of law and custom. And we got nothing for that, an act in good faith, except that the ghost *ranas* attacked two more people. I can't in conscience ask people to disperse under those circumstances."

Tendlathe sighed, jammed his hands into his pockets. It was an act Warreven had seen before—the bluff, good-hearted man from the Stanelands, a little confused by the modern world, but willing to learn—and 3e took a step back, away from the others. 3e wouldn't, couldn't, let 3imself be taken in this time.

"Yesterday was an error, miri, that I admit. An overzealous officer, holding too fast to the letter of the law."

"Under the circumstances," Dismars repeated, "our people will be most upset if they have to disperse again. Especially with nothing to show for it."

"We can talk tonight, if you insist," Temelathe said. "Though I'd've expected a little more consideration for an old man."

"Mir, I wouldn't insult you," Dismars answered, and Temelathe showed teeth in a quick grin. Warreven looked past him to see Tendlathe still standing frozen, hands still in his pockets. The firelight threw the planes of his face into harsh relief, the expressionless stare and the moving eyes.

"But if I must, I must," Temelathe said. "I'm willing to talk all night, if that's what it takes to get this settled."

"We would ask for a preliminary undertaking first," Dismars said.

Temelathe spread his hands. "I'm prepared to talk."

"There are issues that have to be discussed more generally," Dismars said. "At the Meeting."

"The Meeting's out of my control," Temelathe said, but the protest was only perfunctory. "That's a matter for the Watch Council."

"And we know how influential you are, mir," Dismars answered. "But these things need to be discussed, and the Meeting's the only forum where all of us have a voice."

"What issues?" Temelathe faced the younger man squarely, his spread-legged stance—the Captain's stand—apparently relaxed, only the rigidity of his shoulders to betray any hint of nervousness. Behind him, Tendlathe took a single step forward, then seemed to think better of it.

· "A round dozen," Dismars said. "To name a few, there's the question of how contracts are awarded to the pharmaceuticals, there's the whole question of trade—most of all, there's whether or not we should join the Concord. All those need to be dealt with, mir."

"Not everyone agrees with you," Temelathe said.

Dismars looked over his shoulder, the glance as good as a gesture. "All these people are with me. They're not just Bonemarche, mir, we're from all over, *mesnies* as well as the city."

"I could ask the Council to schedule you to speak at the Meeting," Temelathe said. He smiled thinly. "That's your right, after all. But I can't make promises regarding individual issues. The contracts, for example, or trade, those are clan issues, or city issues, those don't belong in the Meeting."

"They affect everyone," Dismars said.

Temelathe shook his head. "I can't make promises for your clans. You're a Maychilder, he's a Trencevent, the lady there I know is Black Stane—you'll have to take this up with your own clans. But I can offer you the chance to speak."

Dismars took a deep breath, and nodded. "And we talk tonight."

"Very well." Temelathe nodded back, the gesture of a man concluding a good bargain. Behind him, Tendlathe smiled.

"Temelathe," Warreven said. 3e didn't raise 3er voice, didn't need to in the sudden silence as 3e stepped out from the group of Modernists. 3e felt the eyes on 3im, the waiting *mosstass* behind the line of the crowd, the crowd itself, not just the people on the barricade and the people who had followed 3im, but the ones still waiting by the *rana* platform and the shanty folk beyond them. 3e realized 3e was still holding the sweetrum bottle, and tipped it to 3er lips, completing Agede's image.

"Warreven," Temelathe said softly. His eyes flickered, taking in both the clothes and the crowd's reaction, the hum of agreement from the odd-bodied to his right. "I hadn't thought of that. The Doorkeeper is a herm."

"I am," Warreven answered, deliberately ambiguous, and touched the bandage over his eye. "And I, and people like me, are suffering for it. That has to stop, and you, Temelathe, are the one who can do it."

Temelathe looked at him, a long, level stare. "So what exactly do you want, Warreven?"

"First, the ghost *ranas* have to be stopped," Warreven answered. "Hunted down and punished would be best, my father, but stopped will do. And then—I exist, people like me exist, and we're not *wrangwys*, not anymore. We are people, and we want a proper name, in law."

There was a little murmur behind him, and then a louder one, as people realized what 3e'd said. Tendlathe made a soft noise, not quite protest, more surprise and anger, and Temelathe glanced over his shoulder, putting out his hand. Tendlathe was still again, and the Most Important Man looked back at 3im.

"I can't promise that, Warreven. You know that."

Warreven took a deep breath. "One man has died, I nearly died last night, I don't want any deaths tonight. But there will be more if you don't take action."

Temelathe looked at him, mouth drawn into a tight line. From behind him, Tendlathe said, fiercely, "Do you stand with him, Dismars? Are you that stupid?"

Temelathe waved him to silence, looked at Dismars himself. "It's a fair question, though. Are you willing to throw everything away, for him? Because I can't meet with you under these terms."

There was a long silence, only the sound of the fire and the breathing of the massed crowd, and then Dismars shook his head. "I'll stick to what we agreed, mir." He looked once over his shoulder, lifted his voice to carry to the crowd. "It's not that we don't recognize that the *wrangwys* have problems, but there are other ways to deal with them."

There was a murmur, almost a moan, from the listening crowd, and someone whistled, a shrill note of disapproval.

"That's not good enough," Warreven said. 3e pitched 3er voice to carry to the entire line this time. "I want those two things—two simple things, Temelathe, to keep the peace and to admit I, we, exist—and I want it now."

Temelathe looked from 3im to Dismars, then back along the line of dockers behind 3im. "Be reasonable—"

"I am reasonable," Warreven said. "There's nothing unreasonable about wanting to exist, my father."

"It's not my business, it's clan business," Temelathe said. He spread his hands, taking in the line at the barricade, the people around him, the platform beyond the bonfire where the *ranas* stood. "I don't have that kind of authority—and you know as well as I do, not everyone agrees with you. The majority of people are satisfied with things as they are."

"They're still wrong," Warreven said bitterly. "You've worn the Captain's shape for a long time, Temelathe, it's time you acted for him. This is simple justice, a simple matter of reality."

"Is it?" Temelathe sounded almost sad.

Behind him, Tendlathe stirred, fixed 3im with a cold stare. "God and the spirits, that's enough. Quit while you're ahead, Warreven."

"And let you pretend I—we—don't exist?" Warreven looked over 3er shoulder again, down the long line of people guarding the barricade. 3e pointed, picking out the first herm 3e saw, then to the person next to 3im, who might have been a fem. "You, and you—" 3e swung around, pointing again to individuals, mostly *wrangwys*, a few faces 3e thought 3e recognized from the bars and dance houses, people who'd done trade, who slept wry-abed, as well as the odd-bodied. "—all of you, can we let him say we don't exist?"

3e got an answering shout, angriest from 3er left, but loud enough from the rest, and 3e smiled equally at father and son, knowing it was more of a snarl. "You hear us. Don't tell me you can't, I know what your power is. You can write us into law. Give us that."

"I can't," Temelathe answered.

"You will." Warreven took a deep breath, feeling the power in 3im, riding the will of the crowd, harnessing it to 3er own desire.

"And if I don't?" Temelathe sounded incredulous. "Are you threatening me, Warreven?"

"I'm opening the door," Warreven said, and was ʒimself answered by another cheer. "It's up to you which one."

Temelathe stared at him for another minute. Behind him, Tendlathe took a slow step forward, and then another, moving closer across the cobbles, until he stood almost at Temelathe's shoulder. His expression was no longer stony, but openly furious, his stare divided between his father and Warreven. The Most Important Man shook his head. "No, not this time," he said. "Not even for you—"

A flat snap cut him off. Warreven blinked, unable for an instant to recognize it, and Temelathe grunted, hands flying to his chest. In the firelight, the blood was already dark on his shirt, spilling over his fingers. He started to say something, mouth opening soundlessly, and then pitched forward onto the worn cobbles of the Market.

"My father—?" Warreven began, and in the same instant saw the flash of metal in Tendlathe's hand. Tendlathe met ʒer stare across Temelathe's body, defiant and triumphant and afraid, and behind him the *mosstaas* tilted his pellet gun toward the sky, fired two quick shots. The sound was drowned in the roar of the crowd, but the muzzle flash lit the night, an obvious signal. The caleche's engine whined as it pulled out, slewing to face the way it had come, and one wing struck the edge of the bonfire, scattering sparks and a chunk of burning wood that shattered as it struck the stones.

"Murderer!" Warreven said, and stepped forward over Temelathe's body. ʒe lifted ʒer cane, swung its heavy length at Tendlathe's head, aiming the weight of it at his temples. Tendlathe ducked, bringing his arms up in automatic defense, and the little gun—a palmgun, small but deadly enough at close range—went skittering across the cobbles. Warreven lifted the cane again, and the trooper shouted, leveling his own gun.

"Get in the car, mir—and you, whatever you are, get back!"

Warreven froze, staring at the muzzle of the rifle. The trooper couldn't miss, not at this range, and ʒe braced ʒimself for the bullet. Then the caleche slid to a stop behind them, passenger door opening, and Tendlathe half-fell into it, one hand to his head. The crowd surged forward, one man throwing himself against the engine cowling, and the *mosstaas* fired at last. Warreven flinched, and the sweetrum bottle kicked in 3er hand, the glass exploding, spilling a great fan of liquid. Some of it landed on the embers from the bonfire and flamed blue, an eerie, alien light, consumed as quickly as it had appeared. The rest of the *mosstaas* were pouring down from the Embankment, and Dismars and someone in dockers' clothes were trying to form the crowd into a line to meet them, but half the crowd didn't seem to realize what had happened and still stood in confusion. And then there were more shots, and people began to run, some toward the side streets, some back toward the Gran'quai. Dismars shouted, his words inaudible at this distance, and someone threw a bottle after the caleche. It missed, broke on the stones, spreading a pool of flames.

Warreven looked back at Temelathe, the body still contorted on the ground, ignored. An ember had landed on one sleeve, and the cloth was smoldering; hardly knowing what 3e was doing, 3e reached out with the tip of the cane and ground out the flame. 3e realized then what 3e must look like, Agede considering 3er latest conquest, couldn't bring 3imself to care. 3e had never meant for this to happen, never wanted Temelathe dead, not when it left Tendlathe in control—

"Raven!" Tatian caught 3er shoulders, swung 3im bodily toward the platform and the stair street behind it. "We've got to get out of here."

"But—" Warreven shook 3imself, trying to get 3er mind to work. The last of the drummers was jumping down from the improvised stage, drum clutched to his body; the flute player stood frozen against the lights, staring toward the Embankment. There was another crackle of gunfire, and she fell or jumped into the crowd below.

"Come on," Tatian said, and shoved 3im toward the platform.

"Warreven!" someone shouted, and another voice answered, "Stop him!"

Tatian swore under his breath. "Leave the cane," he said, and Warreven dropped it. "Look at me."

3e turned, shaking now, the sight of Temelathe falling, the body fallen, and Tendlathe standing over it, caught in the fire-light, still filling 3er mind, and Tatian caught 3er chin. The pain of his fingers on the bruises shocked 3im back to a semblance of awareness, and 3e started to pull away.

"The bandage," Tatian said. "It's too obvious. It's got to go."

Warreven started to nod, but Tatian's hand was already on the corner of the plastiskin, jerking it free. The medipack came with it, spilling what was left of its contents down the side of 3er face and neck, warm and faintly salty on 3er lips. The firelight seared 3er eyes; 3e winced, but turned on 3er own toward the stairs. Other people, dozens of them, were running with them, first in twos and threes, and then in larger groups. Warreven stumbled on the uneven stones, vision blurring, caught the off-worlder's arm for support. As they reached the shantytown, gunfire sounded again, and 3e looked back to see the bonfire scattered, a drift of glowing coals, and dark figures, a neat line and a ragged one, shifting back and forth across it. More people were running toward them, heading for the stairs—heading for all the stair streets and alleys that led away from the Market, and Warreven turned back, climbed blind and aching toward the temporary safety of the rover.

advocate:
> (Hara) man or woman trained in written and customary law, and certi-
> fied by his or her clan as someone who has the right to speak for others
> before the clan and Watch courts.

MHYRE TATIAN

Tatian sprinted up the last few steps to the warehouse street,
shoving Warreven ahead of him. The indigene was moving awkwardly, without coordination, but Tatian pushed 3im on, not daring to stop. He glanced back once, saw more people heading for
this stairway—the *mosstaas* had cut off access to most of the others—and gave Warreven a final shove in the direction of the
rover. Its security field was flashing, warning that the system was
primed and active, and Tatian stopped, swearing, and reached for
his wrist pad to deactivate it. The pulse kicked back across his
chest, and he held his breath for an instant, fighting the pain and
the fear that the interface box would finally fail completely at this
moment. The field stayed clear for a heartbeat, two, and then
faded. He took a deep breath, not daring to admit the depth of his
relief, and said, "Get in, quick."

Warreven moved to obey, and Tatian swung himself into the
driver's pod, triggering the main systems. He kicked the quick
start lever, heard the engine cough and die. He kicked it again,
then made himself take the time to adjust the settings. This time
the engine caught, and he glanced sideways to make sure Warreven was safely in place. The indigene was leaning back against
the cushions, 3er left eye, the only one visible, swollen closed, a
trail of liquid, tears or discharge or the remains of the medipack,
running down 3er cheek. 3e looked bad, but there was no time to
do anything for 3im. 3er door was closed, and the lock indicator
glowed red; he would worry about the rest later. He slammed the

rover into gear and edged out into the street. The hard tires crunched on something, and Tatian saw that the shay parked beside them had lost its side windows already.

He touched the throttle, sent the rover surging forward, and had to swerve to avoid the running figures that loomed out of the shadows. One of them grabbed for the passenger door, but the locks held. Tatian caught a glimpse of a terrified face—maybe a clean-shaven man's, maybe a woman's, too distorted by fear and effort for him to be sure—but knew better than to stop. He touched the throttle again, increasing power, and the face fell away. In the mirrors, he could see more people emerging from the stairway, could hear, even over the noise of the rover's engines, shouts and the wail of sirens in the distance.

"Where to?" he asked, and swung the rover right at the end of the street, turning away from the Harbor.

Warreven didn't answer for a long moment, and Tatian risked a quick look at 3im, then had to swerve again to avoid a running group. 3e was still motionless, slumped against the cushions, but then 3e turned to look at him, 3er good eye open and afraid. "I don't know. God and the spirits, I didn't—" 3e broke off, shook 3er head hard. "Not to my place, anyway."

"No." Tatian took his hand from the steering bar to input a query, searching for the city's traffic system. It was unreliable at the best of times, and he wasn't surprised to see the familiar SYS-TEM DOWN message flicker along the bottom of the windscreen. "The port, then, maybe," he said. If we can get there. "If not, the Nest."

"The Nest?" Warreven was trying to sound more alert.

"EHB—the Expatriate Housing Blocks." Tatian reached for his input pad again, tried to call up a city map. The system fizzed under his skin, produced a cloud of static, hazing the windscreen, and then cleared. He studied the map for a moment, then turned again, heading for the ring roads that would feed into the main road to the starport. There was only one that led to the port complex, and he opened the throttle further, set the rover careening through the narrow streets. The first main street was less crowded than he'd expected; he turned onto it, slowed down behind a shay with company markings. He heard sirens again, glanced nervously into the mirror, and then keyed the surroundings display. Red lights flared on the map, showing the *mosstaas'* reported positions, but the nearest was four streets away. The shay turned off ahead of him, onto a side street that the map seemed to show would be a shortcut to the ring road. Tatian started to follow, then hesitated, looking at the narrow lanes, and kept to the route he knew.

The rover topped the first of the hills, and the road opened out into one of Bonemarche's many little squares. Light flared, streetlights and firelight, and Tatian saw that the central square was filled with bodies. Most of them wore the multicolored ribbons of the Modernist *rana*, and one held a drum, its sides glossy in the firelight. The nearest—a fem, tunic pulled tight and knotted to reveal every nuance of ðer body's curves—pointed and yelled, the words indistinct, muffled by the rover's systems. Tatian hauled on the steering bar, sent the rover skidding around the corner of the square, and saw something shatter in the street behind them. Warreven twisted in ʒer seat, staring back at them.

"They were on my side," ʒe said, after a moment, and settled back into ʒer place.

"I didn't think you had a side anymore," Tatian said. Warreven looked up sharply, face setting into an angry mask, but then, before Tatian could say anything, apology or mitigation, ʒer glare faltered.

"Apparently not."

"I'm sorry." Tatian fixed his eyes on the dark street ahead, very aware of the locked and barred doors to either side.

"I—" Warreven shook ʒer head. "I'm not. I was right—I'm still right about the laws, and I'm right that Temelathe could have done something. But, God and the spirits, I didn't mean for him to die. I didn't think Tendlathe would do that."

"Tendlathe?"

"Didn't you see?" Warreven asked. "Ten shot him, the bastard, he had one of those little guns. In his pocket, I guess."

Tatian took a breath, let it out slowly. He hadn't seen that, had seen only the three of them, Tendlathe, Temelathe, and Warreven, weirdly lit by the bonfire. He had heard the shot—a small sound, he thought, it could have been a palmgun—and seen Temelathe fall. Fall forward, he thought, which I think means the shot came from behind. Tendlathe was behind him; so was a good part of the crowd, but they hadn't seemed that angry yet. And Warreven said 3e'd seen Tendlathe do it. "Do you think anyone else saw him?"

"Do you think it matters?" Warreven shook 3er head again, jammed 3er hands into 3er hair. "The door swings both ways. I forgot that."

Tatian glanced warily at 3im, but saw only the blind eye and the twist of 3er swollen mouth that could mean anything, or nothing. He said, "What happens now?"

Warreven turned 3er head so that 3e was looking out the rover's window. "I have no idea."

Tatian looked away, concentrating on the road. Two streets more, he thought, then one more. . . . And then he turned the rover onto the access road, and braked hard, the rover slewing as it came to a stop, barely avoiding the shay stopped ahead of him. There were more shays beyond that, shays and rovers and heavy company-marked triphibians, warning lights flashing as they tried to edge their way onto the port road. Tatian swore under his breath, seeing more vehicles jamming the port road—not just off-world vehicles, either, not just company marks, but battered four-ups that had to be local. He touched his wrist pad again, changing the parameters of the map, and watched the lines writhe across the base of the windscreen, the same shifts running painfully along his nerves. As he had feared, specks of red light flashed into existence, blocking the port road: the *mosstaas* had already set up a barricade of their own.

"We'll have to try the Nest," he said aloud, and Warreven looked at him.

"What's wrong?"

"There's a roadblock on the port road," Tatian answered, and slammed the rover into reverse, barely missing the nose of a shay as it pulled up behind him. He ignored the driver's angry shout, hauled on the steering bar until the rover swung around again. There was barely room to pass, and he felt the side wheels bump up onto the sidewalk, jolt down again hard. "They move fast."

"Tendlathe moves fast," Warreven said.

That was not a pleasant thought, but it was logical: of course Tendlathe would take over, Tatian thought, and turned onto the first street that led in the right direction for the Nest. And that means real trouble for me—and Warreven, too, of course, but I thought I might get out of this with my job. . . . He blocked that thought—there was no point in borrowing trouble—and fixed his attention on the road.

The Nest's perimeter fences were lit, the first time Tatian had ever seen that, glowing blue against the night. He slowed the rover, for the first time that night glad of the NAPD markings on the machine's nose, and edged up to the entrance. As he got closer, he could see security on the gates—company security—recognizable even without the usual matching uniforms, identifiable by the off-world weapons and the casual competence with which they held them. Company rivalries had been put aside; the Nest would be defended. He lowered his own security field, lowered his window as well as he pulled up to the gate. A tall woman leaned toward him, face shadowed by her helmet, coveralls bulging over body armor.

"Yeah?"

"Mhyre Tatian, NAPD. I live here."

"ID, please?"

He could barely see her face under the helmet, saw mostly the movement of her eyes as she scanned the car. Her stunrifle was still slung, but behind her he could see a mem—not in uniform, except for the badge hanging around þis neck—with a laser cradled at the ready. "In my pocket," he said aloud, and reached, with exquisite care, into the pocket of his shirt. The woman watched, unmoving, took the folder he presented and slipped it into her belt reader.

"All right," she said. "What about ʒim?" She nodded to Warreven, still slumped in ʒer seat.

"ʒe's a friend," Tatian said, and no longer cared what she would think. "ʒe's herm, they're killing herms in the street. I want ʒim safe."

The woman's eyes flickered, and he knew she was thinking of

trade, but then she nodded. "Open your cargo compartment," she said, and he did as he was told. He watched in the mirror as she ran a handheld scan over the empty space, and then stepped back again.

"Go on in," she said. "Park on the lawn by EHB Two, we're out of space in the garages."

I'm not surprised, Tatian thought. "Thanks," he said, and eased the rover through the narrow opening.

The lawn was surprisingly crowded, not just with company vehicles brought in to protect them from the riot, but with shays and three-ups with the indefinable look of local vehicles. Tatian brought his rover into line with the nearest of the three-ups, and was not surprised to see an indigene watching him from the passenger compartment. There were other indigenes as well, some in off-world clothes, some in traditional dress, gathered in a knot around the door of EHB Two. Company employees? Tatian wondered, as he popped the passenger door, or refugees? There were enough of the odd-bodied among them to make the latter possible.

Inside EHB Three, however, things were astonishingly normal. The building had been built around a central atrium, a concession to the local architecture, not much used except for weddings and formal divorces or the biannual contract parties, but the building's governing committee had installed a standard media center and a big-screen display cube anyway. Tatian paused in the doorway, hearing the familiar six-bar newscast theme, and saw what seemed to be most of the building's population crowding under the ceiling-mounted display. In the screen, the Harbor Market was awash in firelight: something was burning offscreen, beyond the scattered bonfire, and more flames showed on the Gran'quai. Tatian winced, thinking of the lost cargoes and heard Warreven's faint, unhappy intake of breath.

"God and the spirits, that's bad—"

"Tatian!" That was Derebought, pulling herself away from the group by the media center's controls. "Thank God you're all right—" She stopped then, seeing Warreven, and her face changed, recognizing 3im.

Tatian shook his head. "You haven't seen me, Derry. You don't have any idea where I am. You can be worried, if you like, but you haven't seen me."

Derebought jammed a hand into her short hair. "That could be a problem, boss. They—the news, the *mosstaas*—they're blaming ʒim for the killings."

"More than one?" Warreven asked.

"So they're saying," Derebought answered. "People killed in the fighting."

Warreven muttered something, turned away, shaking ʒer head. Tatian said, "That's why you haven't seen me. But thanks for the warning."

"Be careful," Derebought said, and turned back to the screens.

Tatian touched Warreven's shoulder. "Come on."

The halls were quiet, as pleasantly cool as ever; the only thing that was missing was the music that usually seeped under the door of flat A72G. Tatian laid his hand on the lock of his own apartment, waited while the lock cycled, amazed by the contrast. He hadn't been gone for twenty-four hours—no, twenty-six, a full turn of the Haran clock—which seemed impossible enough; that the flat was as clean and ordinary as it had been when he left was for a moment utterly unbelievable. He shook himself, shook the thought away, busied himself with the mundane business of playing host. "Sit down, do you want anything?"

Warreven shook ʒer head, but sank onto the long couch, cupping one hand to ʒer eye. "No, thanks."

"Let me see," Tatian said, and pulled ʒer fingers gently away. Warreven flinched, but met his gaze. The swelling looked, if anything, worse than before, and there was dried blood as well as tears on ʒer cheek. Tatian winced in sympathy and went to the media center.

"Not the news," Warreven said, and Tatian shook his head.

"I'm calling a friend. You need a medic."

Warreven made a face, as though ʒe would have protested, but looked away. Tatian turned his attention to the screen. Isabon would surely be in—ðe had to be in, he needed ðer help too desperately, and besides, he told himself, ðe was experienced enough to have seen the trouble brewing and come back to the Nest. The codes flashed past under his fingers, sending pinpricks of sensation up and down his arms, and he held his breath, staring at the screen. Then, at last, it lit, and Isabon looked out at him.

"Tatian! I was hearing all sorts of things."

"Some of them are probably true," Tatian answered. "I need your help, Isa. It could get you in trouble, though."

"Then you were involved in all this." Isabon gestured to where ðer secondary screen would be.

"Yes. I was with Warreven." Tatian waited, knowing he had to give ðer the chance to back out, dreading that ðe might. "ʒe needs a medic."

"God." Isabon took a deep breath. "I saw what ʒe tried to do—why the hell didn't ʒe keep ʒer people under control, it might've worked out if ʒe had."

Tatian heard Warreven laugh softly behind him. "ʒe tried. It wasn't a planned thing, Isa—it was worse than you'd think, believe me. But I—ʒe needs a medic."

"I know someone who'll come," Isabon answered. "Leave it to me."

The medic arrived within half an hour, Isabon at ʒer heels. ʒe was quiet, competent, and quick to agree to Tatian's suggestion that ʒe hadn't seen or treated anyone. ʒe rebandaged Warreven's eye, shaking ʒer head, then helped get the indigene into Tatian's bed. They left ʒim there, already half asleep, as much from emotional exhaustion as the drugs the medic had given ʒim, and the medic left, muttering anathemas on local politics. Tatian went back into the main room with the others and switched on the media center. The camera was still showing the Harbor Market, but the fires seemed to be under control, and there was no sign of angry *ranas*. He shook his head at the screen, at the newsreader's head in the corner of the display, muted the voice that listed the dead and injured and asked people to stay indoors until the crisis was past. He settled himself on the couch, too tired to stay awake, still too keyed up to sleep, dimmed the lights until the media center was the brightest thing in the room. In the screen, the picture changed, became another open space, a square—not the one they had gone through, Tatian thought; this one was bigger, had a fountain and a stand of trees. More people, a trio of herms in the lead, all sporting the rainbow *rana* ribbons, faced a line of *mosstaas*; someone threw a rock, and then a bottle, something that shattered in front of the advancing line. The *mosstaas* kept coming, and Tatian fingered the remote, changing channels before the two lines met.

There was news on every narrowcast channel, though not the same pictures. He looked away, feeling vaguely guilty, as though there was something he could have done. And that, he knew, was stupid. Whatever he had done, Warreven would have gone to the Market, would have made 3er stand—and 3e had been right, was still right about the laws. Nothing he could have done would have changed that. Even so, he sat staring at the media center, riot and fire filling the screen, until he finally fell asleep from sheer exhaustion.

He woke to bright sunlight coming in through the imperfectly shuttered window. He winced, feeling the sweat on his skin, and pushed himself to his feet to close the shutters, flicking the cooling system to full power as he passed the control box. Outside the window, the broad wedge of lawn between the buildings of the Nest was filled with vehicles and people, indigenes in an even mix of traditional dress and off-world clothes. Some would be company employees, of course, taking shelter with their families, but it was obvious even at this distance that a number of them were herms, fems, and mems. There were children, too, lots of them, and someone—one of the companies, or maybe one of the housing committees—had set up a table to feed them. Tatian shook his head, and pushed the shutters closed.

The media screen came back into focus as the light faded, and he worked the remote to bring the voices up again. The Harbor Market filled the picture, empty now, the stones soot-marked from the bonfire, the remains of the barricade piled to one side of the Gran'quai. A drag engine was hauling away the last balks of wood under the watchful eyes of armed *mosstaas*, while in the background silver-suited firefighters prodded at the remains of a large storage shed. That was the only thing that had burned on the Gran'quai itself; Tatian was glad to see that the docked ships and the factors' offices seemed untouched except for the occasional broken window.

"—order was restored," the newsreader was saying. "A few *ranas* remain active, but the Most Important Man has vowed that they will be closed down by noon. We have been asked to remind our viewers that all political activity has been suspended until the crisis is over, and that *rana* bands of any type have been explicitly prohibited until that time."

"Bastard," Warreven said, from the bedroom doorway. 3er voice was a little slurred, more from the swelling than the aftereffects of either the sweetrum or the doutfire. "How bad is it?"

"I haven't heard yet," Tatian answered. "Last night, they were saying thirty confirmed dead at the Market, and another dozen around the city. Plus Temelathe, of course."

"Of course."

"Tendlathe moves fast," Tatian said. It was probably better to get the worst news over with. "Everyone's already calling him the Most Important Man, and he's formally taking over tonight. There's an emergency session of the Watch Council then."

"Bastard," Warreven said again. "Not that I should be surprised." 3e put 3er hand to 3er bandaged eye. "I don't suppose you have any doutfire, do you?"

Tatian shook his head, not for the first time envious of the indigenes' tolerance for their extensive pharmacopeia. "The doctor left some pills. 3e said you could take up to four at a time. They're in the kitchen."

"Thanks," Warreven said, and disappeared through the door.

Tatian watched 3im go, wondering what to do now. He would be recalled, unless Tendlathe expelled him first—someone at the Harbor was bound to have recognized him, and Masani would have to recall him, if ðe wanted to go on doing business with the Harans. However, he wasn't looking forward to explaining this to ðer, no matter how sympathetic ðe had been to the oddbodied. As for Warreven . . . He shook his head. Tendlathe was blaming 3im for his father's death, and he doubted Warreven had enough support left among the Modernists to have much chance of surviving arrest and trial, no matter how many times 3e swore 3e'd seen Tendlathe shoot his father. Could the other odd-bodied, the *wrangwys*, protect 3im? he wondered. They didn't seem organized enough to offer much help, either political support or physical protection, and he had a strong feeling that the latter would be necessary. Tendlathe needed a scapegoat, and Warreven was the obvious one. That left off-world, but there his imagination failed him. He couldn't picture Warreven on any of the Concord Worlds, part of Concord society: 3e was too much of Hara. Maybe 3e could head for the Stiller *mesnies* north of Bonemarche, he thought. Anti-Stane feeling might outweigh everything else. . . .

The communications system sounded then, and he touched the remote, accepted the call without thinking, expecting Isabon or Derebought. Codes flowed across the screen—official codes, the codes for the White Watch House, and he barely stopped himself from canceling the call. He had already accepted it, already betrayed his presence in the flat; to refuse the call would only cause more trouble. At least the Harans had no direct power within the EHB compound, he thought, and braced himself to pretend innocence. The screen lit at last, and Tendlathe's neatly bearded face looked back at him, a narrow bandage running across his forehead. At least Warreven marked him, Tatian thought, and looked down. The reciprocal transmission was already established: too late to do anything except brazen it out.

"Mir Tatian." Tendlathe's voice was cold and very precise.

"Mir Tendlathe," Tatian answered. "What can I do for you?"

"You can stop playing games," Tendlathe answered. "I want Warreven, and I have every reason to think you have him. If you give him up, I'm prepared to overlook your part in last night's fiasco."

"I don't have 3im," Tatian said. He heard a faint noise from the kitchen, suppressed the desire to look, to wave Warreven back out of sight.

"I don't have time for this," Tendlathe said. "You helped Warreven get away, you were seen—you were filmed—doing it."

"Films can be altered," Tatian said. "They're hardly evidence."

"They're evidence here," Tendlathe answered. "And if it comes to that, I'll bring NAPD down with you—I'll be sure they're implicated, as well as you, in conspiracy and murder."

"Anything I did was on my own authority. It has nothing to do with the company," Tatian said, and Tendlathe gave a thin smile.

"I'm sure, but I can make it look otherwise. And I will, if I have to. I told you, I want Warreven very badly."

Tatian looked down at the control bar, glyphs flickering at the edge of the screen. He had no doubt that Tendlathe meant exactly what he said—and I should have realized it, he thought, expected it—and he couldn't risk NAPD's position on Hara. He had no right to jeopardize not only everything Lolya Masani had worked to build, but Derebought and Mats and Reiss, but at the same time, he couldn't give Warreven up. Not now, he thought, and not to these people.

"Tendlathe."

Warreven stepped out of the kitchen doorway, came slowly forward into the camera's range. Tatian opened his mouth to say something, anything, to wave 3im back, but one look at 3er face silenced him. He stepped back against the window, feeling the heat radiating from the shutters, wondering what Warreven thought 3e could gain from this.

"Warreven," Tendlathe said, and there was a kind of grim satisfaction on his face. "I knew you'd be there."

Warreven shrugged. "It doesn't matter where I am, does it? You and I have a lot to talk about—what's it like, Ten, being the Most Important Man?"

"It feels good, thank you," Tendlathe answered. "It feels good to be able to deal with you as you deserve."

"No matter how you got there?" Warreven asked. "I didn't want him dead, and you'll never convince anyone I did, not when it means you taking over. Besides, I saw him die—I saw you shoot him, Ten."

Tendlathe's expression didn't change. "No one's going to believe your lies—"

"And I can't be the only one," Warreven went on.

"The only thing that matters now," Tendlathe said, "is where and how you surrender to me."

Warreven managed a sound that was almost a laugh, and Tatian could see the ghost of ʒer usual humor in ʒer bruised face. "The last thing you want is for me to turn myself in. That would bring everything into the courts, including how and why Temelathe died. Do you really want to open that door?" ʒe laughed aloud this time, sounding genuinely, incredulously, amused. "God and the spirits, maybe I should. It might be worth it, to see how you explain that."

"I can make very sure you don't get a chance to talk," Tendlathe said.

"That's not much incentive to surrender," Warreven answered, and there was a little silence. Tatian looked from one to the other, from Warreven to the bearded face in the screen, but couldn't read anything in their expressions. Tendlathe's face was taut, muscles standing out at the corners of his mouth; Warreven was still smiling faintly, hiding behind ʒer laughter.

"So what do you want, Raven?" Tendlathe said at last.

Warreven took a deep breath, and Tatian realized that this was what ʒe'd been waiting for. "I want this over," ʒe said. "So I'm prepared to make a bargain with you. Let me off-world—I can claim asylum, I know that much about Concord law—and I'll go, and not cause you anymore trouble. You can make whatever deals you want with Dismars, or whoever's speaking for the Modernists now, and I won't interfere. But if you don't let me go, I'll do my very best to make sure you not only have to fight the whole question of gender law through every step of my trial, but I'll make very sure that everyone knows you killed your father."

"No one will believe you," Tendlathe said. "And you are responsible, Raven. None of this would have happened if you'd kept your mouth shut."

"I opened a door," Warreven answered. "You walked through it."

For the first time, Tendlathe flinched, the merest shiver of taut muscles, but Warreven saw it, and smiled. "Plenty of people will believe me, Ten, you're not universally loved. I can make your life impossible—even if we can't fight you, there are enough of us *wrangwys* to guarantee you won't have an easy time running things."

"The Modernists won't help," Tendlathe said. "Dismars has already disavowed your actions."

"I'm not surprised. Issued a bulletin from somewhere safe outside the city, no doubt," Warreven said bitterly. Then ʒe shook ʒimself. "Look, I'm offering you a way out, Ten. You can take what you've got, pull things together, or you can get revenge. I'm prepared to give you that. Either one."

There was another little silence, and then Tendlathe smiled faintly. "Opening another door?"

Warreven smiled back. "I suppose, yes. And there is a price."

"Well?"

"Leave the off-worlders out of this." Warreven tilted ʒer head toward Tatian. "This is our business, yours and mine."

"Mhyre Tatian was seen helping you," Tendlathe said.

"So expel him, or have his people recall him," Warreven said. "If you absolutely have to. But let the company alone."

There was another pause, longer this time, and then, slowly, Tendlathe nodded. "You have twenty-six hours to get off planet, Warreven. After that, the deal's off."

Warreven smiled thinly. "Agreed." ʒe looked down then, looking for the remote, and Tatian touched the key that ended the connection. The screen went blank, and Warreven took a deep breath.

"Look, I—I'm sorry to have gotten you into this. Of everything, I wish I could have gotten you out clean. It's the best I could do—I think it's the best anyone could do, and the company should be fine, but—" ʒe broke off again, shaking ʒer head. "I'm sorry."

Tatian set the remote carefully back in its niche, unable quite to believe what had happened. "The—Masani was bound to recall me anyway, after this. And we do a lot of business with a lot of *mesnies*. We should be all right."

"But will you?" Warreven tipped ʒer head to one side.

Tatian took a deep breath, overwhelmed, suddenly, by the possibilities. Will I be all right? he wanted to say. I'll be better than all right: I can go home—go back to Kaysa, back to Jericho, hell, I can even get my damned implants fixed, and by technicians that I know will know what they're doing. Even if Masani fires me—and I know ðe won't—it'll be worth it. He could already imagine Kaysa's response, laughter first, at the absurdity of it all, and then the sudden fierce embrace. She would be glad to have him back—that had been clear in their last exchange of mail—but not half as glad as he would be to be back with her. . . .

"You didn't have to get involved," Warreven said, "didn't have to do any of this. I'm sorry."

Tatian shook his head, responding as much to the pain in the other's voice as to the words. "No. I—it sounds stupid, but I did have to help you, or try to, anyway." He shrugged. "It's what I said last night, you're right. What you were trying to do is the right thing. I couldn't just stand there and do nothing. Sometimes you have to do something."

"But your job—"

"Masani's not going to fire me," Tatian said firmly. "As for leaving—I'm going home, Warreven. I'm not sorry about that. What about you?"

Warreven laughed then, not a pleasant sound. "I have money, and I can still get at it. Tendlathe can't block the off-world bank networks without annoying the pharmaceuticals even further."

"That wasn't exactly what I meant." Tatian stopped, tried again. "What about the gender laws? You started this. How the hell can you back out now?"

Warreven's gaze flickered, but 3e answered steadily enough, "I already tried fighting him, and look what happened. I don't know how to fight the *mosstaas*, I don't know if we can fight the *mosstaas*, and not all the *wrangwys* were on my side to begin with. Now they certainly won't be, and you'd need all of us, and the Modernists and some of the *mesnies* to beat Tendlathe now. There's no chance of any compromise if I'm here—Tendlathe is stupid enough, no, angry, enough, to make a martyr of me, and that would mean there'd be no way to get the laws changed. Not to mention that I have no desire to be a martyr."

"What about Temelathe?" Tatian asked. "Are you going to let him get away with that—killing his own father, for god's sake?"

"Do you think I have a choice?" Warreven shook 3er head. "It would be my word against his, Tatian—nobody else is going to come forward, no matter what they saw, not if it means speaking against the Most Important Man—and people will believe what they want to believe, anyway. It won't do any good."

"But he won't revise the laws," Tatian said again. "And the Modernists won't push him on it, we saw that last night. Which still leaves people like you—the people you said you were speaking for last night, damn it—outside the system. Not quite human, you said that yourself."

"And I don't have a side anymore," Warreven answered. "As you said last night."

"Haliday, for one, and what's-3er-name, Destany," Tatian said. "Aren't they your side?"

"Hal has money, too, and 3e's in the off-world hospital," Warreven said. "Malemayn can take care of 3im until 3e's well enough to decide what 3e's going to do—and Mal can take care of Destany's case, too, for that matter."

"Can he?"

"He'll have to," Warreven answered. "Do you really think it'll do either one of them any good to have me around? It'll be hard enough to disassociate me from the case—I doubt Mal can win it, now, though maybe he can get Destany off planet as a refugee, ask for asylum, or something. . . ." 3e shook 3er head. "I don't want to abandon them, Destany or Haliday—especially Hal—but I can't help them now. I can only hurt them at this point."

"You can't just walk away," Tatian began, and broke off, shaking his head in turn.

"Watch me," Warreven said. 3e took a deep breath. "For what it's worth, I didn't say how long I'd stay away." 3e caught 3er hair, wound it into a loose twist, then seemed to realize what 3e was doing and released it. "But right now—I opened a door, all right; it just wasn't the one I thought it was." 3e smiled suddenly, almost whimsically. "Which I suppose is typical of Agede, when you think of it. But if there's a door open at all, any chance not to get more people killed, then I've got to take it. I could maybe try to be a demagogue, lead the *wrangwys* in rebellion, but I didn't exactly do it well last night. Look, Tatian, we don't have a tradition for this, for revolution—we don't even have a word for it, like we don't have a word for herms, and I don't know how to make one happen. We've got plenty of words for protest, for objections and obstruction and compromise, all the subtleties of *ranas* and *presance* and clan meetings and the spirits and their *offetre*, and I know how to do all of that. I've trained all my life to manipulate that system, and it's not going to work this time. We need something new—there's going to be a revolution, there's going to have to be one now, because Tendlathe can't keep this system stable forever, but I don't know how to make it happen. Off-world, in the Concord—well, I can learn what I need there."

Tatian said, "Will you?"

"I suppose I have to. I opened the fucking door." Warreven made a face, reached for 3er hair again, twisting the loose strands into a solid bar. After a moment, 3e went on, in a smaller voice, "And, yes, I'm scared, Tatian. It's not just that I don't know what to do, or how to do it, which I don't, but— It's what I said, we don't have a word for revolution or a word for herm, and I'm supposed to invent both of them. I've been a man all my life—yesterday, I was still a man. Now I'm a herm, and I don't know what that means, except that half my own people say it's not really human. How in all the hells can I lead anybody to anything when I don't know what I'm asking them to become? I have to be able to offer something in place of what we've got."

"You always were a herm," Tatian said.

"Yes, but no one said it." Warreven smiled. "As long as no one said it, it—I—didn't exist. But now that it is said, nobody knows what should happen next. And I can't act without knowing. I won't."

Tatian nodded slowly.

"And I'm sorry," Warreven said again, "that I dragged you into it. I didn't mean to do that. Out of everything, I didn't mean to do that."

Tatian looked at 3im, still in black from the night before, black hair wild, the bruises still very evident on 3er face beneath the dark bandage. He could see the shadow of the spirit in 3im, could see, too, the advocate he had run into at the courthouse. Behind 3im, light gleamed around the edges of the shutters, and he was reminded again of the people camped in the EHB courtyards. He still wasn't sure it was right to leave them without a leader, was equally sure it was wrong for Warreven to stay if 3e didn't know what 3e was doing. To stay was a man's solution, in the stereotypes he had grown up with, to stay and fight. Maybe Warreven's way, the herm's way, to retreat to try again, would work better, this time, in this place.

"It's all right," he said. "You were right. That's all there is to it, really. It didn't work—it was the wrong time or something. But you're still right."

"I'll cling to that thought," Warreven answered, but the twist of 3er swollen mouth was almost good-humored. Tatian smiled back, and went to the media center to begin arranging his own departure.

They left for the starport in the first of the pharmaceuticals' convoys, crammed into the cargo compartment of a six-wheeled triphibian along with a man and his two children and their luggage, and a trio of technicians, two off-worlders, a woman and a mem, and a fem who looked at least part Haran. There were more Harans in the other vehicles, and more families: hardly surprising, Tatian thought, shifting on his hastily packed carrycase. The companies were evacuating their most vulnerable people. Warreven had thrown a *shaal* over 3er head and shoulders, sat hunched in the corner of the compartment where 3e could see out the tiny viewport, but Tatian could tell from the sidelong glances that the others had recognized 3im. The father frowned, looked as though he might say something, but Tatian fixed him with a glare, and he subsided. Then one of the children tugged at his arm and he bent to listen to the question.

"—Mommy coming?"

"As soon as she can finish turning over the department," the man answered, keeping his voice soothing with an effort.

"NeuKass thinks it's that bad, then?" one of the technicians asked, leaning forward on the starcrate she was sharing with the mem, and the man nodded before he thought.

"We're just taking precautions," he corrected himself, and nodded toward the children.

"Sorry," the tech said, and leaned back again.

Tatian looked toward the viewport—really more of a strip, a narrow band of armorglass set into the wall of the cargo compartment to let the loaders check the cargo—as the triphibian tilted. They were creeping up the long ramp that led to the port road's elevated section, and he could see past Warreven's shoulder into one of the markets. It was busier than he'd expected, the central area actually crowded, and then he saw the four-up parked beneath the mural of the spirits, and the *mosstaas* milling on the ground beside it. On the wall above them, Madansa poured her bounty from outstretched hands, but Agede and Cousin-Jack stood to either side, offering their blessings as well. Agede, unmistakably, had Warreven's face, and a herm's breasts had been sketched, crudely, on the painted chest. Tatian blinked, and saw a group of workers raise a ladder under the *mosstaas'* supervision. One of them began to climb, dragging a scrubber and its hose, and then the triphibian lurched forward, cutting off his view.

"How the hell did they do that so quickly?" he said aloud, and Warreven looked at him.

"It's easy enough to catch an image from the narrowcasts, use it to make a transfer. We used to do it for elections, things like that."

The Haran technician glanced sideways at ȝim, cleared ȝer throat. "Mir—serray, I mean?"

Warreven tilted ȝer head. "Æ?"

"Will you come back?"

Warreven smiled, the same odd smile he'd worn the previous night. "Yes. Will you?"

The technician nodded, touching ȝer lips in automatic reverence, then blushed and looked hastily away. Warreven blinked, 3er smile changing again, becoming more human, and 3e resettled 3imself against the wall of the compartment.

They reached the port without incident, joined the lines of people hauling their baggage from the entrances to the boarding hall. All the gates were open, and the lines stretched back into the main lobby. Tatian glanced at the overhead screens, noting the extra ships—*Perseus*, converted from freight to passengers by its parent company; *Djinni*, due in orbit by midnight, diverted from Esperanza; and half a dozen others due in over the next few days—and wondered what Warreven had had to pay to get his berth. He himself would be sleeping in a port cubicle for the next two nights, until NAPD's *Polarity* made orbit, but Warreven had managed to get a cabin on the *Djinni*.

"So—" he began, not knowing how, or whether he wanted, to say good-bye, and a voice called from across the crowd.

"Warreven!"

"Malemayn." Warreven held out both hands to the approaching figure. "How's—"

"Hal's safe," Malemayn said, almost in the same instant. "In the port hospital—Oddyny was right—and 3e'll stay there as long as needed."

Warreven's unbandaged eye flickered closed, and Tatian heard 3im sigh deeply. "Thank the spirits."

Malemayn nodded. "I brought what I could," he said, and set an ordinary-looking carryall on the tiles at Warreven's feet. "The *mosstaas* sealed your flat."

"Tendlathe's a petty bastard sometimes," Warreven said.

"And I thought you might enjoy this." Malemayn held out a quickprint sheet, another image of Warreven as Agede, firelit from the night before. Seeing it over 3er shoulder, Tatian had to repress a shudder, remembering what had followed. "These are all over the city."

"Thanks." Warreven took it, folded it carefully and tucked it into a pocket. "Will you be all right?"

Malemayn nodded. "For a while, anyway. There's going to be hell to pay, Raven, there's no way out now."

"I know." Warreven waved 3er hand, the gesture taking in the off-worlders filling the lobby and the boarding hall. "So do they."

"You should get in line," Tatian said. "It's going to take a while to process everybody, and you're going to have to pass the IDCA screening."

Warreven nodded. "I— Thank you. I owe you—not least for being the only reasonable man in Bonemarche, these last few days. I won't forget." 3e hesitated, and Tatian held out both hands. After everything, it felt foolish to part with a mere clasp of hands. They embraced, cautiously because of Warreven's bruises, and Tatian was startled again by the wiry strength of the body under his hands. Then Warreven released him, gave him one of 3er sudden smiles, genuinely amused this time, and turned and walked away across the lobby. Malemayn followed 3im, lifting his hand in farewell.

Tatian watched them go, wondering what he'd seen started. It wasn't over, that much seemed obvious: Warreven's Agede, the herm Agede, had caught people's imagination, would become part of that spirit—would, in Warreven's phrase, Hara's phrase, open the door. If nothing else came of it, it was a beginning, and Warreven could claim that as a kind of victory, imperfect and uncertain as beginnings always were. And if in the Concord 3e could find the ways to translate the off-world concepts, the five sexes and the process of revolution, then 3e would be the person who remade Hara. Even now, he couldn't entirely doubt that 3e might do it. One studied people like that at university, discussed motives and tactics and plans; one did not drag them out of riots, or ride with them to the starport, on the way to exile. Except that, this time, he had. Tatian shook himself then. He had done what he could—what he really had no choice but to do—and he had his own consequences to face. But at least he was going back where he belonged. He lifted his heavy carrycase, thinking of Jericho, of Kaysa, of all the sane, ordinary people, and began walking toward the gates that would lead to home.

GLOSSARY I: Concord Worlds

bi: one of the nine sexual preferences generally recognized by Concord culture; denotes a person who prefers to be intimate with persons of exactly the same and one of the two "opposite" genders.

Big Six: the six major pharmaceutical companies that dominate the Concord Worlds' trade with Hara.

cd, concord dollar: standard monetary unit among the Concord Worlds; circulates in tandem with planetary currencies.

ColCom: Colonial Committee, agency that represents the Concord Worlds' interests on former colonies.

creole: the official language of the Concord Worlds.

demi: one of the nine sexual preferences generally recognized by Concord culture; denotes a person who prefers to be intimate with persons of exactly the same and one of the two "like" genders.

di: one of the nine sexual preferences generally recognized by Concord culture; denotes a person who prefers to be intimate with persons of either of the two "opposite" genders.

end-of-season: shorthand for surplus harvest not included in existing contracts; also the period between the end of Hara's biannual gathering cycles and the beginning of the next, not covered by contracts. Coincides with the Haran holiday periods of Midsummer and Midwinter.

fem: human being possessing testes, XY chromosomes, some aspects of female genitalia but not possessing ovaries; ðe, ðer, ðer, ðerself.

Fifty: generic term for the most important pharmaceutical companies that do business on Hara; analagous to the Haran use of "pharmaceuticals."

FTL shock: collective term for the side effects of passage through jump points, which include disorientation, severe nausea, blurred vision, impaired or oversensitive hearing, di-

arrhea, and incapacitating headaches. Of human beings, 97% experience at least some of these symptoms for six to nine hours after passing through a jump point; of that group, 47% experience symptoms lasting 24 to 72 hours after passage.

gay: one of the nine sexual preferences generally recognized by Concord culture; denotes a person who prefers to be intimate with others of exactly the same gender.

hemi: one of the nine sexual preferences generally recognized by Concord culture; denotes a person who prefers to be intimate with persons of exactly the same and both "like" genders.

herm: human being possessing testes and ovaries and some aspects of male and female genitalia; 3e, 3er, 3im, 3imself.

HIVs: colloquial and somewhat inaccurate term for the cluster of treatable but incurable immune-system diseases endemic to the Concord Worlds; as the viruses are genetically unstable, each planet tends to develop its own set of diseases to which its population develops a certain level of immunity over time. HIVs are generally transmitted through intimate rather than casual contact. Of all human-settled planets, only Hara does not possess a native HIV cluster, nor is its indigenous population particularly vulnerable to outside exposure. Significantly, most drugs used to treat HIVs are derived from Haran sea and land plants; however, the specific factor or factors that create the apparent planetary immunity have not yet been isolated.

hyperlumin-A: original form of the drug used by human beings to control FTL shock. Hyperlumin-A is 99.8% effective in preventing FTL shock, but is highly mutagenic; its widespread use during the explosive First Wave of colonization produced a significant rise in miscarriages and in the number of so-called intersexual births (i.e., of fems, mems, and herms), and is indirectly responsible for the shape of Concord culture. Hyperlumin-A remains in use among certain specialist populations.

hyperlumin-B: second-generation version of the drug used by human beings to control FTL shock. Hyperlumin-B is 78% effective in preventing FTL shock, and only 48% as mutagenic as hyperlumin-A.

IDCA: Interstellar Disease Control Agency. Responsible for preventing the spread of HIVs between planetary systems, the IDCA rules on emigration/immigration issues, administers and enforces medical quarantines, and provides emergency assistance, as well as funding significant medical research.

indigene, indigenes: native-born (indigenous) human population of a planet not a member of the Concord Worlds.

kilohour: standard time unit of the Concord Worlds, equal to 3,600,000 seconds or one thousand (sixty minute or Earth standard) hours.

Lesser Twenty: the "second tier" of pharmaceutical and other export companies operating on Hara.

man: human being possessing testes, XY chromosomes, and some aspects of male genitalia; he, his, him, himself.

mem: human being possessing ovaries, XX chromosomes, and some aspects of male genitalia but not possessing testes; þe, þis, þim, þimself.

mu, mass units: standard unit used in calculating FTL shipping costs.

omni: one of the nine sexual preferences generally recognized by Concord culture; denotes a person who prefers to be intimate with persons of all genders. Considered somewhat disreputable, or at best indecisive.

player: one who participates in trade; a person who does not conform to any of the culturally recognized patterns of sexuality or who wishes to indulge in sexual behaviors and roles not acknowledged by Concord culture, and who is willing to pay professional or semi-professional prostitutes to take on the reciprocal role(s).

pony-show: a one- or two-person company, generally considered to be unreliable or unethical; derogatory.

ser, serrem, serray, serram, sera: honorifics placed before the surname to indicate the gender of the person (man, mem, herm, fem, woman), considered in Concord usage to be part of the person's full name; the generic plural is sersi.

starcrate: a metal shell equipped with a stasis generator and/or

other preservative mechanisms, used to package perishable and semi-perishable goods for interstellar transport.

straight: one of the nine sexual preferences generally recognized by Concord culture; denotes a person who prefers to be intimate with persons of one of the two "opposite" genders.

trade: commercial or "specialty market" sexuality; on Hara, specifically the practice of paying indigenes of any gender for sexual favors and to assume sexual roles not usually taken by persons of that particular gender. Commercial sex is normally regulated by the IDCA, which provides medical and legal recourse for all parties, but Haran trade remains outside Concord law. In conversational usage, "trade" can also refer to the various quasi-legal markets for residence papers, travel permits, etc. that make it possible for Concord citizens to remain on Hara.

tri: one of the nine sexual preferences generally recognized by Concord culture; denotes a person who prefers to be intimate with persons of exactly the same and both of the "opposite" genders.

uni: one of the nine sexual preferences generally recognized by Concord culture; denotes a person who prefers to be intimate with persons of one of the two "like" genders.

woman: human being possessing ovaries, XX chromosomes, and some aspects of female genitalia; she, her, her, herself.

advocate: man or woman trained in written and customary law, and certified by his or her clan as someone who has the right to speak for others before the clan and Watch courts.

assignat, assignats: paper currency issued by one of the five Watches and backed by that Watch's contracts with the various pharmaceuticals; each Watch currency has a slightly different rate of exchange, which varies from season to season, but in general White Watch currency is strongest against the concord dollar, then Red, Blue, Black, and finally Green.

baanket: dinner given at Midsummer by one of the fourteen clans to which all clan members are in theory invited, the original purpose having been for the clan leader to demonstrate his power by his ability to feed all his dependents; in practice, *baankets* are now hosted by the wealthier *mesnies*, and serve to reaffirm status within the clan as well as to renew lineal ties.

baas: informal honorific, used from an inferior to a superior who is in some sense a friend.

babee-story: fairy tale, fable.

bonne, bonne-faitou: female servant, usually related to her employer by clan or *mesnie* ties.

caleche: an expensive, six-wheeled passenger vehicle, with separate compartments for driver(s) and passengers; used as a status symbol.

Centennial Meeting: planetary assembly held once every one hundred years, counting from the year that settlers first landed on Hara; the Meeting stands somewhat outside the normal rule of law and custom, and at least in theory any Haran has the right to attend and address the Meeting.

chanter: man or woman trained to sing the traditional work *chaunts*; still a valued and high-status position despite the increasing mechanization of labor.

chaunt: traditional work-song used to give the cadence for repetitive physical labor (hauling lines, chopping wood, etc.).

clan-cousin: technically, a man or woman within one's own age cohort in the shared clan who is not otherwise related; in common usage, a man or woman of one's clan to whom one feels some tie or obligation, but to whom one is not more closely related; the use of the term generally expresses a sense of affection and kinship between the people concerned.

clan: one of the fourteen political, social, and familial groupings that form the basis of Haran society; although the people within the first clans were not actually related, but chose to affiliate themselves with one of the original fourteen founders, at this point the clans are interrelated in complex and often confusing fashion. Each clan controls a particular territory, and, as one result, surnames are not used on Hara, as the majority of people in any one location would have the same (clan) surname. The original territories varied in the quality and abundance of their resources, and the Stane clan has parleyed their original good luck into economic and political dominance. The fourteen clans are: Aldman, Blithman, Casnot, Delacoste, Donavie, Ferane, Landeriche, Makpays, Massingberd, Maychilder, Newcomen, Stane, Stiller, and Trencevent.

counterpoint: the highest pitched of the traditional dance drums; as the name implies, it usually plays variations on the middle or bass line that carries the dance rhythm.

countre: another name for a counterpoint drum.

coupelet: passenger vehicle, common in urban areas, used by hire-companies to carry middle- and high-status passengers.

coy: literally, "sweetie" or "darling"; a generic and not necessarily intimate endearment with ironic overtones.

dance house, dance houses: a public or private club, sometimes also selling food, drink, and drugs, where patrons meet to dance and frequently to engage in trade.

dandi: colloquial term for a mem or the active partner in a homosexual relationship; the implication is "trying hard, but not really a man."

docker, dockers: man or woman who works on the Bonemarche docks, either as day labor or for the harbormaster himself; this group is outside most of the traditional kinship networks, and has always been both marginalized and highly politicized.

draisine: small, six-wheeled cargo vehicle with either an open or enclosed cargo bed, used to gather and transport the land-harvest; requires minimal roads even in the deep jungle.

Embankment: streets overlooking the harbor and Harbor Market of Bonemarche; the district where most of the city's trade takes place.

entrait: the opening bars of a drummed dance, signaling both the dance and the intended pace.

Equatoriale: the area of the main continent on and south of the equator, mostly deep jungle; the territory was assigned to the Ferane, Newcomen, Blithman, Aldman, and Trencevent clans at settlement, though Casnot disputes some of Newcomen's claims. Historically, the area has been both relatively poor and extremely traditional.

Estaern: the northeastern coast of the main continent, assigned to the Delacoste, Makpays, and Landeriche clans at settlement; Estaern is also the largest urban area in the district, and both district and city have a reputation for avoiding politics at all costs.

faitou, faitous: a servant or servants of either gender, usually related to his or her employer by clan or *mesnie* ties.

franca: the dialect spoken on Hara; not closely related to the Concord creole.

garce: literally an offensive word for boy, used for homosexual women, particularly women perceived as behaving as men, and for mems.

gellion: offensive word for herms, also used for mems and fems, emphasizing the perceived sterility of any relationship; most common in traditional areas.

ghost *rana*: an offshoot of the traditional political song-and-dance groups, conceived as a mirror-image and reversal of their power; unlike a traditional *rana*, a ghost *rana* makes

no noise, but will act, and act violently, to restore its conception of order. Ghost *ranas* tend to be traditional in their beliefs.

gran'mesnie: social structure intermediate between a *mesnie* and the clan; it is composed of from 3 to 10 *mesnies* generally claiming a common line of descent. *Gran'mesnies* are common only in the larger clans.

halving: politest, though still potentially insulting, colloquial term for a herm, and by extension for mems and fems as well; literally means half-and-half, and implies that one is neither man nor woman.

harvest: generic term for the flora collected for export and local use; delivered to the off-world companies twice a year at Midsummer and Midwinter.

Important Man, Important Woman: a man or woman who has, by virtue either of a job or by election, been accepted as someone who can represent or speak for the clan.

ironwood: low-growing tree found in the jungle edge; the wood is naturally very hard, and can, with care, be fire-cured to make it as hard as metal.

jackamie: literally "boyfriend"; always a very casual term that can easily become an insult.

jack, jack-faitou: male servant, usually related to his employer by clan or *mesnie* ties.

jigg: a three-wheeled cart used in both city and back country; carries a driver and one passenger, plus a small cargo.

jillamie: literally "girlfriend"; always very casual, and can easily become an insult.

kittereen, kittereens: a racing vehicle popular on Hara; essentially a small rocket engine mounted on a light frame.

land-spiders: species of crustacean native to Hara which spin a silk that forms the basis of a number of local and export industries.

long-bit: local coin, usually glass or wood, worth .10 meg.

luci: luminscent colony-dwelling sand flies, once used as a light source.

luciole: old-fashioned lamp, usually spherical, designed to house a colony of *luci.*

mairaiche: farm; source of cultivated crops rather than harvest.

marianj: part-time or semi-professional prostitute who plays a passive or woman's part.

marijak: part-time or semi-professional prostitute who plays an active or man's part.

meg: basic unit of Haran currency.

memore: wake, memorial gathering.

mesnie, mesnies: basic unit of (traditional) Haran society, a group of households (i.e., a man, a woman, and their children) living together in a single compound and usually working together at a profession or industry; all the households in a *mesnie* are related, and marriage within the *mesnie* is considered incest and forbidden.

Midsummer: one of the two major holidays on Hara (the other is Midwinter), celebrated by nearly everyone; also marks the beginning and end of most off-world contracts, and clan elections are held then.

mir, miri: traditional term of respect for a man of slightly superior rank; as there is no true generic plural, miri is generally used for groups of mixed gender.

mirrim, mirrimi: traditional term of respect for a woman of slightly superior rank.

mosstaas: literally, "mustache"; Bonemarche's city militia, which also functions as a kind of police force.

odd-bodied: colloquial generic term for herms, mems, and fems.

offetre: literally "offering"; an act or object produced by a man or woman acting as one of the spirits.

pharmaceutical, pharmaceuticals: generic term for all off-world companies doing business on Hara.

player: an off-worlder who is involved in trade, or who is willing to pay for sexual favors; not a common term outside of Bonemarohe and assimilated areas.

presance: a danced or sung commentary on political issues; by staging the comment as a performance, the performers avoid

the legal and customary ban on "frivolous" (i.e., unsanctioned by authority) discussions of politics in a public place or manner; the technique, developed out of the *rana* tradition, has been most commonly used by groups advocating closer ties with the Concord.

rana, ranas, also ***rana* band, *rana* dancers:** a group of men and women who use traditional drum dances to express a political opinion; *rana* performances are traditionally protected by the Trickster, and by custom cannot be stopped unless the *ranas* make an explicit request for their audience to take political action. *Ranas* traditionally wear multicolored ribbons, a mark of the Trickster, as a sign of their special status.

rover: small, four-seat vehicle used to carry paying passengers around the urban centers.

sea-harvest: generic term for the myriad products gathered from Hara's oceans and either used locally or sold to off-world buyers.

seraal, seraals: the harvest territory controlled by a *mesnie;* this may be either a stretch of land with its trails and growing plants, or a stretch of beach and ocean bottom.

seraaliste, seraalistes: the man or woman within each clan who is primarily responsible for negotiating with the off-world buyers; he or she is also responsible for mediating among his or her clan's *mesnies.* This is an elective office.

shaal: length of fabric, often highly decorated, used to wrap head and shoulders in traditional Haran clothing.

shay: most common cargo vehicle on Hara, with a broad, usually open cargo platform and a two-seat driver's cab.

the spirits: celestial beings that occupy an intermediate position between God (defined as ineffable, unknowable, and not terribly interested in human beings) and Man. The spirits intercede for and interact with human beings, and grant favors more willingly, and as a result, their worship, through services and *offetre,* is far more important to most Harans than the distant God. Harans generally believe that a man or woman can take on some of the characteristics of a spirit, either through

dance, concentration, or sheer serendipity, and when in that state, his or her acts are seen as the actions of the spirit.

Agede, the Doorkeeper: Agede's domain is change, death, birth, and healing.

the Captain: the Captain's domain is that of power, action, and battle; he is also the patron of sailors and travelers.

Caritan, the Cripple: her domain is fate and compassion, and she both provides charity and punishes the wicked; proverbially "the Cripple moves slow but she doesn't stumble."

Cousin-Jack, the Harvester, also Cousin: Cousin's domain is the land and its flora, as well as the deep jungle, and he is also the spirit of hearth and home.

Genevoe, the Trickster: he is patron of *ranas* and other performers, and the changeable spirit of holiday and weather; his particular domain is the ocean shallows.

the Heart-breaker: she is the spirit of lust, love, and springtime; her domain is the deep sea; she is also the protector of children and fools.

Madansa of the Markets, also the Marketwoman: she is the spirit of the marketplace, and of kitchens and food; she is generally considered to be Cousin's daughter or wife, and so subservient to his authority in the *mesnie*.

swetemetes: literally, sweetmeats; sexual insult implying prostitution, usually used of men.

three-up: a shay that has been modified to carry at least one more passenger, at the cost of a reduced passenger area.

tonnere, tonnere-bas: the deepest of the traditional drums, and the one that generally carries the dance rhythm.

trade: specifically, the semi-organized business of sex (paid for in money or favors) between off-worlders and indigenes of either legal gender; because these transactions take place outside the normal social systems, and involve unusually large sums of money and/or metal as inducement, an indigene in trade, whether a man or a woman, is not necessarily considered to be a prostitute. By extension, the term also covers indigenes and off-worlders who facilitate the buying and selling of

sexual favors, and the various permits that allow off-worlders to stay on Hara.

vendee: a man or woman who holds customary or legal title to a space in a recognized market.

vieuvant: an "old soul," a man or woman who is recognized as a reliable and accurate conduit for the will of one or more of the spirits; some *vieuvants* speak only for one spirit, others for more than one.

Watch: the largest division of Haran society, based on the original divisions of the ship that brought the first colonists to Hara. There are five Watches: White (command), Blue (medical/scientific), Black (engineering), Green (land-trained colonists), and Red (ocean-trained colonists). Watches retain certain administrative duties, and are also used to determine marriageability; the larger clans are split between Watches to help keep the genetic mix stable.

Watch Council: the closest thing to a central governing body on Hara, the Watch Council consists of three representatives from each of the Watches, elected from the clans within that Watch according to a complex (and variable) formula based on both population and wealth.

wrangwys: literally, "wrong way," generally used to refer to herms, mems, and fems, and anyone whose sexual preferences don't match the male/female model; has been adopted by that group as a self-referential term and is not insulting within the group.

wry-abed: the politest colloquial term for men who prefer to have sex with men and women who prefer to have sex with women.

wyfie: literally, "little wife," implying a less-than-satisfactory substitute; colloquial and offensive term for a fem or a homosexual man.